*Devon Marshall returns
at last . . .*
IN THE LOVE STORY
A MILLION READERS ARE
WAITING

NO GREATER LOVE

In Patricia Gallagher's magnificent bestseller, CASTLES IN THE AIR, beautiful Devon Marshall rose to the peaks of glamour and power in elegant East Coast society, and began her scandalous affair with Keith Curtis, the man she could never marry.

Now, in the long-awaited sequel, NO GREATER LOVE, Devon strives to forget Keith in her marriage to a wealthy Texas Senator and her own flamboyant career as one of America's first women journalists. From the rugged ranchlands of the West to Washington's halls of power, Devon charts her own course, until catastrophe brings her to the gaslit streets of New York—face to face with the man she never ceased to love!

Other Avon Books by
Patricia Gallagher

NO GREATER LOVE

PATRICIA GALLAGHER

AVON
PUBLISHERS OF BARD, CAMELOT AND DISCUS BOOKS

NO GREATER LOVE is an original publication of Avon
Books. This work has never before appeared in book form.

AVON BOOKS
A division of
The Hearst Corporation
959 Eighth Avenue
New York, New York 10019

First Avon Printing, November, 1979

"To lovers everywhere, of all ages and status, who share the beauty and joy of a great love."

CONTENTS

"Thank you, sir, and you'll order tea now?"

"A by later than four o'clock," he presently... would a best budget sit...

PROLOGUE
Summer, 1867

There was a time when the *Delta Queen*'s captain had taken a keen interest in his passenger manifest. But now a lengthy list annoyed him, for there was more profit and less trouble to shipping freight. No longer was he master of the finest steamboat on the Mississippi. Never again could he hope to accommodate such personages as the governor of Louisiana and the mayor of New Orleans. If folks along the great river still recognized the *Queen*'s whistle, they were too busy to wave as she passed Or, perhaps ignoring the blackened smokestacks and battered decks made it easier to forget how she had gotten that beaten appearance.

The first name on Captain Martin's list was familiar. Reed Carter had come upstream with him, boarding at Vicksburg and booking return passage before going ashore at St. Louis. A tall, lean, angular young man, Carter was a Texan by his accent and dress style But he was not a prosperous Texan. His seedy clothes were prewar vintage, and he wore a black string tie instead of a fashionable cravat. His burnished brown shaggy hair had been neatly cropped by the *Queen*'s barber and his scuffed boots polished by a porter, but these efforts only emphasized his general seediness. Grim-faced and preoccupied, Mr. Carter had not disclosed the purpose of his trip but Captain Martin had guessed at it accurately enough. Carter was bankrupt, prospecting for gold in Northern banks Having recently and unsuccessfully panned those mines himself, the captain wished the Texan luck.

The rest of the passengers were perennials—the gamblers who occupied permanent staterooms, their wives or mistresses, and the *Queen*'s small court of entertainers. The others were strangers to Captain Martin and would remain so, though some might share his table and even his berth

Vessels lined the St. Louis levee for two miles or more, a motley armada of freight boats, barges, tugs, scows, and formerly luxurious steamers with which the *Queen* had once vied for river prestige. Now they were all victims of degradation and decay. Commandeered by the Confederacy or captured by the Union, they had served as hospital ships, troop and prisoner transports, even cattle boats, and were fit for little more than scuttling when finally returned to their owners after the war.

Some aspects of the waterfront remained pretty much unchanged, however, such as the warehouses, saloons, and brothels; and the clamor, soot, and smoke from the coal-fed factories.

Hacks and drays, buggies and private carriages converged on the *Delta Queen*'s pier near sailing time, the drivers shouting and cursing one another and their teams. First-class passengers were welcomed aboard by the captain and dispatched to their staterooms by the stewards. The steerage fares had to shift for themselves. Foreigners mostly, speaking their native tongues, toting bundles; every voyage on the Western waterways included these polyglot pilgrims searching for the Promised Land, which some imagined lay in the Territories.

In his third-class cabin, Reed Carter emptied his pockets and counted his funds. Without robbing his reserve, he could afford a few drinks in the *Queen*'s saloon and perhaps even a cheap prostitute if one were available, but he had no real desire for either diversion. There was nothing to celebrate. Four banks had turned him down, their denials so similar one would think they had rehearsed them especially for indigent Confederates. They were sorry, they sympathized, but they could not lend him capital on the nebulous security he offered. They had no proof that his father still owned the land to which he claimed title. The deed might have been forged, or even stolen, or the property confiscated for taxes. They could not justify the expense of an investigation to check the records. Such a slight on one's integrity, however it was phrased, would have incited a duel in Texas. But Reed Carter could not now afford avenging his honor.

"We're bankers, Mr. Carter, not gamblers," the president

of the Mercantile Trust Company had said, shaking his head. "You're asking us to finance a dream."

Perhaps. The inspiration had first come to him in a field hospital in Tennessee, after he had seen the local cattle and realized that even the mixed Eastern breeds of the dairy and beef herds were far superior to the Texas longhorns. His plan had been to import some breeding stock for the Circle C Ranch and establish a purebred herd while continuing to raise the profitable longhorn. The Carters had heard about the Aberdeen-Angus of Scotland, the Brahman of India, and the Hereford of England. All were considered compatible with the climate of western America. Reed fancied the Hereford. But he had nothing to offer the bankers for security. It did not help to mention that his father had once sat in Congress with the great Sam Houston. A man's reputation no longer sufficed in financial matters. His appearance had not impressed the urbane bankers, either. No doubt the ruined rebel was as welcome above the Mason-Dixon Line these days as the carpetbagger below it.

Nor did it help to realize that he was not alone in his predicament and dilemma, that other veterans had returned from battle to find their homes destroyed or confiscated, families separated, sweethearts gone. Those with guts didn't cry over spilt blood and lost fortunes, but picked up and moved forward as best they could.

Vera had made it all more challenging for him. Hadn't she given him fair warning? With uncanny female intuition she had predicted the Confederacy's defeat and the Carters' own ruin. and declared she would not wait in that lonely country while he played soldier and hero.

She hadn't waited a year before riding off with a dashing Mexican smuggler. But she had got her just punishment, the county gossips assured him. Vera had died of typhoid before they crossed the border. Reed thought it ironic that someone who had wanted so passionately to live, had literally died in the act, consumed by her own intense fires before twenty.

"I couldn't stop her," his father had sadly admitted. "I know you set great store by that gal, son, but she just sort of went crazy when that handsome caballero appeared one day, and next thing I knew, she was astride his Spanish pony, behind his fancy saddle, heading south. I felt like shooting 'em both in the ass, but then I figured it was good riddance. Faithless female like that is not worth fretting over, boy. She'd have done you wrong sooner or later, anyway. You're better off without her."

Reed had nodded. "You did the right thing, Pa, letting them go peacefully. I just hope he gave her a decent burial."

"We'll never know," Jason Carter said, "because I sure as hell ain't riding down in that Mescalero Apache country west of the Pecos to find out."

"Me, either," Reed muttered.

God rest her poor soul, he thought, as the *Delta Queen* departed. Vera Madden was the past. What he wanted now was some kind of future, for his father and himself. And, eventually, Reed wanted a woman to love.

At the same time, Devon Marshall, orphaned daughter of Richmond publisher Hodge Marshall, was traveling to New York in the private rail car of Wall Street capitalist Keith Curtis. Burned out of home and business, her father dead by his own hand, Devon had faced burdens that seemed insurmountable.

Ironically, she had faced even more hardships since then than she had bargained for, and could not help wondering what her life would have been if the Confederacy had not lost the war. Would she have married her suitor, Daniel Haverston, and gone to live on his family's Tidewater plantation? Certainly she would not have met the wealthy Yankee, Curtis. Nor would her trail have crossed the impoverished Reed Carter's at President Grant's Inaugural Ball. Both were covering the ball, she as a reporter for the New York *Record* and Reed Carter for the Dallas *Post*.

Much had happened to her since that long-ago summer —love, unwed motherhood, an exciting career. Everything, it seemed, except the one thing she wanted most. Was this desperate decision the ultimate surrender of all her hopes? When painful memories intruded on her resolution, Devon would hum "Dixie," often with tears in her eyes, and tell herself, *"Look away, look away!"*

PART I
September, 1873

Chapter 1

Devon, who in girlhood had dreamed of a traditional wedding, had a decidedly unusual one. She wore a blue-green faille travel suit and matching hat with a curl of ostrich plume. And the civil ceremony, performed just across the Potomac, in Virginia, was witnessed only by the magistrate's wife and small children. Devon looked naively young, solemnly beautiful, and misty-eyed with what her groom hoped was love.

Their first night together was spent in an Arlington hostelry not far from Robert E. Lee's plantation manor—a gross mistake, for it was one of a number of similar places built to accommodate tourists. Entering the Colonial Inn's dining saloon for the wedding supper, Devon feared she might be ill. It was warm with kitchen heat and stuffy with tobacco smoke. They had to wait for a table. Disgusted, Reed suggested they try another place. Devon declined.

"It's all right, Reed."

"But it's not what I wanted for tonight, darling. We'd be more comfortable in Washington, in a decent hotel with good food."

"I'm not hungry," she said. "Are you?"

"No, but we deserve better on our honeymoon."

Devon smiled. "Can we afford better?"

His face became grim. Once he could have purchased a fine metropolitan hotel with the proceeds from one Carter Ranch roundup. Now, thinking of what he would soon take her back to in Texas, he felt terrible. "Not really."

Devon regretted her remark. "I'm sorry, dear. This will do nicely for one night. We'll leave tomorrow, won't we?"

It seemed imperative that she flee the East as quickly as possible, put a great distance between Keith Curtis and herself lest she change her mind even now and go running back to him. Devon had notified her editor of her marriage to the son of Jason Carter, retired senator from Texas, but

4 *Patricia Gallagher*

she did not imagine the announcement would be of much interest to anyone except the staff, her friends in the press . . . and her former lover, should he chance to read it in the New York *Record*.

Reed nodded, glimpsing an empty table and managing to secure it before another impatient young couple could do so. "Hey, there, mister!" the man complained. "We was waitin' for that table!"

"So were we," Reed replied, daring the short, sallow-skinned fellow to make an issue of it. "You take the next free one, sonny, if you can. Come along, darling. God, I hope the chuck wagon has something left to eat and drink, after this stampede. A jug of spirits, at least."

The menu offered fish and sauterne. Neither enjoyed the meal much, and Reed drank most of the sorry wine, muttering, "Wish we'd gone to Kentucky or Tennessee, missed these damn crowds, and got some good bourbon. I'd give my boots for a shot of sour-mash whiskey! But I wanted champagne and lobster for this feast, Devon. Some fancy cuisine like Dijon's in Washington, or Delmonico's in New York."

Devon choked. Why had he mentioned those particular restaurants, and why did her mind rush instantly to Keith and their many dinners there?

"You all right, honey?" Reed inquired solicitously.

"Fine," she lied. "Whatever it was, I swallowed it."

He gazed at her over the guttering candle. Had the cough brought tears to her eyes? He reached across the table for her hand and fondled it. "Shall we retire to our room, Mrs. Carter?"

Mrs. Carter. "Carter" and "Curtis" had the same first initial, which could be embroidered on handkerchiefs and linens, inscribed on stationery, engraved on silver and crystal . . . should they ever be able to afford any. She might even pretend—no, that would be unfair to Reed, a betrayal. She was a Carter, not a Curtis, and any children she might bear now would be Carters. Oh, Scotty! Keith! My baby and my love!

Unable to speak, she could only nod assent.

Reed was tender, gentle, patient. And because hers was an exceptionally passionate nature, Devon was capable of responding. But it was not quite the response he desired, the total commitment he had hoped to inspire in her. He had not expected a virgin, for in the little shack in Virginia where they had taken refuge from a storm, she had implied that there had been—and possibly still was—another man in her life. Reed had assumed it was a desperate alliance due to the war, possibly involving a Yankee. He had assured her that he understood and did not wish explanations. He had proposed to her in that dilapidated house, with the grisly battle souvenirs strewn about the land. Devon had offered herself to him under circumstances he could not then accept.

Consummating the union now, he begged her to reciprocate his love and devotion, to believe that they would have a wonderful marriage. Devon tried to comply. But he tasted tears on his bride's face. Fears plagued him: that she still loved the other man, whoever he was; that a deep bond existed between them that might never be broken, no matter how hard Devon tried.

There was pleading, almost desperation, in Reed's voice. "I love you so much, Devon. I want to give you everything you want, everything to make you happy. All I want for myself is your love . . . and I'll have it, one day. But I don't expect overnight miracles, and I'll be as patient as I can. Meanwhile, all I ask of you is that you be my wife and let me love you. Devon? Say you will."

Devon was sobbing now, heaving against his bare chest. "Oh, Reed, maybe I did you a terrible wrong and should be begging *your* forgiveness?"

"No, Devon, no! It'll work out for us, in time. If I weren't confident of that, I'd take the pistol out of my haversack now and put a bullet through my brain." He paused, holding her close, longing for a drink to drive away the doubts tormenting him. "Oh, God, I love you, Devon."

Finally they slept in each other's arms, and awoke to a clear September morning, a few autumn-tinged leaves drifting past the windows. Reed would have made love to her again, but her reticence deterred him. Was it reluctance? Had he expected too much of her in their first night?

He ordered breakfast sent to the room and studied the itinerary, while Devon organized their luggage for the long journey to Texas. The Eastern railroads and riverboats were in prewar operation, and they would travel by both methods part of the way.

"How big is Dallas?" Devon asked, checking the personal items in her toilet case.

"Several thousand people. But we won't be living there, Devon. Pa moved to Tarrant County, near Fort Worth, last year. He's homesteading some abandoned property."

Her surprise and disappointment were acute. "You never told me that, Reed!"

"Sure I did, honey. You must've forgotten, or your mind was elsewhere."

"Why did he call the newspaper the Dallas *Post*?"

"Because it was printed there, and I lived upstairs in the same building. Pa rode in weekly to help publish and distribute the paper. Several months ago the press was moved and the name changed to the *Prairie Post*. Very wise, since I'll have a better chance in politics in that county. There's less competition."

"Of course," Devon agreed, changing the subject. "I think we're ready to leave."

"I've decided to keep a journal of our trip," Devon said as they journeyed to the depot. "It'll never compare to Washington Irving's *Sketchbook* or Harriet Martineau's *Travels in America*, but someday it may see print. If not, it's still a good exercise in journalism, and a travel guide of sorts."

They moved through the Yazoo Delta, to Greenville.

Viewed at night, the Greenville ruins were as graphic as charcoal drawings. The houses and buildings still standing were dark and lifeless, and the deserted plantations were ghostly.

The silence at Vicksburg, which they reached by steamboat in an early-morning fog, was eerie and ominous. Technically, the South had fallen with Vicksburg, and its surrender had put the biggest feather in General Grant's military cap. The trenches had become the bloody graves of the tenacious defenders, and the victors' flag floating above them now was a specter in the gray mist, symbolizing stillborn futures to men like Reed Carter.

At Monroe, Louisiana, where they had meant to change trains for Shreveport, they learned that a washed-out trestle and derailment would necessitate continuing by stagecoach. Devon and Reed occupied the jumpseats in the center of the Concord coach. Not the most comfortable position, it was still preferable to riding backward behind the driver's box. Devon had not traveled by stage since childhood, and the presence of the armed guard atop the vehicle made her realize that they were on the periphery of the frontier. Luggage space being limited, Devon's two Saratoga trunks had to be left with the freight agent at Monroe, to be shipped later on a wagon train.

Louisianians traveled mostly by water, and Devon observed aloud that she had never seen worse roads, even in the backwoods of the Blue Ridge Mountains.

"You will, ma'am," Lester Barton assured her. He was a rough-looking character in Western regalia bound for the Arizona Territory.

Carla Winston, apparently a widow, was past thirty and quite attractive, with feminine features and bright, alert eyes. Admiring Devon's clothes, she declared, "You won't find anything like that in Texas, my dear. The best you can hope for is a seamstress capable of following a pattern and sewing a straight seam."

Remembering the expensive wardrobe left at the Monroe depot, and her subscriptions to *Godey's* and *Demorest's Mirror of Fashions,* Devon felt vain and foolish. Who would recognize *haute couture* on the frontier? The most style-conscious women were probably the prostitutes and saloon entertainers. Nevertheless, she intended to be well-groomed, despite the rigors of stage travel and lack of hygiene facilities.

The first station at which they stopped could only be called medieval, but Barton commented that it was a model inn compared to the accommodations farther west. Devon sighed. "You make it sound so primitive, sir."

"It is, ma'am."

Sensing Devon's growing apprehensions, Reed growled, "We can do without the travelogue, Barton. This is my wife's first trip to Texas."

"Easterner, eh? Well, I didn't figure she was a pioneer, not with them duds and that magnolia-blossom complexion. What do you do for a living, Carter?"

"I used to ranch."

"Used to?"

"Yeah. Ever hear of the Circle C?"

"Nope. I punched cows on a spread near San Antone for a while after the war, then went up to the Colorado and Montana territories. Never stayed no place long, though. Guess I'm what you'd call a drifter."

"Saddletramp," Reed said contemptuously.

"At times, sure. It's not a bad life, if you got no ties or

responsibilities. A free man can pull stakes any old time and move on. I think I might finally settle in Arizona. The climate agrees with me."

"The gambling climate of Tucson?"

Barton grinned. "Well, I play a little poker now and then. Maybe we can get up a friendly game at the next station, if you can forsake your bride long enough?" Reed ignored that.

Carla Winston complained of the jouncing coach. "We're being pounded to pudding."

"We can make another five or six miles before dark," Reed estimated. "But don't worry, ma'am, we'll camp somewhere for the night."

"Camp?" Devon repeated.

He smiled, patting her knee. "Cowboy lingo, honey. We'll stop at a station."

"When will we reach Shreveport?"

"Tomorrow, if we're lucky. Then we cross the Red River to Texas—and home."

"I can hardly wait," Devon murmured. She did not sound quite as though she meant it.

Chapter 2

The stage was ferried across the Red River on a log raft poled by several black giants. It rocked on the swift-current stream, threatening to topple and drown them. Devon got her first serious fright. Barton's remark, as he gestured toward the receding skyline of Shreveport, did not bolster her mood any. "Take a good look, folks! It'll be many a mile before you see a town of that size again."

Carla Winston, who had taken an immediate dislike to the officious stranger, scoffed. "That puny inland port is hardly a metropolis, Mr. Barton."

"Beats any town in Texas, ma'am, except Galveston. San Francisco is the only real city in the West."

Soon Devon understood what Barton had meant about Texas roads. These erratic trails had been little improved since the migrating buffalo herds had pounded them three feet into the earth over a century ago. Pine forests, deep and dense, enveloped them on all sides. Deer streaked across the path, huge stags with majestic racks escorting harems of does in anticipation of the rutting season. Big black bears lumbered in the woods, and timber wolves howled at night. It was easy to imagine Indians and outlaws lying in ambush. She was certain they did when Reed checked his weapon.

"You expect trouble?" she whispered.

Before Reed could answer, Barton volunteered, "Why do you think there's a man riding shotgun, Mrs. Carter? Many stages are held up, especially if they're carrying gold."

"Is this one?" Carla inquired.

"Well, a strongbox was put aboard at Monroe. Government money, probably, to pay the frontier troops."

"Not necessarily," Reed temporized, glaring at the other man. "It may only contain valuable papers."

Devon thought of the precious jewels in her case, mementos from Keith. She might use them to stake their

9

future in Texas, if Reed would allow it. "Thank heaven for the guard."

"I seen guards picked off perches like sitting pigeons," Barton continued. "And somehow, bandits always know when there's treasure aboard a stage or train."

Devon saw Reed's fists clench. "I'd be much obliged, mister, if you'd keep your thoughts on this subject to yourself. You're upsetting the ladies."

"Christ, man, they're on the frontier now, not back East in a parlor! If they don't realize the hazards, they shouldn't be here."

With these words, Devon lapsed into contemplation, remote and detached.

The food at the Texas stations was like nothing Devon had ever eaten before: fried steak spongy with grease and tough as rawhide, fried potatoes, fried skillet bread. Breakfast was greasy griddlecakes, called flapjacks, served with heavy sorghum syrup, and strong, bitter coffee without either cream or sugar. Texas cows were for meat, not milk. Only babies drank milk, and they were weaned early. Devon's digestion suffered, while Carla Winston experienced a different discomfort.

"If it's not flux, it's constipation," she complained. "And, Lord, how did Eve cope with the menses' curse?"

"I suppose Adam put an immediate stop to it," Devon replied. "But I know what you mean, and if we aren't lodged in a decent hotel soon, I think I shall die!"

They were lucky to find even a pitcher of water and a basin for cleansing. How Devon missed the sanitary and sleeping facilities she had left behind! If the stagecoach were carrying a full load of passengers, unmarried members of the same sex must share quarters. Couples were allowed a room when one was available. The Carters had had only one since their wedding night. The warped door had no bolt, so Reed secured some privacy by shoving a heavy wood chest against it. Devon snuffed the candle, and they undressed partially and got into the sheetless bed, under the scratchy wool blanket.

"Helluva honeymoon, huh?" he whispered, cuddling and stroking her. "Oh, Devon, I wish we were on a luxury liner to the Continent!"

Devon had to curb her emotions, for going abroad with Keith had been one of her dreams. She attempted levity to dismiss the surging memories. "I wonder if this is how bundling originated?"

"Probably, but can you remove more clothing? I want to touch all of you."

She obliged, and the heat of his body warmed hers. For a while they made ardent love on the lumpy hay mattress. Ignoring the wayward straws occasionally pricking her bare buttocks, Devon achieved a climax, then another, though not the number or the intensity she had experienced with Keith. Still, Reed clutched her jubilantly, confident now that all they needed was time and practice.

"That was pretty good for you, wasn't it, darling?"

"Yes," she agreed. "Yes, dear, it was."

"Help me, Devon. Tell me what you like, and I'll try my best to please you. Because more than anything else in our marriage, I want to satisfy you in bed. I know sex is repulsive to many women, a chore. I want you to enjoy it. I haven't had a great deal of sexual experience, and most of it was with paid partners. Maybe we can experiment, and teach each other? Love makes sex infinitely better, Devon."

"Yes," she murmured, glad he had said that love performed these sexual wonders, rather than marriage, which only legalized them. Keith had tried to tell her that, but she had been too puritanical to understand. Why hadn't she listened to Keith? Why had she felt that compulsion to righteousness, sacrificed her child and the man she loved on the altar of conventionality? It was too late now for remorse.

Once they passed out of the timberlands into the broad, flat prairies, the sight of a dark cloud in the sky set the driver to yelling and whipping the teams, jolting Devon out of her reveries. "What happened? A runaway?"

"Trying to beat the rain," Reed explained.

"Does the coach leak?"

"No, but the blacklands turn to gumbo in rain, and we could get stuck. Might even have to get out and walk."

The wheels rumbled in the dry ruts like thunder, and the driver was transformed into a demon piloting a hellcart. Carla beseeched Reed, "Mr. Carter, please tell that maniac to slow down! We'll be turned over at this rate!"

"Wouldn't do any good, ma'am. He's racing the weather."

"He's insane."

Barton, hanging onto a leather strap, laughed. "Lunacy is one of the qualifications for a stagecoach driver, lady. Recklessness is another."

"Then he's qualified," Devon declared, clinging to the jumpseat with both hands.

"Lower them curtains!" the driver shouted as the first huge raindrops pelted the box. "We gonna catch the tail end. Lucky it ain't no tornado!"

The men inside released the leather shades, enclosing the occupants in a warm, moist darkness permeated by perspiration and perfume. "I feel faint," Devon said weakly.

"Give her some air!" Carla cried. "Oh, my God, we'll all suffocate—or be jounced to jelly!"

The ruts filled with muddy water and ran like arroyos, and there was louder swearing and harder lashing of the horses. The coach careened, skidded, bounced threateningly. The passengers bumped around like fish in a barrel, knocking heads and bodies together. Carla cautioned, "Watch your gun, Mr. Carter. It's liable to go off."

"It's not cocked, ma'am, and I assure you I know how to handle firearms."

Devon was tossed onto the floor, and the dimness made her rescue difficult. Barton's assistance infuriated Reed. "Hands off, mister, if you value them!"

"Sorry, sir. I was just trying to help, and it's dark in here. Ungrateful bastard, ain't you?"

"Gentlemen, please," Carla implored. "Don't fight in here, there's not enough room."

"My apologies, ma'am," Reed said, raising a blind to admit light. "But this obnoxious skunk was pawing my wife."

Barton scowled. "Man, I'm glad you're getting off in Fort Worth! I'm heading for Tucson."

"And Boot Hill," Reed predicted, "if I know your type."

Twenty miles east of Dallas, Devon thought the end had come for all of them.

Four Mexican horsemen galloped out of a thicket, shot the weapon out of the guard's hands, and shouted in Spanish to the coachman, *"Alto, alto!"*

Reed poked his revolver through the window, only to find his action anticipated by the cunning leader, who was grinning at him with his finger on the trigger of a long-barreled Spanish pistol. He was a swarthy, black-mustached

man, dressed better than his comrades in the nearly
foppish finery of a *rico*. He spoke English like a don.

"No, señor, I would not do that! Drop your gun, please."

As Reed obeyed, he ordered the strongbox thrown down,
shot off the lock, and directed one of his men to open it,
furious to discover that it contained no gold or jewels, only
some officially wrapped greenbacks difficult to spend in his
native country, documents and mail worthless to him.
"Then the passengers must pay," he decided. "Get out of
the coach, all of you. And no tricks, please, señors. My
boys have the bead on you, and they have not killed anyone all day."

Reed stepped out first. "Long way from the Rio Grande,
aren't you amigo?"

The Mexican sat imperiously in his stolen saddle, a veri-
table throne of hand-tooled leather inlaid with gold and
silver, jade and ivory and mother-of-pearl. Reed thought of
the saddle of the caballero his father had described, the one
on which Vera had ridden away. "Do not call me amigo,
señor. I am not your friend, nor the friend of any gringo
americano, especially Texan I spit on the name," he said,
and spat at Reed's boots. "You have killed our people,
stolen our horses and cattle, our lands, our homes, and
even some of our women."

"You've done those same things to us," Reed told him
grimly, hoping the ladies would not get hysterical and betray their presence.

"*Sí*, and with pleasure, señor. With the greatest of pleasure," he emphasized, as Devon, unable to contain her
journalistic curiosity, peeked from behind a curtain. "And
perhaps we shall do it again."

"You'll have to kill every man here first," Reed challenged, and the others, including Barton, nodded.

"*Silencio!*" the Mexican commanded, as his gang began
to grumble at the delay He beckoned to the females inside.
"Are you deaf? I ordered *everyone* out! My patience is
long but not endless Empty your pockets and purses. My
boys will pass sombreros among you."

Reed swung the door wide, bowing to the occupants.
"Ladies these gentlemen wish to take up a collection for
some needy Mexicans."

"You will be shot in the mouth for that, señor," the *rico*
decreed.

Reed assisted Devon, and Barton the widow, who alighted

making the sign of the cross, beseeching, "Kind sir, we have no money or jewels. We are victims of the recent American Civil War. Everything was taken from us."

Getting a full look at Devon, the leader narrowed his black eyes appreciatively. "That was some years ago, señora," he addressed Carla.

"And we Southerners have been destitute ever since, your Majesty. This is my daughter, on her way to a convent in San Francisco."

"You lie, señora! That is not the habit of a nun!"

"She's traveling incognito, your Highness, because we have come through some Protestant country. Surely you can understand that, sir, since you wear a sacred cross. Well, under my dear daughter's left glove she wears the gold band which wedded her to Jesus Christ only one month ago. I shall enter the abbey with her, having lost my beloved husband, her father, in President Lincoln's war. We shall do missionary work among the poor Mexicans in California. So all we can offer you is our prayers, your Excellency. But do search us if you wish."

He gazed intently at Devon, who contrived an expression of solemn dedication. "Are you mute? Why do you not speak for yourself?"

Carla replied, "She is under a vow of silence, sir."

The Mexican hesitated, while his men mumbled and shrugged, awaiting orders.

"A search will not be necessary, señora. I accept your word as a good Catholic, and will be grateful for your prayers. In your honor, I shall not even kill these American dogs, for I know it would offend you and your daughter, Sister . . . ?"

"Sister Devon, one day to be canonized Saint Devona, for all the good deeds she will perform among your poor mistreated people."

"*Sí*, and you may go in peace now. *Adiós! Hasta la vista!*" He swept off his elaborate sombrero, his pack emulating his gallantry. "*Vámonos, muchachos!*" He signaled, and they put spurs to their wiry Spanish ponies.

Reed bent to retrieve his weapon, dusted it off, stuck it into the holster. Straightening, he met the sly grin of Carla Winston. "What a cool liar you are, ma'am, and fine actress! How'd you invent that clever story so quickly?"

"Would it surprise you to learn that I was a spy during the war, Mr. Carter?"

"On which side, ma'am?"

"The Confederacy's, of course. We had some of the best, you know, and several were female."

"So I've heard."

Barton tipped his hat to her. "You sure fooled me, ma'am, and foxed them bandits."

Carla smiled. "Oh, I've fooled and foxed a lot of men in my time, sir. I may just be in disguise now, in fact."

"If you folks down yonder are done jawin'," the driver called, "try to remember I got a stage to run and a schedule to keep. We're late now! Tom, suppose you bandage up that bleedin' paw with yore bandana and git inside. I reckon Carter or Barton would be willin' to ride shotgun to Dallas, where we can pick up another guard."

"I'll do it," Reed offered.

"No, let me," Barton said in a sudden gesture of heroism. "Your wife looks pale, Carter. Better take care of her."

Resettled in the coach, Carla mused, "They were a long way from Mexico, weren't they?"

Reed nodded "They usually operate in south Texas and along the border, where escape is easier. Just shows how tough things are now. Even the desperados are fanning out. Like the carpetbaggers I don't see much difference, actually. They ought to band together."

On the outskirts of Dallas, a rider hailed the stage, waving a red flag. The driver hauled on the reins, braked the wheels, shaking up the passengers again. "Son-of-a-bitchin' bastard! We'll never make it at this rate! What the hell do *you* want?"

"Smallpox in Dallas," the messenger warned. "Three new cases this morning. Better go on to Fort Worth. None there yet, far as we know."

"The horses will drop dead in their traces."

"So might the rest of you, if you stop here."

"Aw right, goddammit!" He dug furiously in the canvas mail sack for the pouch marked DALLAS, tossed it to the courier. "Take it and tell 'em I'm bypassin' your lousy pesthole!" The whip cracked. "Gidyap, you blasted nags, afore I bust your ornery asses!"

"Any problems, honey?" Reed asked.

"No," Devon answered "I just hope we can avoid contact with that dreadful disease."

"Some people have a natural immunity, darling. Other-

wise they'd all be dead, or pockmarked. I've been exposed
to the pox and never caught it. Pa had it in childhood, a
mild case, hardly any pits visible now."

"That's fortunate," Devon said, thinking that a man
could help conceal the scars with a beard, while a woman
must resort to a perpetual veil. Indeed, some turned to
convents because of such facial disfigurement, and she
prayed there was no ironic prophecy in Carla Winston's
fabrication. Could that be the reason for Carla's own
densely veiled face?

Chapter 3

There was much excitement at the Fort Worth station, where the telegraph wires had earlier relayed a calamitous message. The investment firm of Jay Cooke of Philadelphia, considered a financial Gibraltar, had declared bankruptcy, and gloom and despair clouded the faces of the local businessmen.

The town had suffered during the war, its population dwindling with the receding frontier, shrinking back to a trading-post settlement. The prospect of a railroad that would eventually connect Fort Worth with El Paso, gateway to the West, had stimulated a boom in 1870. Many former settlers returned, along with new ones from the disrupted South. The Texas & Pacific Line, financed by Jay Cooke and Company, was only twenty-six miles away when the dire news struck.

Oh, no! Devon thought, remembering the frantic meetings of the country's leading bankers with President Grant at Long Branch, only a few months ago. Apparently this was the crisis they had been trying to avert. Would the Curtis Bank be affected? She might have to wait days, weeks, even months to learn the answer.

"Well, there goes the railroad," Reed said glumly, "and its promise of prosperity. This means more hard times, more sacrifice."

"I know," she said wearily. "Cooke's failure will likely cause a chain reaction on Wall Street, and eventually spread through the country like an epidemic."

Reed shrugged. "No way of telling yet. That's one of the many disadvantages of living in the boondocks, honey. Unless a catastrophe occurs in the immediate vicinity, it takes a while to hear about it. We don't have any correspondents in New York. That station telegrapher is our hottest news source. Nor can we print extra editions here.

17

We're lucky to go to press weekly, or bimonthly, considering the antiquated equipment and uncertain supply of newsprint and ink."

He gazed somberly at the square, once the paradeground of the dragoons of Camp Worth. Immigrants had moved into the vacated log and adobe barracks after the federal troops were transferred farther west, and merchants had set up shops in the military buildings. Trade routes to the east Texas forests furnished lumber for better structures, but development was suspended in 1861, when the militia left to aid the Confederacy and the Indians began to encroach again. Without the stimulation of a railroad, Reed anticipated poverty. He muttered angrily, "What's wrong with our economy? Why is it always either boom or bust, prosperity or panic?"

Keith Curtis could have explained the complicated mechanics of finance to him, as he had so often tried to enlighten Devon. Once he had told her, "The free capital of the nation is overextended in the construction of railroads, ironworks, and related industries. Hundreds of companies are vying to lay tracks through sparsely settled territories that can't possibly complete or maintain them, much less return fair profits, and the builders are borrowing heavily from British and European banks. That can't continue. There'll be another panic, probably worse than those of '37 and '57. But Grant can't comprehend anything except military strategy. The Treasury secretary is incompetent, and half of the Congress is corrupt and involved in the various real-estate and rail swindles. Too many people are afflicted with a get-rich-quick mania, to the nation's detriment. When will America ever learn the fundamentals of a stable economy?"

"Blame it on human greed and ignorance," she said to Reed.

Travel-weary, Devon was anxious to get away from the crush and confusion of the station. Reed said, "We're located on the Cold Springs Road, darling, and I'll have to hire a buckboard from the livery stable. You might help Mrs. Winston get lodging, while I round up our transportation." He tipped his hat and strode across the barren quadrangle.

Carla watched him admiringly. "Your husband is quite a man, Mrs. Carter."

"Thank you, but please call me Devon. You're not going on to California?"

"Not immediately—that was just a ploy for the Mexicans' benefit. I've decided to stay in Texas awhile. I trust we're good-enough friends to visit occasionally?"

"Of course," Devon happily assured her as they walked toward the Dragoon Hotel. "Let's make it soon and often."

Devon sat beside Reed on the hard, springless plank seat of the small rickety wagon, her valise and his haversack bouncing in the board-bed. "Does the wind always blow this way?" she asked, clinging to her bonnet.

"No, sometimes it blows the other way."

"I'm serious, Reed."

"Sorry. Yes, it's fairly steady on the prairie."

"What a ridiculous place for a newspaper! You should have stayed in Dallas."

"Well, we didn't expect to remain in publishing this long, Devon. A railhead would have made Fort Worth the cattle capital of Texas and put the Carters back into ranching. Now, all that's in abeyance again."

"But I thought journalism and politics would engage us both in the immediate future."

"That's right, darling. I need press exposure in the coming campaign, and I damn well better be elected to office, since the cattleman image is growing dimmer now. It's going to be tough for a while, Devon." He turned pleading eyes toward her. "Just don't hate me when you see what I've brought you to?"

"Don't be silly, Reed. I accepted your proposal, didn't I? I wasn't abducted at gunpoint."

He smiled wryly. "No, but I was strongly considering it as a last resort, if you hadn't agreed."

Devon glimpsed the crude cabin near the creek, where a few weeping willows and cottonwoods stood forlornly. It was the middle of nowhere. Praying that it was some other pioneer dwelling, she felt her heart sink as Reed drew rein and jumped down to assist her.

"Wonder where Pa is?" he said, carrying Devon over the threshold. "Out riding ghost herds on his mythical range, I reckon."

"As a newsman, he should have been at the telegraph office," Devon reasoned.

"Probably was, earlier, and left, aware that the news would spread over the county long before he could print it. The shed behind the house is the press, Devon. Not exactly the New York *Times*."

Or even the Richmond *Sentinel*, Devon reflected wistfully, glad that Keith could not see any of this. It was a thousand times worse than what he had pictured in his jealous rage during their last rendezvous in the Clairmont.

Could she have forced the rigors of the frontier on her helpless son, even if Keith had let her? Denied Scotty the comforts and scholastic advantages his affluent father could provide? Risked his health and maybe even his life in this rudimentary environment?

Should she have waited indefinitely in the shadows of uncertainty, the patient, loving mistress? Adoption had given Scotty his rightful name, heritage, and privileges. And while Esther lived, there was no alternative. Mrs. Stanfield guarded her vegetating daughter like a Cerberus, threatening exposure whenever her son-in-law attempted divorce or commitment. There had seemed no course except the one she had so painfully chosen. But she missed Keith and Scotty in a bewildering, devastating obsession that would have hurt Reed deeply had he known any of the facts.

Most Southern plantations had boasted better slave quarters than this, her new home. Daylight shone through some cracks in the chinked walls, and the frequently patched roof leaked, requiring receptacles to catch the rainwater. Scraps of wood had been nailed or pegged together for furniture. The chairs had horn legs and rawhide seats laced with leather thongs. There was one large room with an adobe-brick fireplace, and a lean-to kitchen with unfinished cupboards and an ancient iron stove salvaged from the discarded cargo of a prairie schooner.

Checking around, Reed cautioned, "You have to watch for snakes, Devon, which sometimes crawl inside. We've found them in the woodboxes, under the beds, even *in* the beds. So be careful at all times. You hear?"

She nodded in mute horror.

"Of course, there're other varmints too, but the reptiles are the worst. We have four venomous kinds: rattlers, coral, copperhead, and cottonmouth moccasins. Moccasins like water and live near rivers and creeks."

"We had the same species in Virginia," Devon recalled,

"but I don't remember any in Richmond, except the political Copperheads during the war."

"Northerners with Southern sympathies," Reed mused, "which made them good snakes in the Confederacy."

"Does your father know you're married?"

"I wrote him of my intentions, but the letter may not have reached him. There's no regular mail delivery." He paused, observing Devon's expression as she surveyed her surroundings. "It's getting near suppertime. Pa and I will help you cook."

"Fine, because I'm hardly an expert on any kind of range, and not yet familiar with the sort of food you Texans eat."

"*We* Texans," he corrected. "You're one of us now, Devon."

Devon had to remind herself that it was a reality. She was actually standing here with her husband, in this pitiful shelter, in the most isolated, desolate country imaginable. The stark landscape stretched on forever.

Reed made a fire in the cook stove and told her, "The fire has to burn down to coals. I'll get the baggage. Make yourself comfortable, darling."

"Thank you," Devon said, clenching her gloved hands. She had read that insanity was not uncommon among pioneers, especially weak women.

The connubial bed, Reed thought ruefully, passing the clumsy frame with linter mattress supported on interlaced lariats. God, what had he done to this lovely, delicate Virginian, whose only experience with horses had been in fox hunts, and who thought cows were for milk, butter, and cheese?

Devon's father-in-law reminded her of a woodcut. He had sharply carved features and grooved skin. White hair brushed his shoulders, and he had a drooping white mustache. His keen eyes squinted perpetually. He grinned widely, sticking out a big friendly hand. "So this is the bride? Son, you picked yourself a beauty! But then, you always did have a sharp eye for horses, cows, and women."

"Not in that order, Pa!"

"No, and I didn't mean it like that, Devon, honey. Despite the tales told about us back East, Texans prize their ladies above all other possessions." He compressed his dry lips. Another *faux pas*. Hell, he must be getting old! Losing

his tact; he probably should be put out to pasture. His
blunder had obviously offended this one. His boy had gotten himself a handful this time This one was a silky-soft,
well-curried thoroughbred, and spirited.

She shook his hand and then embraced him briefly. "It's
a pleasure to know you, Senator."

"Senator," he mused. "Yeah some folks still call me
that. Funny how a title sticks like a brand Was a time
when the Circle C Mexicans called me El Patrón " He
glanced at his son. "I laid in some grub when I first heard
of the plague in Dallas, and not knowing exactly when you
newlyweds would arrive I'm not sure Devon can digest my
chuck-wagon fare, but I'll whip up supper this evening.
That was a mighty long journey, and your bride needs a
rest. Our facilities are primitive, Devon, but we aim to
improve 'em."

Devon knew he meant the tumbling toilet in the weeds
and cactus. After dark and before dawn, she determined to
use the crockery chamberpot She would conceal it with a
catercorner curtain, even if she must devise one from her
garments. Embarrassed, she thought of other things "Can
you cook chili con carne, Senator? Reed tells me it's a
favorite dish in Texas."

"Next to beefsteak " he said. "But chili takes a heap of
seasoning and simmering to make properly. All day actually. We'll get around to the Mexican specialties. Tonight
it'll just be meat and potatoes."

Fried, Devon feared her stomach already queasy. She
craved some creamed vegetables and a crisp salad with
tangy dressing. But the long summer drought had stunted
the garden, leaving only withered greens and a few bitter
roots.

Reed followed his father to the kitchen, asking if he had
heard the news about Jay Cooke and Company.

"Yep, and I know full well what it means to Fort Worth
and other Texas towns begging for railroads Bankrupt
enterprises. fewer new settlers, and old ones moving away.
Well, maybe we can pick up some deserted property cheap,
afford a better home for your wife "

"On credit? Shit. Pa, we're as broke as the rest of 'em!
We'll have to hustle for advertisements to keep the paper
alive. Goddamn that thieving carpetbagger who stole the
ranch! I hope the bastard gets the pox and dies in agony."

"You can't bemoan the past, son. I learned that long

ago. Have to anticipate the future. Hopefully, you'll be in Austin next year, and I'll get some hombres to help me round up some cattle and horses to drive north. How do you think the Circle C got started in the first place?"

"You were younger then, Pa. And stronger."

"I can still ride and rope, boy! And brand. And hit the trail, if necessary. Meanwhile, we'll print the *Prairie Post* and launch you in politics. Always seems to be some money in that game, and not penny-ante poker stakes, either." He gestured toward the bedroom. "I'll bunk in the shed from here on, give you young folks some privacy." He tested the heat of the stove lids with a moistened finger, adjusting the damper. "Excuse me now, better get the griddles hot."

It occurred to Devon that they might have spent a couple of nights in the hotel, to provide a more gradual introduction to this hovel. But perhaps Reed lacked the funds for such luxury and would not accept any of hers, even as a loan. Men and their stubborn pride!

The heavy, greasy food induced a nightmare in which Devon thrashed and moaned before Reed woke her, calming her in his arms. "You were crying, darling. Are you in pain?"

"Just a tummyache," she whimpered.

"Pa's chow," he reasoned. "Christ, I don't know how he has survived his own cooking for this long."

"Did I talk in my sleep, Reed?"

"Nothing understandable. A soda-mint tablet might help your stomach."

"It's better now."

"Well, it'll be morning soon. Maybe we can keep Pa from fixing breakfast. His flapjacks are the worst in seven counties. Harder to digest than iron horseshoes."

"Is he serious about a spring roundup and cattle drive?"

"Probably. Just won't admit his age. I think I'll ride out with him and survey the situation. Wild cattle and horses increased greatly during the war, Devon, and there are millions in Texas now. A man has only to catch and brand them to be in business. But it's a big job to tackle alone— or with an elderly partner. Pa knows that, which is why he's encouraging publishing and politics for right now. If we get the long-promised free election this fall, the Democrats will take over the state capitol, and I should win a seat in the House. We'd be living in Austin in a few months. It's a right nice little town."

"It is?" Devon murmured drowsily, dozing off before he could answer.

Chagrined by her lack of interest, Reed removed his arms and turned on his side, gazing at the dark walls until dawn outlined the cracks. The cabin would have to be repaired before winter. The windows needed panes, but glass was costly and difficult to obtain, as were shingles for the roof. Only recently had his father been able to install a puncheon floor over the hard-beaten earth. The outbuildings consisted of a makeshift stable and a corral shared by the few domestic animals. And there was a chicken coop, where the early risers were beginning to cackle and crow.

Later, saddling his buckskin horse, Reed remembered the many fine quarter horses on the Circle C Ranch. Jason Carter, once the proud owner of the best blooded stallion in the region, was now astride an aging gray gelding, waiting for his son.

"Rebel needs a mate, son. We ought to fetch him a pretty young mare."

"Isn't horse thievery still a hanging offense?"

"I meant a mustang."

"The herd honcho wouldn't appreciate that, Pa. And she might miss her stud and try to go back to him."

"Yeah, I reckon females of *every* species fall in love."

Reed nodded, tightening the cinch on Rebel's belly. "If you're in a hurry, Pa, ride on. I'll catch up with you. Forgot something in the cabin."

The Senator grinned with understanding. "Well, you go after it. I'll just poke along."

Chapter 4

"Bonanza!" Devon cried, opening the bundle of mail Reed brought her from the county post office. There were newspapers, magazines, and a large manila envelope from her former editor containing a ten-page letter and numerous clippings. "Carrie Hempstead promised to keep in touch, and I'm anxious to read everything! Would you like to see a New York *Record*?"

"Darling, that news is over two weeks old! I'll go out and help Pa in the print shed. We have later news from the telegraph station. More new business failures everywhere."

"Any major banks?"

"Several, in Boston, Chicago, New Orleans. The biggest on Wall Street is still all right, however, and said to have more gold reserves in its vaults than the United States mints and Treasury combined."

Devon read that the President had cut short his vacation and rushed to New York to confer with his most trusted economic advisers, including Keith Heathstone Curtis. Grant had then ordered the Treasury secretary to release enough cash to repurchase thirteen million dollars' worth of its own bonds. But the maneuver had had little effect, and economists predicted a snowballing depression that would last for years.

The Bewitching Brokers made news in several ways. Their brokerage firm was a panic casualty, and their publication was in worse financial and legal straits than at any time since their daring exposé of the Reverend Henry Ward Beecher and Elizabeth Tilton love affair. Their best-known supporter, Cornelius Vanderbilt, withdrew his assistance and advice, as did several other wealthy contributors. The crusty old Commodore did not care about the accusations of adultery against America's foremost preacher and the wife of his own best friend, Theodore Tilton, editor of *The Independent,* a religious journal. Old Corneel simply no longer regarded the Claflin sisters as good risks once his determined young wife began to feed him orthodox religion and medicine. She counteracted his faith in spiritualists and magnetic healers, as she had hoped to do.

To Vicky and Tennie, however, the major threat to their fortunes had come over a year ago, when the pastor of Brooklyn's Plymouth Church had denounced Victoria's "Free Love Proclamation" and refused to introduce one of her lectures at Steinway Hall. Retaliation had been their response.

A Washington correspondent when *Woodhull & Claflin's Weekly* had exploded the news bomb that rocked American Christianity to its puritanical foundation, Devon had read the details and knew that many publishers considered the United States marshal's seizure of the copies an infringement of First Amendment rights.

Revenge might be the Lord's province, Vicky and Tennie declared, but the Bible also sanctioned "an eye for an eye, and a tooth for a tooth." Hatred for their sanctimonious persecutor multiplied a hundredfold after their release from prison and, aided by some prominent suffragettes— including Miss Anthony, Mrs. Stanton, and Mr. Beecher's own sister-in-law, Isabella Hooker—they pursued him like the Furies.

Carrie Hempstead felt that the sensationalism would eventually erupt in court, and wrote to Devon, "When that apocalypse comes, I hope you will consider reporting it for the *Record* Meanwhile, the President and Mrs. Grant have set the date for the marriage of their daughter, Nellie, to Algernon Sartoris, for next May 21. Mr. Fitch and I would greatly appreciate your acceptance of this assignment. All expenses paid, naturally, and your fee open."

The White House wedding would be a coveted press plum, and Devon craved it. Could she go?

The fall elections were imminent, and the Senator's son was the Democrats' choice to represent that district in the State House. The Carters were campaigning for him in the *Prairie Post*, and they planned to do some stumping as well.

Devon wanted to work on the paper, but cooking and keeping house for two men kept her busy. Her domestic chores seemed as endless as the dust filtering into the cabin, settling over furniture and floors, enslaving her with broom, mop, and feather duster. Often Devon felt the grit and grime on her skin, in her hair and clothing. Remembering the beautiful Hudson River estate tended by meticulous servants and the immaculate Rhinelander Gardens apartment in Greenwich Village, Devon had to restrain tears. In one of these morose moods, she decided a trip to town might help, and asked Reed to hitch the old horse and shabby buggy his father had bought at auction for a few dollars.

He frowned disapprovingly. "You can't go alone, Devon. This is the frontier, you know, and I haven't taught you how to use a gun yet."

"I'd rather not learn to kill, Reed."

"You'd better. Out here, your life could depend on it. Pa will drive you. He can take care of some business while you shop or visit Mrs. Winston."

"Sure," Jason agreed. "I'll hang around the telegraph station or play cards at the Last Chance Saloon awhile." Somehow, such establishments as the Last Chance were always among the first to arrive in any Western settlement, and the last to leave. "We'll get the rig ready, pronto."

A covered wagon stood in the square, the departing owners disposing of household belongings for which they had no room or further use, selling or bartering them for groceries and other necessities for travel west. The woman wore a plain brown challis dress, a slatted sunbonnet with a wide neck ruffle, and sturdy brogans. Her husband had on patched overalls, a faded denim shirt, and old Confederate trooper's hat. Their furrowed faces and brown, callused hands were at odds with their mid-thirties ages. They had three children, two teenage boys tending the mules and a small girl playing with a dog.

"Might find some bargains there," the Senator told his daughter-in-law. "See anything you like?"

"The cheval glass would be nice, sir. There's no full-length mirror in the cabin."

"Never had much need of one before," he said. "But I know ladies like to view themselves from head to toe."

"It helps us dress properly, without petticoats showing."

"All right. I'll try to buy that thing for you, honey, and figure out a way to get it home in one piece. Go along and visit your friend now."

"Thank you, sir. And you'll come for me?"

"No later than four o'clock," he promised. "Reed wants us back before dark."

Devon was somewhat surprised to find Carla Winston still in residence at the Dragoon Hotel. They greeted each other warmly, embracing.

"Devon, how wonderful to see you again!"

"I was afraid you might be gone, Carla. To Dallas, perhaps, since the plague scare there proved to be simple chickenpox."

"Oh, I've considered it," Carla shrugged. "But living is cheaper here now. I'm one of the few registered guests and I'm treated like royalty. Why move?"

"Sure there isn't some other reason?" Devon teased, removing her veiled bonnet and gloves.

Carla smiled coyly She looked much younger and prettier, in a bustled gown of lilac corded silk banded in purple grosgrain, than she had in the drab black weeds. "Sit down, dear. I'll order tea Or would you prefer wine?"

"Yes, please. I didn't know it was available in town."

"Imported brands aren't," Carla said. "The only spirits the saloon serves are draft beer, cheap cider, and red-eye whiskey strong enough for cattle dip. I brought two bottles of French wine with me, and have been saving it for a special occasion. Your visit qualifies." She produced a straw-white Montrachet whose label and vintage Devon recognized as one of Keith's favorites. *"Voilà!"*

Devon was wistful. "Oh, Lord, Carla! Your presence on that stage was a godsend. A Southerner, too, who speaks my language."

"Native Virginian, sweetie. Born in Norfolk and educated in Richmond."

"Really? I grew up in Richmond!"

"I know, darling Your father published the *Sentinel*. Of course, you were just a child when I went there. I'm at least ten years your senior."

Devon sighed, sipping the excellent wine, savoring its rare bouquet "Fate is strange, isn't it? To think that we should meet on our way to Texas and become friends under such odd circumstances! Were you actually a Confederate agent, Carla?"

Carla raised her right hand, swearing. "Absolutely. I knew Belle Boyd and Rose O'Neal Greenhow, known as Rebel Rose. And Nancy Hart, credited with providing the intelligence for General Stonewall Jackson's cavalry. Brave, clever women, and the South had more of them in government service than the North did. Once I posed as a Billy Yank in the ranks in a baggy uniform with my bust strapped down, but was eventually exposed and thrown into the camp stockade. I escaped by fraternizing with the Union guards, if you know what I mean."

"I think I do, yes."

"Southern women had to do a great many distasteful things in those days to survive, and some are still doing so. My family didn't own a plantation, but we did have several household slaves. My father was a prosperous merchant and chandler. Ours was one of the finest homes in Norfolk, with a beautiful garden and carriage house and stables. After the war we were paupers, like almost everyone else. I went North to find paying work."

"So did I," Devon confided. "It wasn't easy, but I finally got a job as a journalist for the New York *Record*."

"And a damned good one," Carla complimented. "I read many of your articles and followed your coverage of the White House social events and travels with the First Family. You had an enviable career, Devon. I'm curious to know why you sacrificed it for marriage."

"Many reasons, Carla. Some too painful to discuss."

"Love?"

Devon's eyes had been downcast; now she raised them. "Why do you ask that?"

"Because love is often painful. I had the misfortune of surrendering my heart to a married Union officer, with whom I was consorting to gain information for General Lee during the Virginia peninsula campaign. Later, he was captured and confined in Richmond's Libby Prison." She paused in pensive retrospection. "A part of me still loves that damn Yankee!"

"Maybe it's mutual?"

Carla shook her head. "No, Devon. You're a romantic, I'm a realist. When Grant took Richmond and freed the Union prisoners there, my major went home to his wife and kids in Connecticut, and I never heard from him again. It was all pretense for him, you see. I was a sexual convenience, and he also expected to use me in an escape plot. I was posing as a nurse in the Libby infirmary then, extracting what military information I could from the ill and wounded officers, in delirium or in gratitude. But his fevers were mostly raging passions of the groin, and he never revealed anything to me but lust."

"I'm sorry, Carla."

"Don't be. It was part of my job, and I was dedicated. Then I was given another mission, in Washington, where I ingratiated myself with members of President Lincoln's cabinet, primarily the pompous Secretary of War. I attended White House receptions and military balls. I wooed a couple of senators who were in the President's confidence and privy to the communiqués from generals in the field. Neither could resist boasting of his political power when his tongue was glib with alcohol. I not only successfully beguiled the braggarts, but pitted them against each other in the Senate arena."

Devon listened raptly, admiring Carla's skill and courage, thinking that her espionage adventures would make fascinating magazine articles or a thrilling novel. "You're a marvel, Carla! I think I'd have been terrified of discovery."

"I was, occasionally, and I had some close calls," Carla admitted. "Every spy does. It's beneficial to their skill. Makes them more alert."

Carla occupied a two-room suite, the best and most expensive accommodation the Dragoon Hotel had to offer. Red roses climbed the gilt trellises on the wallpaper, and floral carpets covered the floors. Through the open bedroom door Devon glimpsed a brass bedstead, golden oak bureau and chest, and damask chaise longue. The parlor was furnished with a plush settee and matching chairs, a desk, and marble-topped table holding an elaborate kerosene lamp. Two windows draped in gold-fringed crimson velvet overlooked the quadrangle, and Devon noticed a pair of opera glasses on one of the sills.

"What is there to observe in this cow town?" she asked.

Carla laughed. "Force of habit, my dear, and idle amusement. Time drags here."

Devon didn't have much leisure, but she was acquainted with boredom and the curious measures by which people sought to relieve it. "You seem to have adequate resources and income, Carla. In your place, I'd leave this trading post. There's bound to be more action in Dallas—or almost *any* other place."

"Oh, it's not so bad, Devon. The natives are friendly, at least. That's not always true of large cities, as you've undoubtedly discovered."

Devon nodded, sipping her wine. "My husband is running for the state legislature, you know."

"Yes, I was reading the *Prairie Post* when you arrived. Shall we drink a premature toast to his election?"

"By all means," Devon agreed, as Carla refilled their goblets. "My father-in-law will be coming for me soon."

"The old Senator? I've observed him through my lorgnette and am anxious to meet him. They say he was a big man in Texas before the war, both in ranching and in politics. Fought the Mexicans with General Sam Houston at San Jacinto, helped to establish Texas independence from Mexico, and was prominent in the government of the republic."

"Oh, yes. Jason Carter is a local hero. He made some giant strides, and it won't be easy for his son to equal them. But I'm confident that Reed will leave his own imprints."

Carla smiled, lifting her glass. "To your confidence, and to his success!"

Chapter 5

Vast as the prairie had seemed viewed from the cabin, Devon knew her eyes had deceived her. The horizon had been a mirage, and there was really no boundary at all. It stretched endlessly, apparently to the ends of the earth. Now she and Reed were alone on it in the buggy, going to investigate an abandoned homestead northwest of Fort Worth.

Devon was quiet with awe and apprehension, unable to ignore the remnants of defeated humanity strewn about them in the brush and buffalo grass. A collapsed wagon with its fraying cover flapping in the breeze like a tattered white flag; a lone, crumbling adobe chimney protruding from the charred remains of a dwelling; scraps of furniture, clothing, cooking utensils, toys. She tried to overlook the bleaching animal skeletons, including the huge arched ribs of bison and horses, the skulls and horns of cows. The rock-covered mounds with stick crosses were horrifying.

"God rest their souls," she murmured.

"What, darling?"

"Those graves. The poor people in them . . . thinking they could conquer *this* country!"

"Many pioneers have, Devon."

"At what cost? How many lives per mile? How many buckets of blood? And the few who succeed—what's their reward, Reed? More pain and sorrow! The roads west should be marked with cairns."

"They are," Reed said. "But people die everywhere, Devon, and a man under a marble slab in a city cemetery is just as dead as one under a pile of stones in the wilderness. The only difference is, the one out here may have had the satisfaction of dying for something important to him."

"A cause? The South had a cause, Reed, and hundreds of thousands of our men died for it. As many more were maimed, ruined, broken in spirit. What good did our cause do us? Where are our heroes now?" Devon did not realize that she was quoting Keith on the futility of war.

"Postmortems have never changed the course of history, Devon."

"Perhaps not, but fools are often responsible for their own fate."

"Can't argue that," Reed conceded, handing her the reins while he studied the scrap of paper on which his father had drawn a map and scrawled some directions.

"Are we lost?"

"Not yet."

"How can you tell?"

"Well, that lone mesquite and those yuccas ahead are guideposts. Also, the clump of cactus."

"Gorgeous scenery," Devon remarked wryly, returning the lines to him.

"The prairie's not at its best in autumn, darling, and the summer drought was worse than usual this year. But it'll come alive in spring, with blooming sagebrush and wild-flowers. Millions of them, all kinds and colors. Even the prickly pear blooms—pretty yellow blossoms so delicate they last only a day or two. And the fruit is edible. You'll see its beauty then."

But Devon remained cold to this primitive land. She was just glad that the buggy had a top and that she had taken precautions to protect her face and hands. "How much farther to our destination?"

"A few miles. Relax, honey. You're taut as a bowstring."

"Don't mention Indians!"

"I didn't."

"They use bows, don't they?"

"Not when they can get guns."

"Oh, Lord! Drive faster."

"Hush," he whispered, "and listen."

Devon tensed, gripping the seat, hearing a faint rumbling like distant thunder. But the sky was clear as blue crystal, the October sun a brassy glitter. The roar increased, reverberating, shaking the buggy. "What is it?" she asked tremulously.

Reed cautioned silence again, his narrowed eyes scanning the plains. "Mustangs," he said, pointing westward. "Look out there, Devon!"

A magnificent white stallion was leading his mares across the territory in a swift gallop. They came near enough for Devon to see their graceful forms, flying manes and tails.

"How beautiful they are!" she cried, glad she had come along now. "The first real wild horses I've ever seen!" Excitement brightened her eyes. "Do they always run like that?"

"When they're scared of capture," Reed said.

"I don't see anyone chasing them."

"They probably gave up."

"Who?"

He shrugged. "Oh, some hunting party—cowboys, or maybe Indians in need of extra ponies. And a mustang herd stud guards his *manada* of brood mares as jealously as a sultan his harem. They're heading for the hills and won't pause until they get there, even if some drop dead on the way."

"Fascinating," Devon said, wishing she had brought her journal. "How do you spell that word?"

"Like it sounds. Three syllables. *Ma-na-da.*"

"Thanks. I want to record this."

After that spectacular sight, the one they had traveled so far to find was grossly disappointing. A woodpile masquerading as a house, with tumbling outbuildings, broken fences, nature reclaiming the fields.

"It's good ranchland, Devon. The nestors failed because they tried to farm it without water, a common mistake of sodbusters. A few dry spells, and their seeds and labor are wasted. There's a message on the door, but the paint ran. Can you read it?"

"Yes. 'Gone back to Alabama. This here land ain't fit for man or beast. We give it to anybody that wants it, and may God have mercy on them that does.' It's signed Matt and Tillie Boles. I hope they made it home safely."

"To sharecrop on some plantation?"

"It's better than starving in this desolation!"

"Devon, there's an empire here for men with the guts and savvy to establish and hold it! Fortunes will be made in Texas to equal and surpass those of the Wall Street capitalists."

"When cattle kingdom comes?"

"You don't understand," he said. "Shall we survey the situation before posting our claim?"

She stared at him. "You don't expect to *live* here?"

He was out of the buggy and assisting her. "No, Pa can find some Mexican or half-breed squatter, after it's registered in the Carter name."

"Do we have to go inside?"

"Why not? It's open."

"But we're trespassing."

He laughed. "Darling, you read the public notice. Come on, now. And be careful, the step is loose."

Its earlier American counterpart could be found in the Appalachians, Smokies, Ozarks, and Blue Ridge and across the Territories. Hastily constructed from the most readily accessible materials—logs, stones, clay, or mere mud and sticks—it had one room with a fireplace, in which a family of five or six might live. A utility shed had been tacked on to this building.

"Oh, Reed, it's awful!"

"But free, Devon, like manna from heaven. Shall we clean it up a bit?"

"Why?"

"Make it look occupied, to discourage poachers."

A broom of apache-plume weeds stood in one corner. Devon picked it up and began to sweep out the accumulated debris from the living area, while Reed flushed a pair of amorous possums from the lean-to. She laughed as the male charged him, snarling and spitting his rage, retreating when Reed wouldn't be bluffed.

"If he had a gun, he'd shoot you."

"If he were a skunk, he'd have a more effective weapon. Feisty little bastard. Can't blame him, though. I interrupted his fun. Ever see possums mate?"

"I'm a city gal, remember? And I thought possums were supposed to play dead when caught."

"Not when caught copulating, which they do differently from most animals. Wish I'd left 'em alone and let you watch."

"Oh, really!" Devon admonished him, bumping into the blackened kettle still hanging on the hearth crane. Soon her clothes were soiled, and there was a sooty smudge on her cheek.

"You look like a chimneysweep," Reed teased, wiping her face with his bandana. "But cute."

"Get back to work!"

"Hell, I got a better idea . . ."

"Now, Reed, we don't know anything about the last occupants of that bed. It may have fleas, lice, ticks."

He grinned, beginning to strip. "Might as well shuck your duds too, honey. I aim to make love to you, even if lepers slept there."

In truth, Devon was eager, too. Finally they stood naked, viewing their nude bodies for the first time in daylight. Reed said huskily, "You're beautiful, Devon. The most perfect woman I've ever seen, the Creator's masterpiece. We should have a place of our own, where we can do this whenever we please. Even with Pa in the print shop, we're never completely alone."

"You talk too much, Mr. Carter."

"You want action, Mrs. Carter? Very well, you shall have it. Holler when you've had enough. No one can hear you."

The taste of her intoxicated him, as did her readiness to receive him. Mounting her swiftly, he rode high and hard, delivering the long, deep, rapid thrusts in which she delighted, arching her spine and positioning her legs around his torso. Her sensuous cries spurred his own groaning.

"Enough?" he asked, as Devon lay spent in his arms.

"For now," she murmured, surprised at the teeth marks on his shoulder. "Did I do that?"

"Who else?"

"I'm sorry, Reed. I didn't realize it."

"I like it, and hope it leaves a scar. I think I'll make a little branding iron with your initials and burn them into my flesh."

"Oh, Reed, that's barbarian."

"But romantic, too. Wouldn't you like to be permanently marked by love?"

Devon glanced away. How could she admit that she already was? If only she could remove her mental cobwebs as easily as she had cleaned them from the ceiling and walls of this cabin! "We're going to be late getting home, dear."

"Un-huh. But it was worth it for me. For you?"

She nodded against his bare chest.

"I love you, Devon," he prompted.

She smiled at him and sat up, reaching for her clothes. "We'd better get dressed now."

"Yeah." Someday, she would say the words he wanted most to hear. Someday, he assured himself.

A week later, Devon was leaning against the corral as Reed repaired some of the mesquite rails. The prairie grass was drier and browner in late October, and the willows along the Cold Springs Creek hung in long yellow strips. Remembering the brilliant autumn foliage of Virginia and New York, Devon was nostalgic. "Don't you have Indian summer here?"

"Not like in New England," Reed said. "We don't have the trees for it, except the sycamores and oaks along the Trinity and Brazos rivers. This part of Texas is called the Grand Prairie."

"What's grand about it?"

"Nothing, unless you happen to like God's country."

"Looks more like the devil's domain to me."

He smiled slightly. "Plenty of folks would agree with you, including General Philip Sheridan. During his tenure here, he said that if he owned all of Texas and hell, he would rent out Texas and live in hell. But it has its compensations. Look to the east and you'll see one of them."

He meant the wagon train, of course, a flotilla plowing the grassy sea, one of many en route before the panic had struck, and possibly still blissfully unaware of it. From a distance, they resembled an armada, kept on course by wagon-master captains. Canvas covers billowed like sails; flags of drying laundry flew from the bowmasts. Hawks wheeled overhead like gulls. "Prairie schooners," Devon remarked, "and aptly named. But why do they keep coming, Reed?"

He shrugged, preoccupied with his work. "Who knows, Devon? Every pioneer hears a different call. They came in waves after the war, and not all were ruined rebels. They were many Yankees and foreign immigrants, too. Every generation and nationality has its pilgrims, wayfarers, and wanderers. For some, the American West represents freedom and independence. To others, it's a challenge. Most are solid citizens and a credit to the community they settle."

She watched the approaching wagons awhile longer, deciding the occupants were simply afflicted with wanderlust.

"Where's your father?"

"Finishing an editorial. We go to press tomorrow, you know."

"How many pages this time?"

"Six. Ten advertisements from Dallas, several from Waco, Austin, Houston, and Galveston. Enough revenue to pay for the newsprint and ink, anyway. And the county folks are now familiar enough with the name of the publishers of the *Prairie Post* to recognize that name on the Democratic ticket."

"Too bad women can't vote," Devon mused, thinking of her brave suffragette friends with whom she had marched in New York, landing herself in the Tombs.

"Well, I'm afraid that's still in the distant future for this state, darling. But you can discuss it with the ladies at the Harvest Festival next week. I checked the freight from Louisiana while in town this morning, and your trunks finally arrived. That should make you happy."

Happy? Dear God! Did he imagine that pretty clothes were the essence of female happiness? If so, he didn't know much about women, and even less about his own wife. Clothes, indeed!

Chapter 6

"Try to conserve water," Reed advised as Devon prepared her bath. "The cistern is low, and the spring flow dwindling. You can wade across the creek. If it doesn't rain soon, we'll have to haul water from the river."

"Do I use too much?"

"No, but you needn't rinse the clothes twice. Once is enough until the shortage is over. Pa and I will scrub up in the creek, as usual. And we'll dress in the shed for the shindig, allow you more time and privacy."

"Thank you," Devon said. "I'm not really a slowpoke about dressing, I just don't like to rush needlessly."

Using an old flatiron heated on the kitchen range, she pressed a pale amber muslin dress with a scalloped neckline, ruffled sleeves, and yards of fluttering flounces. Discretion forbade her choosing a more fashionable bustled silk gown, whose extravagance might raise doubts of her conservatism and affect her husband's chances in the election. She must also avoid fancy high-heeled slippers and Paris perfume—frivolous vanities to simple countryfolk, and more suitable to harlots than housewives. Lord, if they could see the contents of her trunks—the exquisite lingerie and boudoir ensembles, the silk stockings and French leather gloves, the elegant gowns and cloaks, the expensive furs and jewelry—all the generous gifts of an Eastern millionaire to his beloved mistress.

Suddenly the room felt chilly, the wood washtub so cramped her knees nearly touched her chin. Oh, the luxury of her former ablutions! Soothing salts, scented oils, the finest Castile soap. The Roman tub in Keith's Clairmont suite was Genoese marble, large enough to accommodate two adults, and they had occasionally bathed together, sponging each other, even making love in the warm, fragrant water. Then he would dry her gently with a large

Turkish towel and carry her to the master bedroom. No, she must stop brooding, or go mad!

Bless the Senator for buying her the cheval glass and hauling it home in a rattling donkey-cart, wrapped in old quilts to prevent damage. She stood before it, arranging her hair, which she washed weekly despite the Carters' cautions about wasting water. She would simply mop the floors less often.

She heard the men approaching the cabin, talking loudly to warn her. Devon tucked a pair of topaz-and-seed-pearl *fourches* in her brushed and shining curls, and opened the door.

Reed wore brown canvas pants, a clean white shirt and black string tie, and buckskin jacket. His father was spruced up in his one good dark suit, which he called his "burying duds." Their boots were clean, hats brushed, faces shaved. The Senator had combed his mustache carefully.

"Lucky me, to have two such handsome escorts," Devon complimented, as they lifted her into the buggy and helped to tuck in her skirts.

"We're the lucky ones," Reed said. "I'll be the proudest man in the county! Isn't she beautiful, Pa?"

"A goddess," Jason agreed, mounting his horse. "You'd better keep a sharp eye on the local rustlers, son."

The old armory, scene of the Harvest Festival, was decorated with cornshocks, ripe pumpkins, colorful gourds, Indian corn, and sprays of wheat and oats. The long bare pinewood tables, relics of the dragoons' mess hall, were laden with food furnished by the guests, and several earthenware crocks of native punch.

"Hope they got plenty of this stuff," the Senator said, sampling a dipperful. "I'm parched as the prairie."

"Maybe the dance will break the drought?" Carla suggested, tongue-in-cheek. "Or is that Indian superstition?"

Reed was philosophical. "Oh, it's bound to rain sometime, ma'am. Always does."

"Exactly what is everyone celebrating?" Devon inquired. "Another year of survival?"

"A feat in itself," her father-in-law explained. "But there're other reasons, honey. Even with the dry season, the crops were fair and have been gathered. We had no grasshopper plague, no human epidemic, no rampaging Indians, or Texas fever to quarantine our longhorns in the

Northern markets. That's plenty to be glad about, even if the panic did scare away some settlers and stop the railroad in its tracks only a few miles short of town. Things could be better, sure, but also worse. You got to take the good with the bad, thank Providence for the blessings, and overlook regret."

Reed smiled. "You sound like a circuit preacher, Pa. This is a festival, not a revival. Lester Hale's tuning up his fiddle. Better limber your joints."

"Boy, I can dance circles around you! Always could, and you know it. Compared to me, you've got peg legs."

"Sure, Pa," Reed humored him. "The Hortons just came in. Let's see how things are on the Brazos."

"Howdy, George. Evening, Bess. Anything new in your vicinity?"

"Yep. The Plains Injuns are startin' to sneak around agin. Jed Thompson seen some not more'n twenty mile from the river. Scouts ridin' out from Fort Belknap regular now."

"That so? Reckon we ought to post some guards outside tonight, then, considering the full moon."

"Yeah, and I brought along a couple of cowhands to stand watch. Other fellas can relieve 'em, if they want."

The square was crowded with vehicles, mostly wagons and saddle horses. Those who had traveled more than ten miles intended to spend the night in the building, their children on pallets. There were some strangers among the familiar faces, and the departed families were sadly missed. But the greetings were exuberant, with much hugging, kissing, handshaking, and catching up on local news. Someone mentioned that Ben Becker's barn had burned down, destroying his entire harvest. There would be a barn-raising for the Beckers as soon as lumber and nails were available. Meanwhile, neighbors were sharing their hay and grain.

The appointed master of ceremonies mounted the improvised stage. "Attention, gentlemen! Please remove your hats and spurs, and check your weapons in the artillery room. We don't want no accidents or bruised ladies."

Spurs, gunbelts, knife scabbards came off, some cowboys complaining that they felt naked without these trappings. The fiddler got his signal and began with the traditional "Arkansas Traveler." Monk Saunders began to call the figures in a nasal twang:

> Choose your partner, form a ring,
> Figure eight and double L swing,
> First swing six, then swing eight,
> Swing 'em like swingin' on a gate.
> Ducks in the river, goin' to the ford,
> Coffee in a little rag, sugar in a gourd.
> Swing 'em once and let 'em go,
> All hands left and do-si-do!

The fiddler played by ear, unable to distinguish a written musical note from a cow track. The stamping feet on the puncheon floor kept time. Figures bowing, backing, locking arms, turning, spinning, skipping down the lines to the bottom, then working back up again. Devon had never seen such hearty jubilation.

"So this is a Texas hoedown?" she said as Reed coaxed her onto the floor for the Virginia reel. "I must say we were a little more subdued back home. Where do they get all that energy?"

"It's stored up for months, Devon. This is their sabbatical from work and worry and monotony. Time for fun! They cram as much into it as possible. Harvest festivals had their origins in the Indian ceremonials, you know."

"In this country, yes. Other peoples have been celebrating like this since time began. That's how the Bacchanalia and Mardi Gras originated."

"Yes, my learned love. What a shame to waste all that knowledge on these bumpkins."

"Don't be cynical," she scolded. "I wasn't showing off. Besides, there are some highly intelligent people present. Your father and Carla Winston are getting better acquainted."

"I've noticed," Reed said. "She's a handsome woman in that shining blue gown. Nice shape, too."

Devon smiled. "I predict they'll be seeing more of each other after tonight."

"Maybe sooner. The old wolf has reserved a room at the Dragoon Hotel. I haven't seen such a twinkle in his eye for years."

"Which proves he's not so old, after all."

"Well, not too old, anyway."

Monk Saunders droned on like a mechanical bee:

> You swing me, and I'll swing you,
> And we'll all go to heaven in the same old shoe,
> Chase the possum, chase the coon,
> Chase that pretty girl round the room!

"That's you," Reed whispered in her ear. "The prettiest girl in the room, and after all my chasing, I finally caught you. I'm the envy of every man here tonight," he said proudly, gazing down at her soft fair shoulders, intrigued by the tiny gold-chained locket nestled between her breasts. "That's a pretty trinket, darling. Got a picture in it?"

"No, something more precious to me." But she did not name it, and Reed feared to ask.

The caller broke up their figure:

> Rope the cow and kill the calf,
> Swing your partner a round and a half,
> Swing your partner before you trade,
> Grab 'em back and promenade!

When the rafter-shaking promenade ended, an elderly fellow shouted to the fiddler, "Enough 'Turkey in the Straw,' Les! Play a few waltzes. A medley of Stephen Foster would be jest fine."

"You gettin' winded, Zeb?" Hale hooted from the platform. "Well, I'll oblige."

Waltzing with Reed, Devon asked, "Do you suppose Mr. Hale knows any Strauss?"

"Darling, he's an Ozark hillbilly, and hardly an accomplished musician. Strauss needs a string orchestra of Stradivarius violins and a maestro, not a homemade fiddle and hog-caller."

Devon sighed, thinking of the brilliant ballrooms of Saratoga and the Catskill Mountain House, the sophisticated clubs, theaters, and restaurants of Manhattan, the lavish Washington cotillions.

"Tired, honey?"

"A little."

"Some nourishment might help, and we might as well beat the stampede. Pa and Carla are already at the trough. Shall we join them?"

Carla was eating fried chicken, potato salad, and cole slaw. The Senator's plate was piled with barbecued beef, baked ham, thick slices of sourdough bread, and a wedge of pumpkin pie. Devon couldn't decide what to try first, and picked up a small piece of pound cake on a chipped saucer and a tin cup of punch, grimacing as she tasted the bitter drink.

"Go easy on that," Reed warned. "Too much will make you tipsy."

"What's in it?"

"Mustang grapes and algerita juice. Not intentionally alcoholic, but somehow it just ferments that way."

"'I knew there was something good about it," Carla said, refilling her gourd ladle. "I must get the recipe."

Jason chuckled and patted her cheek. Reed, gnawing on a turkey drumstick, winked at Devon.

A farmer and his wife invited the Carters to a cornhusking party and included Mrs. Winston. Other invitations followed: a barbecue, hayride, taffy pull, a picnic—simple rural entertainments it was expedient for politicians to attend, but Reed accepted out of friendship and genuine pleasure.

As Lester Hale swung into "Buffalo Gal," Carla turned eagerly to Jason Carter. "Come on, Senator! The night's still young, and I feel spry enough for an Irish jig or Highland fling."

"Me too, honey. I'm a wound-up top ready to spin till dawn." He poked a joshing finger at his son. "What's the matter, boy? Can't keep up with your old man? Get out there and shake a leg, both of you!"

"Give us time to eat, Pa, and then we'll see who runs down first. I notice you dropped out of that last promenade."

"Only to quench my thirst," Jason defended. "I've been working up a froth."

"Most old studs do, when pursuing a mare half their age."

"Watch your tongue, boy! There's ladies present. And check your feet—I think you're wearing two left boots."

The newlyweds drove home alone. A great harvest moon beamed on the prairie, and the night was crisply cold. Devon pulled her shawl over her shoulders, wondering if anyone except Carla Winston had realized it was cashmere. She cuddled close to Reed. "Winter is near, isn't it?"

"Yeah, and it's a bitch out here, sometimes. But January

and February are the worst months, and I think we'll be in Austin by then. That's two hundred miles farther south, on the Colorado River." He brushed his lips against her cool face. "Did you have fun tonight, darling?"

"Yes, the people were all very kind."

"Crude, some of them, I know. But life is crude on the frontier, Devon, and a hoedown isn't exactly a formal ball."

"I didn't expect Harvard English and embassy etiquette," she said. "Do you think they liked me?"

"How could they help it?"

"Seriously, Reed. They didn't find me too . . . well, different?"

"You did fine, just the right mixture of modesty and reserve, and they admired you tremendously. We were included in all the invitations."

"And such exciting events, too! What does a lady wear to a corn-husking?"

"Gloves if she values her hands."

Coyotes howled in the distance, and Devon shuddered. She would never get used to that eerie sound. Sometimes they prowled near the cabin, frightening the chickens and livestock, and Reed or his father had to drive them away with gunfire. "Damn those mangy critters!" she cried.

" 'Varmints,' honey. 'Critters' are something else. But you're learning the lingo."

His amusement annoyed her. "Whatever they are, I hate them! Their yelping makes me nervous."

"They're just baying at the moon, or yodeling mating calls. Then again, it may not be coyotes at all."

"Indians?"

"Well, you heard what those folks from the Brazos region said and Indians are experts at mimicry. Some Indian bucks get sex that way in rutting season."

"But that's bestiality!"

"Yep, and old as Scripture. Not limited to savages, either. Lonely men get desperate, and if they can't find a natural mate, well . . . you get the idea?"

"I do, and it's disgusting!"

"Sorry, honey. I keep forgetting your innocence. Such things don't shock wilderness women much."

"Go faster," Devon urged him "I want to get home."

Reed slapped the lines across Betsy's bony rump. "I'm sort of anxious myself," he said, and Devon wasn't sure what he meant until they got into bed.

Chapter 7

"Why all the armament?" Devon asked as the men prepared to go to the polls. "It's an election, not a war."

"Not much difference, sometimes," said Jason grimly.

Reed gazed at her gravely. "You left Virginia before Reconstruction rule assumed full control, Devon. And women don't know much about politics, anyway. But you lived in New York long enough to be aware of the Tammany Hall tactics that kept the Tweed Ring in power. Well, we have a similar situation in Austin now, a bunch of carpetbag crooks robbing the state treasury into bankruptcy. A ruthless state police force works to their benefit."

"You think violence is the answer?"

"We don't intend any violence, unless threatened with it ourselves," the Senator soothed. "Haven't you been reading my editorials, honey? We have no more freedom and independence now than the slaves had. Texas has a chance to regain its own government in this election, and we and our supporters aim to make sure it's fair and square."

"Any man caught trying to cast more than one ballot will draw back a nubbin," Reed declared. "And be lucky if he's not strung up to the nearest trees. We've had a gutful of others taking away our liberties."

"So vigilante committees are forming?"

Reed scowled impatiently. "You used to sit in the Ladies' Gallery in Washington, Devon. You heard the few Southern voices that dared to dissent shouted down in Congress. You've seen the Yankees, determined to grind their heels on our necks indefinitely, humiliate us, rob us of our birthright. How many more years are we expected to endure this treatment?" He jammed his old cavalry hat on his head and stuck a bowie knife in his belt. "Get ready and come with us. You can stay with Carla at the hotel."

"How long will you be gone?"

"Until the votes are in and have been counted under supervision."

"But that could take days!"

"Not in this county," Reed said. "Shouldn't take more than a few hours."

"Well, the time should pass swiftly enough, with all I have to do here."

"You're not afraid to be alone?"

"No," Devon lied bravely. "I can take care of myself."

He smiled wryly. "Yeah, I've seen you shoot. Just keep a loaded weapon handy, and remember which end to hold." That ruffled her, and he hesitated, aware that she was in a difficult mood. He kissed her good-bye. "One of us will be home before dark, darling."

"Good luck," Devon offered, waving them off, her courage waning as they disappeared.

The December day was bitterly cold, the eternal wind whistling across the dry, bare prairie. She bolted the door and stirred the fire, adding another log. Thank God Reed had chopped more wood yesterday, and his father had milked the cow before breakfast. Later on, she might churn some butter and hang out a sack of clabber for cottage cheese.

Right now, she wanted to relax and try to convince herself that she was not pregnant. There were other reasons for a delayed menses, taut breasts, and tart tongue. Her attitude this morning had been waspish and contrary, and Reed had humored her. Did he suspect pregnancy?

Her first confinement had been difficult, even with Keith's medical skills and Mrs. Sommes's midwifery experience. The prospect of childbearing under the current circumstances was frightening.

Devon had just opened her journal to record her maudlin musings when she heard wheels grinding on the lane. She picked up the pistol before peeping through the crack in the door, doubtful she could shoot even if confronted by an Indian. Relieved to recognize Carla driving a livery rig, she discarded the gun and rushed out to meet her.

"Welcome! Providence must have sent you!"

Carla smiled, securing the lines to a hitching post. "I saw your menfolk ride into town alone, and thought you might like some company. Not many ladies out today, and a good thing. Some of those hombres on patrol have blood in their eyes. There's liable to be gunplay."

"I know," Devon said as they entered the house. "The Democrats intend this election to be free and honest."

Carla nodded. "Even if they have to kill the opposition.
—Which is about all the lying carpetbaggers deserve.
They've sacked the South long enough. But I don't want to
discuss politics, dear." Carla shed her handsome wool
cloak, fur-trimmed bonnet, and leather driving gloves.
"Just some friendly female conversation."

"Thank you, Carla. My nearest neighbors are miles
away, and the womenfolk don't have much time for talk."

"Strapped with families, field- and housework," Carla
said sadly. "I felt sorry for them at the festival, Devon.
They looked wasted. And those pitiful homemade garments!
One was wearing an ancient brown hubbard of butternut
homespun, prewar vintage and alluring as a potato sack.
You looked like an elegant court lady among them, and I
felt like a madam in my décolleté satin and French slippers. Maybe some of the gents thought I'd come to establish a bordello." Carla grinned mischievously. "Christ, I'd
go to Dallas, if that were my ambition. There's no money
here. The camp followers service the fort soldiers and officers. The cowboys know every piece of tail for sale in the
territory. And they have other resources. . . ."

"Reed told me that," Devon reflected, "but I didn't want
to believe it."

"Believe it," Carla said. "Every country kid knows it's
true, Devon. I had an uncle who raised sheep in the Shen-
andoah Valley, and his grown boys got more than virgin
wool from their flock. They preferred the ewe lambs and
anchored their hind legs in their boots, getting their fun
without effort when the helpless creatures struggled for
release. I recently overheard some cattlemen talking about
an old miner who inhabits a cave in the hills and fancies a
she-panther, and a local hermit who lives with his jenny.
Lives with her, mind you. They said it was common
knowledge in the county."

"Good Lord," said Devon. "Would you like some coffee,
Carla? The breakfast pot is still hot on the stove, and I
have sweet cream. Our Jersey came fresh several weeks ago
and has the cutest little calf."

"Yeah, I hear it bawling. And the coffee sounds good, if
I can dilute it with warm milk. "I have a weakness for *café
au lait*, a habit acquired in New Orleans. Let's enjoy it by
the fire."

She followed Devon, removing cups and saucers and

pitcher from the cupboard. "This is good china, Devon. English bone?"

"Part of a set bought from a couple on the square, which is how I got the cheval mirror, too. But the platter and sugar bowl had been broken, and I don't have a tray or teacart, either. The Carters are not equipped to entertain, I'm afraid. Reed said they used to set a fine table at the Circle C Ranch, but everything was confiscated for delinquent taxes during the provisional government."

"Those greedy bastards," Carla swore vehemently. "Good thing his poor mother wasn't alive then. Mine grieved herself sick when she lost our lovely home and precious heirlooms. But that's all in the past now, Devon, part of the late, lamented Confederacy, for which taps are long overdue."

They were seated by the hearth, and Devon gazed mournfully into the flames, the embers sifting through the grate and glowing like live rubies on the black stones. "I wonder if anyone ever really forgets the past," she mused. But she was not thinking of the Southland. "What happened to your husband, Carla? You never told me."

"He was killed early in the war, at the First Battle of Bull Run That's when I decided to work secretly for the Confederacy. I was given some training by government operatives, but most of it came naturally. Maybe women have a natural instinct for spying, since they have been engaged in espionage in every war in history. And have suffered a great deal for it," Carla finished vehemently.

At Devon's curious gaze, she explained, "I was ravished early in my spying career by three Yankee soldiers who caught me hiding in a North Carolina hayloft. It wasn't exactly a tea party. They took turns, holding me at bayonet point, until I passed out. When I came to, I was bleeding profusely, and one of the fiends, possibly feeling guilty, was trying to help by stuffing his dirty kerchief into my vagina His buddies had fled. But this one, who couldn't have been more than twenty, took pity on me and directed me to a country doctor. I expected to die of hemorrhage or infection, but I'm fairly tough. I know that kindly old physician cleaned out most of my rapists' sperm—and possibly one of their brats—when he treated me. Anyway, I didn't get pregnant or have a venereal disease, for which I was grateful."

"You're an amazing person, Carla. I realized that on our

first meeting. I value our friendship tremendously. If we go to Austin, I hope you will, too."

"Why not? Most state capitals are fairly lively, at least during legislative sessions. Of course, I'd miss the Senator." Carla winked. "The rascal has sneaked into town several times, and up the backstairs of the hotel to my room."

Devon smiled. "I'm not surprised. He's very fond of you. But stages run to Austin, and where there's a will, there's a way."

"Or vice versa." Carla laughed. She picked up an old issue of *Godey's* and simulated a lorgnette with her fingers. "My dear, this magazine is two months old! I wonder what the stylish ladies of the East are wearing this season? And what of the British and European courts?"

"I suspect, madame," Devon mimicked, "the royal affairs of the Continent are as brilliant as ever, the courtiers eating cake while the commoners scrounge for bread. No doubt Queen Victoria is still mourning Prince Albert in black or deep purple. And Monsieur Worth continues to dominate Paris fashions, although France is no longer a monarchy. And here we sit, sipping coffee instead of tea, with no cakes to munch. Not even curds and whey, because the shiftless servant neglected to make the cheese. Isn't it dreadful?"

Seeing her sudden serious frown, Carla cheered. "Well, I predict young Mrs. Carter will set the style in Austin, with the rest of the ladies copying her!"

"In my months-old costumes?"

"They'll never know the difference, darling. I'll bet you have some gorgeous clothes in your expensive trunks. I didn't know journalism paid so well."

"It doesn't," Devon replied ruefully. "I had a very wealthy and generous friend."

"Benefactor?"

"In a sense."

Her visitor waited, expectant. But Devon only offered more coffee, and tried to resume their farce. "Would you care to hear our luncheon menu, Mrs. Winston? Leftover pinto beans seasoned with salt pork. Cornpone. And crab-apple cobbler sweetened with blackstrap molasses. Alas, no sugar or spice. Supper will be the same."

"Sounds delicious," Carla said, appraising her friend's wan face. "You look pale, dear. Feeling well?"

"Just a little tired."

* * *

They cooked, cleaned the kitchen, and did some other chores, and then it was time to light the lamp. Devon polished the glass chimney, a daily task, glancing apprehensively at the old clock on the wall, its brass pendulum marking the time. "It's getting late, and Reed promised that one of them would return before dark. I hope nothing went wrong."

"The polls don't close until seven," Carla reminded. "And the Senator knows I'm here, Devon."

"You're not afraid?"

"After my experiences in the war?"

"But this is the frontier, Carla."

"And Indians have been seen near the Brazos River, according to some settlers. But that's miles away, Devon. Besides, I've heard some of the tribes are friendly– and the military dispatches are posted at the telegraph station. If the scouts' observations are correct, the hostile Comanche are in winter camp on the High Plains, the Kiowa are in the Red River region near the Oklahoma Territory, the Apache are down around the Pecos, and the forts and outposts are keeping watch on all of them. I'm not worried about the savages. And the other outlaws, usually white, are seeking money and valuables, which they'd hardly expect to find here."

The rising wind rustled the reedy grass, and the whippoorwills and bobwhites cried plaintively. Later, the coyotes came. They were not as large as the gray timber wolves of the forests, or the Mexican lobos, but they were as fierce as their ancestors. Ordinarily, coyotes avoided human beings, but it was winter now, and the chickens clucked uneasily in the coop. The cow bellowed anxiously to warn her calf. "Those varmints fancy the tender victuals out there," Carla surmised. "Don't you have a watchdog?"

"Ranger took off after a bitch in heat last week, and we haven't seen him since."

"Typical of the male of every species."

"The coyotes are advancing, Carla."

"Not toward the cabin, Devon. But we'd better be prepared." She removed a derringer from her reticule.

"You always carry that?" Devon asked.

"Always, and it's deadly if your target is close and your aim steady. No woman should travel without a weapon,

Devon. My trusty little companion has saved my life on
several occasions. Can you handle a gun?"

"Not very well. Reed gave me some lessons, but I have a
horror of them."

The howls grew louder, hungrier, then suddenly ceased,
as the cunning creatures crept toward the outbuildings,
pausing, stalking, awaiting their leader's signal.

Within minutes the flimsy shelters were stormed, the
cackling layers snatched from their nests, fought over, de-
voured. The penned cow lowed, butted, gored, while her
helpless calf was mutilated. The frenzied sow's efforts to
protect her squealing litter were also futile. A pair of coyotes leaped upon the stable roof, deciding to risk the hooves
of the dray horse.

A pale moon shone on the grotesque scene, and Devon
cried, "Carla, they got the hens, calf, and piglets! Now
they're after the horse, and they'll get yours, too!"

"Not if I can help it!" Carla grabbed the rifle out of
Devon's frozen hands, propped open a window shutter, and
fired. But the trigger only clicked. "The goddamn pin is
stuck, and they're too far away for the derringer! I'll try
the Colt. Get some more ammunition handy!"

"Oh, Carla! The men left it in the print shop after loading their weapons this morning!"

"My God! Well, I have some extra bullets in my muff,
but every one has to count, Devon. Rattle some tin pans—
the noise might frighten them."

But as Devon dug in the cupboards, the crazed pack
charged the cabin, growling, clawing the logs, bouncing
against the door and walls. Devon screamed. "They're trying to get inside!"

"Must be starved, or rabid," Carla shouted, emptying the
revolver into their midst, killing and wounding several. "If
I could get the leader, the rest might leave." She cocked
her derringer. "Come on, big boy!"

The leader attempted to leap through the window, and
she fired into his snarling fanged mouth. He hit the ground
with a heavy thud. His mate's mournful yowling drove the
survivors berserk. They ran around in rage and confusion,
attacking one another and their own shadows. The hitched
mare broke her tether and fled across the prairie, dashing
the vehicle and shafts to pieces. A few more shots scattered
the coyotes, leaving only their yelping echoes on the wind.

Carla dropped the wood shutter and latched it. But Devon, hysterical, continued to clatter the utensils until Carla removed them from her hands and gently shook her shoulders. "It's all right now, honey. The jackals are gone."

Her eyes were glassy. "Are you sure?"

"Positive. They got most of the chickens, except those on the high roost, and the poor little calf. But not the cow or that nag in the stable. Mine broke loose and ran off, however, so I'm stranded."

"I'm sorry, Carla." Devon was nauseous and too dizzy to stand. She eased toward the bed and sat down gingerly. "I . . . I think I'm bleeding."

"Menstruating? Me, too, a week early! Can you lend me some protection?"

"All I have are rags and safety pins, Carla. In the lower bureau drawer. Help yourself."

"Thanks. If Madame Ellen Demorest would employ her genius to devise some convenient sanitary aids, she'd earn a million dollars and the gratitude of every female from puberty to menopause. I despise wearing the rag every month, as every other woman must. You need anything, dear?"

Devon clutched her cramping belly. "I may be miscarrying, Carla."

"Miscarrying? Jesus Christ, you're pregnant?"

"I'm not sure yet. I've only missed one month."

"Maybe it's just excitement, Devon. Lie down and try to relax. I'll elevate your feet." As Devon obeyed, Carla placed the pillows under her legs. "Does Reed know?"

"No, I haven't told him yet."

"Why in hell not? He's the father, isn't he?"

"I wasn't sure."

"That it's his child?"

"That I'm pregnant."

Carla sighed. "And you didn't want to worry him ahead of time? So you let both hombres ride off and leave you alone in this godforsaken place?"

"They wanted to take me along, but I was stubborn."

"Oh, shit, Devon! Women are just silly fools about such things. They hate to bother their menfolk with their 'female problems,' even though the sons of bitches are responsible for *most* of them! I bet Adam was out hunting a fresh apple while Eve was bearing his brats in agony. That just proves God is a man!" Carla paced. "Do you feel any better now?"

"Some."

"Still think you're bleeding?"

"No," Devon murmured weakly.

"Let me check." Carla examined her undergarments. "I don't see anything, Devon. If you were pregnant, you still are. But in your shoes, I'd welcome a miscarriage. This might be a great land for men and horses, but it's hell on women and children!"

Around midnight they heard thundering hooves on the dark lanes, and Devon said, "The fellows must be coming."

"High time!" Carla muttered.

"Don't mention our ordeal, please."

"Devon, the laying hens are gone, the calf is dead, there are seven stiff coyotes outside, and the bloody entrails of a few are decorating the cabin. And you don't think they'll suspect anything?"

"They're probably too drunk or too elated to notice now," Devon reasoned. "They're giving the rebel yell and singing 'Dixie' at the top of their lungs. That means Reed won his race, and they've been celebrating at the saloon."

Carla nodded, smiling wryly. "Men, the lucky bastards!"

The words were hardly off her lips when male fists were pounding the door. "Hey, in there! Wake up! It's us, and we've got great news!"

Carla removed the plank bar to admit them. The Senator swung her off her feet and kissed her, while his son went to his wife. "Guess what, darling? Your husband won by an overwhelming majority!"

"Congratulations," Devon said, and Carla added hers.

Reed sat down beside Devon, started to remove his boots. "Anything wrong, honey?"

"No, Carla and I were just preparing to retire."

"Oh. Well, maybe you ladies would be more comfortable in here. I'll bunk with Pa in the shop."

Jason laughed, jubilant with victory and bourbon. "I can think of better sleeping arrangements, Representative Carter. But I got a stashed jug of red-eye out there that might help to console us. Good night, ladies. Pleasant dreams."

"Likewise, gentlemen." Carla watched them weave out the back door, and then burst into laughter. "Boy, tomorrow morning when they look around this yard, they'll think they had nightmares!"

Chapter 8

Devon did not know what had awakened her. There was no sound from the coop or stable, and the cabin was still in darkness. She rose and cracked a window. The strange glow in the west was puzzling, and she woke Carla.

"The sun seems to be rising in the west."

Carla sat up, yawning. "It's too early for sunrise in any direction."

"Please, Carla. Get up and look."

"Oh, all right. I guess anything can happen in this crazy place. And nothing would surprise me after last night." She gazed at the odd glimmer in the distant sky. "Lightning, probably. A storm coming."

"I don't hear any thunder."

"It's too far away."

"Maybe it's a fire?"

"Maybe. Or Saint Elmo's light. We're both exhausted enough to be having hallucinations, Devon. Let's go back to bed. We haven't slept over four hours."

"I can't sleep anymore." Devon lit a candle and began to dress. "Anyway, it's almost five o'clock. The men will be up soon."

"Hah! They're embalmed. I doubt if Gabriel's horn could wake them. Even the roosters aren't crowing yet!"

"The hens are gone. What do the cocks have to crow about?"

"You're right." Carla stripped off her borrowed flannel nightgown, shivering as she put on her clothes. Then she rekindled the fire. "Better warm up this igloo, make it nice and cozy for the snoring bulls."

"I'll start breakfast," Devon said. "They'll wake up when they smell the coffee boiling."

"I know a better way," Carla decided, opening a window and blasting two shots over the print shop before Devon could stop her. "That'll rouse them."

55

It did. They came out half-dressed, carrying shirts, jackets, and boots. Jason stumbled over something in his path. He swore lustily, straining his eyes in the breaking dawn. "God Almighty! There's bodies everywhere, son! We must've had a massacre last night!"

"Pa, those are dead animals! Wonder who killed 'em?"

"Whoever fired those shots just now, I reckon. They were shots, weren't they?"

"Yep, and I think I know who did it."

"Good morning, gentlemen!" Carla greeted them cheerily at the kitchen door. "Did you rest well?"

"Not long enough," Reed replied. "That wasn't my rifle or pistol, ma'am. Sounded like a lady's toy."

Carla grinned. "I was playing with my derringer, and it accidentally went off. Sorry I woke you boys."

"No matter, sweetheart," the Senator said. "It was about rising time anyhow. Nice day, too. Pretty red sky already."

"Pretty, hell! Focus your eyes, Pa. See what I see?"

"Holy smoke!"

"Yeah."

"Is it a fire?" Devon asked anxiously. "We weren't sure."

Reed glanced at Carla. "Weren't you? But don't worry, it's miles away."

"Don't worry?" Devon cried. "Haven't you seen the slaughter outside! Do you have any idea what we went through last night?"

"Sure, honey, but you managed, didn't you?"

"Thanks to Carla!"

"Well, that's over now, Devon. There's another problem that could be worse than a few coyotes."

She wanted to hit him. "Enjoy your eggs this morning, dear. There won't be any more until the pullets start laying. There's nothing left of the nest hens but feathers."

"I figured that," he drawled, and Carla knew Devon was too upset to realize the affected nonchalance was for her benefit. "And the way Millie's mooing, she's got a full udder and no calf to relieve her. Guess I'd better milk her. Get yourself some chow, Pa, and then ride to town. The horses are still saddled."

Jason shook his head, befuddled. "Imagine, forgetting to unsaddle our mounts! How you feel, boy? I think I was trampled in a buffalo stampede."

Reed laughed. "That wasn't sarsaparilla we were drink-

ing. There was a horn and hoof in every swallow, and we
owe the dear ladies an apology."

By daylight, clouds of dark smoke were drifting toward
the cabin. Flocks of birds, flushed from cover, flew overhead, and other wildlife scurried out of harm's way. Settlers had seen the terrifying glow in the sky long before
they heard the community church and school bells, and
were rapidly organizing to fight the menace. Every horse,
every available vehicle, brought volunteers. Farmers, ranchers, vaqueros, carried sacks, old blankets, and tubs full of
water.

Devon and Carla stood outside in the harsh December
wind, watching the parade.

"How far away is it?" Carla called to a passing horseman.

"Hard to tell, ma'am! But no matter how far, it's still too
goddamn close!"

"Can it be stopped?" Devon called through cupped
hands.

"God knows," he answered, spurring his mount.

"Maybe we should try to help, Carla."

"The men ordered us to stay here, Devon."

"That doesn't mean we have to obey."

"Bravo! But just what could we do out there, besides get
in the way?"

"Join the bucket brigade."

"Devon, if you're pregnant . . ."

"Oh, Lord! I forgot about that."

"Well, try to remember it. You scared the devil out of
me last night."

Devon tried to ignore the vultures feasting on the coyote
carcasses and the remains of the calf. "Poor Millie, still
crying for her lost baby." She shuddered. "I'm cold. Let's
go inside."

"Might as well," Carla agreed.

Smoke obscured the sun. Soot and cinders and debris
floated in the haze, sifting down on the cabin. "What if the
fire comes this way, Carla?"

"Then we run the other way."

"If this place burns, we'll have to begin all over again,"
Devon worried.

"Well, it won't be like trying to rebuild the Taj Mahal,
darling. This isn't much of a spread."

"I know, but it's all the Carters have."

"The land won't be destroyed. Besides, you'll be living in Austin soon, and might never return."

"This is Reed's district. We have to maintain a voting residence."

"Not this wretched hovel, Devon. You could stay in Fort Worth." She paused as more riders and wagons passed.

Devon said, "I can't stand this sitting and waiting, Carla! We can take some coffee and food in the buggy. And medical supplies, in case of injuries."

"The Florence Nightingale and Clara Barton of the prairie? I'm sure there are plenty of Good Samaritans on the scene already, but a couple more can't hurt."

The holocaust was only a few miles away now, and the spavined horse was in no hurry to get there. Indeed, he preferred not to go at all. Carla had to urge him with the whip, and the picture they made was one the plainsmen would never forget.

Reed reined in Rebel. "Weren't you told to stay at home, ladies? The wind could change at any moment and blow this thing completely out of control. You could be encircled, trapped, and burned!"

"We thought we might help," Devon argued. "And there are other women here."

"Pioneers who know what to do."

"We brought some butter for burns and an old sheet for bandages."

"We have buckets of lard and bandanas for that. So far there are no disabling casualties. If so, we may need your aid. Meanwhile, I forbid you to go beyond that fireguard those farmers are plowing. If your cloaks caught fire, you'd burn like bales of wool."

He spurred Rebel, offering over his shoulder, "You might have better luck with that critter, Carla, if you'd use a prod. A mesquite branch with the thorns applied to a certain tender spot under the tail works miracles."

The firefighters worked in crews and relays, beating the burning grass and brush with whatever was handy, including hats, chaps, and stamping boots. The flames fought back, advancing on the wind. Someone had to act as fire chief, directing the battalion, and the command fell on former Confederate cavalry captain Reed Carter. Having fought his first prairie fire at ten, and many others since, Reed was an experienced veteran.

"Some of you men start another backfire!" he ordered. "The team on the right get some drags ready!"

Carla eased the buggy closer to the forbidden area, and was immediately halted. "Whoa, ma'am! That's far enough. I really wish you'd leave, for your own safety. I assure you, we can manage without you."

Devon set her chin. "We brought some food and coffee."

"No time to eat!" Reed yelled at her. "What we need most is water."

"We have a jug."

"A jug?" He laughed grimly. "Bring us the Trinity River, or the Brazos."

The men built the backfire, setting torches of flaming weeds to a strip about thirty feet wide, ahead of the principal blaze. As it caught and burned, guards stood ready to whip it out when it had progressed far enough. The flames would automatically die on reaching the razed barrier. But vigilance was necessary to prevent the flying embers and exploding cow and buffalo chips from landing in free areas and igniting new blazes.

Devon was writing in a lined book.

"Scratching your journalistic itch?" Carla asked.

"I'm a reporter, Carla."

"You *were* a reporter, Devon."

"Just the same, I intend to record this firsthand. I've never witnessed a prairie fire before, and hopefully never will again." She talked as she jotted notes. "They're fighting fire with fire now. It's an old technique, effectively employed during the Great Fire of London, and in Chicago two years ago. But it's not always effective, because of wind changes." She stopped, and they watched the fire drag.

A small herd of longhorns, too few to constitute a stampede threat, was roaming the region. Several cowboys rode out, lassoed a couple, and brought them to the scene. The cattle were killed, the heads severed, and the carcasses split in half lengthwise. Ropes stretched the fore and hind legs to saddlehorns, and the bleeding sides of beef were dragged up and down the lines of fire, smothering much of the peripheral blaze. Men followed on foot, beating out the residual flames with wet sacks and blankets.

"Is that brutal tactic necessary?" Carla asked Reed.

"Sometimes, ma'am. Animals were sacrificed in the Bible, weren't they? Well, this is a form of sacrifice to the fire god of the frontier, and we hope it appeases him."

Devon studied the buckskinned figure of her husband astride the buff-colored pony, man and beast seeming to blend as one, like some fantastic centaur native to the American West.

"All male, your man," Carla whispered to Devon. "And so's his sire. Look at him out there, working like a mule. He'll drop dead!"

"No, Carla. These folks are accustomed to calamity, and take it in stride."

"That's right, ma'am," said a bowlegged old cowpoke standing near the buggy, too crippled with rheumatism now to assist in the operation. "I seen cowboys and buffalo hunters survive prairie fires before, and if you kin bear the gruesome details, I'll tell you how. They killed cows or buffalo, whichever was handy, gutted 'em partially, crawled into the belly cavity, and waited for the flames to pass over 'em. The hair was scorched off the hide and the stench was enough to make a Christian puke, but blood, piss, and sweat kept 'em moist and alive. Faith alone didn't protect or save 'em, though. Guts and savvy did. And that's the truth of it, ladies. The Lord heps those who hep theirselfs."

Devon began to retch, and quickly clamped a kerchief over her mouth. "Dear God," she prayed aloud, "why am I in this terrible place?"

"You married a Texan," Carla said quietly.

For a time it seemed the fire would burn forever, resisting all efforts to extinguish it. The drags were grated to shreds, only fragments of hide and bone remaining, and fresh ones were made. The sacks, blankets, and tarpaulins were beaten to tatters. Men's faces and hands were burned, but they scorned attention. A vaquero's breeches caught fire, had to be ripped off, and now he worked in his underwear with *chaparreras* shielding his legs. The intense heat felled one townsman, smoke several more. Reed carried the victims to safety, and Devon and Carla ministered to them.

"You're good nurses," Reed complimented.

"What if you can't stop the fire?" Devon asked.

"Then we can't," he replied, squinting against the blinding glare. "We can't contain it forever, Devon. Don't risk your own life. Leave, both of you, before it's too late."

Without waiting for a reply, he galloped off and roped a longhorn yearling, shot and butchered it with a savage fury. He had just attached the gory drag to his saddle and was about to run the rim of the fire again, when suddenly the wind shifted, blowing westward across the blackened breaks. The fiery dragon, finding nothing more to consume, starved itself to death.

Its breath was still hot upon the ravaged earth, but gradually the smoke cleared. There were hundreds of acres of charred prairie, fields, and several homesteads, each containing all of the families' possessions. Soon the buzzards would come for the slaughtered cattle.

Carla turned the buggy toward the cabin. The men trailed on horseback, faces and clothes smeared with dust and soot, sweat and blood. They were weary, but proud in victory. The men were all ready for celebration.

Devon was tense and silent, clinging to the bouncing seat. No doubt about it this time: she was bleeding. It had begun when Reed killed the last animal drag in what appeared to be an act of ruthless violence.

"Drive to the hotel and get a doctor," she told Carla in a surprisingly calm voice.

Carla was the excited one now. "Reed is right behind us, Devon. I'll flag him down."

"No, I'd rather you didn't."

"Devon, he has to know!"

"Yes, but not now, Carla. I'll be all right, I know I will. Just get me to town."

It was several hours before Reed and his father returned from the firefighters' jubilee in the Last Chance Saloon. The doctor had just left. Devon was lying in Carla's bed, sipping hot beef broth. She had aborted the embryo, about six weeks old, without much pain or danger. When Reed was told, he rushed in to see her, angry and distraught. "Why didn't you tell me?"

"I wasn't sure."

"But you must have suspected, Devon."

"Only vaguely."

"I warned you not to go to that fire!"

"It was a combination of several things," she said. "Whatever the cause, it's over, and the doctor says I'll be fine in a few weeks."

"Doc Randall? What does he know about women? He

was an army surgeon. Maybe we should transfer you to Dallas. There's a very good doctor there."

Carla heard from the parlor, where she had been talking with Jason. She entered the bedroom. "She'll be better off here, Reed. I'll take care of her. Moving her now would do more harm than good."

He sat on the edge of the bed, elbows on his spread knees, face in his hands. "I wanted a child so much, Carla. Was it a boy?"

"It was too early to tell."

"There wasn't anything Randall could do to save it?"

Carla shook her head, feeling sorry for him. "Now, I think we'd best let Devon rest. The last twenty-four hours have been quite an ordeal for her."

"Yes." Reed bent and kissed his wife's cheek, pale and cool as snow. "Darling, I'm sorry. . . ." His voice choked. He touched her hair and left before she saw the tears in his eyes.

PART II

Chapter 9

It was a week before the ballots were counted all over the state, confirming the almost unanimous Democratic victory. Devon recuperated rapidly, dispelling Reed's fears that she might not be strong enough to make the move to Austin. They had a tacit agreement not to speak of the miscarriage.

When alone, Devon was melancholy. She would open the locket containing a snip of Scotty's hair, and remember the glorious days in the house on the Hudson, when the three of them were a family! There was a void in her life that nothing could fill, not her husband, nor a dozen other children.

The devastated prairie was no inspiration. The landscape appeared more desolate than ever under the wintry skies, filling her with gloom. A change of scene would help, she decided.

Reed tried to help. "I know you miss your career, Devon, and there are no newspapers in Texas to offer comparable opportunities. Anything but a large metropolitan daily would be anticlimactic. But I imagine the New York *Record* would welcome your coverage of the big event at the White House next May."

"The Grant-Sartoris wedding? As a matter of fact, they have offered it to me, Reed. But Washington is far away, and the Texas legislature would still be in session, so you couldn't accompany me."

A wry smile crossed his face. "I'm not particularly interested in any of the Grants' social affairs, my dear."

"You wouldn't mind if I went alone?"

He would mind very much, more than he could admit. But he felt this was important to her, if only to convince herself that she could still handle it and keep her by-line active. "Only if you didn't come back to me," he said tentatively, observing her carefully.

"Reed, how silly!"

"Shall we assume, Mrs. Carter, that fate intends you to witness that Potomac shivaree for the *Record*?"

"Bless you, dear." She embraced him and kissed the cleft in his chin. "You're so understanding."

His tightening arms bruised her. "I love you so much, Devon, sometimes it frightens me. I get strange notions. I wonder if you might want to leave me one day." He forced a smile. "Let's change the subject. How would you like to go to town this evening? Register at the hotel. Order champagne, if they have any. Toast our future. We haven't celebrated my election yet, you know, and it's been over three weeks."

"That's the best invitation I've had today, sir, and I accept! I'll wear a lovely dress and take along some seductive lingerie."

Reed tried to disguise his tremors in humor. "Then prepare for seduction, ma'am."

"Promise?" She smiled archly, tossing her golden curls and tilting her green, amber-flecked eyes.

She *did* want to resume her career, and this was his reward for obliging her! He ought to paddle her pretty little rump, rather than patting it. "Get ready, my love, and we'll be on our way."

The few guests in the Dragoon's dining room recognized the district's new state representative and offered congratulations, the men declaring that Reed Carter could have whipped his Scalawag opponent "hobbled and hog-tied."

Carla Winston came over from her table to clasp both their hands. "What a handsome pair of celebrities!"

"No flattery!" Devon laughed, wagging a finger. "It might be misconstrued as bribery. Will you dine with us?"

"Darling, I wouldn't think of horning in on your private celebration!"

"Then you must come for Christmas dinner, if you like wild turkey and cornbread stuffing!"

"I'll be there with jingle bells on," Carla declared. "Enjoy yourselves this evening!"

When they were seated and their order taken, Devon said, "Your constituents love you, Representative Carter."

"Premature honeymoon," he mused cynically. "It's inevitable in politics. I hope my popularity endures."

"But you're skeptical?"

"There's so much to be done in Austin, Devon, and I'm not a miracle worker. We've had Radical rule for eight years, and every newly elected Democrat will be besieged with requests to turn back the clock, reverse all the wrongs and deliver rights. Texas has experienced more crises than any other state in the Union. We've served under six flags. Nothing will improve overnight."

Later, in their room, after the champagne, Devon prepared to retire. But Reed removed the chiffon peignoir ensemble from her hands. "You won't need this fluff tonight."

"Not even the nightie? It's chilly in here."

"I'll warm you, Devon, and we have a cozy comforter to snuggle under." But once in bed, he hesitated. "Are you sure it's all right to make love, darling? Not too soon?"

"I'm perfectly well now, Reed." She bit her tongue before saying more. Why did she always conjure the same images in her mind? A kingly railcar rolling away from Richmond, toward Washington. A luxurious bed, rocking like an adult love cradle. Speeding to Bagdad on the Hudson, and to Babylon on the Potomac. To heaven and hell, and all the stations in between

Vaguely she heard her husband's voice. "I'll be careful, anyway. Tell me if I hurt you."

Oh, God. *Let* there be pain, suffering, torment. Torture would blur the memories, would make its own impression.

"It's all right." She smiled up at him.

But it wasn't all right. Would it ever be all right again?

Chapter 10

The stage passengers were assembled, their hand luggage atop the coach. The driver yelled, "All aboard!" and the armed guard mounted the box. The six-mule team, their manes and tails whipped by a high wind, plodded over the frozen ground at the rate of ten to twelve miles per hour. Miles of open country lay ahead, and Devon could understand why so many railroad companies had gone bankrupt trying to build tracks across Texas. Ice crystals glistened on the prairie, the temperature was steadily dropping, and Devon worried about sleet or snow delaying them.

"We should have left sooner, before the holidays."

"No hurry," Reed said. "There's almost two weeks before the new legislature convenes."

"And possibly longer," Carla suggested, "if the incumbents don't vacate easily."

Reed cast her a wary glance, not wanting to alarm his wife. "Where'd you hear that scuttlebutt?"

Carla did not confide her ability to send and decipher Morse code, nor the "situation precarious" the telegraph keys had tapped out at the Fort Worth station. "From a wise old horse's mouth."

"Pa? Yeah, his sensitive political ear can pick up vibrations like a divining rod."

"He's very astute," Carla allowed, "and I'll miss him."

"Oh, he'll be in Austin for the inauguration, ma'am, and periodically thereafter, if I know Pa."

They all fell silent until they reached Waco. Set in the broad, fertile Brazos Valley, Waco was the only town of any size on the route between Fort Worth and Austin. Its character had changed drastically since the war. Formerly a quiet, Southern-influenced village, it was now a rip-roaring frontier town. The transformation had occurred in 1870, when Waco became a gateway for travelers journeying west. Cheap hotels behind gaudy facades, wild saloons, gambling halls, and brothels mushroomed. The streets teemed with restless cowboys and lawless buffalo hunters, and duels were fought at the drop of a hat or the turn of a card.

"Most dangerous place in Texas now, except for El Paso, on the Rio Grande," Reed drawled as the stage pulled in behind a wagonload of buffalo hides.

Devon winced. "So naturally we'll spend the night here?"

"Sure, honey. It's the principal stop on our way."

"Oh, fine!" Carla quipped. "I was afraid we might not have any excitement this trip."

Reed grinned. "We'll be safe enough, if we stay indoors after dark."

Their sleep was disturbed several times by the banging piano in the hotel saloon, the rambunctious ovations for the female entertainers, and random shots. Devon sat up, startled, and Reed soothed, "Gentle down, honey. It's just some trigger-happy cowpokes testing their skill."

"They'll kill each other!"

"That's the object of the game."

"What game?"

"The fast draw."

"Dueling? Isn't that against the law?"

"What law? And who could enforce it, with every man toting weapons?"

"Oh, Lord! What a wild, desperate land! It'll never be tamed!"

Reed was listening to the masculine laughter and feminine giggling issuing from an adjoining room. "Sounds like that hombre's got him three or four gals in there!"

"What would he need with that many?"

"Oh, there's ways of using 'em. Right now, he's probably just chasing 'em around, playing cowboy. Some strange characters like to do that with women, make 'em strip bucknaked, and lasso 'em on the run. I knew one bronco stud that wanted his filly to wear nothing but his hat and boots and prance before him while he flicked a quirt at her teats and ass. Peculiar, huh?"

Perverted, Devon thought, remembering the lecherous old bookstore owner's collection of erotica, including illustrated versions of the Marquis de Sade's books, which he had tried to force her to view the night a blizzard had stranded her in the shop—and Keith's explanations of some people's weird sexual perversions and fantasies.

"Go complain to the management," she said. "How can we sleep with that ruckus in our ears? The walls are paper-thin, and they might frolic all night. But we have a long distance to travel tomorrow."

"Well, I'm awake pretty good now," Reed said, as Devon tried to burrow her head under the pillow. "Might as well have us some fun, too."

"Maybe you envy that lecher and his wild harem?"

"Nope, one's enough for me."

"Have you ever had more than one woman in bed with you?"

"I don't remember."

"Oh, yes, you do! You have, haven't you?"

He shrugged. "Hell, I reckon so. A couple maybe, when I was a young buck and full of piss and firewater. But I'm older now, and that kind of romping is too strenuous. I sure don't envy that fellow his whores, when I've got a lovely little wife who can wear me out fast when she wants to. Come on, honey, give me some loving. . . ."

Loving? This was the gratification of lust aroused by the antics of strangers. Devon knew, because she was similarly motivated, and not by love.

The journey ended on the third day, without significant incident, and only a few hours behind schedule.

Devon was pleased with the small frame bungalow the realtor had located for them. She liked the white Colonial siding and green window shutters, the shingled roof and railed porch, the fenced yard and garden. Plant some ivy on the walls and ramblers on the pickets, and she'd have a vine-covered cottage on the Colorado. She might have had a castle on the Hudson, she teased herself.

Carla took rooms in a nearby boardinghouse, within view of the Carter residence. She unpacked her spyglass, which had a longer range than her lorgnette.

On her first visit, she found Devon writing in her journal. Without the constant blowing dust of the prairie, house-keeping was easier, and a convenient bakery provided the daily bread at two cents per loaf. Domestic help was available, and Devon promptly hired a Mexican laundress and charwoman, paying them out of her own funds.

"Confiding to Dear Diary again?" Carla asked. "You'll have a book thicker than the Bible before long."

"Well, I have more leisure now."

"Where's your husband?"

"Trying to take his seat at the Capitol."

"That should prove interesting," Carla predicted, with her knowledge of the brewing furor. "Meanwhile, let's go sightseeing before the walls come tumbling down."

"Good idea," Devon agreed, getting a hooded cloak.

The government buildings reminded the Virginians of Richmond. The Capitol, with its Greek Revival portal, stood on a hill at the top of a broad, unpaved thoroughfare called Congress Avenue. The Governor's Mansion was classic antebellum: six tall Ionic columns supporting the double veranda, the walls of painted white brick, dignified and beautifully symmetrical.

Among the other tourist attractions were the Land Office, a formidable pile of native stone; the Texas Military Institute; and the state insane asylum. The only public structure of Spanish influence, it was of soft gray sandstone, with landscaped gardens, paths, and benches for the inmates.

"It looks like a great villa," Carla marveled. Most mental institutions were dismal places.

For culture and entertainment there were a library, an opera house, a theater, several civic and social halls, schools, and picnic areas along the wooded banks of the river.

"Right nice little town," their guide remarked, "considering it was just a buffalo camp in 1838, and protected by a stockade until '45."

Devon asked if the trails leading into the bluish hills were bridle paths.

"Only for cowboys and Comanche," he replied. "Them red devils ain't been conquered yet. They still make occasional raids on white settlements along the streams."

"Then where do the local ladies ride?"

"Nowhere alone, ma'am. There's some riding done over at Barton Springs, but the trails are mostly lovers' lanes."

"I'll have to remember that," Carla whispered *sotto voce*, "when Jason comes to town. My Spartan landlady made it clear that she frowns on gentleman callers on her unchaperoned female guests." The absurdity of it evoked laughter from the worldly Carla. "Can you imagine me, at my age and with my experience, requiring a chaperon?"

Devon echoed her amusement. "I've had enough touring for one day, Carla. Let's go home and have some hot tea. I found a pound in the store yesterday and bought it all! Genuine pekoe! I just hope it's not stale."

"It would still beat Texas-style java," Carla answered, rapping the driver's seat and giving the Carter address.

On the fifth of January, the Democrats knew there would be no orderly transition of government. The Radical-appointed state supreme court declared the election law unconstitutional and the results of the December balloting invalid. And Governor Davis issued a formal proclamation forbidding the Fourteenth Legislature to convene.

Davis wired President Grant and appealed for federal troops. But Grant's interference in the internal affairs of Louisiana and Mississippi had taught him a bitter lesson. He denied the request, declaring that the people had spoken at the polls and that that ought to be enough.

But the Radicals would not yield.

"Looks like trouble," Reed told Devon.

"And I suppose you'll be in the thick of it?"

"Well, I'm not a coward."

"But that's what the carpetbaggers want, Reed! If there's insurrection, the President would have to intervene."

His jaw was set grimly. "There won't be enough time, if we move swiftly. Any federal troops would probably come from San Antone, and that's over eighty miles away. Besides, Grant has already refused."

"Stay out of it, Reed. Please?"

Her concern moved him. "I'm a part of it, Devon. You don't understand Texans. We do what we feel is right."

"Like at the Alamo? Heroes, every one. *Dead*, every one."

He checked his weapons and put on his hat. "Stay in the house, Devon—and this time, *obey* me!"

"What if you're killed?"

"Then, Mrs. Carter"—he grinned, kissing her good-bye —"you'll be a poor widow."

For three days the town was an armed camp, ready for action, and women and children were warned off the streets. Davis telegraphed more urgent appeals to Washington, but to no avail. Moreover, his own supporters began to desert him, and the local militia joined the opposition.

At the first sound of gunfire, Devon grabbed a shawl. She was about to run to Carla when she saw her friend rushing to her home. They embraced in the yard, and then Carla ushered Devon back inside.

"It's begun, Carla, and Reed is with them!"

"Naturally. Where would you expect him to be? He's a man, isn't he?"

"Texan," Devon muttered, "and they're the gamecocks of the breed! Fighting is what they do best."

Carla laughed. "Oh, I don't know about that. Some of them are also good at other things. Sit down, Devon, and have some tea. Frankly, I'd prefer something stronger."

"There's some bourbon in the kitchen cabinet."

Carla found the whiskey, poured two generous portions, and handed Devon one. "Take it slowly—it's neat."

Suddenly an ominous silence fell, and the women glanced at each other. "Maybe it's a truce," Devon said hopefully.

"I think it's mostly hand-to-hand combat, Devon. Fists and gunstocks. I've heard the Democrats spiked the cannon on the Capitol grounds, so the Radicals couldn't use them. They didn't want the Capitol fired on, because of the mementos of Texas heroes inside."

"The carpetbaggers don't care about that, Carla. They're in the building, using it as a fort, still hoping the United States Army will come to their aid."

Devon gulped the whiskey, coughing.

Carla patted her back. "I should've diluted that poison for you, honey."

"No, it's good. I'll have some more."

"You'll pass out."

"Who cares? If there's bad news, I'd rather be sedated."

Late that afternoon Reed returned, with a bullet hole in his hat, a rip in his breeches, and blood on his shirt. Devon was lying drowsily on the sofa, eyes half-closed, seeing only the condition of his clothes. She tried to rise, but her feet, her body, seemed leaden. "Oh, Reed, you've been shot!"

"No, baby, just my hat. Some midget next to me thought he was firing in the air and clipped my crown." He poked a finger ruefully through the charred space. "Damn near ventilated my skull, and sure as hell ruined a perfectly good hat! But it's all over, ladies, and we won!" He was grinning happily. "The Radicals finally surrendered. There were some bloody noses and broken bones, but nobody got killed. Davis knew better than to try to fight it out with old

Rip Ford and the Rangers! Reconstruction rule is over in Texas! Over, at long last."

"Congratulations," Carla sighed. "Will there be a celebration?"

"You bet! A militia parade and dancing in the streets. And the first act of the Fourteenth Legislature will be a resolution thanking President Grant for respecting our state's rights."

"Bravo and olé!" Devon cheered giddily. "Maybe they should also present Davis' ears to the President. Wouldn't that be the supreme gesture?"

"For a toreador," Reed agreed, "and that's what some Texans wanted to do with Santa Anna's ears after San Jacinto, but General Houston was too Christian to allow it." He glanced anxiously at Carla. "Is she all right?"

"I think so. Just partially tranquilized. That stuff should have a warning on the label. Maybe even a skull and crossbones."

"Green corn," Reed said. "It'd kill a horse. Any left?"

"A few good slugs." Carla accompanied him to the kitchen. Lowering her voice, she said, "You have a rare and delicate flower, Reed, the kind that thrives best under cultivation. I doubt that she could ever be transformed into the field variety native to this land."

Reed quirked a dark, quizzical brow. "Don't chew your cud so long, Carla. Spit it out."

"Devon is not like other women, Reed. She's a unique species, one of a kind. And I believe she must return—at least periodically—to her origins. Or else perish."

Reed drank. "I agree, ma'am, and she'll be going East in a few months. I hope you'll go with her."

Carla smiled. "I'd be delighted, sir. Shall we shake or drink on it?"

"Why not both?" he replied, grasping her hand before passing the whiskey.

Chapter 11

Reed was soon elected speaker of the House of Representatives, an honor which kept him so busy Devon scarcely saw him in daylight hours, except on Sunday. Often he worked late at night in his Capitol office, as if the burden of restoration were his responsibility alone. The Democrats had inherited a political and economic mess that would require years to repair.

"The Union will never forgive us our sins of secession," he told Devon. "Our national representatives will always be the whipping boys of Congress. God knows when, if ever, another Southerner will occupy the White House. The Virginia presidential dynasty is a part of the past now."

"All these problems can't be solved in a month, Reed. Or in a year, or ten. You'll wreck your health working so hard. I never see you."

"The speaker is the ramrod, Devon, and his job is tougher than any other House member's. But there is some recreation coming up, a big celebration on Texas Independence Day, with a reception at the Governor's Mansion. That's March 2, you know."

"Oh, Reed, how wonderful!"

"Naturally, Pa will be invited and want to escort Carla. That should please her."

It pleased both women immensely, and they were in a pother over what to wear to the various entertainments. Texans celebrated their independence from Mexico even more vigorously than America's from England. There would be picnics and barbecues during the day, fireworks and dances at night, climaxed by the Governor's Ball. Seamstresses had been busy for weeks. No calico, gingham, or homespun frocks for this occasion!

Devon chose an elegant ivory brocade trimmed with Brussels lace, one of the last gowns in her wardrobe for which Keith had paid the bill. But when she draped the matching lace scarf over her head, Reed shook his head. "No mantillas or rebozos tonight, Devon. Too Mexican. Don't forget the reason for the celebration."

"Sorry," she apologized, hoping that Carla would remember and leave behind the beautiful fringed Spanish shawl she had intended to wear.

It was the first time Devon had seen her husband in formal wear. Though he looked handsome, he lacked Keith's urbanity. Reed would always be more comfortable in range clothes. She could not visualize him in tails and top hat, with an opera cape and gold-hilted cane, the mode compulsory at White House receptions.

But she was proud to arrive at the Governor's Mansion on his arm, as Carla was proud to appear with his father. They were all impressed by the Cokes' gracious welcome. Later, as Mrs. Coke escorted her through the house, Devon commented with surprise on the tasteful decoration.

"Oh, the executive residence has been improved considerably since Washington-on-the-Brazos, my dear. You know, I'm sure, that Texas had several capitals before Austin was selected as the permanent site? Some were rather crude and primitive. In Houston, for instance, the First Family lived in a simple log cabin. But this has been the official home of our governors since 1855, and contains some cherished mementos."

Devon touched Stephen F. Austin's desk, and the great American Empire bed constructed of native woods for Sam Houston. When she mentioned that she would like to write an article about the mansion, Mary Evans Coke encouraged her.

"I'm confident your talent would do it justice, Mrs. Carter. Is it true you're going to Washington to cover the wedding of President Grant's daughter?"

"Yes, I'll be leaving next month."

"How exciting! Of course, the guests will be mostly prominent Republicans. Southern Democrats won't be very well represented, I'm afraid." Music signified the opening of the ball, and her hostess said, "The gentlemen will be seeking their ladies. I admire your gown, Mrs. Carter. May I ask the name of your *modiste*?"

Devon hesitated. Considering the present condition of the state treasury, it would hardly be wise to say it was a Worth original created in Paris. "I bought the material and pattern before I left New York and found an excellent seamstress in Dallas. Unfortunately, she closed her shop after the panic and returned to Manhattan."

"What a pity! Texas is hardly a style center now, but someday our ladies may be among the best-dressed in the country, if not the world."

The grand march began with "Dixie" and "The Yellow Rose of Texas," tunes which had not been heard in the Governor's Mansion for eight years. Then came the sentimental Stephen Foster melodies. Devon waltzed with the governor, the lieutenant governor, and every statesman who could seize the opportunity.

The new regime was toasted with imported champagne and with Tennessee and Kentucky bourbon. Watching some of the single girls dance and flirt with Reed, Devon felt a sudden twinge of jealousy. One pretty wench in particular was trying to monopolize him, and her youth and vivacity reminded Devon that she was older. Now she could better understand Esther Curtis' reaction when they had met at the Fifth Avenue Hotel, during the Curtises' ball for President and Mrs. Grant. Esther had undoubtedly realized the identity of her husband's mistress.

Carla interrupted her brooding reverie. "Something amiss, dear? You look as if you'd seen a ghost."

"I'm thinking of interviewing Mrs. Coke," Devon replied quickly, "and doing a story on the Governor's Mansion. I'm sure Carrie Hempstead would publish it in the *Record*."

Reed approached and smiled dubiously. "Do you honestly believe New Yorkers care what's happening in Texas?"

"Some of them," Devon replied.

"Sure. Financiers interested in loans at usurious interest rates. But that social pap is for the ladies."

"Half the people on this earth are female," Carla reminded him, smiling over her shoulder as she left.

"Thank God for that half," he said, reaching over to kiss Devon's cheek. "You made a big hit tonight, Mrs. Carter. Pa and I were both very proud of you. We'll be invited to more parties now than I care to attend. Decline as many as you can graciously. I'm no social lion, and I'm too busy with government business to pursue frivolities."

"You weren't exactly beating off that bevy of young belles," Devon accused. "You danced four times with Melissa Hampton!"

"That many? I wasn't counting."

"Well, I was!"

"Her father carries some weight in the Democratic party of this state."

"About two hundred and fifty pounds of it!" she snapped. "And I gather the Hamptons' invitations are to receive priority? You are aware, Mr. Speaker, that your wife is leaving Austin in April?"

"What has that to do with the Hamptons?"

"Nothing, I hope." But she knew that Gore Hampton's wife had been dead for some years and his charming young daughter was his official hostess.

Reed laughed, his arm circling her waist. "If that's jealousy, Mrs. Carter, I'm pleased. Very pleased."

The hack delivered them to their small white bungalow, and Reed spoke of buying their own carriage when they could afford it. He paid the driver, and Devon waited for him to open the door and light the kerosene lamp in the parlor. Taking a glowing candle from the mantel, Devon went to the bedroom, undressed and donned a warm nightgown, and crawled promptly under the feather comforter.

Soon Reed joined her, naked, and asked, "Why the flannel tent?"

"Decent wives cover themselves in bed in winter."

"But not in summer?" His fingers fumbled with the buttons, ripping off several in his haste and frustration. "Help me, or I'll tear the damn thing off!"

She lay defiantly still. "And rape me?"

"I'm not a rapist."

"Every man is, on occasion."

"Every man? How many have raped you?"

"Many, in their minds. Several this very evening, in case you didn't notice."

"I noticed, and I'm not referring to mental violations, Devon. I mean physical reality. I know I wasn't the first man to possess you. Did you give yourself willingly to the original seducer, or were you forced?"

She stared at him aghast. "Why are you asking me this?"

"Because it's been eating my guts out, like lye! I know you don't love me, and never have. Did you love the bastard who got your virginity?"

Devon remained silent, glaring at him in the smoking light of the bedside candle. She hated quarrels, and turned her face aside. Tears shimmered in her eyes.

"I'm sorry for the outburst, Devon. I must've drunk too

much. But you started it, with all that business about Melissa Hampton, implying there might be something between us. Good Lord! I only met her this evening! I've seen her in the gallery, but paid no attention. A pretty young girl, sure, but she means nothing to me. All I want is you . . . and *your* love. Yet I know I have neither, not really. How long do you think a marriage can survive such a one-sided situation, my dear?"

"Do you want a divorce?"

"Certainly not! Do you?"

"Maybe it would be better for both of us, Reed."

"Don't say that! This is all my fault, Devon. Please forgive me, it won't happen again. It's just that . . . Well, when you rejected me physically, I guess it riled me. Bruised my ego. I didn't think you resented sex with me."

"I don't," she exclaimed. "Have I ever denied you?"

"No, and at times you act eager. Other times, you seem merely submissive, even reluctant. And when you mentioned rape . . . well, it was a spur in my heart. I don't want marital duty from you, Devon. Frankly, I'd prefer love without wedlock than vice versa. Can you understand that?"

"Yes," she murmured. "I can. I'm just upset, Reed. It was a long evening, and I heard some rumors . . ."

"What kind of rumors?"

She shrugged. "I was eavesdropping on a political conversation and heard your name mentioned as a gubernatorial appointment to the Senate."

His laughter was a relief. "Christ, I thought it was some romantic gossip, which would be utter nonsense. That presumption is premature, Devon. It may or may not materialize. If it does, I promise you'll be the first to know. Is that what's bothering you now?"

She nodded, and he kissed her mouth, slipping a hand into the nightgown to fondle her breasts. "Any objections?"

"No."

"Forget the ring and the vows, Devon. Do you want me as a lover? If not, this is as far as I'll go."

"You *did* drink too much."

He thrust a leg between her thighs. "Answer me."

"Oh, Reed, we can't really talk under these circumstances. If you want relief—"

"Relief?" He leaped from the bed. "*Relief?* I can get that at a whorehouse!"

"Why are we fighting, Reed? Provoking each other? I don't honestly know."

He sighed heavily and knelt beside the bed. "Because I'm a fool crazed with jealousy, I guess. Saying things I don't mean." He took her hand. "Why do you put up with me?"

She smiled, touching his face. "You've been working too hard, Mr. Speaker. So you're tense and anxious, and need a sounding board."

"I could sleep on the sofa," he said sheepishly.

"It's not long enough for you. Get back in bed, before you catch a cold."

He snuffed the candle and took his place beside her. "I don't deserve a wife like you, Devon. But right now I think I'm the luckiest man alive, and the richest. I couldn't be richer if I owned the Comstock Mine in Nevada, or the biggest bank on Wall Street."

A cry rose to her lips, but she stifled it.

"If you're not mad at me anymore, honey, I'd like to hold you. Just hold you . . . you know?"

"Yes," she said, moving into his embrace. "Hold me, Reed, and don't let me cry. *Please*, don't let me cry. . . ."

Chapter 12

Happily for Devon, Carla made the journey to Washington with her. Reed escorted them to the depot, bidding his wife a fond farewell before hurrying back to the Capitol. The train would carry them to Houston and then to Galveston, where they would board a ship to New Orleans, after a few days of shopping, they would continue by Mississippi riverboat to Memphis and then by rail to Washington. Devon had some hoarded greenbacks in her baggage, and Carla always seemed to have sufficient funds to live where and how she pleased.

Again she traveled as Mrs. Winston, in widow's weeds, explaining that she liked to keep in practice should she ever return to her former profession. Devon suspected the disguises merely amused her. Demure in a gray-blue tissue wool suit with a floral chip hat, Devon could have passed for her daughter. "Did Reed and his father persuade you to accompany me?" she asked.

"I didn't need any persuasion, Devon. I was as eager as you for this trip. And thank heaven we're not making it by hellish stagecoach!"

The rattling railcar was hardly luxury, but spring was already in central Texas. Redbud and laurel brightened the hazy blue hills around Austin, and the Coastal Plains were vast scenic murals of bluebonnets, pink and yellow buttercups, purple verbenas, crimson winecups, and vivid red-and-yellow Indian paintbrush. They slept in their straight-backed wood seats, wakening the next morning in the deep green pine forests and marshes near Houston. The lavender hyacinths growing wild in the glades and bayous were considered a perennial nuisance to be ruthlessly eradicated with machetes. The town itself, recently flooded by heavy April showers, lay in a watery basin, and Carla exclaimed, "Great Scott! Is this swamp what the Carters envision as a future metropolis?"

"Texans must believe that miracles will happen in this state, else why would they live here? I'll just be glad to get to Galveston and on that ship!"

It was smooth sailing across the Gulf of Mexico and up the wide mouth of the Mississippi to New Orleans, and they could hardly wait to visit the shops in the Vieux Carré. Devon bought some new additions to her wardrobe. On Royal Street she found a bottle of her favorite French scent, jasmine and ambergris, blushing when Carla teased, "One would think you expected to met an old beau, *chérie.* Or a new one?"

"Well"—Devon affected nonchalance—"this is supposed to be the place for liaisons, isn't it? Where every prominent man has a mistress?"

"Many of them black." Carla nodded.

"Only according to the miscegenation laws," Devon said. "Reed went to school here and told me about the annual quadroon balls, where the gentry select the beautiful young maidens and negotiate for them with their shrewd and ambitious mothers by *written* contract! The stipulations guarantee a comfortable home, generous allowance, servants, carriages and horses, and the education, in the North or abroad, of any offspring. And Mama gets a nice pension, security for herself. And the gentlemen are often quite proud of the arrangements, flaunting their golden-skinned beauties in public."

Entering Jackson Square, Devon decided that she wanted to meditate a few minutes in St. Louis Cathedral and light a votive candle in memory of poor, sweet Mally O'Neill. Pregnant, abandoned by her faithless lover, she now lay in a pauper's grave.

"What happened to her?" Carla asked as they came out of the dim church into the sunshine.

"According to the police report, her gas jet leaked during the night, and she was asphyxiated."

"Lonely girls in large cities seem prone to such 'accidents,'" Carla said sympathetically. "Many are suicides, and their home folks never learn the awful truth."

Devon sighed. "Some are alone, Carla, or their families don't care. It's tough on single women everywhere, if they must scrounge for a living."

"Yes, but let's not depress ourselves with such dismal conversation, darling! I think we have time to go to the

French Market before our boat leaves. I'm hungry for some jambalaya. I relish Creole food—or is that Cajun?"

"I'm not an authority on New Orleans cuisine." Devon shrugged. "But I enjoyed the breakfast at the Court of the Two Sisters, and that wonderful dinner at Antoine's last evening. I'm surprised they let us in, unescorted."

"A dowager duchess and her protegée are welcome anywhere, my dear."

"Oh, Carla, what a joy you are! And a guardian angel couldn't be a more diligent protectress."

While they were eating, a foppishly dressed gentleman strolled over, tipped his tall hat, and bowed from the waist, addressing the older woman in a strong Gallic accent. "May I present myself, madame? André Dubois."

"Monsieur Dubois," Carla acknowledged sedately.

His eyes rested covetously on Devon. "May I also request the honor of an introduction to your daughter, *s'il vous plaît?*"

"You may not, sir," Carla replied sternly, as any proper matron would in a public place.

"A thousand pardons, madame." Chagrined, he bowed again, clicked his heels smartly, and departed.

Carla smiled behind her thick black veil. "The bold cock! Not that I blame him, wanting to meet you. I wonder how many duels his effrontery has occasioned? Sometimes I think Frenchmen thrive on arrogance and challenges."

"That's what some people say about Texans," Devon said.

"With good reason, I suspect."

A steamer whistle blew, and Devon forgot everything else. "That's our signal, Carla. We'd better hurry!"

They shared a comfortable stateroom on the new riverboat, dined in the flamboyant salon, strolled on the fancy-railed promenade deck. Devon attracted much male attention, which Carla's chaperonage promptly discouraged. At Memphis, now considered the toughest town on the Mississippi, Carla put away away her widow's garb—but not her derringer.

Now they were on the last leg of the journey, taking the same rail route that Devon and Reed had traveled to Texas. Devon saw again the grim battle sites, so numerous in Tennessee, where Captain Reed Carter had fought with a

Texas cavalry unit. Chattanooga? Chickamauga? Shiloh? He had told her, but Devon had forgotten. How could she forget a major incident in her husband's life, yet remember minor ones in her Yankee lover's?

As the train finally chuffed into Alexandria and across the Potomac to Washington, Devon's rueful sigh and pained expression puzzled her companion. "Headache?"

"Fatigue. It's been a long trip, Carla."

"And we both need some rest. But since we've arrived several days early, I suppose you'll have to cover some of the prenuptial parties?"

"Not necessarily. The *Record* has Associated Press service. My concern is the main event."

They bought local papers at the depot, managed to hire a hackney despite the heavy traffic, and proceeded directly to the Willard Hotel. The envelope the desk clerk presented to Devon upon registration contained a warm message of welcome from Carrie Hempstead and the staff, a press information sheet and badge, and a liberal draft drawn on the Curtis Bank.

From her windows Devon could see the Capitol and the still-unfinished Washington Monument on the Mall, the White House, and the Treasury next to it. There she had witnessed President Grant's first Inaugural Ball and had met Reed Carter. The Clairmont was also visible, a view she could neither resist nor long endure. *Was he there now?*

Carla's room adjoined, and they relaxed over a late luncheon, scanning the newspapers. Devon recognized the by-line of female correspondents with whom she had traveled in the First Lady's retinue, attended White House functions, and sat with in the press galleries of Congress. The elaborate accounts of the entertainments for the celebrated young couple suggested extravagance hardly befitting a nation struggling with a depressed economy. But only the antiadministration press dared criticize the President's expenditures.

While Devon organized some notes, Carla read aloud from the long list of Nellie Grant's trousseau. "East Indian shawls, ivory-handled parasols, lace sacques, one hundred dresses of silk, muslin, gauzes, grenadines, hats and shoes for each costume, numerous sets of handmade lingerie, and thirty trunks to carry it all on the European honeymoon.

My God! The bridal costume alone cost five thousand dollars! Could that be a misprint?"

"Not likely. Nellie is her father's darling."

"I'd like to witness that wedding. Do you suppose I could sneak in with the press corps?"

"I'm afraid not, Carla. Every reporter must show a pass, and anyone caught abusing his privilege would be automatically and permanently barred."

"Perhaps I could purchase a counterfeit pass?"

"Well, it's been done. And someone with your ingenuity would know how," Devon said. "But it's risky."

Carla affected horror. "Oh, I wouldn't want to take any *risks!*" she cried.

Cupid could not have arranged better weather for the occasion, Devon thought, seeking a lead for her story. The massive marble buildings reflected a dazzling whiteness in the bright May sunlight. Like the famous Old World capitals, Washington had its great river. Pennsylvania Avenue this morning was its Appian Way, incensed with blooming magnolia and catalpas.

The seventy splendid equipages arriving for the eleven-o'clock ceremony carried about two hundred guests—relatives and friends of the First Family, Cabinet members, statesmen, uniformed warriors, and beribboned diplomats. British Ambassador Sir Edward Thornton would sponsor the bridegroom. The bride's older brother would serve as best man. The bridesmaids included the daughters of General Sherman, Admiral Porter, Senator Conkling, and Secretary of State Hamilton Fish.

Police and soldiers guarded all entrances to the White House grounds. Joining the female press in the main hallway, Devon was greeted by Gail Hamilton, Nell Hutchinson, Kate Field, Olivia Briggs, and others, all of whom were pleased that she had come.

At Mrs. Grant's bidding, they were given a preview of the East Room, scene of the rites. A rich rug from the sultan of Turkey covered the dais before the great eastern window, where the vows would be spoken under a floral arch and large bell of snowy blossoms. Masses of white flowers and greenery decorated the chamber, festooning the walls and elaborate crystal chandeliers. The fragrance of thousands of gardenias, tuberoses, and lilies of the val-

ley was most intoxicating. Preoccupied with her pad and
pencil, Devon barely glimpsed the familiar faces being ushered into the East Room. The bridal party was her primary
concern, and the procession began with the Marine Band's
rendition of Mendelssohn's "Wedding March."

Reverend Tiffany was already on the dais. Mrs. Grant
appeared with her sons Ulysses and Jesse. Still mourning
her late father, Julia Grant wore a dark silk gown, bustled
and trained, unadorned except for lavender ribbons and
her favorite lilacs. Her luxurious black hair was swept atop
her bare head, with a few ringlets coiled at the nape. The
bridesmaids entered in gowns of corded white silk, with
looped sashes and tulle-draped overskirts, carrying blue-
and-pink nosegays.

Colonel Frederick Grant was in military uniform. Mr.
Sartoris wore a proper striped suit and cutaway coat. His
brown hair was parted in the middle, his gray eyes solemn,
his brown mustache waxed, and he was holding his own
bouquet, with LOVE in gilt letters on the streamer, an unprecedented and somewhat astonishing innovation.

A reporter whispered that Algy looked older than his
twenty-three years, rather pale and dissipated, giving more
life to the rumors that he was an excessive drinker. Olivia
quipped, "That gives him something in common with his
father-in-law."

When finally the bride appeared on the President's arm,
the cost of her costume did not seem quite so outrageous.
Nellie was a vision in white French satin and point lace,
her dimunitive figure completely enveloped in a cloud of
veiling crowned with orange blossoms. She wore her parents' gifts, diamond necklace and earrings, and carried a
pearl-and-lace fan. Pink rosebuds centered her white bouquet, which also bore the curious LOVE banner. It was as if
the young couple must convince the pessimists, including
their respective families, that they were happy. Grant wore
a sad, dubious expression, and tears were visible in Julia's
eyes.

The ceremony was quite brief, the whispered exchange
of vows inaudible except to those nearest the platform.
Disappointed, Olivia muttered, "Good grief! All that preparation and expense for those few minutes? What a waste!"

Gail Hamilton, remote kin to the Grants, jibed, "Put
that in your report, dear. Then you won't have to cover

any more White House affairs for the duration of the administration."

"Hah! You know my editor would strike it out, just as yours approves everything you write."

Miss Hutchinson grinned. "Welcome back to the club, Devon. As you can see, it hasn't changed much."

Devon smiled. It was as though she had never been away. "I wonder what the gentlemen of the Fourth Estate thought of Algy's bouquet?"

"Something libelous and censorable, no doubt."

"I found it rather touching."

"You were always a romantic, Devon. I'm hungry. Too bad we can't attend the wedding breakfast in the State Dining Room."

"I'd love to snatch one of the gold-on-white satin menus," said Olivia. "And I'm sure"—taunting Kate, Nell, and Gail—"the spinsters among us would like a piece of the wedding cake to place under their maidenly pillows? Ah, well, at least we have the privilege of viewing the gifts in the second-floor library. Shall we proceed, ladies?"

Mounting the stairs, Nell asked Devon, "How do you like Texas?"

"I haven't seen all of it yet, Nell. It's a vast land, you know, and most is still uninhabited wilderness."

"But you're living in Austin now, aren't you?"

"Since January." Devon nodded. "My husband is speaker of the state House."

"Wonderful! I knew Reed Carter would become important in politics, even before I read it in the New York *Record.*"

"Thanks," Devon said, wondering who else had read Carrie's news items about the Reed Carters.

White cloths garlanded with flowers covered the tables. Devon had not seen such a display of wealth and splendor since the marriage of Boss Tweed's daughter. The estimated value of $100,000 seemed inadequate. There was gold and precious jewelry. Ornaments of vermeil, ivory, and jade. Exquisite china and porcelain vases, bowls, dishes. Crystal pitchers and goblets. Cut-glass decanters. Silver. Bolts of fabulous materials. Rare paintings, bronze and marble sculptures. As Devon moved about, reading the donors' name cards, she came across a familiar one engraved in Old English script. She was wondering whether or not to mention it in her report, when the unforgettable baritone voice spoke softly behind her.

"Mrs. Carter, I believe?"

Devon froze, unable to face him, then melted as his hand under her elbow gently forced her to turn. "Hello, Keith," she quavered. "I didn't notice your arrival. Were you present at the ceremony?"

"Yes. A potted plant must have obstructed your view. How are you, Devon?"

She swallowed to moisten her dry throat. Except for a few more silver strands in his dark, wavy hair and a bit more cynicism in his brooding eyes, he had not changed. He was . . . still Keith. His clothes, as always, were impeccable. Devon knew no other man with such *savoir faire*. "Fine. And you?"

"Well enough. I must say you look extremely fit, and lovely as ever."

"Thank you. But it hasn't been long enough for me to age, Keith."

He smiled ruefully, and her heart fell at his feet. "No, it only seems so to me, Devon."

Her eyes pleaded eloquently for answers to questions he must surely sense, but he only shook his head. "This isn't the time or place, Devon."

"Can't you just tell me . . . ?"

"Not now," he insisted. "We'll be in town a few days. At the Clairmont."

"We?"

"Scott and I. And Miss Vale."

Weakness engulfed Devon, threatening to overtake her. It might be a tragic mistake, but she wanted to see her child. She *had* to see him, even if it killed her. "May I come tomorrow?"

"Do you think that's wise, my dear?"

"I've never been wise, Keith. You should know that better than anyone else."

"Don't humble yourself, Devon. I couldn't bear it. What's done is done. I have some business appointments in the morning, but anytime after two in the afternoon would be convenient."

Her eyes misted.

"Smile, Devon, and pretend to write. Olivia is watching us, and God knows she's the biggest gossipmonger in Washington. Unless you can convince her that this is a professional interview, we'll be an item in one of her columns. Oh, Christ! Here she comes like a tropical storm—"

"Why, Mr. Curtis!" she gushed, rolling those eyes that missed very little of a scandalous nature. "I hope you're not giving my competition a scoop of some kind? You told me at the Hamilton Fish soiree the other night that you were here only as a wedding guest."

"That's correct, Olivia. Mrs. Carter was just inquiring about the progress of the Brooklyn Bridge since she left New York."

"Oh, that monstrosity! I doubt it'll ever be finished."

Devon picked up an engraved poem. "Have you seen this, Olivia?"

"Whitman's tribute to Nellie, 'A Kiss to the Bride'? Yes. Poor Walt. I suppose it was the only gift he could afford. And I haven't seen a thing from Mark Twain, who frequents the White House." She winked at Devon. "You may not be aware, having been in the hinterlands for some months, that since the demise of Jay Cooke and Company, Mr. Curtis is the Baron de Rothschild of America. His bank is now the Wall Street Gibraltar, evidently an impregnable financial citadel."

"Wasn't it always?" Devon asked demurely.

"Ladies, please," Keith implored. "Money is such a vulgar subject."

"Not in Washington!" Olivia retorted. "Nor, for that matter, in New York." She consulted her printed schedule. "The bride and groom will leave at one-thirty for the Baltimore and Ohio Depot, and you know Grant's penchant for promptness. If we're going to witness the send-off, we'd better dash downstairs immediately."

"I'll be there," Devon said, a promise she meant for Keith, not Olivia.

The newlyweds left the White House in the state carriage, in a shower of rice and rose petals. Church bells pealed "Hail Columbia!" and "God Save the Queen." Admirers waved, blew farewell kisses, and flung flowers along the route to the station. There, the Pullman palace car built for the Vienna Exposition and now decorated with American and British flags waited to take them to New York and the honeymoon ship in the harbor.

Devon returned to the Willard to prepare her story. Carla knocked.

"Quite a spectacle, wasn't it?"

"Let's talk later, Carla. Right now I must write my impressions, while it's all still fresh in my mind."

"Don't bother, dear. I was there."

"You were? How did you manage?"

"Guess."

"I can't imagine, and I'm no good at riddles."

"Well, here's a clue. There was a feeble old lady in black, with a cane and ear trumpet, who had lost not only her invitation *but* her five sons in the Union cause. The poor soul almost had a seizure when the White House doorkeeper tried to deny her admission. She begged to see Mr. Lincoln. So Thomas Pendel, who had held the same position under President Lincoln, sniffed back his tears and passed her through to the East Room, where a very handsome and chivalrous fellow gave her not only his seat—while he stood behind a tubbed palm—but his place at the wedding breakfast as well. Isn't that nice?"

Devon was amazed. "Do you happen to know that gallant gentleman?"

"No, do you?"

"Slightly," Devon admitted.

"In that case, you might like his menu as a memento," Carla suggested, presenting it to her. "I'll keep the piece of wedding cake to dream on, since I'm still single."

Chapter 13

By the time the Otis steam elevator reached the top floor of the Clairmont, Devon's heartbeat was audible in her ears, and her expanded lungs thrust her ribs against the tight corselet so that it was difficult to breathe. The contoured bodice of her lemon-colored *peau de soie* dress, another of her New Orleans purchases, enhanced her high, conical breasts, and the cascading bustle gave her lithe hips a titillating sway. A large netted yellow silk rose topped her sunbright hair, which was coiffed in the latest *al greco* style featuring a cluster of loose side-swept curls on the neck.

The operator glanced at her admiringly, and Devon was suddenly intensely jealous of the other women who must periodically ascend to this suite.

"Which way?" she asked the operator, suddenly confused. "Right or left?"

"Don't matter, ma'am. Mr. Curtis has the entire floor. Owns the building, in fact. But his foyer entrance is to your right, and there's a knocker."

"Thank you."

Devon hesitated before the refurbished portal of carved oak with bronze fittings, then timidly tapped the monogrammed knocker, praying that Miss Vale would admit her, that Keith had decided to be absent. Then the door opened and he stood there, incredibly handsome in a lounge jacket of hunter's green over gray broadcloth trousers, the memorable odor of his French shaving lotion on his smooth tan face. Her feet felt cemented to the marble corridor, and he had to assist her across the threshold.

"The yellow rose of Texas?" he asked, taking in her costume.

"The Virginia jonquil," she replied. "They grow wild in the meadows around Richmond, you know."

"Is there a song about them there?"

"Not to my knowledge."

Glancing about, she saw that the entire suite had been redecorated. New furniture, carpets, draperies, mirrors, paintings. Had some other woman supervised the decor?

"You've changed things," she said.

"The Clairmont's a profit-making organization now, Devon. A residential hotel, with a waiting list and never a vacancy."

"Your quarters, too?"

"No, nor any part of this floor. I'm presently discussing plans for a glassed-in terrace and roof garden."

"That will be delightful."

"I think so. Washington is expanding in all directions, and I'll have a better view of the city." He waited, as if deliberately tormenting her. "Scott is napping, and Miss Vale is out on some errands. She's a member of the family, almost. We couldn't manage without her. The boy loves her dearly."

Devon swallowed ruefully. "How long does he nap?"

"An hour or so."

"Could I just peek in on him?"

"Better not," Keith advised. "Sometimes he's cross if disturbed prematurely." He indicated a Louis XIV sofa. "Make yourself comfortable, Devon. Miss Vale prepared tea before leaving, or would you prefer a glass of wine?"

"Madeira or Montrachet would be fine."

Seated, Devon remained silent while he poured wine for her and cognac for himself. She kept her gloves on, trying to disregard the slight ridge of her wedding band, and held the stemmed crystal goblet with both hands, lest her tremors cause comment. "How long will you be in Washington, Keith?"

"Until I finish my business and get some definite bids on the terrace-garden project I mentioned." His eyes focused longingly on her mouth. "And you?"

Devon shrugged. "I'm traveling with a friend, Mrs. Carla Winston, whom we met on the trip to Texas. We may visit New York for a few days, I'm not sure. The *Record* would like me to consider more assignments."

"Why didn't your husband accompany you?"

"Reed is speaker of the Texas House of Representatives, and the Fourteenth Legislature inherited a terrible mess from the carpetbag regime."

"You live in Austin with him?"

Devon nodded, sipping the Montrachet, wishing that

Scotty or Miss Vale would appear before the conversation drifted into reminiscence.

Keith, opposite her in a winged armchair, crossed his long legs. "I thought the Carters intended to establish a crusading newspaper? Set the journalistic frontier on fire?"

"Jason Carter—the old Senator—publishes a small weekly. But the panic hit Texas severely, ending railroad building."

"The entire West, Devon, except for the great lines, with big money and power politics behind them. Chinese coolies still arrive by the thousands in San Francisco, to work on the Western rails. Jay Gould is planning to connect Fort Worth and El Paso, eventually. But weren't you supposed to live in Dallas?"

"We got detoured," Devon explained.

He gazed at her gravely. "Didn't we all! Are you happy, Devon?"

She dared not meet his eyes. "I'm not unhappy."

"Forgive me if I don't quite believe you."

"What is happiness, Keith? I thought I knew, once, but I'm not sure anymore!"

"Happiness is love, Devon, and you know it as well as I. It matters not who or what you are on this earth, it takes love to be truly happy. That's not philosophy. It's a human fact. You said almost the same words to me once. Apparently you don't remember when or where."

But she did, and told him so. "It was the night you found me in the Gilded Cage."

He nodded grimly, his voice suddenly hoarse. "Oh, God, Devon! What happened to us?"

"Life," she answered sadly. And since his wife was a part of that life, she had to mention her name, knowing that he would not willingly do so. "How is Esther?"

He responded reluctantly. "A complete physical and mental invalid. Almost catatonic, and a mirror must be held before her mouth frequently to detect breath. The physicians say the general paresis of dementia is gradually setting in, and she can't last more than six months. They've been mistaken before, of course, but this time I believe the prognosis. The only sustenance she receives is through a tube into her stomach. She weighs about sixty pounds, or less. We have day and night nurses, and her mother is also in constant attendance—in fact, when Henry Stanfield died several months ago, Hortense refused to leave Esther even to attend his funeral. I went to Boston to make the arrangements.

"I'm afraid the long ordeal has also unbalanced Mrs. Stanfield's mind somewhat. Evidently there's a fine balance between sanity and insanity, and it doesn't take much to tip the scales. Prolonged melancholy, obsession, even nostalgia can adversely affect the mind, Devon."

And profound love? she thought. A day did not pass without thoughts of him and what might have been. And now they were together again, could they part and go their separate ways? Try once more to forget? *Forget?* Dear Lord, there *was* no forgetting. That was the trouble.

A small nightshirted figure appeared in the doorway, rubbing dark-lashed eyes. "I woke up, Daddy, and Miss Vale wasn't there. But I can dress myself." Then he glimpsed Devon, who was staring at him. "Mommy? You look just like my mommy."

Within seconds Devon was on the floor and cuddling him. "Scotty, darling! I *am* your mommy. And you do remember me, don't you?"

His arms curled about her neck. "You are her, you are! I heard your voice in a dream, and you came to me!"

"Yes, precious, I came to you." Devon held him tightly, planting kisses on his soft cheeks. Soon the child was kissing and hugging her with all his might. "I've missed you, Mommy. Where have you been so long?"

"It hasn't been so long, darling, only a few months." But she knew even a few days could be an eternity in childhood. "Mother was away on a trip, working for a newspaper. But I'm back now, and I've missed you too, Scotty. More than I can ever tell you."

Keith resorted to his defense against painful emotion—a stoic mask. "Get dressed, young man! You can't parade around in your nightclothes before a lady."

The boy's response was quick and logical. "It's all right, sir, because she's my mother. If Miss Vale can see me this way, I guess Mommy can, too."

Devon's great concern that the child might already have forgotten her was mercifully relieved, but not the ache in her heart.

"Come along, Scotty," she said. "Mother and Daddy will help you dress."

One small hand in each of his parents'. Scott led the way to his room. It was no longer a nursery, but a boyish chamber sturdily decorated with nautical touches similar to those in his cabin on the yacht. There was a standing globe, a school desk, books, a large slate with some new words, and several mathematical problems Devon would have thought too advanced for his age.

"What a bright boy you are, Scott! Can you select your own clothes?"

"I've been doing that since I was four, Mother." He opened the wardrobe, where rows of garments hung in easy reach, sorted through them until he located his favorite navy-blue sailor suit, white linen shirt, and light blue tie. Next came the standard black stockings and polished high-topped boots. "I can even button my own shoes, if Miss Vale hasn't misplaced the hook. She does that sometimes, when her mind wanders."

Devon wanted to weep, lamenting all the delightful childish sayings she had missed.

Keith was smiling slightly, the pride in his expression almost tangible, and suddenly Devon wished she had borne twins or triplets. Maybe then he would have let her have one child. But, no, he would have adopted them all, doubling or tripling her loss and her sorrow.

Scott was now removing a set of clean underwear from the lower drawer of his chiffonier. "Excuse me, please. And don't worry, I can fasten the flap and garters. But I'd rather do that in the bathroom."

"That's the proper place, son. Go ahead, we'll wait here."

Soon he emerged, completely dressed, except for the tie, which he held in his hands. "I'm not very good yet at making the bow ends come out even."

"I have trouble tying my cravats occasionally," Keith told him. "Let me help you, son."

"No, please," Devon cried. "Let me!"

"Of course, Mother. But you needn't kneel, Miss Vale sits on the valet bench, and I stand before her. I'm big enough, you see."

"Indeed you are, Scotty! But Mother likes to be on her knees sometimes."

"That's for praying."

And penance, Devon thought, tying a neat bow under the wide linen collar.

A key grated in the lock, and Heather Vale entered her private suite, adjoining the child's. The "errands" had been an invented excuse to allow the parents some privacy. Her greeting was sedately cordial. "Good afternoon, madam. It's nice to see you again."

"Likewise, Miss Vale. I want to thank you for taking such splendid care of Scott. He's a perfect little gentleman."

"I'm glad you're pleased, madam. But his father deserves equal credit. In no other position have I witnessed more conscientious paternal devotion."

Embarrassed, Keith said somewhat brusquely, "I think you might take Scott for his usual airing now, Miss Vale. If you're not too tired from the shopping?"

"Not at all, sir. I found everything in one department store on Pennsylvania Avenue. The purchases will be delivered tomorrow. The city is about back to normal today. It was a bedlam yesterday, and you were wise not to take the child into the crush. Come now, Master Scott. We'll have a pleasant stroll in Lafayette Park. Perhaps you'll find some nice playmates."

"Will I see the President, too?"

"No, dear. President and Mrs. Grant are in New York to bid their daughter and her new husband bon voyage."

Miss Vale took her charge's hand, denying him the lollipop he requested. "It'll ruin your appetite for dinner and is bad for your teeth. British scientists have already discovered this in their people, who consume more sweets than any other people in the world."

"I don't care, I just want some candy."

His eyes beseeched his parents, who shook their heads, although Devon was tempted to shower him with bonbons. And when they had gone, she asked, "Does he understand Miss Vale completely? She speaks to him as if he were an adult."

"That dental speech was primarily for my benefit, lest I indulge his sweet tooth," Keith explained. "But, yes, Scott understands her. He's something of a prodigy, Devon. He has already assimilated more knowledge than many youngsters twice his age. Even Miss Vale, who's not given to exaggeration, rates his intelligence far above average. Naturally, I consider him brilliant and expect him to be a genius."

"Financial wizard, like his father?"

"Not necessarily. Whatever field he selects will please me, as long as the decision is his own. I just want him to be happy."

"Oh, yes, Keith!" She sighed, touching some of her son's clothes and toys. "Do you still have the *Sprite*?"

"Yes. Scott loves the water and sits with me when I take the helm. He enjoys sports, Devon. Sailing and riding. He has graduated from his Shetland pony to a small Banbury mare. I've taught him to swim. And what a thrill when he caught his first fish in the brook that runs through the estate! I can't wait until he's ready for some deep-sea fishing and real hunting."

Devon was pensive, walking through the connecting passages to his suite. Taking her leave now would be sensible, sparing the child and herself a tearful parting. But she did not want to go yet, and Keith was surely aware of her reluctance.

"Every boy should experience the outdoors," she said, "and have some sporting skills. Scott is lucky."

A frown darkened his face. "He could be luckier, Devon. I try to compensate for your absence and would probably spoil him rotten without Miss Vale's stern supervision. The death of a parent can be rationalized to a child, but how does one expain this situation? With lies!"

They were in his rooms now, and Devon understood his dilemma. "You were right, Keith. This meeting was unwise, and you should have refused me permission."

"I couldn't, Devon. I've never denied you anything."

"Anything, Keith?"

"Except that, and you know the reason!" He paused, scowling. "Besides, you can have legitimate children now. I had imagined you were already pregnant."

"I lost a baby," she said quietly.

"When?" he asked instantly.

"Last December."

He was visibly shaken. "Was it . . . ?"

"Yours? No, Keith."

"What happened?"

"Miscarriage. Mrs. Winston could tell you more. She has saved my life several times, bless her. Carla's a remarkable person, Keith, and one of the bravest, most self-sufficient women I've ever met. Would you believe she was a Confederate agent in the war?"

"That is remarkable. What's she doing in Texas now?"

"I often wonder. She's a native Virginian and seems to have the financial means to live anywhere. I think she's rather fond of Reed's father, despite the vast difference in their ages."

"Is it mutual?"

"Apparently, but I'm afraid his plans don't appeal to Carla. The Senator's homesteading some land near Fort Worth, you see, and running a weekly paper."

"In a cabin on the prairie?"

Devon glanced away. "It's only temporary, until he can establish another ranch."

"Devon, the war has been over for years, and Jason Carter is an old man. Don't be like some ostrich Southerners, who still expect the South to rise again. It never will."

Her eyes flashed emerald fire. "No, the Yankees would not allow that! But at least Texas is finally rid of the carpetbag rule and will ultimately prosper."

"On Northern money," he said. "Our banks are making loans in Dallas and Houston. And when that halted railroad eventually reaches Fort Worth, Texans can thank Yankees."

"Including the Wall Street Midas?" His nod further provoked her. "The magic Curtis gold! I might have known."

"I'm a banker, Devon. Banks finance progress."

"And expand on interest and foreclosed mortgages."

"Not always, although we're hardly charitable institutions. And surely you'll concede the superiority of iron horses to transport cattle and crops to market? And people to their destinations? The stagecoach is still the principal method of travel in the West, including the Carters' territory."

"You've been studying Texas?"

"Investigating it, and why not? I have some investments there and am considering more. Maybe I'll build some bunkhouses and corrals, hire a foreman and cowhands, and start a ranch." He smiled wryly. "I just might get some high-heeled boots and a tall Stetson hat and play rancher."

"Texans don't 'play' at ranching, Keith. They take it very seriously."

His manner was arrogant, but Devon knew it was a facade. It was no more effective than her attempts to camouflage her own desperation. How much longer could they affect this masquerade? She had better leave, before lost control carried them to the point of no return. But as she rose and hesitated, he asserted himself in one swift motion. Instantly Devon was in his arms, his mouth hungrily on hers, and she responded with equal passion. Her husband became a vague image, receding, dissolving.

"You still love me!" he exulted triumphantly, and Devon could only nod, savoring his searching kisses and caresses. Consumed with pent-up want, she was barely conscious that he had swung her off her feet and was rapidly approaching the master bedroom.

He was undressing her when reality intervened—the rapping knocker. "Ignore it," he whispered. "Whoever it is will go away."

But reason had returned, and Devon shook her head. "No, Keith! We can't, it's wrong!"

"Don't fight me, Devon. It's no use. We love each other too much. Darling, please?"

The intruder persisted, sounding urgent. Keith swore and went to answer, straightening his clothes. Devon jumped up from the rumpled bed, astonished to behold her half-naked body and glittering eyes in the mocking mirrors. Composing herself and garments as promptly as possible, she was back in the parlor before Keith, deliberately delaying, opened the door.

"I'm terribly sorry to disturb you, Mr. Curtis," the governess apologized. "But I forgot my key, and Master Scott seems somewhat ill. He complains of headache and nausea and feels feverish. I thought it best to bring him home immediately."

"Certainly, Miss Vale." Keith picked up his son and carried him to the nursery. "Summon the house physician at once."

"Yes, sir." Heather Vale rushed out to the elevator, descending to the lobby so the desk clerk could have the Clairmont's physician paged.

"What do you suppose is wrong with him?" Devon asked.

Keith sought to calm her anxiety. "Probably a cold or upset stomach. We'll have to wait for the medical diagnosis."

Dr. Zimmer, who received his comfortable suite gratis, soon arrived and examined the patient. "Relax, Mr. Curtis. We have an epidemic of measles here every spring, and your son has the classic symptoms. But he's a healthy lad and should recover easily with proper nursing. The rash will appear in a day or two. I'll give Miss Vale instructions for his care and will be back tomorrow, unless you need me before then."

"Thank you, Doctor. I appreciate that."

Zimmer replaced his instruments, pretending not to notice Devon. He was aware that Mr. Curtis occasionally entertained ladies at the Clairmont, but not, to his knowledge, when the boy and his governess were present. There must be some special reason for this beauty's company today, none of which was any of his business. "I'll show myself out," he said, picking up his expensive leather satchel.

The parents were visibly relieved. They talked to Scott, petted and cheered him, promised many gifts, and then allowed Miss Vale to prepare him for a fortnight of confinement.

Once again in Keith's rooms, Devon said seriously, "I want to help nurse Scotty, stay in town until he's well. Miss Vale will understand my presence, and you can explain it to the doctor however you wish."

"I don't explain my private life to anyone, Devon. You should know that. But I'm glad of your decision. It will benefit the child."

"Has he been ill much?"

"Fortunately not, and never seriously. This is his first childhood disease. He doesn't have much contact with children in the country."

"But you can't isolate him to prevent contamination, Keith. Scott needs playmates his own age."

"He needs brothers and sisters, my dear, and should have had several by now."

Devon said nothing, but in her heart she agreed with him. Regardless of the circumstances of their relationship, she could have given him a small family. How much worse off could she have been as his mistress than she was now, married to one man while loving another?

Chapter 14

The time had come to confide in Carla, and Devon now wished she had done so long ago. As the sun lowered over the Potomac, casting a rosy hue over the city, she told Keith, "I'm going to the Willard."

"I thought you intended to stay here."

"At night?"

"I have a guest room, you know. But if using it would bother you, I also keep other accommodations available."

"For unexpected visitors?" she asked, piqued.

"For privileged ones," he replied. "The Clairmont has often accommodated dignitaries visiting the White House. There was a surfeit of them at the wedding, and several lodged here, including a British duchess."

"The Duchess of Sussex?" Devon had included her in the list of distinguished guests, briefly describing her elegant gown and jewels. A very attractive woman, no more than thirty, with auburn hair and an exquisite complexion. "She's lovely, Keith. Why wasn't the duke with her?"

"I didn't ask. Perhaps he was on business for the Queen. Or ailing. He's much older than she."

"You know her well?"

"Barbara's a friend."

" 'Barbara,' is it? Did she have a retinue?"

"A small one, including two maids." He smiled at her petulant curiosity. "And, no, I didn't visit with her alone."

"I wasn't thinking of that."

"Weren't you? Anyway, she left for New York on the same train as the Grants, and will sail to England on the same ship with Nellie and Algy. The suite she occupied is just below this floor, and would be convenient for you."

"Thank you," Devon said. "I'll bring some things."

Carla registered no surprise at the confidence. Rather, she was sympathetic and understanding, agreeing that Devon belonged with her ill child and his father.

"But what about Reed?"

Devon shrugged. "I don't know, Carla. But we can't leave Washington on schedule."

"Don't worry, dear. I'll handle it."

"How?"

"According to the message, which I'll wire promptly with your signature, I've contracted a stubborn case of dysentery, which naturally precludes travel. Plausible?"

Devon nodded, putting clothes and toilet articles in a valise. She felt guilty about the lie. But there was no alternative, and the emergency warranted it.

The itchy red rash appeared in due course, and they placed cotton mittens on his hands to prevent scratching. When his temperature soared, Devon kept a twenty-four-hour vigil until it subsided. Keith sat with her while the governess rested, and they drank coffee and spoke in hushed tones. Once, weary and apprehensive, she began to cry. "What if he goes into a worse stage?"

Keith patted her hand. "The fever is not alarmingly high, darling, and the doctor is in the building. You're exhausted. I'll wake Miss Vale in an hour or so, and then you're going to sleep."

"I couldn't, Keith."

"You will, if I have to go to bed with you."

"All right," she murmured.

"All right, what?"

"I'll try to sleep."

At first Scott's appetite was slack and his diet largely liquid. But on the fifth day he complained of hunger, which Dr. Zimmer regarded as a good sign. "He's doing fine, Mr. Curtis. Just keep him warm, keep the shades drawn to avoid light damage to his eyes, and continue the prescribed medication. I anticipate a rapid recuperation. Indeed, you may have difficulty confining him for the required period. But it's necessary, to prevent complications."

"I understand, Doctor."

It was apparent that Devon's presence was an important factor in the child's convalescence. Hugging her, he said, "I'm so happy you came back to me, Mommy. Don't ever leave me again."

"Oh, Scotty! Baby darling." She pressed his face to her bosom. "I'm not sure Mother can stay with you always, nor even very long. But you're such a big brave boy, and you know how much Mother loves you and thinks of you, no matter where she is."

"Then stay with us," he pleaded, clutching her. "Daddy says you have a job somewhere. But you don't need to work, Mommy. Daddy has a whole bank full of money! I saw it, when he took me into the vault. There's gold and silver and greenbacks, and lots of pretty jewelry. We're rich, Mother, so you don't have to work."

"You don't understand, precious."

"You said you love me!"

"I do, Scotty, more than life."

"And you love Daddy, too?"

"Yes, darling. With all my heart."

Devon was cradling him in her arms, rocking him gently, when she realized that Keith was standing on the threshold. She blotted her tears. "Miss Vale is fixing your supper now, Scott, and I want you to eat every bite. Your dessert will be ice cream."

"What flavor?"

"Name your favorite."

"Chocolate," he announced unequivocally.

Picking up a ruler, Devon waved it like a magic wand. "Your wish is granted, Master Scott! But remember, you must eat your meat and vegetables first."

"I promise, Mommy. Then will you tell me a story?"

"At bedtime, sweetheart."

"You know wonderful stories, Mother. I like those about wagon trains and stagecoaches and cowboys and Indians best of all. Miss Vale talks mostly about fairies and elves, kings and queens and little princes, and some English boys named Tiny Tim and Oliver."

Devon kissed the silken crown of his head, where the dark curls grew in clusters, one lock falling over his forehead like his father's. His lessons had been suspended for the duration of the malady, and he was not allowed to look at his picture books or use his slate and crayons, lest he strain his eyes. Stories and sedentary games were his only amusements.

"What did you tell your tall Texan?" Keith asked when she joined him.

"A tall tale," she answered.

"And he believed it?"

"Reed has no reason to distrust me, Keith. Besides, it was Carla's idea. She has an inventive mind."

"Most operatives do—it's their stock-in-trade."

"You must meet Mrs. Winston, Keith. Actually, you already have. She was the little old lady whom you befriended at the wedding. A disguise, of course. She's ingenius that way. In many ways, really."

The women kept each other informed via messengers. The mail that Carla sent to the Clairmont included congratulations from Carrie Hempstead and notice of several reprint offers for her article, invitations from local hostesses who imagined that Miss Marshall was again the New York *Record*'s Capital social correspondent, and a telegram from Reed regretting Carla's indisposition, wishing her well, and hoping they would both be able to travel soon.

The Grants had returned from New York, saddened not only by the departure of their beloved daughter but also by the depressed economy, visible everywhere. Hundreds of banks and insurance companies were in receivership. Some five thousand American factories, mills, mines, shops, stores, had closed. Unemployment was rising drastically, and Union veterans, unable to exist on their meager pensions, threatened to march on Washington. Not since the firing on Fort Sumter had the nation been so perilously near revolution.

Grant was in a quandary as to how to cope with the crisis. But he was certain of one thing: Secretary of the Treasury William Richardson, in office less than a year, was already under congressional investigation for irregularities concerning the Internal Revenue Division! Grant would have to request Richardson's resignation and try once again to persuade Keith Curtis to accept the post.

When the White House summons was delivered to the Clairmont, Keith responded immediately. The conference took place in the President's office, where Grant sat at his desk nervously puffing a cigar. "You know why I sent for you, of course?"

"I think so, Mr. President."

"Good Lord, how could Richardson fail me this way! Congress is hot on his tail and will demand he leave. The Treasury can't be without a secretary. What am I to do for a replacement?"

"There are many able men, Mr. President."

"None better qualified than you, my friend."

"I wasn't including myself, sir."

Another refusal, even before the offer. And the reason would be familiar: too many personal obligations that would interfere with a total commitment to the position.

"I see." Grant sighed. "Then I must search elsewhere, and the pickings are slim. Jay Gould is shrewd, but the public hasn't forgotten his involvement with Jim Fisk in Black Friday, the Erie Railroad stock frauds, and numerous other scandals. August Belmont knows finance, but he's a Democrat allied with Tammany Hall. William Astor is also a Democrat, and a wheeler-dealer. Commodore Vanderbilt is too old, and hardly trustworthy."

"You're just considering the capitalists, Mr. President. Americans are obsessed with money and the power it wields in government and society. Lacking royalty, we have created an aristocracy of wealthy idols. There's a social register of robber barons in New York whose methods of achievement rival Bluebeard's."

Grant, himself an ardent admirer of the class under discussion, sat bemused, wondering how much of this was aimed at his misplaced adulation, which had frequently led him to select the wrong men to serve in his administration.

"What you say is true. But the fact remains that Richardson must be replaced. Have you any recommendations?"

"Well, there's a Kentucky lawyer, with whom I've had some fair dealings, who might be a responsible choice. Benjamin Bristow is a Republican, competent, and highly respected in his state. I'm not guaranteeing his performance, however, merely proposing his name."

"What does he know about finance?"

"With all due respect, sir, what did Richardson and his predecessor know about it?"

"You're right," Grant said. "I'll get in touch with Mr. Bristow promptly. I appreciate your comments, Keith, and trust you'll remain available in an advisory capacity?"

"Of course, sir."

"Thank you kindly. And if you're free this evening, Mrs. Grant and I would enjoy your company at dinner."

"I'd be honored, Mr. President. But my little son is with me on this trip, and presently confined with the measles. Has your youngest boy had this pesky disease yet?"

"I believe so, although Julia would know that better than I. In any case, use your own judgment. Melah always prepares a feast, even when the family is dining alone.

What the other servants don't consume is wasted, a practice which must cease. With so many hungry citizens eating out of slop barrels, the White House can't afford prodigality. The opposition is still ranting about the extravagance of Nellie's wedding, and I understand the Grants have been hanged in effigy in some Tammany wards. My hopes for a third term might not amount to much."

Keith silently concurred, unaware until then that Grant entertained such precarious ambitions. As his secretary announced the arrival of another appointment, Keith stood and shook hands, feeling sorry for the harassed and bewildered general, who had botched the most important mission of his career.

Returning to the Clairmont, he appeared tired and introspective; Devon suspected he'd had to make a difficult decision, possibly even disappointing the President. "How did things go?" she asked.

He shook his head gravely, fixing a drink at the cellaret. "Not well. Somehow I've acquired the image of a messiah who can miraculously cure the ailing economy."

"That's because your fiscal prophecies of the past are coming true with a vengeance. According to this morning's papers, Prime Minister Disraeli has invited you to a conference in London."

"France has been economically shaky since the deposal of Napoleon III, and naturally concerned about the Bourse and other European markets."

"Have you accepted the invitation?"

"I could hardly decline it, Devon."

"Then you'll be sailing to England soon?"

He nodded, savoring the Scotch.

"And taking Scotty and Miss Vale along?"

"Yes. We'll visit Heathstone Manor."

The ancestral estate in Sussex, a part of her son's noble heritage. How Devon wished she could accompany them! She averted her eyes, lest they reflect her longing. "That's wonderful, Keith. Do any of your mother's family still live there?"

"My grandparents, and an uncle and aunt. It's time Scott met them."

"Yes," she agreed.

"I hope you won't mind, my dear, but I've ordered dinner from Dijon's. Everything, as I recall, that you used to enjoy. I thought a little celebration appropriate, since the boy is recovering so nicely." He did not mention the White House invitation.

Devon nodded happily. "We don't get much French cuisine in Texas. Mostly steak, fried or barbecued. The veal is fairly tender, but the longhorn beef is usually tough."

"The ranchers should crossbreed the cattle, import other stock, and establish new strains."

"That's what the Carters would like to do," Devon confided. "But it takes capital, and few Texans have money to invest *now*."

"I make loans, Devon, if the collateral warrants it."

"We have no collateral, Keith. Anyway, I think Reed has temporarily forsaken ranching. He's good at politics and may end up in Washington."

"By gubernatorial appointment?"

That surprised her. Had he already heard the rumors? "Possibly."

"Well, anything that would get you out of Texas would be a blessing."

She blushed. "Oh, it's not so bad, Keith. Some people even like it. It's still largely a wilderness, of course, and harder to tame than a shrew."

He smiled ruefully, his penetrating gaze becoming disconcerting. Unable to sit still, she moved about the room, touching a jade tiger, a marble stag, a teak cigar box, the best-selling novel he had been reading. "Do you think it's possible to circle the globe in eighty days?"

"Jules Verne makes it seem so."

"Critics pan his fantasies."

"But they're popular, probably because they provide a fictional escape from harsh reality. I've just finished Mark Twain's *Roughing It*, about the Overland Trail, Nevada miners, and other Western lore. I suspect some of the adventures you tell Scott are inspired by Twain and Bret Harte."

"He enjoys them, Keith."

"Naturally. Most children like unfamiliar tales, including ghost stories. They make traditional fare, which Miss Vale sanctions, seem dull."

"She's an excellent governess, though. You made a wise choice, Keith."

"Heather Vale was hired solely on references, Devon.

You know that." He was pouring his second drink when a knock heralded the arrival of dinner. "Ah, finally! I'm famished."

"Me, too," Devon lied.

The uniformed waiter wheeled in a portable steam cart that held precisely the same menu Keith had ordered for them on their first night together in Washington, including the vintage champagne and tiny silver tree hung with fresh plump strawberries and the silver dish of powdered sugar. What a memory he had, and how cleverly he had revived hers!

Devon knew she must leave quickly this evening, lest it end with her in his bed, making love by candlelight. She also knew, as surely as he sat intimately surveying her across the white-clothed table and glowing tapers, that he would do nothing physical to detain her. He would simply bide his time, confident that she would ultimately come to him. What if, as usual, he was right?

Chapter 15

In Austin, the legislature was preparing to adjourn. A great deal had been accomplished in the short session, and the members were being congratulated by a round of entertainments, topped by Judge Hampton's grand ball at his river estate.

Everyone in Travis County knew of Hampton House. It rivaled the Governor's Mansion, and some Texans wondered how Gore Hampton had managed to retain his wealth and property and even to accumulate more, while others were reduced to poverty. The answer suggested some conspiracy with the carpetbaggers, but if so, Hampton had been clever enough to conceal it.

A number of former Hampton slaves were now employed on the estate. Cared for by a mammy since birth, young Melissa was still waited upon by a black maid. A black valet attended her father. The staff also included former slaves as butler, housekeeper, cook, and handymen. All were as servile as ever they had been in slavery.

Cherishing his late wife's memory was regarded as one of the judge's more favorable attributes, and the portrait of her sedately posed in a velvet chair occupied a prominent place in the drawing room. Although a gracious lady, Prudence Hampton had been unable to number beauty among her assets. Nor was her husband handsome. Yet they had created a beautiful child. Melissa was the only one out of five to survive adolescence, which explained the judge's fanatic fatherhood.

Melissa was totally spoiled. She knew exactly how to coax and tease her father into obliging her whims and wishes, often sitting on his lap and tickling his whiskers, hugging and kissing him as she had in childhood. He was never able to resist her, and would promise "Anything you want, baby. Just don't ask for the moon and stars, because Daddy can't get them for you." Even as a child Melissa had not craved these celestial intangibles, and since puberty her desires had become solidly worldly.

Melissa addressed the Carters' invitation personally, in her own Baltimore-finishing-school hand. She told the black houseboy, "Take this one to the Capitol and present it to Mr. Reed Carter himself. Understand?"

Skeeter nodded. What he didn't understand was why this envelope was more important to Miss Melissa than the others, which he was merely to deliver to their respective residences. "Should I wait for a reply?"

"No, just be sure you hand it to *him*."

"Yes, miss," Skeeter said, and started off on his errands.

Although Melissa had included the customary *RSVP*, she did not expect anyone to send regrets. Judge Hampton's invitations were tantamount to social subpoenas. Ordinary folks had as much chance of receiving one as commoners a royal summons. She was confident that Reed Carter would respond. Worried, however, that Mrs. Carter might return at the last moment, she had the passenger lists of the trains from Houston checked until the day of the ball.

Judge Hampton was very proud of the way his daughter had assumed the role of mistress of the house. In a frothy white lace gown, with tiny fresh pink rosebuds in her thick brown hair, Melissa greeted the guests as her father's hostess. But she did not relax completely until Reed Carter's arrival, alone. Her prayers had been answered! Apparently her heavenly father couldn't refuse her petitions any more than her earthly one could.

Gore Hampton called genially, "Reed, my friend, welcome to our home!"

"Thank you, sir. Good evening, Miss Hampton."

Melissa beamed. "We're delighted you could come. Mr. Speaker!" She glanced about him, pretending surprise and disappointment. "Mrs. Carter is still away?"

"Yes, due to unfortunate circumstances. Mrs. Winston, her traveling companion, was taken ill in Washington."

"What a shame! We mailed your father an invitation, but perhaps he didn't receive it. The postal service is so unreliable. Of course, it's a long trip by stage from Fort Worth, and the Senator is getting on, isn't he?"

Reed smiled. Naturally, anyone past sixty would seem ancient to Melissa. "Well, he's not exactly Methuselah yet, Miss Hampton."

"Oh, please, call me Melissa. But not *Miss* Melissa, which is a tongue twister. Say it rapidly three times."

"You're right," Reed agreed, silently trying it.

"Drives the servants mad!" Melissa chuckled gleefully. "If you'd like some refreshment, there's a large variety in the dining room, sir, where most of the guests are congregated now. The ball will begin shortly."

"Please reserve a dance for me, Melissa?"

She raised flirtatious brown eyes. "Only one?"

"Several," he amended chivalrously, moving on.

The host was a big bearded man who obviously enjoyed the fruits of life—a glutton in every respect, Devon had characterized Gore Hampton.

But whatever the judge's character, his daughter was a charming coquette. Any man would be flattered by her attentions, and Reed found her delightful. But Miss Hampton intended to do more than just entice him, and her conduct was part of a design she had lain awake nights to perfect. She wanted Reed Carter and, one way or another, she had always gotten what she wanted.

In the middle of their third waltz together, she suggested a hiatus on the veranda. Escorting her from the ballroom, Reed solicitously inquired if she felt faint. "Heavens, no! I never swoon—that's for delicate, unhealthy females who overlace their stays! It's just so stuffy in the crowd, and unseasonably warm."

"It's June, my dear. Time to get warm in Texas."

"But the nights are still pleasantly cool, especially near the river. And I'm an outdoor girl who enjoys fresh air."

"This is a fine location," Reed remarked on the broad, columned gallery, "and Hampton House is beautiful."

Melissa took it all for granted, as her birthright. "Well, it's home to us."

The manicured grounds were a smaller version of the Hampton cotton plantation's lawns in east Texas, with perennial flowerbeds and borders in bloom, a rose garden, and an intricate, precisely clipped privet labyrinth. The air smelled of roses and spicy pinks, magnolias and wild cedar, and moonlight glinted like gold dust on the great river flowing beneath the bluff.

"Excellent view," Reed commented.

"It's better from the gazebo," Melissa said tentatively. "Daddy had it built on the best vantage, so it could also serve as a watchtower. Let me show you."

She took his hand to lead the way down the steps and across the pebbled paths. The hexagonal wood structure was large enough for a bandstand. The supports and railings were ornately carved, the floor varnished, the west wall latticed. There were rattan settees, chairs, tables. Flowers and ferns trailed from hanging baskets and ornamental pedestals, and there was a flagpole atop the quaintly peaked roof, where the Lone Star banner waved on important occasions, as if Texas were still an independent republic.

"I spend hours here," Melissa confided, "idling away lonely days."

"Lonely? A girl like you? You're lucky, Melissa, having everything you want."

"Not quite everything, Reed. There are some things Daddy can't buy for me." Unexpectedly she asked, "Do you miss your wife?"

Caught off guard by her directness, he nodded. "Very much."

"Seems strange for her to leave you so long."

"Mrs. Carter is a journalist, Melissa. She went to Washington on an assignment, and then she was unavoidably detained."

"Oh, I know she used to work for a New York newspaper. But she was single then. I understand she still writes under her maiden name."

"It's an established by-line."

"She's a career woman, isn't she? One of those feminists —always demanding the vote, marching in the streets, and making public nuisances of themselves."

"We'd better return to the ball, Melissa."

She promptly apologized. "I'm sorry if I've offended you, Reed. I didn't mean to criticize your wife. Mercy, no! If *you* don't mind her activities, why should anyone else?"

"No offense, my dear."

But she gnawed on the subject, as a tenacious dog on a juicy bone. "It's just that . . . well, some of your colleagues' wives feel differently. They think a married woman's place is in the home, with her husband."

Reed snorted. "Half of my colleagues' spouses were left behind, Melissa, for financial or other reasons. Do the gossipmongers slander them, too?"

"Probably. Idle tongues just naturally clack, you know."

"Well, let's not risk having them chatter about you,"

Reed said, turning toward the house. "I'm married, remember?"

"They wouldn't dare spread rumors about me," she assured him confidently. "Daddy would punish them through their men."

"But you must admit this interlude looks suspicious, Melissa, and Daddy can't monitor people's minds."

Melissa shrugged her bare shoulders, softly pink and alluring above the low-necked gown. Her body was fully matured, from voluptuous breasts to curvaceous hips, and Reed had sensed her sexual maturity when they danced together. She was lusciously ripe, and spoiling to be plucked. Still a virgin? Probably, since any fellow trifling with her reputation would risk the judge's wrath and his own ruin. The thought made him quicken his pace.

Melissa entered the ballroom fanning herself, her intimidating glare silencing any suspicions among the matrons and wallflowers. Her father was perspiring, his face and bald pate florid above his dignified Vandyke.

"Where you been, sugar?"

"Outside, trying to catch my breath and cool off."

"Daddy's little girl getting hot?" he asked indelicately, and Reed had to suppress a grin.

"Well, it's really quite stifling in here, Daddy."

"It sure is, honey. Refresh yourself with some iced punch, and then dance with me. My pretty baby can't let the evening pass without dancing with her old daddy."

Watching them on the waxed floor, Reed detected more than paternal pride and affection in the way the judge held Melissa and in the glow in his eyes when he smiled at her. He was aware of the mental quirks of some doting fathers who, deprived of their wives, transferred their desires to their daughters. Was Melissa too young to realize his attachment? She was certainly equipped with all the female essentials, and she seemed to enjoy teasing Daddy. It could develop into a messy situation, and Reed wanted no involvement in it. After a stiff drink of Hampton's best bourbon, he paid his respects and went home to the little frame cottage on Congress Avenue. In his restless sleep he called Devon's name and reached out for her, waking with her pillow in his arms.

A few days later, as he was leaving the Capitol with a portfolio of government papers in hand, Reed pretended not to see Melissa's wicker pony cart, the only one of its kind in Austin, waiting at the foot of the granite steps. But it was difficult to ignore Melissa when she wished to be noticed.

"May I offer you a lift, Mr. Speaker?"

He approached the curb and tipped his hat. "Good afternoon, Miss Hampton. Thank you, no. I need some exercise."

"Don't be silly! You're as slim as your name. And why so formal today? The other night it was 'Melissa.' "

"I don't think your father approved of the informality," Reed hedged

"Daddy? Why, he's as fond of you as of a son, Reed! He told me so himself! He'd be insulted if you refused my hospitality now."

"Melissa, I have work to do! The legislature is adjourning this week."

"Well, you certainly can't finish everything on the agenda before then, can you? Come on, get in! Your timidity is making us conspicuous."

"It's not timidity," he muttered, climbing in beside her, feeling foolish in the white-and-gilt feminine contraption, his long legs cramped. Even the horse was white, a beautifully curried Arabian mare, with ornamental silver-and-white leather trappings.

"What, then?"

"Common sense, Melissa."

"Pooh!" She giggled, slapping the reins across Scheherazade's sleek flanks. "If you're concerned about Daddy, he's visiting the Widow Hensley, and will likely be away most of the night. He does that sometimes. I don't know why."

Probably to keep from raping you, Reed thought, gritting his teeth. Surely she knew about incest?

"You're going the wrong way," he advised, as Melissa headed out of town. "I live in the other direction."

"So I'm taking you for a little ride, Mr. Speaker. Any law against that? How do you like my chariot?"

"Charming, but you drive it like a hellcart."

"Too reckless? I should think a former cowboy and cavalry officer would be accustomed to recklessness."

"I prefer to hold the reins, miss."

She started to relinquish them, then changed her mind, afraid he might spoil her fun. "Relax, sir. I'm an excellent driver. A terrific equestrienne, too. I can ride bareback, and I despise that fancy English sidesaddle the local ladies started using a few years ago." This barb was aimed at his wife and Carla Winston, whom Melissa had seen riding in elegant Eastern habits.

"You're a paradox, Melissa, scorning feminism one minute, and flouting convention the next."

"I resent rules."

"That's obvious, my dear. And just what is in your rebellious little head now?"

"Mischief, maybe." She laughed.

"You need a spanking, young lady."

"Oh, Daddy spanks me often, playfully. I don't mind. I rather enjoy it, in fact. Sometimes I wish he'd do it harder, use a crop, hurt me a little." Removing the whip from its ivory holder, she lashed the horse, crying, "Hang on!" as the cart careened on the rutted dirt road.

"Slow down!" Reed shouted, grabbing at the lines, but she only laughed and cracked the whip harder.

A wheel hit a rock, nearly overturning them. "Goddammit, Melissa! You want to get killed?"

His anger further excited her, adding a fillip to the adventure. She hoped to provoke him into violence. "Ah, that's the good old Texan spirit! Remember the Alamo!"

The horse was traveling rapidly now, almost at runaway speed, the lightweight vehicle bouncing like a crate along the wooded lane toward the green hills. Reed feared that if he attempted to wrest control from Melissa, they would be injured. How could he explain such an accident to her father? They rumbled at breakneck speed across a narrow bridge, the iron hubs sparking against the flintstone sides. Trees grew thickly here, arching overhead, and they had to duck to avoid the low-hanging branches. Approaching a steep incline, the frothing animal slowed for the climb, finally descending into a pleasant valley and trotting to a nearby creek.

"Scheherazade is thirsty," Melissa said, grinning at Reed's scowl. "No harm done, Mr. Speaker."

"Only because the horse has more sense than its owner."

"I'd like a drink, too. Wouldn't you?"

"Yeah, something stronger than water." Reed got out, ignoring her outstretched hand.

"Such manners," she chided.

"You're not helpless, Melissa."

"I think you're afraid to touch me," she taunted.

Grimly silent, Reed cupped his hands to drink, then splashed cold water over his sweating face. He wiped it with his kerchief, his blue eyes appraising the position of the sun.

"Hot under the collar, Mr. Speaker?"

"Stop calling me that, and drink if you're thirsty. It'll be dark before we get back."

"And me without a duenna! Gracious, how terrible! The gossips will say I've been compromised."

"Hush, Melissa, and hurry. I'll drive back."

"If you wish, sir." She lapped slowly, like a puppy, then perched on a rock, kicked off her slippers, and began to remove her stockings.

Reed yelled, "Melissa! What the devil do you think you're doing?"

"I want to wade."

"There isn't time."

Already barefoot, she hoisted her skirts above her knees and stepped into the shallow stream, tickling her toes on the ferns. Reed watched her, furious but intrigued by her brazen antics. She was a tempting combination of hoyden and enchantress, as bold and charming as Vera. He strode toward her, his eyes cautious as a scout's, pretending fury. "Get out of there! There are Indians around here, and I'm unarmed. You want to be captured? Scalped or raped?"

"Do I have a choice?"

"Melissa!"

"Oh, all right." She sighed. "But we're playing this drama in reverse, you know? *I'm* supposed to be the reluctant maiden."

"Are you?" he asked unexpectedly.

"Reluctant?"

"A maiden."

"Well, I'm not married."

"That's not what I mean."

Her wide dark eyes challenged him. "Interested, Mr. Carter?"

"Presumptuous, and I'm sorry. Forgive me."

"I'll grant you a conditional pardon," she decreed. "Don't frown. There's only one condition—that you carry me to my shoes, so I won't get my feet dirty."

"Come to the bank," he agreed.

"Yes, sir."

As Reed lifted her from the brook, her arms lassoed his neck tightly, and her lovely lips parted in a smile, inviting his taste. Despite his resolutions, Reed felt an ache in his groin, a tantalizing desire surging beyond control, and an inexplicable rage at Devon for leaving him prey to such temptation. Melissa's body was soft and pliant against his, her bare smooth wet legs visible above her wide-legged drawers, and he had a sudden compulsive urge to kiss her dimpled knees.

Knowing his thoughts, she urged, "Why don't you?"

The roar in his ears, created by his racing heart, was almost deafening. "What?"

"Make love to me."

"I can't."

"You look capable," she coaxed.

"But I can't, Melissa!"

"Physical impairments? Wounded in the war? Kicked by a mustang?"

"No," he said vehemently.

"Then what's the problem? I know you want me, Reed. And you wouldn't be the first, if that's hindering you."

The news both relieved and disappointed him. "There was someone else?"

"Un-huh. When I was twelve, although Daddy never knew. The boy was only fifteen, the son of family friends, but big for his age and precocious . . . like me. We had a secret place in the attic, where we played house on some old quilts. It was fun, but he was just a boy. I've never had a man do that to me, and I think you would like to. Now."

Reed paused, gazing intently into her provocative eyes, his own darkening with quickened passion. As if magnetized, their mouths drew together. She was squirming, as eager for sexual release as he, and Reed knew he was going to oblige.

Selecting a grassy spot, he lowered her gently to the earth beneath him. While he unbuttoned his trousers, Melissa exposed her body. She proved expert at coordinating her movements, moaning and gasping in repeated spasms, truly sorry when the playing was over.

"I could do that forever with you," she praised him.

"Nothing lasts forever, my dear, especially not that."

"But while you were inside me, we were one person,"

joined by the act," she murmured dreamily, longing to lie with him all night, even on the ground. "Isn't that a wonderful feeling, darling?"

"Wonderful."

"And you do like me?" she asked anxiously.

"How could any man not like you, Melissa?"

It wasn't at all what she wanted to hear, but it would do for now. "Then we can be together again?"

He shook his head. "No, something might happen, and I couldn't do anything about it."

"Can't you be careful?"

"Carefulness doesn't always work, Melissa. I only hope to God nothing happens from this time. I wouldn't want to hurt you, or my wife. I'm in love with her, Melissa."

She began to tidy her garments, brushing the leaves and grass from her tangled hair. "It didn't seem so a few minutes ago."

"I know," he said ruefully. "But sometimes the devil gets the better of a man, and he weakens. I didn't intend it to happen." He retrieved his hat from the ground, knocking off the dirt fiercely. "Now, we simply must leave! The sun is down. Maybe we can sneak into town unnoticed."

"Who cares?"

"I do. And you should." He helped her into the cart, and drove as swiftly as caution and dusk would allow. "I'll get off at the city limits and walk home or catch a horsecar."

"Suit yourself."

"Melissa, don't sulk. Be fair about this. It wasn't entirely my fault, you know."

"Are you blaming me?" she demanded, not waiting for his response. "Just because I wasn't a virgin doesn't mean I'm an easy slut. A convenient whore for any man's lust!"

Her bonnet and pretty sprigged-muslin dress were sullied, but more so her pride. Embarrassment made her hostile. Reed felt compassion for her, and remorse at his own conduct. She was young and impetuous, and *he* was old enough to know better.

"Certainly not, Melissa. No such inference was implied. You're a lovely, vital, charming girl and must have scores of suitors begging for your hand. Please try to forget this incident. I promise you, no one will ever know unless you betray yourself."

"What if I'm pregnant?" she accused bitterly.

The prospect gave him violent shivers.

"How long did you carry on sex with that boyfriend?"

"Several years," she admitted.

"What sort of precautions did you take?"

"None."

"Well, there's your answer."

"No, it isn't!" she cried, distraught. "I was caught, once, but got rid of the brat."

"How?"

"Abortion."

Good Lord! Was she lying? "And your father never suspected?"

"No. An old Mexican midwife helped me. I paid her ten pesos and a garnet brooch."

"How old were you?"

"Fourteen."

"And you and the boy continued your relations?"

Melissa nodded, biting her lips, twisting her hands. "It never happened again."

Reed's relief was almost audible, but he pitied her. Perhaps the unskilled operation had sterilized her. He dared not suggest this to her. Did she suspect? "Melissa, I'm sure everything will be all right."

"But it won't," she sobbed. "Because I . . . I love you, Reed. Truly, I do."

His hands strained on the reins, but he affected calm. "Not really, Melissa. You only think so now. I'm flattered. But you realize the situation, and why I can't reciprocate your feelings. Besides, I'm much too old for you. Why, I'm forty," he lied desperately, "more than twice your age!"

"You're not either," she sniffed. "Anyway, I like older men."

"You poor child."

"I'm not a child!"

They had reached the edge of town. Reed halted and handed her the lines. "With your driving expertise, I think you can take it from here." He hopped down, portfolio in hand, before she could protest. "Good night, Melissa, and good-bye."

"I hate you!" she declared miserably. "I hope you die! I hope your wife dies, too!"

"You don't mean that."

"No," she retracted. "Not about you. Oh, Reed, please believe me. I love you very much."

"I'm sorry, Melissa."

He walked rapidly toward Congress Avenue. In a few moments she passed him, whipping the horse furiously, venting her rage and despair on the helpless animal. In such a mood, Melissa was capable of any violence, even self-destruction. Reed tried to stop her. "Wait, Melissa! I'll take you home!"

But she did not hear him, and soon all he heard were echoing hoofbeats. He could only pray that her tantrum would pass before morning, and without consequences.

Chapter 16

To the extent that she was capable of mature emotion, Melissa did love Reed. She kept their secret, as much for her own sake as his. But her loyalty did not extend to his wife, whom she now blamed for her inability to have Reed Carter for herself. Her hatred focused on Devon. She had often heard her father say that the easiest way to defeat an enemy was to first make a friend of him, gain his confidence, maneuver him into a vulnerable position, and then annihilate him. Melissa began to think about it.

Reed avoided most of the social and civic affairs where they might meet, but in those he could not ignore, Melissa was the soul of tact. The escapade in the valley might never have occurred, and he decided that she was more sophisticated than he had imagined. She was formal and discreet in the presence of others, addressing him as Mr. Speaker or Mr. Carter.

Gore Hampton smiled on him benignly, and Reed believed that the judge would support his coveted senatorial appointment in Washington. In gratitude, he complimented Miss Hampton: "You're a fine, generous person, Melissa, and I appreciate your adult attitude."

"Thank you," she replied sedately. "All your colleagues consider you an honorable man, Mr. Carter, and a worthy replacement for that renegade Republican senator. I'm not fully aware of all the political intricacies, but I understand he's guilty of some malfeasance in public office and indiscretion in his private life as well. He deserves his disgrace, don't you agree? I hope such an ignominious fate will never befall you, sir."

Her tongue had a razor's edge. Still, Reed did not regard the innuendos as a real threat. The cunning little witch had something else in mind. Another rendezvous? Well, he had an effective deterrent.

"Mrs. Carter is on her way to Austin," he said.

"Really? How nice! I hope we shall all be great friends. I want to congratulate her on the Grant-Sartoris article. As you know, it was reprinted in several Texas papers, including the Austin *Gazette*."

"That would please her, Melissa."

The beguiling smile concealed her malice. "Will she be accepting future assignments?"

"Perhaps." Reed bowed and surrendered Miss Hampton to the next partner on her program, a young politician from the Houston area. "Well, if it isn't Mr. Paul Thaxton! The youngest and most eligible bachelor of the Texas House! Only twenty-two, and with an exceptionally bright future. . . ."

Bullshit, Melissa thought, unimpressed by Thaxton's age, appearance, or personality. And surely Reed knew her father's opinion of the callow representative from Harris County. He was a greenhorn, a dullard lacking the qualifications essential to success, a political pawn of a powerful clique. He would remain in his seat only as long as he cooperated with the district demigods who had elected him. Mr. Thaxton was a tool for stronger men. The judge would never consider him as a prospective son-in-law.

Indeed, Reed knew all this, but he was desperate to interest Melissa Hampton in someone else. Anyone else.

Trouble was, the strong-willed girl had ideas of her own. Reed was astonished to see Melissa and a small group of chattering women at the station when the train pulled in from Houston. "Waiting for someone?" he inquired.

Melissa explained that since Devon Marshall Carter was a local celebrity, the Austin Ladies Social Society had organized a Welcome Home Committee. "Won't she be surprised and honored, Mr. Speaker?"

"Yeah," Reed muttered. "But will you give me a chance to greet her first, Miss Hampton?"

"Of course, sir! We wouldn't think of invading your privacy at such a delicate moment."

Nevertheless, the reunion was restrained. Reed's kiss and embrace were less than vigorous. For Carla, he had only a handshake, remarking that she appeared in excellent health.

"I had fine medical care," she said, issuing instructions to the porters. "Are our petticoats showing? Why are those women over there staring at us?"

"It's some kind of unofficial committee," Reed explained.

"Oh, Christ! They're descending on Devon—get her away from here as quickly as possible."

Devon was scrutinized, touched, questioned. She might have panicked, except for her press experience. And she now marveled at the equanimity of some of the public figures she had interviewed. "Thank you, ladies! I appreciate your kindness and wish I could accept every single invitation. Unfortunately, we'll be leaving for Fort Worth soon and won't return until the legislature reconvenes."

Melissa stepped forward, presenting a bouquet from the Hampton gardens. "You mean Congress, Mrs. Carter? Your destination seems more likely to be Washington than Austin."

"Well, in that event, you must all visit us there!"

As they chorused assent, Carla interrupted, "Please excuse us, ladies! There was a case of cholera on the ship, and then an epidemic of it in New Orleans, so . . ."

"Oh, my! Oh, mercy!" The group scattered, clucking like frightened hens. "Good-bye! Good luck!"

Reed frowned, assisting them into the hack. "Is that true, Carla, about the cholera?"

"No"—she grinned—"but it worked, didn't it?"

Devon appeared even lovelier than when she had left, and he was eager to get her home. But after they had dropped Carla off at her address and were alone together at home, they were reticent, almost shy. Reed was smoking more than usual, puffing on his second cheroot. He broke out a new bottle of whiskey. As for Devon, the bungalow and furniture seemed strange to her, as if she had been away much longer than she had. After the Willard and the Clairmont, how was she ever to return to that miserable cabin on that desolate prairie? The prospect made her shiver.

Reed did not notice her tremors. "I've missed you terribly, Devon. I couldn't tell you how much at the station, with that damn committee observing us."

"I wonder what really motivated them?" Devon mused.

"Fans of yours, darling."

"Oh, Reed," she scoffed. "Melissa Hampton *my* admirer? Surely you realize that little demonstration was more for your benefit than mine? That girl has a crush on you."

He glanced away, shaking his head. "Well, it's not mutual and never could be. Anyway, she's a child."

"Not exactly, dear. And there's something about her I just can't like. I think she could be treacherous."

"Devon, why are we discussing Melissa Hampton? My God, we've been apart over two months! Is that silly girl all we can talk about?"

"No, of course not."

"Are you glad to be back, Devon?"

"Yes," she replied after a slight pause.

"You hesitated. Why?"

"Did I? It's just that . . . well, you seem a little different, somehow."

He gulped his whiskey, set the glass on the table, and moved toward her with open arms. "Just lonely for you, darling. Don't ever leave me for so long again."

Devon let him kiss and caress her, but she felt no burning desire, as she had with Keith. "Is it true, as Melissa said, that we'll be going to Washington soon?"

"Unless something—or someone—changes the governor's mind before then," Reed told her.

"Someone?"

"Well, you know politics. Every power in the party has his favorite for the position."

"And whom is Judge Hampton supporting?"

"Me, presumably."

Devon pursed her lips and fluttered her lashes, mimicking the judge's audacious daughter. "With Daddy's little darling's approval, no doubt."

"Stop it," Reed ordered abruptly. "This should be a happy occasion for us, Devon. Why are you tormenting me?"

Why, indeed? she wondered, ashamed. Because of a guilty conscience?

It had been horrible, leaving Keith and her beloved Scotty. And Keith hadn't made it easier for her.

"I have no choice, Keith."

"Yes, you do, Devon. Leave Carter. Return to New York with us, to the Hudson estate. The servants are still there, everything is just as you left it . . . waiting." He began to plead his case, eloquent as always, and she could only listen and regret her actions. "Esther cannot possibly survive much longer, even with forced feeding. As I told you, she's terminal, and I pray for a merciful end to her ordeal. But Mrs. Stanfield still believes her daughter experienced a miraculous, if temporary, cure at Lourdes and burns votive candles before a statue of Bernadette. In her senility, she probably expects her sainted child to be bodily received into heaven. So I have two demented creatures in Gramercy Park, and spend most of my leisure in the place I consider my real home. And yours, too. It's beautiful, Devon. I've bought some adjoining acreage and landscaped it, improved the stables and added more outbuildings, and a private landing for the *Sprite*. But the house lacks its mistress. Without you, the estate will never be complete."

What could she say? That there was a man waiting for her in Texas, missing and needing her, a husband to whom she certainly owed some loyalty? He was not responsible for her errors. She was his wife, legally and morally, and she could not desert him, not without a reasonable explanation. Could she?

"Oh, Keith, don't tempt me this way. Please! You know my weakness concerning you and Scotty. In Reed's place, would you want me to do what you're suggesting now?"

"No," he admitted ruefully. "But I'm selfish about you, Devon. Always have been, always will be. I don't care about Carter's feelings, and I would be lying if I pretended otherwise. I just want you to be *mine* again, Devon."

After a while, Devon lost her composure, bursting into deep, wrenching sobs. Keith watched her somberly, powerless to console her or himself.

Devon's good-bye to Scotty had been just as heartrending. . . .

Throughout her anguished reverie, Reed had been absorbed in an agony of his own. He sensed a schism between them, but could not decipher its source. Had he inadvertently betrayed himself with regard to Melissa Hampton? If so, he was unaware of it. But Devon was perceptive, gifted with that uncanny talent called female intuition, and just naturally suspicious of Melissa's behavior. Damn Melissa! He would have to tread lightly around her, praying that he had not made her pregnant. Already the wench had spoiled his reunion with his wife.

Or *was* it all Melissa's fault? Somehow, he felt an additional reason for the gulf opening between Devon and himself.

What could it be?

Chapter 17

Upon learning that the Carters planned to leave Austin soon, Melissa pestered her father to host another entertainment before the majority of the legislators returned to their district residences. "Just an informal shindig," she coaxed, gently blowing in his ear. "A barbecue and some outdoor games. Baseball, boating, riding, horse racing."

"Whatever you want, honey," he agreed. "Long as you invite the right folks."

"Naturally, Daddy."

Melissa knew the Cokes would be unable to attend, however, for such events exhausted the frail first lady, who must conserve her energies for the demanding duties of her position. But her absence would not discommode Miss Hampton, who had no patience with delicate females.

Devon wanted to send regrets, but Reed felt compelled to accept, with or without her. Irritated, she demanded, "Is this a command performance?"

"Do you want me to go to Washington, Devon?"

"Yes, of course."

"Well, every other Democratic hopeful will be there, my dear. I don't want to lose by default."

"Very well," Devon acquiesced. "But I don't think I'll do any riding."

"Don't deprive yourself, darling. You're a fine horsewoman, and you love to ride."

"Not astride."

"The judge has sidesaddles."

"You've been in the Hamptons' tack room?"

"No, but they used to fox-hunt in East Texas, where the ladies prefer sidesaddles."

For aesthetic reasons, Devon thought, particularly during certain periods of the month. But apparently he had already forgotten her indisposition, and damned if she would remind him! Some Texas girls seemed unaffected by

Eve's curse, and one would think Melissa Hampton was immune to it. Melissa engaged in all sorts of strenuous sports, such as baseball, for which she wore black sateen bloomers, a white blouse sans bandeau to restrain her bobbing bosom, and canvas shoes. Devon had seen Eastern women in this garb at resorts, playing croquet and lawn bowling, but it had never been popular in fashionable circles. Most scorned it as unflattering. Nor would any real lady disport herself in a tailored linen shirt sheer enough to reveal the contour of her unbound breasts!

Devon wore a summer gown sashed in moiré ribbon the color of the dainty violets sprigging the dimity, and a large leghorn hat to ward off the fierce sun. Fortunately, the estate boasted many great shade trees—monarch live oaks trailing long mauve-gray boas of Spanish moss, tall pecans which grew wild throughout the state and attained impressive size along the waterways, magnificent magnolias, cypress, and pines transplanted from the Hampton plantation.

Appetizing smoke wafted from several long pits in the earth, where Negro and Mexican cooks tended the beef, pork, turkey, and chicken roasting over hickory and mesquite coals. Cedar tables and chairs stood under the leafy umbrellas. There were cold beer on tap from Austin's new German brewery; stronger liquors for the gentlemen who preferred them; and iced tea, fruitades, and spiced punch for the ladies and children. A fully equipped chuck wagon provided the ranch atmosphere the judge liked to give his informal feasts. His property was often the site of local fairs, festivals, political rallies, holiday celebrations, horse races, rodeos, turkey shoots, and other sporting events enjoyed by Texans.

Reed was appropriately dressed in denim pants and shirt, boots and bandana, and new Stetson hat. Devon could easily spot him in the crowd and tried to disregard the frequency with which Miss Hampton eyed him, and her indifference to the young bachelors who swarmed about her.

After plates of barbecue, beans, potato salad, and relishes, Devon and Carla sat in a wicker swing attached to a stout sycamore limb, sipping frosty lemonade garnished with fresh peppermint and fanning themselves leisurely. "It must be a hundred degrees in the shade," Devon estimated, plying her pleated silk fan. "We should have brought palmetto fronds! These dainty things are meant for parlors."

Carla agreed, dabbing tiny pearls of perspiration from her exposed skin and hoping she had applied enough alum to prevent dampness and odor in her armpits and between her legs. How could anyone remain fastidious in this heat? Some of the men were as smelly as animals, and Carla pitied the women forced by nature to take extra precautions. "Do you suppose our hale-and-hearty hostess ever had the cramps, or vapors, or female complaint?"

"Certainly not the green sickness," Devon said. "I feel anemic beside Lady Godiva."

"Godiva's bosom was better concealed by her hair! But maybe she didn't have as much to conceal, or *reveal*. I haven't seen bigger teats except on cows."

A horn sounded, and Gore Hampton mounted a platform to announce the entries in the first horse race. There were seven contestants, with Speaker Carter riding the judge's favorite steed, a swift black stallion named Beelzebub, and his daughter on her spirited white Arabian mare. The spectators moved toward the track edging the estate, and Devon and Carla tagged along, unfurling parasols.

"Want to guess the winner?" Carla asked drolly.

"I don't need to guess."

"But that's dishonest!"

"Expedient, dear."

The horses were paraded to the post. Bets were made, and sealed with handshakes. A blank cartridge was fired into the air, and the racers were off. Reed dashed immediately into the lead, and for a while Devon thought he would maintain it. But midway on the stretch she realized that he had ceased spurring Beelzebub and was actually restraining him. Melissa had increased her speed, her wide bloomers flaring in the breeze, hair flying beneath the jaunty green-and-yellow jockey cap. Every pair of male eyes was glued to her bouncing breasts as her mount broke the crepe-paper streamer across the finish line a full length ahead of her nearest competitor. Cheers, whistles, clapping, lauded her victory. She grinned triumphantly as her father pinned a blue ribbon on her chest and a lackey placed a wreath of yellow roses around Scheherazade's frothing neck.

Dismounting, Reed congratulated her and surrendered Beelzebub to a groom. Then he glanced sheepishly at his wife, stung by her expression of disgust. When he tried to take her hand, she brushed it off negligently, accusing, "You threw the race!"

"So did the others, Devon, out of chivalry."

"Or cowardice? Fear of political reprisal by the judge! It's sickening the way everyone kowtows to the Hamptons. No other woman could wear that obscene costume! And don't pretend you haven't noticed. You've been positively leering at her."

"Like every other man not blind," he admitted. "But that doesn't imply admiration, my dear." Anxious to change the subject, he suggested a boat ride and maneuvered the ladies toward the landing. "I hear there'll be dancing on the *Melissa* this evening. That's the family paddle-wheeler."

"Which doting Daddy bought as a toy for his little girl?" Devon quipped. "I presume the *Melissa* has already had her maiden voyage!"

"Several, I'd say." Carla grinned wickedly. "I wish the Senator were here today."

Walking between them, Reed said, "I'm sure he does too, ma'am. But there's so much to do at home. I'll be glad to get back and help him."

Devon asked grimly, "Will you, dear, with all the allurements in Austin?"

Reed glanced at her warily, grateful for Carla's presence. "It must be hard on Jason, living alone out there."

"Not really, Carla. Pa loves the prairie, and wants that land for his descendants. It's the only heritage he can leave us. Not much of an inheritance now, but someday it'll be valuable."

Devon no longer cared much about "someday," the irretrievable past, or the tenuous future: she cared about today. She bitterly regretted the time she had missed with Keith and her child. They were almost two thousand miles apart again, and the only reason she could endure Reed's subservience to the arrogant Hamptons was because it might eventually reduce that vast distance.

She sat in the rowboat, skirts spread modestly, hat and parasol shielding her face and arms, while Reed plied the oars. Carla remained on the pier, chatting with people who had inquired about Jason Carter. A few sailboats and other craft were on the wide blue Colorado. Devon removed a white glove and trailed her fingers in the cool sparkling water, thinking wistfully of the *Sprite* and the great scenic Hudson. How she longed to see the Jersey palisades from the Dutch farmhouse again, the continuous parade of river traffic to and from Albany and the ports between, the sealike Zuider Zee, the picturesque precipices of the Cats-kill Mountains.

"You make a lovely picture," Reed complimented. "Like a calendar illustration for a summer month."

Devon smiled.

"Still peeved at me for letting Melissa win the race?"

She affected a nonchalant shrug, although the incident still chafed. "Maybe she beat you fairly, dear. She rides like the Furies."

"Better," he muttered wryly. "But I had the faster horse and it was difficult curbing him."

"Then why did you?"

"Because the prize I'm after is more than a blue ribbon, Devon, and I want it for us."

"I know, Reed. But I wonder if it's worth all the com-promises."

He laughed. "Throwing a non-purse race to a saucy girl? That's hardly a crime, darling."

"Not in itself, no, but it has sinister implications, Reed. It might have been a test, to determine your vulnerability, how easily you would concede in serious issues."

Reed rowed faster, clearing his throat. "Devon, once I get to Congress, I'll be my own master, just as my father was. Gore Hampton can help to put me in the United States Senate, but only my actions can keep me there. I don't intend to disgrace the country."

"Ahoy, there!" It was Melissa, bareheaded and bearing down on them in a birch canoe with a sailfish painted on the bow. "I'll race you to the rapids!"

Reed gave her a friendly salute. "Not now, Miss Hamp-ton. I have a passenger."

"That's no excuse, sir! You also have an advantage of about seventy pounds of muscle and sinew."

The intrusion and provocative challenge infuriated Devon. Melissa's youthful verve and audacity and utter disregard for the elements made Devon want to discard her own beauty precautions, strip, and plunge naked into the water. She was suddenly bored with modesty and decorum, with behaving like an elderly matron before this precocious, carefree nymph. "Go ahead," she prompted Reed. "Take her on, and compete in earnest!"

"Devon, this is a heavy, clumsy rowboat, and that's a light, well-designed canoe."

"But you're a man, and stronger. Or are you, either one?"

His face darkened. "That's a hell of a thing to say to me, Devon! And disregarding the difference in craft, I'm carrying extra weight."

"Excess cargo? Well, jettison me!"

"What's the matter with you?"

"Nothing. Race that little bitch in heat, and don't dare give her any quarter."

"Devon—"

"Row!" she muttered between clenched teeth.

Glaring at her, Reed signaled Melissa and worked the oars with all his might. Sweat soon soaked his clothes and streamed down his face, dripping off his long sideburns. Melissa laughed, enjoying the contest, and paddled her canoe with the skill of an Indian. They remained abreast for some fifty feet, but even Devon realized that the unwieldy flat-bottomed boat was no fair match for the sleek canoe. Her rage subsided, and she was urging Reed to concede when she glimpsed the rapids ahead.

"White water!" she cried, gesturing. "Slow down! Turn around!"

"Make up your mind," he drawled, still angry, pulling the oars desperately.

Melissa gained and glided past, able to aim for shore before reaching the treacherous current. Devon screamed, clutching the sides of the boat, while Reed struggled to steer them out of harm's way. Ahead were huge, jagged rocks and a raging cascade tumbling into whirlpools. Melissa had safely beached her craft and was running downstream with some men carrying paddles and long poles to assist the Carters, who were now drifting helplessly in the main channel, headed for disaster.

"Hang on, Devon!" Reed shouted. "And stay with the boat, if possible, no matter what happens!"

He stuck out an oar to avoid a boulder and grazed it, splintering wood. Devon was terrified. The river was very deep below the falls, a descent of some twenty feet into perilous eddies that had claimed many victims, including Indians, trappers, and settlers.

The hull banged and screeched against rough stone mounds, was hung up briefly, then abruptly released. Reed ordered Devon to lie on the bottom, for she was obstructing his view, and she obeyed, clinging to the loosened seat board.

"Remove your shoes and most of your clothing," he told her, too busy to pull off his own boots.

Now the boat was plunging over the roaring cataract, and Reed was trying to balance it upright, deaf to the voices yelling advice from the banks. As they took on water, Devon tore frantically at her drenched garments with numbed hands, succeeding only in hopelessly knotting her long sash. By some divine miracle the vessel remained intact and afloat, and escaped the dark, violent vortex threatening to suck it under. Then, as Reed piloted it toward calmer waters, the bottom struck and split on a submerged boulder.

Jolted out of her stupor, Devon screamed shrilly and began to sob. Luckily the river was fairly shallow here, less than eight feet, and the wreck lodged securely between the rock and a cypress stump. The dislodged passenger seats floated away, along with Devon's cartwheel hat and Reed's expensive new Stetson. A crowd had gathered at the scene, with an anxious Carla in front. They extended hands, sticks, poles, oars. Reed got Devon to safety first, and then himself. Melissa embraced them both, declaring herself on the verge of diving into the maelstroms to help save them.

Devon was shaking hysterically, her teeth chattering, her hair hanging in wet skeins on her exposed shoulders. Her dress was a ruined rag, one sleeve ripped off, severed skirt flounces and petticoat ruffles dragging the ground.

"You poor thing," Melissa crooned. "We'll get you to the house and into some dry clothes. Oh, what a tragedy! You might have drowned, dear, except for your heroic husband."

Devon was stupefied, unable to speak or move. Reed carried her, grimly silent, water sloshing in his unemptied boots. Melissa walked beside him, sharing in his heroism, and more enamored of him than ever. Aware of his wife's wretched appearance, she smoothed her own mussed hair, hitched up her bloomers, and discreetly fastened her shirt.

Her father met them on the gallery, exclaiming, "Good God! What happened?"

"An accident, Daddy. Where's Doc Harper?"

"He had to make a call, but he'll be back soon. Take Mrs. Carter inside and make her comfortable."

Assisted to Melissa's rooms by a maid and Carla, Devon was appalled to see herself in the cheval glass. Angry red scrapes and bloody scratches scored her body. Fortunately, her face had escaped serious injury, although there were bruises. Never had she been more embarrassed, nor felt so foolish. Even in her misery and humiliation, she recalled the cruel chiding that had precipitated the calamity. Her rash tongue might have killed them both! And, ironically, Melissa would probably benefit from her shrewish behavior. Indeed, she was acting the perfect hostess now, offering her guest a choice of apparel.

"Do you like this blue voile or the pink dotted swiss? The maize organza is adorable on, and the green muslin would go with your eyes. You can borrow some lingerie, I have oodles of it. I hope some of my shoes will fit—your feet are a bit smaller than mine. But then, I'm also taller than you."

"The muslin will be all right," Devon murmured, suffering Melissa's generosity, still suspicious of her. "Anything to get me home."

"You're not staying for the dance on the riverboat?"

"Dance!" Carla cried. "Can't you see she's hurt and still in shock? She may have internal injuries."

"Of course, and the doctor will examine her."

Devon started to protest, but Carla insisted that she needed medical attention. She had towel-dried Devon's hair and was now tenderly brushing the damp curls. Then they helped her into a nightgown and wrapper and put her to bed.

Dr. Harper was sure the injuries were largely superficial. "You'll have some discomfort until they heal, Mrs. Carter, but I can't detect any broken bones or other serious damage. I'll give you some laudanum for pain and sedation, if you need it."

"Can I go home, Doctor?"

"I would prefer that you recuperate here for a week or so. The Hamptons have plenty of room, and I'm not far away."

"Please," Devon implored weakly, "I'd rather not—"

But Melissa interrupted, addressing Carla. "Dr. Harper is right, and she shouldn't be moved yet. The Carters shall be our guests. And you too, Mrs. Winston, if you wish."

It thrilled Melissa to think of Reed sleeping in her bed, even without her, for she was certain that his wife was in no condition for lovemaking. Furthermore, she herself would help to nurse the patient, making sure that she took her sleeping potion early in the evening.

Reed was talking with her father when she and Dr. Harper came downstairs. "How is she, sir?" he inquired.

"Hurt, but not badly. No internal injuries indicated. As a precautionary measure, however, I'm confining her here for the present. And though I know you folks planned to leave for Fort Worth tomorrow, I certainly wouldn't advise any lengthy stage travel for a couple of weeks."

"Whatever you recommend, Doctor. Is it all right with you, Judge?"

Hampton assented jovially. "You heed this old sawbones, Mr. Speaker. He's a graduate of Harvard Medical College and knows his anatomy. You and the missus are welcome to stay as long as you please. Mrs. Winston, too."

"Thank you, sir. Now I reckon I'd better dash home and pick up some dry duds."

"I'll go with you," Melissa offered, "and fetch some things for Mrs. Carter."

"That won't be necessary, Miss Hampton. I can take care of it. May I borrow a horse, sir?"

"Sure, son. Take Beelzebub. And, Melissa baby, you know Daddy needs his little girl as hostess. The accident preempted the baseball and croquet games, but the dancing will go on as scheduled, from sunset to dawn. There's a full moon tonight, and I want you to wear a nice dress, sugar. Those pantaloons might be practical, but they sure ain't pretty."

Melissa tweaked his beard. "They're bloomers, Daddy, and perfect for sports. But I'll wear a lovely gown this evening," she promised—more for Reed's sake than her father's. "You will be back, Mr. Carter?"

"Later." He nodded.

Also battered in his battle with the rapids, Reed rode Beelzebub gingerly. In addition to various cuts and bruises, he had strained some muscles and tendons that made sitting saddle uncomfortable. Further festivities did not especially appeal to him, and he would have preferred to relax with a few drinks and mull over the events of the day. Devon's attitude hurt and puzzled him. Something had affected their relationship, and he blamed her trip to Washington. The separation had estranged them to a disturbing degree. He changed clothes, put some personal articles for

Devon and himself in the saddlebags, and rode back to Hampton House, arriving before sundown.

A supper tray of chicken broth, veal in aspic, charlotte russe, and milk had been brought to Devon. She was sitting up in bed, Carla coaxing her to eat, when Reed arrived.

"Feeling better, darling?"

"Some," she answered. "I don't especially like being confined here, though."

"Doctor's orders, Devon."

"So we shall all be the Hamptons' houseguests? And you and I, Mr. Speaker, will share the bedchamber of the judge's daughter." She waved a flaccid hand with swollen wrist and fingers. "Isn't that cozy?"

Her tone prompted a frown, but he quickly smoothed it away. "The accident was not my fault, Devon."

"No, indeed. It was mine, and this is the consequence and my punishment."

"No one is being punished, my dear. We're lucky and should be grateful. It could have been much worse, you know."

"Yes, they might be dragging the river now for our bodies. Mine, anyway. I couldn't have saved myself, Reed. I realize that." She glanced at the rows of dolls on Melissa's shelves, then dropped her eyes in shame. "I'm sorry for what I said to you earlier. I was venting a childish tantrum. Please forgive me."

"Forget it, Devon. Just rest and get well. We'll have to remain in Austin awhile yet, but it doesn't matter."

Doesn't it? Devon thought. Was he so beguiled by Melissa, oblivious of her intentions?

She noticed his dark suit, clean white suit, and carefully tied cravat, and the scrapes across his chin and forehead. "You feel like dancing tonight, dear? You were hurt, too, you know."

"Not really, but I'll put in a brief appearance out of respect for our genial host."

"And durable hostess," she added, wincing at a sudden pain in her bruised breast.

He let that pass, addressing the pensive Carla. "Will you be my companion?"

"If you're willing to share me with the judge, who has also requested my favor."

Reed nodded, smiling, and bent to kiss his wife's trembling lips. "Dr. Harper prescribed a sedative for you, darling. I'll try not to disturb you when I come in. Good night."

"Good night," she quavered.

Observing his limping departure, Carla predicted, "He won't do much dancing, Devon. He's pretty banged-up, too, though he'd never admit it. God, what a man, and how he handled that emergency! What were you apologizing to him for?"

"Something I said."

"Unkind?"

"Insulting."

Her eyes widened in surprise. "But why?"

Devon shrugged. "I wish I knew, Carla. Just spite, I guess."

Since Devon's confidences in Washington, Carla had been tempted to confide some secrets of her own. But professional ethics and the agency's strict code of conduct forbade her doing so.

Chapter 18

During the next few days Devon's discolorations spread and the lacerations had to be treated to prevent infection. A natural process, Dr. Harper assured her, along with the increased body soreness and aching discomfort. Self-conscious about her bluish cheekbones and dark-ringed, partially closed left eye, Devon longed to leave Hampton House.

She decided that the judge's daughter was instrumental in her continued confinement. Melissa was a genius at manipulating older men. Her father was wax in her clever hands, and even Reed appeared malleable, vexing Devon. For although Carla's surveillance indicated that he spent most of his leisure in the library perusing the law volumes and discussing politics with their host, Devon knew he accepted Melissa's invitations to ride with her and stroll on the grounds. Indeed, he seemed to be enjoying their stay at the fine estate: the excellent accommodations, delicious food, and the attentions of the servants. Melissa's accomplishments included the piano and guitar, at which she entertained after dinner, often singing Texas folk songs in duet with Reed. And Gore Hampton had taken a fancy to Mrs. Winston, whom he found attractive and intelligent. Carla could easily have made another conquest, had her heart not still belonged to Jason Carter.

"Hurry and get well," she urged Devon, "so we can hit the road north."

"I'm strong enough now, Carla. I think Dr. Harper's extra precautions are influenced by . . ."

She paused as carriage wheels grated on the gravel driveway, halting under the porte cochere, and they heard familiar voices and laughter. "She went with him to the Capitol," Carla explained, "to clear his desk. She follows him around like a lovesick puppy, and he's too kind to push her away. Melissa has a penchant for older men."

Devon gave a forlorn sigh. "There's not such a great difference in their ages, Carla. Eighteen and thirty-two. After all, I fell in love with a man eleven years my senior."

"And I with one thirty years mine!" Carla marveled. "Does Melissa bother you, Devon?"

Devon admitted that she did. "I didn't expect to encounter an 'other-woman' situation so early in my marriage, Carla. We haven't even celebrated our first anniversary yet, you know. Not until September."

A knock interrupted them, and Reed strode in, carrying a portfolio of government papers. Devon instinctively averted the worst side of her face, so that he viewed a somewhat sullen profile. Carla excused herself and left.

"Look at me, Devon," Reed gently coaxed.

She refused.

"Have you been up today?"

"Some."

"Good. Why not join us at dinner this evening?"

"To be stared at, and compared to Melissa? No, thanks."

"Don't be so sensitive, Devon. You're healing nicely, and still beautiful despite what you think."

"Spare me your chivalry, Reed. There are mirrors here, and I'm not blind. Was Melissa a big help in your office?"

"I didn't need any help, Devon."

"Then why did you take her along?"

"She invited herself, and it was her carriage."

"Not that conspicuous pony cart!"

"No, the family victoria, and the coachman drove."

"The governor should have such fine transportation!"

"I agree, but the budget doesn't allow for it. The Cokes will have to manage with the old equipage until the next legislature can appropriate sufficient funds for a state coach."

He sat on the bed and took her hand. "Would you like me to dine here, Devon?"

"I'm sure you're expected at the table, Mr. Speaker. Has the hostess placed you at the head yet?"

"The judge sits there," he replied, irritated. "I'm a guest in this house, not master of it."

"Well, the butler will be announcing dinner soon, and guests shouldn't be late."

"Goddammit, Devon! I wanted to be with you this evening, and talk about whatever is troubling you. But obviously you're not ready for conversation or anything else." Abruptly he stood. "Perhaps you'll be in a better mood tomorrow. May I wash up, madam?"

"By all means! Shave and put on a fresh shirt. I think Miss Hampton is bathing in cologne."

"Enjoy your supper," he said, entering the lavatory.

Her tray arrived, loaded as usual. Devon left all but the consommé and custard. At dusk Carla came to bid her good night and inquire if she needed a sedative. Devon did not think so, but later the music and singing—Reed and Melissa harmonized to the strumming of her guitar—kept her awake and restless. She swallowed a pill and relived the horror of the rapids in a realistic nightmare.

After the impromptu musicale, Reed went out on the veranda to smoke, and Melissa tracked him. The judge and Carla were engaged in a tight game of checkers in the library. The warm night was cloyingly scented with honeysuckle, jasmine, and magnolias. Melissa suggested that it would be cooler by the river.

"Isn't it your bedtime, young lady?"

"Oh, Reed, don't tease me about my youth! Lots of girls my age are married and mothers." Remembering her pregnancy at fourteen, Melissa changed the subject. "Walk with me to the bluff?"

"It's dark," he hedged, although scattered kerosene lanterns on iron posts prevented total darkness even on moonless nights, "and there might be snakes in the garden."

Melissa smiled, taking his arm persuasively. "The handyman beats the grass and bushes for snakes, and he receives a bounty for any venomous ones killed on the property. Daddy even imported a pair of Asian mongooses once and tried to breed them, but they didn't survive long enough to become acclimated."

"Too bad. We could use thousands of them on the plains and prairies."

A railed and lighted stairway descended to the dock, where the paddle-wheeler was moored. Melissa had plans for the vessel which bore her name, and this time, to her surprise, Reed seemed quite willing. Their initial embrace on deck was spontaneous and a mutual invitation. Wordlessly Melissa led him to her cabin, where they undressed in the shadowy light filtering through the windows and lay together on the comfortable berth. Stimulating him with her hands and mouth in ways that seemed perfectly natural to her, she stoked fires banked by Devon's recent coolness.

"Oh, I love you!" she cried, wrapping her legs around his hips as he entered her, hoping he would make a similar declaration. But he was silent, intent on pleasure, relishing her body as much as she did his. Thoroughly enjoying sex, Melissa did not want the act to end. But she knew it must, and consoled herself with the belief that, whether or not Reed admitted it, he was falling in love with her and would desire her again . . . and again. Certainly his guilt was less now, a promising sign.

As they were dressing, she ventured tentatively. "This is a nice rendezvous, isn't it?"

"Convenient," he agreed, buttoning his shirt. "Have you put it to this use before?"

"No, but Daddy does, rather regularly. Do you suppose anyone missed us?"

"Not enough to check, apparently. They probably think we've retired."

Melissa chuckled, enjoying her forbidden fruit. "That's what I implied when I told them good night."

But Reed was suddenly rueful, conscious that he had not only betrayed his marital vows again but abused the judge's hospitality. "Your guests will be departing shortly, my dear. Dr. Harper tells me that Mrs. Carter will be able to travel next week."

Her disappointment was irrepressible. "I think he's wrong, Reed. She's very delicate, like all Virginia ladies. You should have married a native Texan, someone accustomed to our climate and customs."

"But I didn't, Melissa, and Devon is stronger than she appears."

Though it hurt, Melissa had to pose the painful question. "You still love her?"

"Of course." And, as his behavior contradicted him, he hurried on. "I'll always love her."

"But you love me, too!" she insisted, pleading. "I know you do, Reed. It was different tonight."

"Yes, it was, Melissa. And I do care for you, more than I should. That's reason enough for me to leave Hampton House."

Melissa heard nothing except that he cared for her. She was determined to be adult and reasonable. "It'll work out for us, darling, if we're patient."

"You don't understand, Melissa."

"Not everything, no. But I'm sure you'll find a solution for our problem. You're so brilliant. I'll wait forever, if necessary."

The night watchman, who patrolled the estate with a brace of trained German shepherds, was approaching the landing, a pine-cone torch in his hand. "We've got company, Melissa."

"That's just Remus on his regular rounds. He knows we're here and wouldn't dare intrude or talk, lest I have his tongue slit."

As the sentinel and dogs passed, Reed guided her out of the boat and up the cypress steps. They separated before reaching the house, Reed to smoke another cheroot on the veranda, while Melissa slipped up the back stairs to the room she was presently occupying. She smiled smugly as she crawled into the canopied mosquito-netted bed, convinced it was only a matter of time before Reed Carter would be all hers.

In her youthful confidence, Melissa could even bear his temporary absence from Austin and insisted on accompanying the Carters and Mrs. Winston to the station. Shaking hands, her eyes focused keenly on Reed's mouth. She was mutely assuring him that she understood why he could not kiss her good-bye. They must be circumspect before his wife, to whom Melissa now felt superior, positive that the poor fool suspected nothing. Peering through the wispy veil covering Devon's face, Melissa tried to pick flaws in the harsh sunlight, hoping the facial abrasions would leave permanent scars, that her fair skin would quickly wrinkle, her honey-gold hair fade, and her lithe figure turn to fat.

From the sidelines Melissa waved and blew kisses to the passengers. As the stagecoach rumbled northward, past the Capitol, Reed glanced back, and Devon asked quietly, "Did you forget something, dear?"

"Nothing important," he replied, looking at her, pleased that she did not turn away. She had been an enigma for the past few weeks. Undoubtedly Hampton House had affected her adversely, and exposure to Melissa had not helped. Anxious to mend the breach, he made tentative advances when they stopped for the night, and Devon was receptive.

"Do you feel well enough, darling?"

A playful smile dimpled the corners of her mouth. "For what, sir?"

"I thought we might renew our acquaintance, madam."

Disrobing, Devon tossed a tiny slipper at him. He caught it and came to remove the other, then her stockings and lace-edged drawers. "Welcome back, Mrs. Carter. For a while I feared a part of you had been lost somewhere. I missed you, my love. Terribly."

Most of her injuries had already disappeared without a visible trace, and Devon need not flinch nude in the lamplight. Though less voluptuous than Melissa's, her body was infinitely more desirable to Reed, and he kissed and caressed her lovingly. His lips tasted the soft flesh of her inner thighs, traveled to her stomach and navel and breasts, teasing the taut pink nipples, and returned to the pubic region, his tongue exploring secret places. While Devon did not reciprocate in all respects, as he wished, it was an ardent evening. Reed felt relaxed, drained naturally of the seed unnaturally wasted with Melissa. He hoped Devon's pregnancy would result. As he lay with his wife, the unbidden reverie of another woman disturbed him, as an invasion of privacy. There she was in lifelike image, wearing that curious, complex expression that could portray anything from love to mockery to menace. How in hell had he become entangled in her tantalizing web? And could he ever extricate himself completely? More worrisome, did he really want to be free of her fascination?

Arriving at the cabin in a hired buckboard, they discovered why his father had not met them in Fort Worth: his left leg was in a splint cast, and he walked with a homemade crutch. "Busted the damn thing several weeks ago," he explained, shunning the women's sympathy. "It's almost healed now. Set it myself, good as any doctor could. Made the surgical equipment, too."

"Why didn't you let me know, Pa?"

"You were busy, son. Wasn't anything you could do, anyway. I've had broken bones before, you know, more than I can count. Lucky this wasn't my hip."

"How did it happen?" Carla asked after her greeting kiss.

"Well, one day I saw some mustangs grazing on the prairie. There was a pretty little mare, with a golden coat and white mane and tail. I decided she'd make a fine mate for Reed's buckskin and went after her."

"A mustang?" Reed shook his head. "Jesus, Pa, you should know better!"

"Oh, I caught her, all right, with a pound of sugar. She wasn't too reluctant and may have been somebody's stray that just got into the remuda. I brought her home to Rebel, which suited him fine, because he's been hankering for a mate a long time. He was just waiting for her to come into heat. Trouble was, so was that honcho stallion. He tracked her at least ten miles, arriving the next morning. I was inside rustling up some grub when I heard him whinnying, pawing, and snorting. Somehow he managed to open the corral gate. He challenged Rebel, with blood in his eyes. I grabbed my rifle and went out to referee, but they were already fighting, and I was afraid I'd shoot the wrong one."

Reed frowned. "Did he injure Rebel?"

"They both got some battle scars. After all, Rebel was a mustang and herd stud himself until you captured him. But a tamed animal can never defeat a wild one, and the conquistador won and started off with his prize. I tried to lasso her, missed, and slipped in a pile of manure. The ornery son of a bitch stomped on my leg and snapped it like a twig! While I sat there, the two critters galloped away. Rebel came over and nuzzled me, but I could see he was mighty disappointed and maybe even tempted to follow their trail. You have to ride him tomorrow, Reed, and cheer him up. He's pining." He winked at Carla. "I've got something in common with him, though I'm somewhat handicapped now."

She laughed. "Not too much, I'd say, Senator."

As Devon removed her veiled bonnet, the old man stared at her face and then at his son. "Is the honeymoon over?"

"No, Pa, it's nothing like that," Reed answered. "We had an accident, too. You know those rapids on the Colorado, downstream from Hampton House?"

Jason nodded. "Don't tell me you were fool enough to try to run 'em with your wife in the boat?"

"Of course not! I'll tell you about it later, Pa. It's been a long, hard trip for Devon, and she needs rest. Carla will spend several days here, to help out, so we'll be bunking in the print shop again. How's the paper doing?"

"Surviving, bimonthly, on patent medicines. A country journal couldn't exist without those advertisements."

"Some city dailies thrive on them, too," Devon said, thinking that large portions of quackery mixed with yellow journalism contributed to the healthy circulation of the New York *Herald*.

Jason Carter had more important matters to discuss with his son, but had to wait until they were alone that evening, lest the ladies become alarmed. In late June, while Devon and Carla were away, the Plains Indians had gone on the warpath, besieging a buffalo hunters' camp for three days. Ironically, the warriors were led by Chief Quanah Parker, the half-white son of Cynthia Ann Parker, who had been captured as a child in 1836 and eventually became the wife of Peta Nicona.

"I reckon you heard in Austin about Adobe Walls?"

"Not until the battle was over," Reed said.

The Senator hawked and spat into a battered old spittoon. "Hell, nobody except the Indians knew in advance! But their carbines were no match for fifty-caliber Sharps rifles. Twenty-eight hunters and one woman in the camp managed to kill at least twenty braves and wound lots more, including Quanah himself."

"Do you think there's danger here?" Reed asked.

"Oh, we're vulnerable, Reed. But fortunately, we don't have too many hide hunters in this county. As you know, the richest game areas are beyond the Brazos, in the panhandle and near the Canadian River, and we're going to need more than Rangers and armed citizens to defend us. Congress and the President must recognize this, and establish more frontier forts. This should be one of your prime missions when you get to Washington."

"I'm not there yet, Pa."

"But you will be, son. I've had some communications with the governor and other powerful Democrats. You're fated."

"And what do they expect of me? A combination of Sam Houston and Jason Carter? That was a different era, and Texas had a friend in the White House. We wear the Confederate brand now, almost a renegade stigma. The Mason-Dixon Line still divides North and South."

"We're talking about the West now, son, and it's all one country, one people."

"Bullshit! You think the Easterners give a damn about

the Territories? Or that the Wall Street capitalists who dictate to Congress are interested in outposts? I doubt if a senator could even get the floor to address this issue, and he'd probably be shouted down if he did."

"Just don't yield. Filibuster, if necessary. Congress, state or national, is an arena. You've got the vital rhetorical weapon, son, and I'm confident you'll use it."

Reed smiled skeptically. "You're the eternal optimist, Pa."

"At my age, you've got to be, boy. Once you give up, you're a goner and might as well be dead." He hobbled on his whittled oak crutch to a cabinet. "I had to kill the pain of this goddamn fracture with liquor, but I think there's enough left for a few slugs. Let's drink to your future in Washington."

"A bit premature, isn't it?"

"Like you said, I'm the eternal optimist."

PART III

Chapter 19

That summer, while Texans worried about the Indian Wars, personal problems plagued Washington politicians. The Crédit Mobilier and Union Pacific scandals of '72 had not yet been laid to rest when new charges of malfeasance in office arose against public officials from nearly every state in the Union. The Back Pay Grab, in which Congress increased their own salaries and the President's retroactively, while the national economy was at its lowest ebb in the century, infuriated the press and the people. The Sanborn Contracts, comprising illegal tax collections with the tacit consent of the Treasury Department, further riled tempers. And rumors of yet another major conspiracy were brewing in the distilleries. More congressional investigations were promised. One Texas senator announced that failing health necessitated his retirement to private life before the expiration of his term, and concluded, "I trust that my state's governor will not play party politics in selecting my successor."

The statement smacked of intimidation to Democrat Richard Coke, who promptly and defiantly appointed the speaker of the Texas House to fill the vacancy.

Reed was repairing the cabin roof when a courier delivered a wax-sealed envelope from the executive mansion in Austin. His father accepted it and waved it in the air. "Come on down! I think this is it!"

Reed pointed to a dark cloud overhead. "I better finish this job first, Pa. Won't take long." Securing several more hand-hewn shingles into place, he climbed down the ladder.

The Senator could hardly contain himself. "Well, am I right?"

Reed nodded slowly, his deep blue eyes grave under the brim of his old nutria hat. "Pray God I'm worthy of the trust the governor has placed in me, Pa."

Jason stuck out his hand. "Congratulations, son! Just do

your best for your country and state, and neither God nor man can fault you. If you make mistakes, be sure they're honest ones and admit them freely. Now, go tell your wife the happy tidings. I think I'll ride awhile on the prairie. No better place for prayer than God's country."

Devon was in the kitchen kneading dough. Her sleeves were rolled up, an apron protected her gingham dress, and flour dusted her hair and face. "Do we have a visitor for lunch? I heard hoofbeats on the lane."

Slipping an arm around her waist, Reed kissed the back of her neck.

"I'm busy now, dear, and a mess, too! Making our daily bread is a chore. At least they have a bakery in Austin."

"And many in Washington, Mrs. Carter. That horseman came on state business. May I present the new junior senator from Texas, ma'am?"

Devon whirled about, joy sparkling in her eyes. "That's wonderful, Reed! I'm so proud of you. What a marvelous anniversary gift! When do we leave?" Tomorrow would not be too soon for her.

"Well, first I must wire the governor my official acceptance, then tender my resignation to the Texas Legislature. Finally, I must be seated in the United States Senate, without opposition."

"How could there be opposition? Surely your character and qualifications are satisfactory?"

"But I'm a Southern Democrat, remember, and Republicans have the majority in Congress now."

"They can't refuse to recognize you because of your party affiliation, Reed."

"Not constitutionally, no. But they can drum up other reasons. It's not likely, of course. But you should be aware of political chicanery by now, Devon. You were a Capital correspondent long enough."

"Yes, and there may be some dissenting voices from the North, mostly token objections. It's traditional. You'll be sworn into office, though, Senator Carter, and I'll applaud you from the gallery. We'll have to find a suitable residence and buy some new furniture. Will your father move with us?"

He shook his head. "No, Pa has to homestead this land for three years before it's ours, which he intends to do. Besides, he has already had his Washington experience."

Devon guessed at another reason. Jason Carter did not

want people saying his boy couldn't handle the job alone, that he required sideline coaching from the old man. And perhaps it *had* all come too soon. But this was no time for misgivings.

"We'll manage," she assured him.

"It'll be a whole new life for us, Devon. Oh, God, I want to succeed!"

"Determination is half the victory."

"What's the other half, wise one?"

"Who knows, in politics? Luck, possibly. Or friends." She paused thoughtfully. "I wonder what Carla will do now?"

Reed shrugged, preoccupied. Catching his eye, Devon knew his intentions. "We're alone, honey, and I'm feeling amorous."

"I haven't set the bread yet."

"It'll wait, but I can't."

Devon clucked her tongue. "Such impetuosity—and from a supposedly dignified United States senator!"

He grinned, untying her apron strings.

As news circulated of Reed Carter's Senate appointment (Jason printed a special edition of the *Prairie Post*), letters poured into the Fort Worth post office with congratulations, invitations, petitions, supplications. The Hampton House stationery, gray vellum engraved in maroon ink, was familiar. Melissa had added her best wishes to the judge's, and begged to fete the Carters before their departure for Washington. Devon penned polite regrets, blaming the pressing time element, and hoping the wench could read between the lines.

Naturally, there would be some entertainments. But Devon did not fret unduly about the prospects at Hampton House, assuring herself that Reed had too much at stake now to be led even temporarily astray by the wily judge's daughter. Furthermore, she expected the old senator to counsel the young one and curb any impulse toward indiscretion.

"Miss Hampton will have to cast her bait elsewhere," she told Carla. "The fish she wants to hook is headed for other waters."

They were having tea in Carla's sitting room at the Dragoon Hotel. "Well, don't be surprised if the cunning creature follows him to the Potomac."

"He'll be too busy to notice, Carla. Most congressional novices are in love with their constituency and with ideals. Addressing Texas problems will consume most of his time and energy."

"The novelty will wear off," Carla predicted, adding milk to her tea. "Especially when he finds his colleagues yawning during an impassioned speech on which he worked weeks."

"I don't think so, Carla. Reed is tenacious. You know how seriously he took the speakership in Austin. He'll be so devoted, I doubt if Melissa Hampton or any other siren could lure him from duty."

Carla arched a brow. "That's a beautiful wifely tribute, Mrs. Carter. Have you fallen in love with your husband?"

A long silence ensued, during which Devon absently crumbled a cookie. "Unfortunately not, because life would be so much easier if I could, Carla. And I've tried—truly, I have. But it's impossible, and you know why. This morning, when I consigned our trunks to the freight agent, I couldn't believe only a year had passed since I came here as a bride. It seems infinitely longer, and I feel as if I've aged greatly."

"Nonsense! You can match youth and beauty with any woman in Washington."

Devon indicated the trunks, valises, and hatboxes scattered throughout the suite. "Have you finished your packing?"

"Just about. Thank heaven there's a train from Dallas now and we can travel by rail all the way!"

"I just hope we can find a decent place to live," Devon said, sweeping up the crumbs of a few moments ago, while Carla watched thoughtfully.

"Do you have a preference?"

"Well, I like the Southern atmosphere of Georgetown, but Reed might want to be nearer Capitol Hill."

"Oh, it's just a good brisk walk for a rangy Texan, and I may be able to help you find a place there."

"Really? That would be marvelous, Carla!"

"I can't make any promises yet. I must make some contacts first."

"When will you know?"

"Maybe not until we reach Washington," Carla replied.

* * *

No more was said about it, and Devon assumed that their friend had either forgotten or failed. The Carters arrived in Washington prepared to hunt, grovel, and barter for the limited housing available. Registering at a small grimy hotel near the depot, they embarked on an exhausting, unsuccessful search.

"Every available space is taken," Reed complained. "Attics, basements, carriage houses, even stables. We might have to pitch tent on the Mall or camp in Rock Creek, as I did on my first trip here. Remember, you thought I'd freeze in the snow?"

"I didn't know you had slept on the ground on cattle roundups," Devon explained, perusing the real-estate section of the Washington *Star*.

"Well, we better retire early tonight, so we can hit the trail again at dawn. We might have better luck fanning out, honey."

After a frustrating week, Devon was in despair, and Reed suggested they settle for a grubby rooming house on Maryland Avenue.

"I hate boardinghouses!" she cried.

"But there's not even a vacant park bench!" He clamped on his hat. "If by some miracle we discover something better, we can always move. I just hope that greedy old harridan hasn't already rented it to someone else."

Devon was morosely munching a piece of cold chicken in their room when Carla appeared jangling a ring of keys. "*Voilà!* Your open-sesame to Georgetown, Mrs. Carter."

Devon leaped up, tossing the drumstick into the wastebin. "Oh, Carla, you're a genius! I want to see it!"

"The carriage awaits, milady." Carla chuckled as Devon grabbed bonnet, gloves, and reticule, and they hurried outside.

Devon loved the red-brick-and-white-limestone house on the hilly, tree-colonnaded street. The autumn elms were golden, the maples scarlet, the oaks bronze. There were two stories and a basement, a symmetrical pair of glistening bay windows, and an intricately spoked glass fan over the pilastered entrance. Inside, Devon admired the wide polished mahogany stairway, the fine furniture, rich carpets and draperies, the simple elegance and impeccable order. But her spirits quickly ebbed. They could never afford it, even if she went back to work!

"Come see the garden," Carla invited, as if she owned the property.

The courtyard was planted with Southern trees and shrubs, roses and fall flowers in bloom, ivied walls showing a tinge of purple, and several sculptured English box-woods. It was all reminiscent of Richmond, and Devon's sigh was deep.

"Like going home, isn't it?" Carla asked perceptively. "But, of course, Washington was once a part of Virginia, and will always retain some of it. You can see the foothills of the Blue Ridge Mountains from these heights."

Devon had a sudden intuition. "Is this by any chance your property, Carla?"

"Mine?" She laughed as they went back inside. "I should be so lucky! No, Devon, but I know the owner, and when I mentioned my good Texas friends' need of a residence here, he responded gallantly."

"Where does he live?"

"Various places. He was abroad when I first tried to contact him, which is why it took a while. We keep in touch, however. And, incidentally, he employs custodian service, so there won't be any exterior or interior main-tenance."

"But we insist on paying rent, Carla."

"Darling, he'd be insulted! And he's far too wealthy to bother with that. The place is yours for as long as you need it. Enjoy it, Devon, and don't look a gift horse in the mouth."

Still incredulous at their good fortune, Devon sat on the Sheraton sofa in the high-ceilinged drawing room, one hand caressing the luxurious damask upholstery. "Reed will be skeptical, you know."

"I'll explain the situation, Devon. It's either this or a ratty hole in the wall somewhere."

"But it'll seem like bribery!" Devon protested.

"Only if it came from a lobbyist with ulterior motives, my dear. This man has no need of political favors."

"Reed won't take it for nothing, Carla."

"Oh, very well, Devon. Shall we say fifty dollars a month? That shouldn't strain your budget too much, on a senator's salary. You can send your payments to the Capi-tal Real Estate Corporation, on Pennsylvania Avenue."

"Does our generous benefactor have a name?" Devon asked curiously. "Like 'Santa Claus'?"

"He prefers to remain anonymous."

"Eccentric?"

"No, just a very private person. His philanthrophies and endowments are secret. And his enterprises are so vast I couldn't begin to name them. This house is peanuts to him, Devon, and you'd be a fool to refuse it."

"I realize that, Carla. But since it's your friend, you should take it. What are your plans?"

"Nothing definite." She shrugged. "A trip to Norfolk to visit my family, and then . . . well, maybe New York. According to the *Police Gazette*, experienced female operatives are always in demand at Pinkerton's and other detective agencies."

"But that's dangerous work, Carla! You could find safe employment here, with the government."

"Clerking in a civil-service office? I'm afraid that would bore me, Devon. Sleuthing is exciting, and I've always been an adventuress."

"What about Jason Carter?"

Carla's expression mellowed. "I rather expected him to propose, but he didn't. A good thing, too, because I might have been tempted to accept, and we weren't compatible enough for marriage. I'm no more the frontier-frau type than you are, Devon, and would have gotten cabin fever eventually, just as you did. Anyway, Jason's too goddamn old for me!" she finished, abashed at her sentimentality. "And love, contrary to the poets, does not really conquer all obstacles. But we'll remain friends—and lovers, should we meet again."

Sadness overcame Devon. "I'll miss you, Carla. We've been through so much together. What shall I do now?"

"You have a profession, Devon. I know journalism and politics don't mix well, and you're a senator's wife. But you can steer clear of the Capitol controversies and personality conflicts. You're an excellent social correspondent. But if you crave more action, you know where to find it."

"In Brooklyn"—Devon nodded—"when Theodore Tilton's alienation-of-affections suit against the Reverend Beecher goes to trial. I may oblige the *Record* for the extra income." She paused. "Don't forget your promise to explain this house to Reed?"

"Is *that* still bothering you? Oh, Devon, what a pretty paradox you are! One minute a free and independent spirit, the next deferring to your husband. Don't worry, dear. Just leave everything to your fairy godmother."

There was some perfunctory opposition to the seating of Reed Carter and, ironically, his strongest support came from a New York Republican. When a Yankee colleague objected, questioning the legality and propriety of an appointment by a former Confederate military officer whose own election to the governorship of his state had been bitterly opposed, Roscoe Conkling's commanding voice silenced him.

"I respectfully remind the gentleman from New Hampshire that President Grant settled that Texas dispute in Richard Coke's favor when he refused incumbent Davis' request for federal troops. And he acted similarly in the decision of the Brooks-Baxter case in Arkansas, to cite additional precedent. The gentleman from Texas is fully qualified to be a member of the United States Senate and must be seated."

It was a brave political bull that would lock horns with the ferocious Conkling in his own arena. The few dissenters abstained from further protest, and Senator Reed Carter, Democrat of Texas, took the oath of office in the first session of the Forty-fourth Congress, in the Vice-President's presence.

Devon smiled at her husband from the gallery, where she sat with the Ladies' Press Corps. In another section, Kate Chase Sprague, recently home from a European tour and beautifully chic in a Paris costume of bronze moiré, beamed on her fiery American Cicero. But their protracted love affair no longer stirred much comment among the columnists.

"What a proud moment for you, Devon!" Jane Swisshelm exclaimed after the swearing-in ceremony. "Congress needs new young blood, and I trust you'll be viewing the Washington scene from this vantage again?"

"In the future, perhaps, Jane. At present, however, I'm busy just being a housewife."

"Which is quite a chore in itself, my dear."

"That it is," Devon acknowledged. "Especially when your income is limited and you must chase around hunting bargains."

"Really?" Olivia drawled cattily. "Your residence doesn't suggest any financial problems."

Already Devon found herself on the defensive. "It's not our home, Olivia. We're only using it in the owner's absence. A good friend obtained it for us."

"How fortunate, considering the deplorably inadequate housing situation here! We'll look forward to your first official entertainment, Mrs. Carter. Of course, you realize that Mrs. Sprague is still the number-one hostess in this town. The first lady has never actually been first in that respect, although she deserves plaudits for her efforts. The White House lost its main attraction when Nellie moved to England. The Grants are still brooding about that. And then elder son Fred took a bride in Chicago. Poor Julia, her chicks are leaving the nest."

The senators were leaving the chamber. Devon caught Reed's signal. "Excuse me, ladies."

"Join us again," they chorused.

"I shall, thank you."

Reed met her at the foot of the ornamental stairway, and, after a visit to Statuary Hall, they left the Capitol. Outside, Devon asked, "Did you thank Senator Conkling for his support?"

"Yes. I can't say I like him much, though. He's a pompous man."

"And probably the most influential politician in Washington, next to the President."

Irony and chagrin showed in his frown. "I'd rather have been championed by a Southern Democrat, but they're conspicuous by their absence. I saw Mrs. Sprague in the gallery, but not Mrs. Winston. Has she left town already?"

"Yesterday," Devon said.

"Sometimes I wonder about that woman, Devon. The way we met, and the things she has done for us. Acquiring that nice home at such reasonable rent. How does she do it?"

"It's easy, if you know the right people, Reed. Carla just happened to have an accommodating friend."

"A realtor collects our monthly check, but *who* is our landlord?"

"What difference does it make? We have a good address in Georgetown and can afford some domestic help with the savings. Do you approve?"

"That's your department, madam. Just don't go over-board."

"Oh, no! I'll be very discreet and economical, Senator. What about transportation?"

"We'll see," he said. "Maybe Carla can wave her magic wand again and turn a pumpkin into a carriage."

Chapter 20

Congress recessed for the Christmas season, and Devon hung a holly wreath tied with red ribbon on the Carters' front door. They received greetings from Carla in Virginia, Devon's *Record* friends in New York, and from many Texans, including Governor and Mrs. Coke. Devon was tempted to destroy the pretentious card from Hampton House, with Melissa's personal message on the back, but she placed it with all the rest on the hall table, along with calling cards and invitations.

Kate Chase Sprague's traditional *dansante chandelle* was held at Edgewood, her late father's beautiful estate on the Potomac. Washington society eagerly anticipated this annual event, which generally surpassed even the grand balls of the White House. As on other occasions, the host was not Kate's husband, Senator William Sprague, but her lover and Sprague's foe in the Senate, Roscoe Conkling.

The guests waltzed to a string orchestra in the splendid ballroom, which was aglow with the myriad candles for which the dance was named. There was an elaborate buffet, much appreciated by all.

The Grants put in an appearance before midnight, and Devon noted for the *Record* the first lady's gown of scarlet velvet trimmed with ermine, and her glittering diamond-and-ruby jewels. Kate's exquisite creation of white satin and drifts of white chiffon suggested snowy purity. To live in the White House had been her ambition since girlhood. Four times Chief Justice Chase had failed to win the Republican nomination for the presidency. He had virtually died in the attempt. Kate realized that her husband would never achieve the office, either, but she believed that Roscoe Conkling might. She had cast her lot with him, despite his having a wife and family in upstate New York.

"Hell of a situation, that," Reed remarked in the hired carriage jouncing over the dark, icy streets to Georgetown.

"I guess Sprague was too embarrassed to show his face. It's a wonder he has the nerve to appear at his desk in the chamber. Of course, he's usually drunk. I can't understand why Rhode Island continues to reelect him. But I don't suppose he's the only cuckold in Congress."

"Nor the only drunkard," Devon mused, huddled in her cloak. "And he has chased his share of petticoats."

Capitol Hill was thick with so-called married bachelors who had left their wives back home. There was no shortage of attractive women for them in Washington. Nor was much significance attached to these social arrangements, unless an alliance was flaunted. A number of politicians had appeared at Edgewood this evening with women on their arms who were not their wives.

"That's different," Reed said of Sprague.

"You mean infidelity is all right for Sprague but not all right for his wife?"

"I didn't mean that. But are you defending Kate's conduct?"

"Maybe there are extenuating circumstances."

"Maybe," he agreed, dropping the subject. "I'm sorry I couldn't afford a better gift, darling—some jewelry or a fur. Perhaps I'll be more prosperous next year."

"The writing portfolio is very nice and will come in handy when I'm away. I'll write to you on the monogrammed stationery, and you must answer on your letterhead, Senator. Someday our correspondence may be famous."

"Do you mind if I work awhile tonight?"

"Not if you think you should."

While he burned the gaslight in the study, Devon lay in bed thinking of Scotty. Had the box of presents arrived in time to be placed under the tree? Shopping for the toys, trying to imagine something he did not already have, had given her extreme pleasure and intense pain, because she could not witness his reactions when he opened the brightly wrapped packages. She did not even know if he still believed in Santa Claus. Almost six months had passed since she had seen him and Keith, but she would be going to New York soon, and maybe . . . Maybe.

The Beecher-Tilton case was set to go to trial in Brooklyn on the eleventh of January. And since it had no political implications and was expected to be of short duration, Reed had agreed to Devon's covering it for the *Record*.

Devon's career these days took her to morning coffees and afternoon teas, music and poetry recitals, dramatic readings, lectures, and the theater. She attended a suffrage rally at Lincoln Hall, where Anna Dickinson spoke brilliantly on women's rights. Devon was pleased to see Mrs. Grant in the audience. Julia Grant had never reversed her initial stand on this highly controversial issue and continued to publicly support it. It meant a considerable risk for a lady of her position, and Devon admired her courage and loyalty.

January in New York! Frosted rooftops, icicles dangling from eaves and trees, glazed church spires etched like pristine crystal against the leaden skies. Traffic stalled. Men muffled in greatcoats and beaver hats hurried to business. Cloaked and muffed ladies shopped on Broadway. It was all familiar to Devon, yet so exciting she scarcely felt the sting of the harsh wind off the harbor as the hansom cab passed City Hall and turned into Park Row and Printing House Square.

Before the panic, the *Record*'s building had been enlarged, and the paper had a new steam press. Devon was proud to enter its grand portals as a journalist. After a warm welcome from Mr. Fitch, Carrie Hempstead, and others of the staff, Devon offered a poignant little speech telling them how pleased she was to be back, if temporarily. She exclaimed over the fine daily the *Record* had become. There was applause, and then Tish Lambeth passed coffee and doughnuts, which the men had bought themselves.

Two years of publicity had preceded the sensational drama about to unfold in the Brooklyn City Courthouse, on which *Woodhull & Claflin's Weekly* had scooped every other newspaper in the country. And during the long interim some astute editors and columnists observed that not once had the Reverend Henry Ward Beecher publicly refuted the charges. Rather, he ignored them, continuing to preach to his ever-expanding congregation at Plymouth Church. This year's sale of pews was the largest in the parish's history. Even nonbelievers came to hear America's most famous minister, now accused of breaking the Seventh Commandment with his best friend's wife. If Beecher thought the bitter cup would pass, he underestimated the server.

Victoria went on lecture tours, with Tennie as her advance booking agent, filling the halls with the prurient and the curious, recouping some of their lost fortunes through steep admission fees. From platform and stage, Vicky declared, "The hell of which the Reverend Mr. Beecher so zealously preaches will freeze over before I am silenced about his adultery, apostasy, and hypocrisy!"

Not even the hard winter weather discouraged attendance in the courtroom on the opening day of the trial. Ferries from Manhattan, now dubbed "Beecher boats," were loaded to capacity. Hundreds of spectators unable to gain entrance lounged on the steps and milled on the grounds, where a carnival atmosphere prevailed. Vendors hawked newspapers, pamphlets, sandwiches, coffee, peanuts, hot chestnuts, pinwheels, posters, and balloons painted with the faces of the principals. People proclaimed their sympathies with buttons and plaques. One organ-grinder's monkey sported a Beecher cap.

Devon sat in the reserved press section, with reporters she either knew or recognized, as well as strangers from far away. Prominent ecclesiastics, jurists, politicians, businessmen, financiers, feminists, and socialites were present. Nothing in America since the outbreak of the Civil War had generated as much interest. Religion was a vital part of daily life, and ordained ministers were revered, and considered beyond the temptations of ordinary mortals.

Beecher was surrounded by a battery of legal counselors. A grandfather and nearing sixty, he had white hair and wore a conservative black suit. He did not appear worried. A committee from his church had already exonerated him in a private investigation, and had excommunicated Theodore Tilton for filing suit against him.

Devon had never liked Beecher, nor seen anything to admire in his brand of fire and brimstone. His pinkish moon face and sensuous mouth suggested the cunning, prurient cupids in Roman art. And she could never forget his outrageous stunts to promote his sister's anti-South novel, *Uncle Tom's Cabin*. Her father had deplored his lopsided principles, his professed love of the common man while courting the favor of wealthy and prominent citizens. But Devon was there to report the facts of the case, if indeed they could be ascertained at all from the confusion encompassing them!

Mrs. Tilton, concerned for her four children, alternately

admitted and denied her infidelity. Her marriage was destroyed, her reputation sullied, her sanity threatened. She was a small, dainty, attractive brunette, and her husband a handsome blond giant. How she had fallen in love with the aging preacher was just another of the many mysteries of this strange case. Devon pitied Lib Tilton, wondering how she herself would have reacted in a similar situation.

The person everyone most wanted to observe was absent. Neither legal side could subpoena her, even had they wished to do so, for Victoria Woodhull was still lecturing in the Midwest. But Susan Anthony and Elizabeth Cady Stanton, her loyal friends, who had first told Victoria of Elizabeth Tilton's tearful confession, were daily attendants. They acknowledged Devon's presence in the press box with nods and smiles, and invited her to lunch during court recesses.

"Lib is being victimized, as women usually are in adultery cases," Mrs. Stanton said. "She was a good and faithful wife until Beecher seduced her with his glib tongue. He actually convinced the poor, naive soul that there was nothing wrong in her submitting to him, that it was almost a holy union because of his consecration!"

"The man is an infidel and a hypocrite," Miss Anthony stated unequivocally, spooning her potato soup. "And if there's any justice, he will come tumbling down from his exalted pedestal."

Devon asked, "Do you think Vicky will testify?"

"Oh, she'd be eager to!" Mrs. Stanton replied. "But the attorneys are afraid of her since her public announcements of affairs with both Tilton *and* Beecher. Victoria is honest about her philosophy of sexual freedom for both sexes. And whatever her faults, lying is not one of them."

The trial gave indications of a long run, and the proceedings so absorbed the public and press that even Washington news couldn't compete for the front pages. In the evening Devon returned to her hotel room and wrote her impressions of that day, sending them by messenger to the *Record*. Often her hand ached with writer's cramp, and she wished for one of the new Shoal typewriters, which had been demonstrated last year and were currently in production by the Remington Company, although not yet available. She determined to memorize the keyboard and learn to operate the miraculous machine as soon as it was obtainable.

No matter how fatigued she was, she wrote to Reed

regularly, and he answered impatiently, "Is that three-ring circus up there going to play forever? If so, you'd better forget it and come home."

Riled by the veiled command, Devon replied, "As the son of a publisher and a former journalist, you realize my professional commitment to the *Record* is ethically binding. Only an emergency could force me to abandon it."

To his curt demand, "Create one!" Devon responded, "How are things in Congress, dear? We don't hear much about it here now. This trial takes precedence over everything."

Devon glanced habitually at the Manhattan journals, where the Curtis name was likely to appear. And one day she saw an item that stunned her.

Mrs. Esther Stanfield Curtis, wife of Wall Street banker and capitalist Keith Heathstone Curtis, is dead at the age of 37. The former socialite, once among New York's most popular hostesses, succumbed in her sleep last night, at the family residence in Gramercy Park, after a long, confining illness.

Private memorial services will be conducted in Grace Episcopal Church tomorrow morning, after which the remains, accompanied by Mrs. Curtis' husband and her mother, Mrs. Hortense Clayton Stanfield, will be sent to her native Boston. Interment will be in Mount Auburn Cemetery.

Her father was the late Henry Alder Stanfield, and the family was well-known in Beacon Hill society. Friends desiring to send flowers are requested to contribute instead to their favorite charities.

Devon sat down, the paper rustling in her tremulous hands. Esther was gone, and Keith was free, at long last. Her love, her child's father, her heart's desire was single— but *she* was not! The knowledge pounded in her mind. She felt sick, dizzy. Nausea seeped into her throat, and a sudden fierce pain throbbed in her temples and at the base of her skull. She began to retch, finally vomiting up her supper into the commode.

Even if she could skip a few hours of the trial, she dared not appear at Keith's home, the church, or the railway station. Mrs. Stanfield, already partially unbalanced, might become violent. So the next day, as the Grace bells tolled for the funeral in Manhattan, Devon took her seat in the dingy, crowded court chamber in Brooklyn.

It happened also to be the occasion of the Reverend Mr. Beecher's first appearance on the stand, and what impressed the reporters most was his refusal to swear on the Bible. Declaring that he had scruples against such oath-taking, Beecher insisted on the New England form of upraised right hand. More of his clerical theatrics, Devon wondered, or a clever ruse to circumvent the truth? There was a dramatic stirring among the astonished audience, as one of Tilton's attorneys declared, "The Reverend Mr. Beecher is well aware that 'Thou shalt not lie!' is *not* one of the sacred Commandments!"

Beecher wept briefly, but one could not be sure whether the tears were genuine or mere histrionics. Printed and verbal testimony to the contrary, including the introduction of his clandestine letters to Lib Tilton and a written apology to her husband, Beecher denied any wrongdoing with Mrs. Tilton or any other female, including that "free-loving prostitute," as he contemptuously referred to Victoria Woodhull. Under cross-examination he slandered both women, stating that each had tried to force her attentions on him, but that he had nobly resisted their improper advances.

Numerous bouquets from his faithful congregation, most of whom staunchly avowed his innocence, were delivered daily to his table, and Beecher held a nosegay of violets in his hands during his testimony, causing one columnist to describe him as "a dunghill covered with flowers." Another commented, "Man has been falling since Adam, but not until Henry Ward Beecher did he reach the ultimate depths."

Devon listed the dialogue for the *Record*. It was alternately fascinating and ludicrous:

Judge Fullerton: Were you in the habit of kissing Mrs. Tilton?

Beecher: I was when I had been absent any considerable time.

Fullerton: Were you in the habit of kissing her when you went to her house in the absence of her husband?

Beecher: Sometimes I did and sometimes I did not.

Fullerton: Well, what prevented you upon the occasions when you did not?

Beecher: It may be that the children were there then.

Fullerton: Did you kiss her in the presence of the servants?

Beecher: Not that I recollect.

Fullerton: Then the times you did embrace Elizabeth Tilton were occasions when the two of you were alone in the house?

Beecher (shrugging and smelling the violets): I don't remember the exact circumstances.

Fullerton: Try.

Court recessed, and Devon rushed outside into the slickered and umbrellaed crowd. Cold rain was falling, but no matter the weather, hundreds gathered every morning in the hope of somehow gaining entrance. A well-dressed man offered Devon a hundred dollars for her press badge, and a slovenly woman tried to steal it. A police detail was assigned to keep order, but the men had to concentrate primarily on the pickpockets, tramps, whores, and religious fanatics. No doubt the law wished more fervently than anyone else for an end to the Beecher business.

Devon had forgotten her galoshes, and the icy water soaked through her shoes, chilling her feet and legs. She longed for a hot bath and full night's rest, but was able to realize only one wish.

A letter from Reed required an immediate answer. He wrote: "My bill has reached committee. Some senators consider it an isolated problem to be handled by individual states and the territories. I maintain that the national government is responsible for the safety and defense of all citizens, and Texans are carrying more than their share of frontier burdens. The floor debate should be interesting, and I hope you will witness it from the gallery. You've been gone long enough, honey. Too damned long, in fact, I need you. Come here! Your loving but lonesome husband, Reed."

She tried to placate him with reasonable explanations and soothing promises, concluding: "When that glorious day of debate dawns, rest assured I'll be there, Senator. The trial can't last much longer, and should go into summation soon. Please bear with me. Your busy and harried wife, Devon."

Reed fired a curt, impatient wire. "Court is not in continual session, madam. You have some leisure, and there are daily trains to Washington."

Her response was even briefer: "They run both ways, sir."

Chapter 21

In March, King Kalakaua was on his way back to Hawaii, Congress passed its fourth Civil Rights Act since the war, and official Washington was anxious about rumors of a vast coalition of distillers and revenue agents who were systematically defrauding the government of thousands of dollars in taxes. But mostly America's attention was still focused on the Beecher-Tilton case. Illicit sex was more stimulating than untaxed alcohol, clerical adultery more exciting than congressional chicanery. The Brooklyn City Courtroom attracted more illustrious spectators than either the House or Senate galleries, and some formerly obscure journals sprang into national prominence with their sensational coverage of the trial.

By being the first to publish Mrs. Tilton's pathetically incriminating letters to her husband while Theodore was away lecturing between 1866 and 1870, the Chicago *Tribune* gained the reputation of the greatest newspaper in the Midwest, even outshining many of its larger Eastern competitors. Not to be eclipsed, Charles Dana burst a bombshell in his New York *Sun,* accusing a certain Mrs. Morse of having "connived to procure an abortion for poor Lib Tilton's love-babe," and declaring that this fact was common knowledge among local editors and journalists too squeamish or fearful of reprisal to reveal it. Unsure how to handle this touchy aspect in her articles, Devon merely quoted the *Sun* and let the readers draw their own conclusions.

The clever Claflin sisters were now home from their lucrative tour. Their tabloid was humming on its press and selling every copy before the ink was dry. The prurient public, itching for Victoria Woodhull's appearance in court, finally forced jurisprudence to subpoena her, not as a witness, but to produce whatever relevant evidence she possessed.

The President could hardly have attracted more notables to the scene for this long-awaited and eagerly anticipated debut. James A. Garfield, General Benjamin Butler, Edwin Booth resembling the brooding Hamlet for which he was renowned, other famous stage and opera stars, leading novelists and poets, Protestant and Catholic prelates, Jewish rabbis, Wall Street bankers and brokers all rushed to the courthouse as if the fate of the nation rested on Mrs. Woodhull.

To the disappointment of Beecher's admirers and his attorneys, the "notorious hussy" did not look the part. She was fashionably dressed in a dark blue promenade suit, with narrow bands of black velvet decorating the basque. A small tearose, Vicky's fragrant trademark, graced her throat. Her chic black straw hat was veiled in deep blue net. Even her most caustic critics had to admit that she was lovely, elegant, and poised.

"Put the harlot on the stand!" screamed a crazed female worshiper of Beecher's.

"Hang the witch!" chanted her rabid companion. In another era, Victoria Woodhull might have been stoned or burned at the stake.

The gavel rapped for order, and the disrupters were threatened with eviction. Victoria, sedately ignoring the outbursts, was in her element. She wished to take the stand, but counsel for neither the defense nor the plantiff would allow it. After cursory examination of the correspondence that implicated their client in the notorious lady's love life, Beecher's lawyers tossed it aside.

Victoria shrugged nonchalantly. "Very well, gentlemen. I am not the judge of their suitability for admission. And while they may not do for Mr. Beecher, you were anxious enough to have them."

Lifting her veil dramatically, she focused her eloquent purple eyes on Beecher and then walked serenely from the courtroom accompanied by her pretty sister, Tennie. Rejection of the letters as evidence had increased their commercial value, and they planned to auction them. James Gordon Bennett had already offered a substantial figure for exclusive rights of publication in the New York *Herald*.

The highlight of that particular session had been reached, and court was recessed.

Devon made her routine exit and trip to the hotel, elbowing her way past the gawking outsiders. It was early

May. Trees and grass were green, flowers and shrubs in bloom. She yearned for a respite in Prospect Park. But her editor was anxiously awaiting her account of Mrs. Woodhull's day in court.

Devon had just completed her report and given it to the *Record*'s messenger, who sped off to the Fulton Street ferry. She was in a wrapper, brushing her hair and preparing to bathe, when the bellboy delivered a familiar card, slipping it under the door and inquiring if there were any message. "No," she answered, but immediately changed her mind. "Yes! Tell the gentleman I'll be down shortly."

Shortly was forty-five minutes, time enough for the gentleman to have a drink in the hotel bar and smoke a cigar. He was seated in the lobby reading a paper when Devon finally came down. The gas chandeliers were lighted, and the dining room was preparing for evening patrons.

He rose and bowed, smiling. "Good evening."

"Good evening, Keith," Devon replied.

"Have you had dinner yet?"

"Not yet."

"Will you do me the honor?"

Devon nodded, taking the arm he offered, discovering that he had already reserved a secluded table. After consulting Devon, Keith ordered seafood appetizers, châteaubriand, asparagus tips in Mornay sauce, and champagne.

"You know about Esther?" he asked.

"Yes, I saw it in the paper."

"I'm surprised there was space enough, with the Beecher-Tilton spectacle absorbing everyone's attention. How can you endure that, day after day?"

"It's my job."

"So much of the coverage is disgusting, Devon. Journalism in its lowest form."

"Mine, too?"

"Not what I've seen of it, no. You haven't lost your technique. But you must admit there is plenty of muckraking. Even the attorneys engage in disreputable legal tactics. This trial will set a record for unethical conduct. I suppose The Woodhull gave her usual flamboyant performance today?"

"She was quite decorous, actually."

"That's a part of her act."

Devon tasted the French-style steak, which was tender,

juicy, and delicious. "Victoria has never denied her principles of free love, Keith. On the contrary, she proclaims them from the platform and in print."

"Good advertisement," he muttered. "And so Mrs. Tilton has left her home and children to stand by Beecher. How did her husband's defense phrase it? 'You'll always find the adulteress with the adulterer!' That statement should have been objected to as prejudicial to the jury and stricken from the record."

"Why?"

"Because it's conjecture, and presumptuous. And not *always* true, is it?"

Their eyes locked across the table. "There are exceptions," she allowed.

Why didn't he mention their son? Surely he realized his silence was torture. "How is Scotty?"

"Fine."

"No ill effects from the measles?"

"None. He's as strong and healthy as ever."

"Thank God." She waited. "Will you bring him to Gramercy Park now?"

"Occasionally, but he prefers the country, the woods and animals. And it's better for him. A child is happier in a familiar environment."

"I imagine so," Devon agreed.

"How is the senator?" he asked grudgingly.

"Who?"

"Your husband, Mrs Carter."

"Oh." She blushed. "Quite well, thank you, and waiting for the Committee on Indian Affairs disposition of the bill he introduced in February. Texas and the entire frontier need more protection, or better-kept treaties."

"That's primarily a military matter, Devon. He'd have better luck going directly to the White House."

Devon bolstered her nerve with champagne. "Why did you send me your card this evening, Keith? Surely not just to dine with me?"

"Of course not. You know the reasons, Devon." Laying his napkin aside, he gazed at her with longing. "The *Sprite* is docked in the East River. I thought you might consider a weekend cruise, for a change of pace and scenery."

"Alone?"

"Except for the captain and crew."

Nothing could be more appealing, and her mind divided into two separate yearnings. Could she have Keith and still not hurt Reed?

"Your invitation is intriguing, Keith, but—"

He quickly interrupted. "You needn't decide now, Devon. Just think about it."

"Are you staying in town?"

"On the yacht," he said. "That's how I came. No sane person would risk those overloaded ferries. It'll be a miracle if óne doesn't capsize and drown hundreds of people."

"You should see them debark from the 'Beecher boats' in the morning," Devon told him. "Like cattle out of a shoot, stampeding one another on the trail to the courthouse."

"Dessert?" Keith asked, as the waiter stood by. "They have one of your favorites—cherries flambé. And a variety of crepes, cakes, pies, ice creams."

"Too fattening. I'm watching my weight."

"Nonsense," he scoffed "You haven't gained an ounce in a year, Devon. Indulge yourself a little. Take some sherbet, anyway, while I have a brandy."

An hour later, they parted in the lobby, with only a clasp of hands, and Devon's promise to send a message to the *Sprite* if she intended to join him there.

Indecision tormented her for two days and nights, and in the end she went, hoping their son would be aboard.

But he was not, and when she asked why, he said, "The meeting in Washington tore you both apart, darling. You were devastated, and Scott cried most of the way home. He's too young to understand these things, Devon. Why hurt him and yourself more than necessary?"

Logic could not assuage her painful disappointment. "Why didn't you tell me this the other evening, Keith?"

"I said we would be alone, remember?"

"But I didn't realize you meant that."

"You expected a chaperon?"

"No," she cried angrily. "I expected to see my child, with or without his governess! I don't think I'll stay, Keith."

"It's too late, Devon. We're casting off."

"Put me ashore in a dinghy!"

"Don't be absurd."

"Well, if you imagine this is going to be a romantic interlude, Mr. Curtis, you're badly mistaken! I'll not share your quarters."

"Choose any stateroom you please, Mrs. Carter—as far away from mine as possible, if that's how you feel."

"That's precisely how I want it," she snapped.

"Rufus will be serving luncheon at two o'clock. You're welcome, madam."

"Thank you, sir."

Refusing his assistance with her portmanteau, Devon flounced down the passageway to the last cabin. All were luxuriously fitted, with comfortable berths and compact furniture, and fully equipped with the latest sanitary facilities. The one Devon took was artfully decorated in green and blue to complement the Renoir paintings on the birch-paneled walls.

Once again her heart had ruled her head where Keith was concerned, impetuosity overriding prudence. Common sense had warned her that it was unwise to board the *Sprite* under her present circumstances, but she *was* aboard now, and might as well enjoy it. Sulking would be silly.

Setting the table, Rufus greeted her with a broad grin. "It's a real pleasure seeing you again, Miss Marshall! Where you been keeping yourself, besides the Brooklyn courthouse?"

"Various places, Rufus. And it's nice to be aboard the *Sprite* again, too. I hope we'll have fair weather."

"Yes, ma'am. That blue sky and balmy breeze means smooth sailing."

Keith entered, in white trousers and dark blue brass-buttoned blazer, black-billed white seacap in hand. Devon smiled. The years had not aged him. No other man seemed as desirable. Visualizing her son in his image some thirty years hence evoked sadness. Would his parents still be alive then? Still apart? And still desperately in love?

"Captain Bowers won't be joining us," he said. "He's at the wheel."

Glass expanses had been added to both sides of the commodious dining and lounge area, and Devon could view Manhattan and Long Island from the table. Rufus, in immaculate white jacket, served several of his culinary specialties. In this delightful atmosphere Devon forgot the earlier spat, though not the reason for it. Her child was never long out of mind, and cruel gremlins taunted her that Keith was using this knowledge in his effort to bring them together again, permanently.

He remarked ruefully, "Ironic, isn't it, that our problem

still exists, after all these years and our attempts to solve it? Only now I'm free and you are not. We seem to be victims of a perverted destiny, Devon."

"Did you feel anything when . . . when Esther died?"

"Relief," he said honestly. "Nothing but relief. Death was only a formality for her, Devon. In reality, she had expired long ago. I could scarcely remember knowing her, much less loving her. I was glad her mother insisted on burying her in Boston, with the Stanfields. She did not belong in the Curtis-family plot and would not have rested easily."

"How will Mrs. Stanfield manage now?"

"Well enough, on the pension I've provided for her. She can be a recluse in her home on Louisburg Square, with her faithful servants and her memories. She's more than eccentric, you know, and her daughter inherited her affliction. Esther was many different persons, Devon. Her personality changed periodically and radically, alternating between brilliance and lunacy. She was mentally ill when I married her—I realize that now. I'm thankful we never had any children together." A pensive pause. "That's also why Scott is so important to me. I just wish he had some blood siblings. I have nightmares about losing him."

"Oh, don't say that!" Devon cried, for the same horror sometimes beset her. "Don't even think it, Keith. I was nearly wild when he had the measles."

Rufus moved unobtrusively between the galley and salon, and Keith said, "In Washington, I asked you to leave Carter. Now I shall ask you again. Divorce him and marry me."

"I've thought of it," she answered slowly. "But he's a good man, Keith, and I have no legal reason or—"

"You don't love him, Devon, and marriage without love is immoral. Little better than prostitution. Fornication—and often rape—sanctioned by law."

Devon grimaced. "That's what Victoria Woodhull says."

"I speak from personal experience, knowing the misery of a loveless union."

"It hasn't been exactly that kind of ordeal for me," Devon proclaimed in loyal defense of her husband. "Perhaps because Reed loves me, and I don't dislike him. It was different in your case, Keith."

He opened the silver container Rufus had earlier filled with chipped ice, dropped several pieces into a glass, and filled it with Scotch. "And is that enough, Devon? Can you be satisfied with a one-sided love for the rest of your life? Can Carter? Granted that you don't hate him, or find him repulsive, how often have you been together as man and wife in the past five months? He never looks at another woman, even in your absence?"

Devon thought of Melissa Hampton, and her suspicions. "I don't know, Keith. He did mingle in Austin while I was away, and he does in Washington now. Politics and parties are synonymous, you know."

"So is surreptitious sex in that Babylon on the Potomac! I've proposed a logical and simple release from your marital trap," he went on.

"Simple? It takes an act of Congress to get a divorce in the District, Keith!"

"That can be arranged, my dear."

The statement struck Devon as arrogant.

"We're not at that stage yet," she said hurriedly.

Keith knew when to press and when to refrain. "Enough on that subject! We're in Long Island Sound now. Shall we go on deck?"

Devon nodded, eager to change the discussion and their surroundings.

Chapter 22

Captain Bowers saluted from the helm, and the crew recognized the passenger with courteous nods. Her reputation was safe on the *Sprite*: discretion was a prerequisite of any Curtis employee.

They lounged in canvas deck chairs, watching the sun slip behind the wooded hills and farms of the Bronx. Once they had visited the Edgar Allan Poe cottage at Fordham, where one of Devon's favorite poems, *Annabel Lee*, was composed while Poe's tubercular wife was dying. Somehow the mournful ode to eternal love spoke for her own bouts with sorrow.

She removed the pins from her upswept coiffure and let the bright tresses tumble to her shoulders.

"You look sixteen," he said admiringly.

"You didn't know me at that age."

"I have a keen imagination." His eyes lingered on her tempting coral lips, then traveled leisurely over her figure. "Also a graphic memory. I haven't forgotten anything about you, Devon. You have dainty feet and kissable toes, dimpled knees, a tiny mole on your charming buttocks, and a pair of the prettiest, sweetest—"

"Hush," she cautioned, glancing warily around.

"Breasts," he whispered, leaning toward her. "Ah, my love still blushes like a maiden! Has she forgotten our frequent perusals of *Gray's Anatomy*, and that marvelously illustrated text I consulted in delivering our baby?" Her flush deepened, and Keith visualized the taut pink nipples. "I think I shall prolong this cruise indefinitely . . ."

"Keith, you wouldn't! I have to be back in Brooklyn Monday morning, and you promised . . ."

Grinning, stroking an imaginary mustache, he asked, "Did I?"

"Oh, you villain! Does it please you to tease me?"

176

"It excites me," he said. "As you surely know, your eyes change color with your moods. They are varying shades of green, from jade to emerald, and the flecks go to amber, topaz, and gold. Fascinating in anger, delightful in joy."

"Will we sail all night?"

"No, we'll anchor in a harbor. Dolph Bowers knows the best ones. We'll have a late supper. Anything special you'd like?"

"Does a cold buffet appeal to you?"

"Bread and water would appeal to me, if we shared it."

A wagging finger admonished him, though not too severely. "Don't spend your compliments so extravagantly, lest you exhaust your repertoire before the cruise ends."

Seagulls circled, glided, scavenging for galley refuse. Masted and rigged ships and fishing craft ringed the horizon, flying foreign and domestic flags. Their horns and whistles echoed for miles.

"The Sound is beautiful," she remarked.

"You've seen it before, haven't you—from another yacht?"

So she had, but had almost forgotten the occasion and the weird experience aboard Commodore Vanderbilt's boat. "Good heavens! You do have a memory!"

"That ridiculous séance off Fire Island to contact Margaret Fuller's spirit in Davy Jones's locker was the joke of Wall Street for weeks," he reflected. "Especially the participation of intellectuals like Kate Field, Horace Greeley, and George Ripley."

"Miss Field is an occultist herself, Keith. And many learned people attended the 'Rochester Rappings' of the Fox Sisters, including James Fenimore Cooper, William Cullen Bryant, and George Bancroft."

"Primarily out of skepticism, I suspect. But Vanderbilt actually believes in spiritualism, Devon, and is forever trying to communicate with his mother and other relatives on the other side. The Bewitching Brokers hoodwinked old Corneel in more ways than one. But either he's less gullible in his dotage or the witches have lost some of their enchantment, because they couldn't persuade him to rescue their paper when it was floundering in red ink. They had to take to the lecture circuits to save it."

"I've seen the Commodore in court a few times, and he

still seems fairly spry. About eighty, isn't he? I think his young wife put a halt to his friendship with Vicky and Tennie."

"High time, too."

Purple twilight lingered, and as dusk descended, lighthouse beacons beamed on the shore points. Rufus brought refreshments and inquired about supper. Keith replied that they preferred a late buffet, which Rufus could prepare and leave on the table before retiring.

"Yes, sir," Rufus said, returning to the galley, where the regular cook was fixing the crew's chow.

Devon sampled her drink. "Why, it's planter's punch! It's delicious!"

"Rufus knows you're a Southerner. He can concoct a fine mint julep, too, mild enough for a delicate lady."

"Bless him." But Devon thought Keith had suggested these cocktails to his valet, to help ease her inhibitions. Soon a resplendent moon appeared, shimmering like liquid mercury on the waves. Devon felt vibrantly alive, eager for the joys of life. She even forgave Keith for luring her aboard with an unspoken invitation to see her child again. Suddenly she chuckled. "This is so good, I may get tipsy this evening! I hope Rufus prepared a whole barrel of it."

Amused, Keith reached over to drape the scarf about her shoulders. The Atlantic breezes were sweeping across the deck, but Devon hardly felt the chill. "One would seem to be your capacity, darling." He grinned.

"Do you know that Washington ladies drink almost as much as the gentlemen at parties?"

"Well, living in the Capital can be difficult. And I've heard that Texas is a great place for men and horses, but hell on women. Did you find the ladies indulging there?"

"At times," she acknowledged. "Especially on the prairie. Our home was a primitive cabin, in the middle of desolation."

"Sounds wretched," he said, lighting a Havana cheroot.

"Oh, there were some nice aspects: friendly folks and homey entertainments. But mostly it is drudgery. Eternal winds and dust. Bitter winters, scorching summers. Miles to the nearest store in Fort Worth, to buy staples at exhorbitant prices. Not a decent ladies' shop, and only one in Dallas, some thirty miles away on the east fork of the Trinity River. Terrible roads. Indians and bandits and fevers. And yet, despite all the horrors, most of the natives love Texas and would defend it to their death. The old senator intends to remain there and be buried on the lone prairie."

"And the young senator—what are his aspirations?"

"Well, not ranching anymore," Devon said. "But his political career will depend largely on his performance on Capitol Hill. That failing, I suppose he would return to Texas and local politics. He made quite an impression as speaker of the state House."

"Yes, I read the *Record*, Devon. Carrie Hempstead printed that news, along with other items about the Carters."

While they dined, Rufus lighted the bronze wall lamps in her stateroom and prepared the lavatory with her favorite French soap and salts and Turkish towels. The ship's bells were signaling midnight when Devon retired. The euphoria diminished during her preparations, and the bad imps returned to plague her. She dreaded the end of the cruise. Without her restrictions, they might sail for months, sail around the world and over the rainbow.

She luxuriated in the commodious berth, the pale green satin sheets soft and sensual against her bare, scented flesh. She would never have slept *au naturel* had the *Sprite* been in motion and subject to emergency abandonment of ship. But Captain Bowers had put into Cold Springs Harbor for the night, anchoring off Centre Island, and only the brazen moon dared peer through the portholes.

An hour dragged by, and still sleep eluded her. Counting stars didn't help. She adjusted and readjusted her pillows. Did Rufus and the others wonder why she and Mr. Curtis were quartered separately? What a thing to worry about! she chided herself. But she couldn't help it. She imagined other women on the *Sprite*, eagerly sharing his stateroom. And what was her husband doing tonight? Had he accommodated some persistent hostess with an unescorted female on her hands? Could he continually resist the temptations of Washington? Had he successfully resisted Melissa Hampton?

Oh, God, why couldn't she conquer her own physical cravings now, suppress them! Drifting in helpless confusion, she was unaware of her visitor until she heard his low, gentle voice. "Am I disturbing you?"

"No, I was awake. But I didn't hear a knock."

"There was none," he explained. "Your door was unlocked. Did you forget?"

"I didn't consider it necessary."

He crossed the carpeted floor and stood looking at her a few moments in the moonbeam, before sitting down on her berth. "If you want me to leave, tell me now, Devon. In words."

Her silence spoke eloquently, but more so her embrace. She could not divert her mind, nor did she try. Her fires were spontaneous, rapidly burning away her guards, threatening to consume her. Stripping the sheet from her body, he exulted to find her nude, as if she had been waiting for him. His own garments were promptly discarded.

"Don't let me hurt you, darling."

"I'm not a virgin, you know."

"But it's been so long," he said, his arms enveloping, crushing her, "I may get violent."

There was some initial violence, almost ravishment, and she gloried in it, her passion and desire pacing his. Then exquisite tenderness and artistry, prolonged and repeated paroxysms of ecstasy that transported her to another plane, unreached since their last intimacy. Only his consummate skill could fathom the true depths of her sensuality, evoke the ultimate sensations. And Devon knew, as she had always known, that for her, love made all the difference. Love created the perfect union. Without it, she could not commit herself totally to any man—husband or not.

Afterward, her body continued to quiver in his arms. "That's one thing we had, Devon."

"Not the only thing, though."

"No, but one of the most important, wonderful, and vital. I won't ask you if—"

"But you want to know. No, darling, it was never the same with him. You warned me our last time at the Clairmont that it wouldn't be, remember? Well, you were right. Not because he was ignorant or selfish or brutal. But something was always missing. Was it the same for you, with anyone else?"

"Never. There were other women, of course. I had to try to forget you somehow. Usually it was just release. Sometimes I pretended my partner was you, but it didn't work. No one could ever replace you for me, Devon. You were an integral part of my existence, even before our child linked us, and I don't believe either of us can ever forget the other." More slowly now, he said, "I don't give a damn about Carter. You were mine first, and I want you back. Whatever the cost, I intend to have you as my wife and Scott's mother. I've regarded our separation as temporary, your marriage as a desperate venture. Circumstances have changed, Devon. I won't try to force an immediate decision, but I won't wait indefinitely, either."

They made love again, and yet again, before he left her at dawn to dress in his own quarters. The sun was up and the yacht steaming on the Sound when Devon joined him.

Chapter 23

Portfolio of notebooks and sharpened pencils in hand, Devon was in the press section of the courtroom at eight o'clock Monday morning. The Reverend Mr. Beecher, accompanied by counsel and a police escort, acknowledged his cheering admirers with smiles, nods, and blessings. Many people, unable to crowd into Plymouth Church for his Sunday sermon, had stood outside. The simple red-brick edifice, built without a steeple, in the tradition of the first New England meetinghouses, had become a tourist attraction. The flamboyant pastor amply compensated for the austere architecture. His treasury's wealth was now compared to the Vatican's.

There had been snowstorms in January and February, thundershowers in March and April. Now, as summer approached, a premature heat wave hit the East Coast. The courtroom was hot and stuffy. Spectators plied fans and kerchiefs. The winter wardrobe Devon had brought with her had been shipped back to Washington and replaced with seasonal apparel for which she shopped when she could.

On Friday afternoons the *Sprite* docked in the East River, beckoning, but Devon could not always follow. Reed came up once in May, and she went to Washington the first weekend in June. On both occasions they alternately quarreled and reconciled. He accused her of putting her career before her marriage.

"Goddammit, Devon, your place is with me! Who the devil cares about Beecher, anyway?"

"The entire country, judging from the news coverage."

"The political morality of America should concern the press more than one parson's peccadilloes," Reed argued. "He's not the first or last clergyman to sin like other mortals. Even popes have fallen off their infallible thrones into the arms of amorous women. Lust is a human instinct."

Devon nodded in rueful accord. "The trial can't go on forever, Reed. Everyone concerned must be sick and tired of it by now, including the judge and jury. Please, let's not dwell on it any further. I'm anxious to hear about your Indian bill."

His mouth twisted grimly. "It was scalped in committee."

"I'm so sorry, Reed. I didn't know. Couldn't Senator Conkling help?"

"He's involved in other matters. Senator Sprague's wife, for one, and Sprague himself. They've practically come to blows in the chamber, and both carry pistols now. Sprague is making an absolute fool of himself, giving speeches attacking Conkling's character, without mentioning the real reason for the vendetta. And Conkling thinks he's Mark Antony in the Forum. The fresh flowers on his desk every morning are delivered from her conservatory, and he keeps a page busy sending her messages. Meanwhile, Congress sits on its complacent ass, the economy worsens, and graft and corruption continue in high places."

They were in the Georgetown house, the beauty of which Devon had almost forgotten. Cook had served dinner in the muraled dining room, with flowers and candles on the table, and wine in crystal goblets. A silver service and set of fine china were included in the furnishings, along with some valuable paintings and art objects. "Have you met our landlord yet?" she asked over the demitasse and delicious Bavarian torte.

"No, I just pay the monthly rental according to Mrs. Winston's instructions."

"Dear Carla. I wish I'd hear from her."

"So does Pa," Reed said. "But the mysterious lady seems to have disappeared, at least from our lives."

"Well, she was there when we needed her, thank God."

"I think Carla Winston was at loose ends, wandering, and our paths chanced to cross, Devon. That happens frequently out West. Pioneers meet on wagon trains or stagecoaches and become staunch friends. Cowboys riding mutual trails will stick together for hundreds, even thousands of miles, fight and die for one another—then go their separate ways. Such relationships go with the territory. One can't expect permanence of them."

"I suppose not," Devon agreed, although she had thought it was different with her and Carla.

When they went upstairs, the bed in the master suite was

turned down, and Devon knew there was no avoiding the inevitable. Reed would not be distracted, and she had no plausible excuse. A sudden compulsion to confess her infidelity dissolved in fear of the possible consequences. It might provoke the same sort of mess now transpiring in Brooklyn. Therefore, she accepted his approach, yielded, and even pretended to enjoy it. But her pretense only increased her guilt, and her conscience threatened to betray her. Her soul felt as nakedly exposed as her flesh, and she reached for her nightgown.

"Modesty?" he teased. "I'll just have to remove it again, later. Since you're leaving again tomorrow, we must make the most of tonight."

Toward the end of June, the Beecher-Tilton case went into its final phases. But if the woman responsible for its beginning witnessed its finale, she did so incognito—a credible-enough feat for the versatile Victoria, whose artful disguises had enabled her to enter assemblies where she was forbidden to speak, eluding guards and police with warrants for her arrest.

Whatever The Woodhull's theatrical abilities, however, some considered Henry Ward Beecher a better actor than Edwin Booth. With a phenomenal memory in the pulpit, capable of quoting entire chapters of Scripture verbatim, he was forgetful on the stand. In the six months of the trial, journalists counted more than eight hundred instances in which he had responded to questions with "I don't know" or "I can't recollect."

Tired of evasions, the plaintiff's counsel berated the defendant's convenient mental lapses, and the harassed judge decided to quote some of his own words to him, reading from a copy.

" 'It is often better that past crimes should slumber, so far as the community is concerned. There be many things that are great sins, grievous and wounding, which, having been committed, the conscience of the actor leads him to feel that there is a kind of expiation, or, at any rate, a justice, which requires that he should, with open mouth, confess that which has hitherto been secret. Forsake, surely; to God confess, but it does not follow, especially when your confession would entail misery and suffering upon all that are connected with you, that you should make confession merely for the sake of relieving your own conscience.'" Judge Fullerton paused, peering at Beecher. "Do you recollect preaching a sermon of which that is a part?"

"Well, I regard it as sound doctrine."

Warning that he would countenance no discursions, Fullerton inquired, "Will you tell me the date when that sermon was preached, if you please?"

Beecher's memory was suddenly accurate. "Sunday morning, October 4, 1868."

Judge Fullerton spoke to Chief Justice Neilson. "There is generally not much done, sir, after the sermon but the benediction."

Neilson asked, "Will the jury get ready to retire?"

"There has been no collection take-up!" Beecher exclaimed.

This time his levity produced no laughter. His entire conduct had fallen short of the dignity of his profession.

Audible sighs of relief arose from the jurymen as the bailiff escorted them out. Press and spectators then filed out to await the verdict. No one expected a rapid decision. Devon went to the hotel across the street, into which she had moved when the attorneys began their summations.

Never in her career had she been more anxious to conclude an assignment. Summarizing the day's proceedings on paper, she gave it to the *Record*'s messenger. Then she opened the windows to admit some fresh air. The heat was suffocating. Scarcely a leaf moved on the dusty trees of the courthouse square. Perspiring reporters clung to branches and hung onto the roof and ledges of the building, trying to peer into the jury room. Some camped on the steps and slept on the ground.

For eight days Devon slept partially clothed, ate in her room, took sponge baths, and observed the courthouse, often through a lorgnette. One juror collapsed from the heat, several others suffered colic from tainted food, and a doctor had to be summoned. Devon was weary and half-ill herself when finally the panel trudged back to the jury box and the reporters dashed madly inside.

The foreman reported no clear-cut decision. After fifty-two ballots, the vote was nine to three in favor of Henry Ward Beecher. The Plymouth Church section rejoiced wildly, hugging and kissing one another, sobbing and praising the Lord. Beecher thanked his counselors, while his wife wept at his side. Elizabeth Tilton was not present. Her husband left the courtroom quietly, refusing comment.

Nothing definite had been established, nor would ever be. Preparing her final article on the *cause célèbre*, Devon wrote tersely: "Guilty or innocent? Only Mr. Beecher and Mrs. Tilton know. And God."

Chapter 24

Before leaving New York, Devon begged Keith to let her see Scotty again. This time he relented and ordered Captain Bowers to take the yacht up the Hudson to his private landing below the estate.

Mrs. Sommes and her daughter, Enid, welcomed their former mistress with joy. The handymen, Lars and Karl Hummel, shook her hand warmly and said how much they had missed her. And though Devon had once resented the country, feeling bored, it now appealed to her as a haven. She appreciated, as never before, the peace, beauty, and seclusion. The old Dutch farmhouse of fieldstone and silvered oak seemed infinitely more beautiful than when she had lived there. The gardens, designed by the planner of Central Park, rivaled any of the castle grounds on the Hudson.

There was another tearful reunion with her son, and another heartbreaking parting. The child, crying and pleading to go with his parents "on the big boat," had to be wrenched from his mother's embrace by the governess. Devon was so shaken that Keith had to carry her aboard. He swore that it would never happen again, and told her so after calming her sobs in his quarters.

"No more visits, Devon. It's worse than the rack. If you want to go there again, be prepared to stay. Understand?"

She nodded, her hysteria subsiding. It was his ultimatum, and she understood.

Devon wondered if she should tell Keith about the conversation she and Reed had had recently, the talk about Reed's efforts against large businesses. But no, that would be unfair to Reed.

"Let's travel together," Keith urged, reluctant to release her, "as far as Philadelphia, anyway. You can always make connections there, Devon."

She was tempted. There had been no mandate from

Reed to return home immediately after the trial, and Devon surmised that his new antimonopoly project involved him. Once he got his teeth into something, he held on as tenaciously as a prairie wolf to a jackrabbit. She feared nothing short of death could dissuade him in his current fight.

"I'd like to, Keith. But a delay might seem suspicious. And you'll be in Washington soon again, won't you?"

"In a couple of weeks, probably. You'll continue as Capital correspondent for the *Record*?"

"Yes," she said. "Mr. Fitch was so pleased with my coverage of the trial that he gave me an appreciation bonus and offered a foreign post. I declined it, of course."

"We'll be docking soon, Devon. One last good-bye?"

She flung her arms around him. "Oh, yes, darling! But don't make it sound so final. It's only temporary, you know. I've always thought the French have a much better expression for partings, especially between lovers."

"Is that our destiny, Devon? All we'll ever be? Lovers, meeting and parting."

"No, no! But for the present . . ." She heard the *Sprite*'s distinctive whistle as they approached the New Jersey harbor. "Kiss me, Keith, and love me! Oh, please, love me always!"

The Capital station was packed with departing passengers. Even men forced to remain in Washington for the summer sent their families to healthier climates. The city was hot, humid, and fetid during this season, and besieged by mosquitoes and flies from the stagnant pools along the canal.

Ordinarily the Grants would already be in Long Branch, but the Whiskey Ring furor had interfered with their vacation plans. The honor of the White House was in jeopardy again, and Mrs. Grant was embarrassed and bewildered. Julia felt that her husband was surrounded by rogues and opportunists constantly taking advantage of him. More than ever the President needed a friendly press, and the first lady did her utmost to ensure it through the columnists who attended her receptions.

Devon rummaged in her large reticule for her key, gave up, and hammered the knocker on the white Georgian-Colonial door. To her astonishment, Melissa Hampton opened it, wearing a lime organza tea gown fluttering with feminine ruffles.

"Oh, Mrs. Carter! When did you get in?"

"An hour ago," Devon replied, entering. "My bags are still at the depot. When did *you* arrive, Miss Hampton?"

"Last week. Daddy and I decided to detour through Washington on our way to Saratoga Springs, to visit the Carters."

"I see." Devon stripped off her gloves. "I'm sorry I wasn't here to welcome you, my dear. I trust my husband has been a genial host?"

"Ever so kind, ma'am. Daddy has been to Washington many times, but this is only my second trip, and Reed—I mean, Senator Carter—has been showing me the sights."

"How nice! And where is the senator now?"

"At the Capitol, with Daddy. The maid just wheeled the tea cart into the parlor." Melissa extended her hand. "Won't you join me?"

The invitation infuriated Devon, as if Melissa were mistress of the house. "Thank you, Miss Hampton. I believe I can find my own way."

Melissa giggled. "How silly of me! You do live here, don't you? Occasionally, anyway. I hear you've been in New York the past six months, reporting that Beecher thing in Broklyn. The papers were full of it, even in Texas. Would you like me to pour, Mrs. Carter?"

"I'll preside, thank you, and let's drop the formality. I think we know each other well enough, Melissa."

"I reckon we do, Devon." Melissa admired the room—the hand-screened silk wall covering, delicate mahogany and satinwood furniture, an exquisite Aubusson carpet. "My, this is a lovely place! And weren't you lucky to find it?"

"Yes, although it doesn't compare to Hampton House."

Another irrepressible chuckle. "No residence in Texas does, honey, except maybe the Governor's Mansion and Hampton Plantation manor, after which it was modeled." Melissa sipped her tea with finishing-school etiquette, appraising her rival over the Spode cup. "Your face healed nicely, Devon."

"No scars, Melissa."

"Nowhere on your body, either, after that awful accident?"

"None."

"Oh, but you must have some slight imperfections?"

Melissa persisted. "A teensy mole or birthmark somewhere? Mother Nature rarely creates a perfect specimen."

"Not even in your case, Melissa? I shouldn't think nature would dare flaw Daddy's little girl!"

Melissa lifted her hair off her graceful neck, sighing as the heavy brown mass fell again. "Lord, talk about Texas heat! This beats any I ever saw."

"Summer is not the time to visit Washington."

"When is the time?"

"Any other season. Most of the entertaining is done in winter and early spring."

"We'll have to come back then," Melissa said tentatively. "The Carters can fete us, and you can write it up for the journals. Daddy's a mighty important man back home, you know."

Devon resented the reminder. Her anger at Reed for not apprising her of this situation was boiling by the time he and the judge returned, and she had difficulty suppressing it in their guests' presence.

"Look who's here!" Melissa cried, jumping up at their entry. "Isn't this a jolly surprise?"

"Sure is," Reed agreed, kissing his wife's cheek. "If I'd known, honey, I'd have met your train."

"A mix-up in communications, apparently." She shook hands with Judge Hampton. "How are you, sir?"

"Just fine, ma'am, and happy you're back. Sure would've hated to leave without seeing you." His arm circled his daughter's waist, nudging her breast. "Ain't that right, sugar?"

Melissa smiled faintly, her eyes on Reed. "Why, missing Mrs. Carter would've been just awful, Daddy! I don't think I could've stood it."

Devon winced at the honeyed barb, wishing she could reciprocate. How long must she defer to this sly little slut, tolerate her sarcasm, cultivate her specious friendship? And why didn't Reed come to her defense at these malicious goadings?

Obviously uneasy now, and seeking to avert a clash, Reed invited the judge to share a drink and a smoke in the library. "If the ladies will excuse us, please?"

"Certainly, dear." Devon forced a gracious smile, but she intended to collar him later.

*   *   *

Judge Hampton insisted on treating them to dinner that evening, at the Metropolitan Hotel. "As a token of appreciation, folks, for your kind hospitality."

"Just repaying a favor, sir," Reed said, referring to the week spent at Hampton House after the boating mishap. "We'll never forget that, will we, darling?"

"Never," Devon murmured, irked at the prompting, certain that Melissa would never let her forget anything the Hamptons had done for them.

"The city looks so pretty at night," Melissa remarked as they rode along Pennsylvania Avenue vis-à-vis in a leased landau. "*When* will Austin get gaslight, Daddy?"

"In a year or so, baby. They're building a gasworks now. But wait till you see New York! There're more lights on Broadway than in all of Washington. I reckon Devon could tell you about that town, seeing as how she used to live there."

"I just had the most scrumptious idea, Daddy!" Melissa fondled his plump, stubby-fingered hand. "Why don't we invite the Carters to go to Saratoga Springs, as our guests? It'd be marvelous fun, the four of us there! You and Reed could go to the horse races and casinos, and Devon and I could ride, play croquet, take the waters together. In the evenings we could dance in the ballrooms!" As they passed a streetlamp, she leaned toward Reed, her globular breasts almost bouncing out of her low-cut bodice. Devon longed to slap her fawning face. "How does that sound to you-all?"

"Delightful," he said, clearing his throat, "particularly since I've never been there, only heard of its many pleasures. But I have a heavy schedule right now, Melissa."

"Couldn't you get away for a week or so?"

"We have no reservations," Devon demurred.

"Daddy can get some," Melissa said confidently, and the judge nodded smugly, convinced of his influence everywhere.

Glancing at his wife, Reed detected a decisive refusal. He hoped it was imperceptible to their company. "We're both disappointed that we can't accept, Melissa. But as your father knows, the state of the Union is anything but healthy now. The economy is in utter chaos. The Whiskey Ring will soon be investigated, and no telling how long that'll last."

"Yeah," Hampton lamented, "the people are getting real finicky about every little government irregularity. Hellfire! Some malfeasance is natural in public office. It's called 'feathering one's nest' and used to be expected. I'm not a Grant supporter, but damned if I don't pity the poor devil now. Seems to me Congress is just stirring up a tempest in a booze barrel!"

"Must we talk politics now, Daddy? I'm famished, and the Metropolitan has good food."

"You've been there before?" Devon inquired.

"Last night," Melissa replied, "Which is why I wanted to go again this evening. They have a fine orchestra in the public ballroom. The Willard and Kirkwood House do too, but I like the Metropolitan best. We haven't tried the Clairmont yet, however. It looks too fancy for us plain Texans, and Reed says it's patronized mostly by New England snobs."

Devon cast her husband an oblique glance, fuming. "It seems you've been entertaining our guests quite well, dear. I hope they'll enjoy this occasion, too."

Although the meal was palatable, the chef was not in the class of Dijon's or the Clairmont's. Nor was the wine cellar as well-stocked. After dinner, Devon waltzed with Reed, but he seemed reticent and preoccupied. They changed partners, and Devon cringed at Hampton's sweaty touch and too-tight clasp. Now and then he tried to press his beefy thighs indecently against her body, and his lascivious smile and obese panting repulsed her. How could Reed subject her to this? And what was he saying to Melissa now that evoked so much lilting laughter? His energy paced hers, and he looked healthy and youthful, obviously enjoying her company. Devon could no longer delude herself. It was not just a young girl's flattering infatuation for an older man. Something deeper had developed between them.

It did not surprise Devon to discover that Melissa occupied the guest chamber across from the master suite, while the judge was down the hall. "Who assigned the sleeping arrangements?" she asked casually as they prepared to retire.

"The housekeeper, I suppose."

"With Miss Hampton's assistance?"

Reed shrugged, removing his cravat. "I wouldn't know, Devon. I wasn't here when they arrived."

"Why didn't you let me know, Reed?"

"You were involved in Brooklyn, remember?"

"Nevertheless, you might have informed me by telegram. I am your wife, after all, and this is my home!"

"Is it, Devon?" Tossing his white shirt on the blue velvet chaise longue, he unfastened his belt and then his trousers. "And how much of a wife have you been to me since January?"

Devon turned away, smarting. "Not much," she admitted. "But you know the reasons, Reed."

"Not all of them," he drawled.

She tensed, facing him again. "What does that mean?"

"Simply that I went to Brooklyn one weekend, only to find my wire hanging on your hotel door! When I inquired at the desk, the clerk said you had left the day before, with some luggage. Where were you, Devon?"

A lie was the only alternative. The truth right now might turn his new antitrust bill into a personal feud. "I was on another assignment."

He smiled cynically. "An interesting one, I presume?"

"Believe what you like," she told him, entering the dressing room to finish disrobing.

She emerged in a nightgown, which he did not try to remove. Nor did he touch her when she got into the fourposter beside him. He lay on his side of the mattress, arms folded beneath his head, gazing at the dancing shadows on the ceiling.

"Any more questions, Mrs. Carter?"

"None, Senator. Snuff the candle."

But the next morning, after he went down to breakfast, she discovered a strand of long dark hair on her pillow. It had escaped the chambermaid, and its source was hardly a mystery. They had slept together before Devon's return, and probably every night since Melissa's arrival, in this or the other room. She could imagine their intrigue, waiting until her father was snoring soundly, the secrecy adding zest to their embraces. How dared he take the bitch in their marital bed? Commit adultery, and then let his wife sleep on the soiled sheets? Enraged, Devon summoned the servant and ordered an immediate change of linens.

She remained upstairs most of the morning, pondering

the situation. This evidence confirmed her original suspicions that Reed and Melissa had been intimate during her absence from Austin last year, and probaby on other occasions, perhaps even while she was confined at Hampton House. And she had denied Keith and herself the same privilege at the Clairmont during Scotty's illness! But what could she do now? How could she accuse him in the face of her own infidelity?

Tying on a large Milan straw hat, she went down to the courtyard with a basket and pruning shears. The men had already left for the Capitol, where many legislators gathered even though Congress was not in session.

"We missed you at breakfast," Melissa said, joining her in the garden and offering to help cut flowers.

"I'm sorry. I overslept, and Reed was too considerate to disturb me."

"Fatigued, honey?"

"I've been on a strenuous assignment," Devon said.

"And I reckon a delicate lady tires easily, at your age."

"Don't worry, Melissa. I'm in no danger of death."

"But you are rather pale and nervous, Devon. Your cheeks could use some rouge. I never resort to it, myself."

Devon snipped a scarlet rose. "No, but you might try some buttermilk and lemon juice, occasionally. It's a marvelous bleach, and your skin seems a bit sallow."

"That's Texas tan, from the outdoors! Our men don't cotton much to frail females, you know. They admire sturdy women who can take the elements in stride without pampering themselves." Piqued by her rival's criticism, Melissa impetuously declared, "As a matter of fact, your husband admires my brunette coloring and robust constitution. He told me so himself!"

"Indeed? When was that, Melissa?"

"Many times! Last night, while we were dancing, was one."

The girl could use some lessons in diplomacy, and a curbed bit on her audacity. "And do you number Senator Carter among your male admirers, Miss Hampton?"

"I think he's the most wonderful man I've ever known!" she stated emphatically. "Moreover, I don't believe you appreciate his many fine qualities. And I'll tell you something else, ma'am. You're going to lose him."

The passionate outburst was an admission of love, and of competition. Devon gazed at her, tapping a long-stemmed red rose against her chin with an equanimity Melissa could not comprehend. "At any rate, my dear, I'm sure we understand each other much better now. Shall we gather a few more bouquets, and then have luncheon? Afterward, if you like, we can go shopping, sightseeing, or riding in Rock Creek Park."

"They have rental stables?"

"Several, and the trails are almost as primitive as those in Texas," Devon said. "Reed and I used to ride them together when he was a journalist here for his father's newspaper."

"But he's not just a reporter anymore, Devon. He's a United States senator now!"

"Thanks to Daddy?"

"I didn't say that."

"You didn't need to, Melissa. I trust you brought some English habits along and can enjoy a sidesaddle, because that's how ladies ride here and at Saratoga."

"You've been there?"

"Oh, yes. It's lovely." Her eyes were suddenly wistful. "You should make part of the trip by steamboat up the Hudson River—the scenery is spectacular. And there's a resort hotel in the Catskill range, called the Mountain House." Her voice ebbed. "The blooms are withering. . . ." She sighed. "We'd better go inside, Melissa."

Chapter 25

After the Hamptons' departure, Reed plunged directly into his work. When he was not in his office at the Capitol, he was in his study. His assistant, Mason Forbes, came frequently to the Georgetown address with books, notes, documents. He was a tall, thin, gangling youth of twenty, with sandy hair, acne-pitted skin, and thick spectacles on a long aquiline nose. A brilliant mind compensated for lack of physical attractions. One day he would surely be a highly competent lawyer. Digging into family backgrounds and corporate structures like a determined archaeologist into historic mounds, he discovered precisely the kind of data that Senator Carter required—accurate, and fully substantiated.

Reed was engaged in preparing his bill, and trying to garner support from the Southern members of his party. Devon's suggestion that he was driving himself too hard and might do well to take a short rest with the Hamptons in Saratoga Springs was summarily dismissed.

"I don't have time to gallivant on vacation, Devon. I promised the people of Texas some action, and I intend to keep my word. I've had some valuable experience since my Indian-affairs bill was killed. I've observed the strategy of both houses. It's imperative to obtain some staunch allies *prior* to the crucial floor debate."

Their relationship was definitely declining. Reed was civil in public and private, and Devon did not divulge her discovery of his betrayal. A few times she caught an expression of rueful yearning in his eyes, followed by remorse, as if he regretted his errant behavior.

He brooded in her presence, especially in the bedroom at night, while she brushed her hair or buffed her nails, and Devon sensed that he was uneasy alone with her. A fortifying drink usually preceded his sexual advances, which were hesitant and sporadic. Did alcohol reduce his fear of rejection, as submission assuaged her guilt? Whatever the reasons, their intimacies had become almost mechanical. He no longer insisted on her nudity or cooperation in the act, too proud to beg favors and apparently hoping she would oblige him of her own accord. His gratification was automatic and assured, hers frustrated. Afterward they quickly separated, as though embarrassed.

Melissa sent long chatty letters from Saratoga, describing the entertainments, fashions, new acquaintances. There were frequent references to her father, which usually began with "Daddy says . . ." "Daddy thinks . . ." "Daddy wants . . ." She still hoped that the Carters would be able to join them, for a brief respite at least.

Devon placed the letters on Reed's desk, to read and answer if he wished, and did not care if he did either. Deeply immersed in his project, he scarcely had time to correspond with his father, a task which Devon assumed, because she liked the Senator and was sorry he was alone on that desolate prairie. Jason wrote that the Indian menace had diminished somewhat in Texas, as the warring tribes moved north of the Red River to the Midwest Plains, as if in pursuit of the cavalry. With the assistance of a hired hand, Jason was successfully homesteading his land and even acquiring additional abandoned plats. Did he still dream of another Circle C Ranch?

As Reed had predicted, Orville Babcock was acquitted in the distillery-fraud trials through the President's voluntary deposition and unqualified belief in his innocence. Grant was especially fond of Colonel Babcock, who had delivered his last letter before Appomattox to Robert E. Lee. He was a family friend and confidant, beloved of Julia and the children. Only three of the numerous conspirators were eventually punished by fines or imprisonment.

The unholy aura of the Whiskey Ring was still hanging over the White House when another dark specter arose. Many honest citizens had wondered how Secretary of War William Belknap and his adored wife, Puss, could live in splendor and spend freely on his mediocre salary. Then came the sordid revelation: certain arrangements had been effected with the frontier traders, who were beholden to the War Department for their appointments. These stores were essentially mercantile monopolies allowing the operators to do business without restraint as to the price or quality of the merchandise—provided Belknap received a substantial

kickback from their profits. A House investigation resulted
in public indignation and impeachment demands, and once
again the President was stunned, humiliated, and bewildered. There seemed no end to the traitors he had chosen
to serve with him.

"Jesus Christ!" Reed swore in disgust. "The country is
on a carousel of corruption! And so even the post trader-
ships are monopolies? Well, that's just more fuel for my
bill."

Devon knew the House of Representatives must formulate impeachment proceedings against Secretary Belknap
before he could be tried in the Senate. It would postpone
the introduction of Reed's ambitious legislation for a while,
perhaps indefinitely. Devon was relieved.   .

Keith was in and out of Washington that summer, conferring with the President, whose aspirations to a third
term now appeared dim. In troublous times Grant invariably summoned his loyal friends for counsel and support,
hoping they would rally around him as had his military
officers during the war. One of his greatest disappointments, however, was his inability to persuade Keith Curtis
to enter his administration in any official capacity.

The lovers met publicly on the social scene, and pri-
vately when it could be discreetly arranged. But the reporters kept a curious eye on Keith's visits to the White House
and the Treasury, and pursued him for statements. His
responses were invariably vague. Persistent or impertinent
queries received a curt "No comment!"

There was one "accidental" meeting in Rock Creek
Park, where they rode side by side for over an hour, not
daring to dismount and embrace, nor even to join hands
across the bridle path, lest a press spy be hiding in the
bushes. The area was still quite rugged, not nearly as well-
developed as New York's Central Park, and a primeval
wilderness compared to London's Hyde Park and the Bois
de Boulogne of Paris.

They managed a couple of trysts at the Clairmont.
Devon admired the architectural changes, especially the
beautiful roof garden, redolent of exotic plants. Plans to
include some rare captive birds had been abandoned, however, lest they remind Devon of the Gilded Cage. Once
they made love on a large terrace lounge under the stars,
and she refused to glance at the lighted Capitol dome,

which signified that Congress was in night session. She knew that Reed, who had a perfect attendance record so far, was at his Senate desk, once occupied by Sam Houston and his own father.

"What's happening in Georgetown?" Keith asked reluctantly, and Devon knew what he meant.

"Not much."

"But you're still living with him?"

"Just barely, Keith. We share the same house."

"And bed?"

She hesitated. "Not really."

"You don't sleep together?"

"Yes, but—"

His jealousy boiled. "Then he still makes love to you!"

"What you would call 'release.' It's not my idea of lovemaking, and I don't think it's his, either. But that's how things are between us now." She told him about Melissa Hampton. "I can't honestly blame him, though. He knew when he proposed that there was someone else in my life, whom we both expected the rites of holy matrimony to exorcise. Some wives do fall in love with their mates after marriage, but I just couldn't. Then along came this pretty young girl, who adores him. I'm inclined to believe it's mutual."

"In that case, you have legal grounds for divorce, Devon. Shall I put an attorney on it?"

"Not just yet, Keith. There might be disagreeable repercussions. He's suspicious of me. It seems he came to Brooklyn one weekend during the Beecher business and found me gone. I was with you, of course."

"I see." He frowned. "That could complicate things. But how much longer must we wait, Devon? How much more time must we forsake, time for each other and our child?"

She could only sigh and shake her head forlornly. Reed had never even broached the subject of divorce. Perhaps he had discussed it with Gore Hampton and been advised to maintain the status quo. Even in morally lax Washington, divorce could be hazardous to a neophyte politician's career. In the rural and religious South, it could mean political oblivion.

Mrs. Grant was strikingly gowned in black satin and diamonds for the traditional New Year's Day reception. Devon attended with her husband, as guest and social columnist. Though the first lady was as gracious as always, there was sadness in her eyes. The anti-third-term resolution recently passed by the House had quashed Grant's hopes of remaining in the presidency. Even the solid North seemed to have turned against Lincoln's general, once the greatest hero in the Union. For his wife's sake, Grant affected relief that Congress had made the difficult decision for him, declaring that he had never really wanted the office to begin with. Julia seemed to take some consolation in announcing that their dear daughter-in-law, Mrs. Frederick Grant, was expecting in June and hoped to bear the child in the White House.

For the *Record* Devon described the Worth costumes of both Mrs. Belknap and Mrs. Sprague, one of silver brocade, the other of emerald velvet trimmed with sable. Charming Puss Belknap did not appear particularly concerned about her husband's troubles, and Kate Chase Sprague, along with many others, was now confident that Roscoe Conkling would be the next occupant of the White House. As always, the diplomatic corps glittered with ribbons, medals, and gold lace.

Devon caught her breath as Keith Curtis arrived, suavely handsome in a formal black suit, tall silk hat, and white-satin-lined opera cape. Unaware that he was in town again, she suspected that he had come primarily to meet her husband. This he did, introducing himself while Devon pretended to be absorbed in conversation with Mrs. Hamilton Fish, wife of the Secretary of State. She could not hear what the two men in her life said to each other, but their handshakes were plainly less than cordial, their expressions grim and speculative, each taking the other's measure. Her pulse raced erratically. She longed to excuse herself and move within range of their voices, but feared her composure might slip.

Instead, she approached the British ambassador's serene and attractive lady, admiring her mauve moiré gown and court jewels, and politely inquiring, "I trust the Queen is well, Lady Thornton?"

"Her Majesty was in excellent health and spirits when last I saw her, Miss Marshall. Oh, pardon me, please. It's Mrs. Carter now, isn't it?"

"Yes, milady. But I still write under my maiden name."

"And how is the women's movement progressing here? Some of our ladies have been on the verge of a feminist rebellion since Mrs. Woodhull's visit last year. Does she honestly believe that she also is a Victoria destined to rule?"

Devon smiled. "It's one of her more bizarre concepts, derived from spiritualism."

"Rather presumptuous. Although she does seem to be an extraordinary person, a magnetic personality, and utterly dedicated to the liberation of her sex. I hear one can become mesmerized during her lectures."

"Mrs. Woodhull is a gifted speaker," Devon acknowledged. "British women have been engaged in the fight for their rights much longer than their American sisters, haven't they?"

"Quite, and Mary Wollstonecraft is revered as their Joan of Arc." Lady Thornton evinced some of her keen wit. "Actually, my dear, I think it began with Lady Godiva."

To Devon's grateful relief, the meeting between Reed and Keith was soon interrupted by the Treasury secretary, who wanted some private conversation with the Wizard of Wall Street. Mr. Curtis and Mrs. Carter nodded and smiled in passing, mere acquaintances. No one, not even the eagle-eyed Olivia, was the wiser. Yet each was intensely aware of the other's presence, and they had to practice rigid discipline. Devon could hardly keep her eyes off him, and Keith was conscious of her every movement. He heard her whispering taffeta skirts and inhaled her familiar fragrance.

Devon approached Reed. "So you finally met Mr. Curtis?"

Reed scowled, grinding his teeth, then spoke in a low tone. "It was his idea, not mine. I wonder if he has somehow gotten wind of my intentions. I've sworn Mason Forbes and the Southern Democrats in my camp to secrecy, but the Capitol cloakrooms are clearinghouses for rumors. I think a Wall Street spy stalks every corridor."

"Well, what do you think of him?" she inquired nonchalantly. "Does he seem a dangerous creature who must be crushed?"

"Like most men in his class, he's courteous, cultured, and extremely intelligent. An aristocrat, and far above the majority of robber barons who operate by tooth, claw, and club. But giving the genteel devil his due doesn't cover up his basic character. He's no less ruthless than his competitors."

"How could you deduce all that in a few minutes?"

"The specimen has been under clinical observation for months, Devon. Forbes discovered that Curtis is a silent partner and major stockholder in a number of American corporations, and that he also controls many foreign companies through loans and mortgages. He's a giant financial octopus. His oil and refinery holdings rival Rockefeller's, and he owns enough railroad and shipping stocks to dictate freight rates on any commodity he chooses. The thing that worries me most is that he can afford to buy lobbyists and legislators wholesale. It's common knowledge that votes are for sale in Congress and that many of the men who enter those hallowed halls with empty pockets miraculously emerge with full ones." Reed paused, objectively contemplating a certain tall, straight, broad-shouldered figure across the Blue Room. "I'm going to cut Curtis down to size!"

Or vice versa, Devon thought, dreading the confrontation.

Chapter 26

Congress reconvened with a full slate of unfinished business to settle before any new proposals could be considered. Both houses joined efforts to repeal the ten-year-old Southern Homestead Act, on which they wrangled for nearly two months. This postwar law, conceived in hostility, was supposedly designed to guarantee every emancipated slave his promised "mule and forty acres." But it had been so grossly abused and unfairly administrated on all levels of government that many disillusioned freedmen complained, "We didn't get no mule, no forty acres, no nothing."

The chief recipients were Northern capitalists, industrialists, and speculators, who acquired vast tracts of virgin timberlands, cultivated farms and plantations and ranches, depriving the rightful owners and heirs of properties belonging to their families for generations. Now the repealed act removed all legal restrictions, leaving the South in worse straits than ever, victimized by the powers in office. Protests and pleas for help poured into Washington.

Jason Carter had warned his son via telegrams and correspondence that this would happen, and eventually came in person to learn what had gone on and why the Democrats had not realized the situation before it was too late.

By then the House had impeached Secretary of War Belknap, and the Senate was preparing for his trial. "I don't have time for postmortems," Reed told Jason in terse frustration. "We have another issue to decide now, Pa."

"Belknap? Goddamn thief," Jason swore lustily, "and you know what we do with horse thieves in Texas!"

"We can't hang him, Pa."

"No, but honest men will vote for his conviction."

"The President supports him, and the Republican faction will exonerate him, as they have every other party cohort," Reed predicted. "He's already resigned his post."

"Yeah, I've been reading about it in the Eastern journals, which contain more bullshit per square inch than Western cattle range per square mile. Belknap belongs behind bars, along with the other crooks in this administration."

"The most powerful senior senators are defending the secretary."

"Especially that fork-tongued Conkling, who champions all of Grant's appointments. Where are the Daniel Websters, Houstons, and Clays?"

"Dead. And only their ghosts remain in the Capitol. Congress and the country are still divided. God knows when they'll be reunited. You can't legislate unity, Pa. But I'm glad you came, and I have something important to discuss with you, once the Belknap business is off the agenda."

"I won't be around that long," Jason surmised. "Got to get back before nature retakes the place or some squatters move in." He shook his leonine head ponderously, the long white mane brushing his shoulders. "Somehow I wish you had stayed in Austin, son, as speaker of the House. They're calling a convention to adopt the new state constitution, and you could have contributed so much to it. Sad to say, you haven't shone very brightly for the Lone Star up here —at least, so far."

Devon glanced up from the novel she was reading. "That's not quite true, sir, or fair, considering the time he's been here. But Reed did help to focus national attention on the frontier Indian problems."

"I yield to that partially, ma'am. Their attacks are only sporadic since Adobe Walls. But the Rangers and vigilantes are due more credit than the United States Army." Jason stamped around the room on his now permanently game leg. "Might I inquire the trouble between you two? Gone sour on each other already, or just too blasted busy to make a baby? I expected a grandchild by now!"

Devon blushed, fingering the book. Reed frowned and shuffled some papers.

Jason arched craggy white brows. "So there is something wrong, eh? I can see it in your faces."

"That's personal, Pa."

"Damn right! You kids are all I've got in this world, for which I'm not long. Naturally, I'm concerned." He glared at Reed, his voice roaring like thunder. "You been straying off the home range? I know the temptations in this territory would try St. Peter himself, but you got the prettiest and sweetest little gal I ever saw, and if you're stupid enough to go roaming in other pastures, just remember the grass is never greener across the fence unless there's a water hole!"

Reed's anger flared. "Hold on! We have a few problems, sure. Every married couple has. But we'll solve them. Put on your hat and coat and take a walk. I've got some work to do."

"With that law student? He's a bright young fellow, all right, but I think—"

"Mason Forbes is my aide, Pa, in the drafting of a bill I've been considering for months now. The one I'd like your opinion on before you leave Washington."

Jason cleared his throat, embarrassed by his meddling. "Well, sure, I'll be happy to oblige. When do you expect Forbes?"

"After dinner."

"Dinner now, is it? In Texas, we still eat supper. What're you paying your scholar?"

"A few dollars a week. Can't afford more on my salary. But he'd work for nothing. Wants the experience. He hopes to be in Congress himself someday, after graduation from law school."

Jason snorted. "Why does every jackleg lawyer want to be in politics?"

"Why not? Every legislature is a body of lawmakers, isn't it? I wish I had more practical knowledge of the law myself."

Devon rose to adjust Jason's shawl, tucking it into his woolly sheepskin jacket. "Better bundle up. It's cold out today, and there's grippe in town."

The old man scowled, though plainly enjoying her attentions. "See how she's mothering me, like I was a six-year-old with a snotty nose! Needs a few youngsters to tend, that's what. Oh, don't snort and paw, son! I've had my say. Got other things on my mind, anyway, which proves I'm alive despite my age." He squinted at Devon. "Whatever became of your charming friend the Widow Winston?"

Devon shrugged wistfully. "I wish I knew, Senator. She seems to have vanished. But I keep hoping she'll appear."

"If she does, give her my fondest regards, honey. I sort of miss that gal."

"Me, too," Devon admitted, kissing his leathery cheek above the flowing white mustache.

"Go to a barber, Pa," Reed admonished. "Some senators are joking about having Buffalo Bill Cody or Wild Bill Hickok in the gallery."

"I think he looks like a biblical patriach," Devon defended. "Don't be late for din—supper, Senator. Cook is preparing some of your favorite dishes."

"Beefsteak with chili and beans, I presume," he said, clamping on his dusty old Stetson before striding out.

A few days later, while checking Reed's wardrobe for cleaning and repairs, Devon accidentally discovered evidence of regular correspondence between him and Melissa Hampton. The clever wench had used her father's stationery, addressed Reed at the Capitol, and marked the envelope PRIVATE. Unable to suppress her curiosity, Devon read enough of the personal and incriminating letter to wonder at Reed's indiscretion in carrying it in his coat.

Certainly she had tried to be more discreet in her relationship with Keith, and was confident that her husband had no inkling that the man he intended to persecute "as an example for other monopolists" was his wife's lover.

The official Centennial ceremonies opened in May, in Philadelphia, with the singing of Sidney Lanier's "Centennial Hymn" and a grand march. Then President Grant, escorted by General Sheridan, threw the master switch on the giant Corliss steam engine, the chief mechanical wonder of the Exposition. It powered all the exhibits in the great Machinery Hall. Many foreign dignitaries were present and marveled over American ingenuity and the inventions of the past hundred years. There were steam-driven locomotives, ships, printing presses. The telegraph and Atlantic cable, cotton gin, sewing machine, gas for illumination—all had been invented during the last one hundred years. Vehicles for public and private transportation as fine and efficient as any that could be imported. Working models of Edison's stock ticker and automatic pen duplicating system, Remington's typewriter, and Bell's telephone, so new and intricate they were considered futuristic novelties.

Separation of the Women's Pavilion from the Main Hall irked the feminists, as if women's contributions were of less importance to civilization. Victoria Woodhull viewed it as belittlement, and Susan Anthony wondered if women were expected to be grateful for any representation at all.

Madame Demorest's pavilion was the most imposing, with four bronze nymphs adorning the classic Ionic pillars of the white-marble-and-plaster building. Lifelike wax images of famous American ladies, as well as of Queen Victoria and the former Empress Eugenie, displayed exquisite gowns on a richly carpeted and decorated stage. Elaborate fluted pedestals supported leather-bound copies of the Demorest publications, and polished walnut cabinets held her famous patterns, innovative corsets, skirt suspenders, shoulder braces, bosom aids, and cosmetics.

Devon interviewed Ellen Demorest for the *Record*, and interviewed the chic and cosmopolitan Miriam Leslie, wife of the publisher of *Leslie's Illustrated Weekly,* and the representatives of Godey's and Buttericks's handsome pavilions. Devon was kept busy indeed.

The *Sprite* was anchored in the Delaware River, its owner sponsoring an exhibit of Curtis Enterprises in Machinery Hall. There were an oil derrick and drilling equipment; a model of the Bessemer furnace, which was currently revolutionizing the iron and steel industries; new materials and methods employed in the engineering of bridges and buildings; and examples of new tools for use in industry, agriculture, and science.

Though the *Record* provided comfortable accommodations for Devon in a good hotel near Independence Square, she spent some nights on the yacht. These were beautiful evenings, in which they renewed their love. Keith had brought Scott along, and they toured the amusement section of the fairgrounds, taking in the sights and games and clowns and puppet shows.

Devon no longer cared much if she and Keith were seen together, or her press associates grew curious. Her marriage must ultimately be dissolved legally. The only worrisome questions were when and how. She knew she would bear the brunt of public censure, inflicted primarily on her sex in such cases. The facts were indelibly imprinted upon her mind: Elizabeth Tilton was a pariah now, living alone in poverty and disgrace—an adulteress excommunicated from her church and shunned by society. But her accused seducer still preached in his pulpit and enjoyed respect. As

Miss Anthony said, "His ersatz martyrdom has made him a hero, if not a saint, in the eyes of his congregation." *Woodhull & Claflin's Weekly* expressed it somewhat differently: "Alas, the flowers have indeed effaced the male dunghill, but the stench will forever cling to the victimized female buried beneath it." Lying in Keith's arms in his stateroom, Devon wrestled with her conscience.

One evening, as they relaxed over her sherry and his brandy, Keith mentioned that he planned to purchase stock in the Alexander Bell Telephone Company, currently forming. Devon tried to dissuade him.

"You have so many interests already, darling. Are you aware that a certain senator is devising a bill to break up the trusts in this country?"

"I've heard a rumor to that affect, Devon. The junior senator from Texas has some mighty ambitions."

"It's more than personal ambition, Keith. He considers cartels destructive to free enterprise and damaging to individuality."

"Do you agree?"

"I don't know enough about the subject to have an intelligent opinion."

"It's worthy of thought. And Carter will garner plenty of publicity and establish his name in politics. But I don't believe his efforts will result in actual legislation. Whatever their faults, corporations are an integral part of the national economy, Devon, and, in some respects, vital to progress. Certainly they absorbed many small firms since the panic, and their methods of merging are not always ethical. Pressure and coercion are frequently applied, and that's wrong. But they are not all voracious monsters gobbling up helpless little vendors, shopkeepers, and family businesses. Scoundrels though some capitalists are, the world would probably still be in the Dark Ages without them. They are responsible for most of the industrial accomplishments currently awing visitors in Machinery Hall."

"You mean there are two sides to every issue, and nothing is ever all black or all white?"

"Precisely."

"Darling, what's going to happen when Reed rises on the Senate floor to denounce you? I think I shall attempt to silence him, by whatever means necessary." Devon frowned.

"No, Devon," he said sternly. "Let him alone. Spare

yourself the humiliation. I can handle anything he throws at me personally, but I don't want you or Scott involved in any way. I won't enter the arena unprepared. I'll have lobbyists, congressional allies, and legal counsel. Let's forget it for now, my love. Did you finish your Centennial article for today?"

"Yes, while Miss Vale was tutoring Scotty and you were busy with business."

"He's delighted to have you aboard, Devon. We're a family now. He looks forward to dinner with us in the main salon, and our tucking him in at night. You know that petition he includes in his nightly prayers?"

Devon nodded, recalling the little boy's plea to have his mother present always.

"He expects it to be answered, Devon."

"It will be," she promised.

"When?"

"I don't know, Keith." She sighed. "I wish I did."

Chapter 27

In mid-June, after much debate at the Republican Convention, Ohio's Rutherford B. Hayes was nominated to head their 1876 ticket. Behind the scenes, Kate Sprague employed all her wiles to comfort Conkling, assuring him that he was still young, there would be another day.

A delegate to the convention, Keith told Devon at a Hayes' victory celebration, "I think Grant was actually relieved to be exempt from the wrangling and turmoil. But Conkling could barely conceal his bitter disappointment and anger at his allies for deserting him. Ulysses had wanted primarily to please his Penelope, as he sometimes calls Julia. They're both fond of Homer's *Odyssey*, you know, and often read it together."

Devon nodded, aware of the Grants' literary tastes. "Well, Mrs. Grant will have some consolation in another grandchild. But how does a man, once idolized, accept expulsion gracefully?"

"The general will manage," Keith was confident. "So will his lady. Their extraordinary courage enabled them to endure the war together."

Later that same month, a terrible fight occurred in Montana, and once again Grant mourned the death of an old and beloved comrade. General George A. Custer and every one of the 265 men of the Seventh Cavalry were killed by Sitting Bull's Sioux Indians at the Battle of Little Big Horn. Flags flew at half-staff. The Colorado Territory petitioned for statehood, and the shocked nation knew the West was not yet theirs. Jason Carter sent his son a terse telegram: "Maybe now we'll get those extra fortifications we've been pleading for, to no avail!"

* * *

With one-third of the Senate running scared in the shadows of the tainted Grant administration, Reed told his aide, "The time is not yet, Mason."

"I wonder if it ever will be, Senator."

Reed shrugged, dubious himself. "I hope I'll have enough political savvy and strategy to know, Mason. All I know now is that this is not it. With most of Congress on the campaign trail, it's difficult to assemble a quorum in either house. But don't get discouraged."

"No, sir. But if you manage to ramrod the Carter antitrust bill through all the various channels, you'll either be immortalized in American political history or a martyr."

Reed removed a cigar from the box on his desk, whittled off the end with a bone-handled penknife, and struck a match. Aromatic smoke filled the office, hanging like a pungent cloud as he puffed and then contemplated the glowing coal. "Neither prospect appeals to me much right now, and I'm beginning to wish I'd kept my ass in Texas." A few moments of silence ensued, while the law student waited for clarification. "Oddly enough, I never really wanted to be anything but a rancher. I went to war because the Confederacy was in trouble."

"The United States Capitol has many exits, sir, but I doubt you'll ever use any. You're a winner."

Reed gave his bony shoulders a brotherly clap. "Thanks for your confidence, Mason."

As the November elections approached, the people were restless, agitated by cold and hunger and unemployment, labor strikes and street riots. The atmosphere favored a change in government leadership, and Tilden received a plurality of almost 300,000 votes. The Republicans refused to concede, however, on the grounds that the returns from four states were incomplete. The election was still in dispute a month later, while President Grant was delivering his Speech of Apology to Congress, blaming his mistakes in office on inexperience and his failures as "errors of judgment, not of intent."

"The people don't know where they stand," Reed told Devon over dinner a few evenings later. "Democracy? Jefferson and Jackson must be turning over in their tombs. The country's falling to pieces, and Congress is doing nothing to hold it together. Still, I hear the Grants' final New

Year's Day reception will be the grandest in the administration's history, as if they were leaving in triumph rather than disgrace. Do we have to attend, Devon?"

"You don't, but it's part of my job."

"And you should be escorted by your husband," he said reluctantly.

"Not unless you want to, Senator, or consider it important to your political image."

"That sounds cynical," he accused. "I realize I've been coasting in the Senate, and ineffectual, but national affairs have taken precedence in both houses."

"I'm not criticizing your performance in the Senate," Devon protested. "Nor do I want to quarrel with you over politics, Reed. I just wish you wouldn't consider me a fool, oblivious of your affair with Melissa. You went to Philadelphia with the Hamptons primarily to be with her, and they returned to Washington and this house for the same reason."

"And where were you, Mrs. Carter? In New York, covering a suffrage convention!"

"The movement thought the centennial year a good time to call attention to their own declaration of independence," Devon explained. "They have been struggling for equality for a century now. As Sojourner Truth declared in her marvelous speech, women of all races are still in social bondage, and her white sisters are no freer from their male masters than their black ones were in slavery."

"Well, I wouldn't consider you exactly dominated, madam. You're pretty damned independent, it seems to me, accepting assignments without even consulting me anymore."

"You agreed that I could work," she reminded him, "and we need the extra income. That's not a criticism of your salary. It's simply a fact."

"Sure, there are men who spend ten times my annual pay in one poker game. Five thousand dollars would be pocket money to Keith Curtis. Forbes learned that he wagered twice that much at the first Kentucky Derby last year, and even more at the second one this year."

Devon maintained a bland expression. She was beginning to dislike Mason Forbes and his tactics, and she wondered how much, if anything, he had discovered about her and Keith. Nothing definite, evidently, or Reed would surely have confronted her with it by now. She had just given him the perfect opportunity, with her reference to the judge's daughter. Or perhaps Mason assumed that, like Caesar's wife, Senator Carter's was above reproach?

A blizzard was raging in Washington on the first day of 1877, and the Carters arrived at the White House, as did many other guests, in a sleigh. Illuminated inside and out, the great mansion was visible even through the thickly flying snow, and Reed muttered, "I bet this place hasn't been so bright since the British put the torch to it."

Fires blazed in every hearth, hundreds of gaslights gleamed in the massive crystal chandeliers tinkling with myriad pendants. Numerous bayberry-scented candles and beeswax tapers in ornate silver, gold, or cut-glass candlelabra flickered and glowed on the marble mantels and polished tables. For weeks Mrs. Grant and the domestic staff had been taking inventory of the house, meticulously cleaning and preparing it for their successors, stocking the pantry and wine cellar, determined that the next mistress, whoever she might be, would not fault the previous one.

The exquisite Blue Room, where the Grants received, was springlike with bright flowers and fresh greenery from the conservatory. A diamond cross set off Julia's jet-embroidered black velvet gown. Daughter Nellie glowed in claret velvet with a long-trained skirt and high basque clasped in front with diamonds. Fred's attractive wife, Ida, had chosen celestial blue silk overlaid with rare white lace, pearl jewelry, and white camellias in her dark hair. The entire Grant family was present, including the newest addition, six-month-old Julia Dent Grant, who was carried in by her nurse in a long mull and Valenciennes dress once worn by her famous grandmother at White Haven.

Snow flaked Keith's hat and caped coat, and Devon, in champagne satin shining like her pale glossy hair, had to restrain her impulse to rush toward him. This time Reed offered no handshake, and Keith ignored him. At Mrs. Sprague's entrance, in buttercup yellow velvet with a queenly jeweled tiara on her titian locks, Roscoe Conkling deserted his political clique to join her. Later, to no one's surprise, they left together in his handsome carriage, a pair of torchbearers lighting their way in the storm. Olivia made no comment about her good friends, who frequently visited in her Maple Square home. And Devon merely mentioned their attendance in her newsletter. Their romance was accepted in Washington society now, and they were always invited to the same social events.

An Election Commission had been appointed to examine the returns of the states in question, so Devon could relax awhile longer. But sometimes it seemed as if she were being deliberately tormented by the delays. She was certain of it when she and Keith met in March, after Hayes had been declared President and quietly inaugurated, with no speech, parade, or ball. On that occasion, Keith suggested that it would be wise if the Carters moved from their Georgetown address.

She stared at him, astonished. "But why? We could never find a place like that on our budget, even if one were available anywhere in Washington."

"Nevertheless, I think you should consider it, Devon."

"You mean living there could have political implications?"

"Yes."

"Oh, dear God!" she cried, clasping her hands to her forehead in sudden comprehension. "You own it, don't you?"

Keith nodded.

"The furnishings, too?"

"Everything. I also pay the custodians."

Devon began to quiver. "How could I have been so stupid? It seemed a miracle. And Carla Winston convinced me that the owner just wanted to help her Texas friends." Her jaw dropped, and she accused, "Mrs. Winston is in your employ too, isn't she?"

"No, she's an operative with a Manhattan detective agency."

"But you hired her services? That's why she was on that stagecoach to Texas!"

"For your protection, Devon. I knew Carla's experience. After all, you were going to a frontier wilderness."

"I had a husband to protect me!" she reminded in fury.

"Indeed? Where was he when the wolves attacked your prairie hovel? Celebrating in a Fort Worth saloon!"

"Reed had just won a state election, Keith. He and his father spent most of that day and night guarding the polls."

"At least she was with you while your male protectors were otherwise occupied."

"That's true," she ruefully admitted. "All true. And we did become close friends, Keith. But now I wonder if her friendship was because she liked my company . . . or was paid for it!"

"Carla loves you, Devon, as a sister. It broke her heart when her mission ended in Washington."

"Which, of course, was 'finding' that impressive address for the Carters, at the incredibly low rental."

"Would you prefer the alternative, Devon? Like the Gothic Arms in New York, which you inhabited once? How in hell could I know your Texas knight would go on a capitalist witch hunt, and begin with me? And what am I supposed to do when we joust in earnest—let him run a lance through my guts?"

"Reed's not a savage, Keith."

"No? I think he'd enjoy devouring the Wall Street tycoons alive!"

"We can't move," she decided quietly. "It's too late, Keith. Surely someone important is already aware of who owns the Georgetown place?"

"It was purchased through one of my trusted attorneys, for the Capital Real Estate Company. But enough persistent probing could reveal my interest in the firm, Devon, and conceivably connect us. You realize this?"

She nodded, sighing. "But leaving now would be even more suspicious, wouldn't it? If it becomes an issue, we'll just have to face it."

"Well, the honorable Senator Carter is not exactly pure Sir Galahad," Keith reminded. "Miss Hampton could be subpoenaed, you know. Hasn't she stayed there while you were away?"

"With her father, Keith. I told you that."

"She didn't sleep with Daddy, though, according to the evidence you found. The servants must be aware of what went on. Our affair could be counteracted with his."

Her brows arched quizzically. "Do you have a spy in the household?"

"Darling, even royal residences have domestic spies, and no doubt the White House has its share. I assure you, if Carter drags private matters into this, he'll regret it."

Devon struggled, dashing tears from her eyes. "Before it's over, there may be a great deal of remorse on all our parts."

"Are you strong enough to take it, Devon? You could avoid the whole ordeal by going abroad."

"Without you?" She shook her head.

"I can't leave the country now, Devon. I can't flee. But you could take some foreign assignments for the *Record*. If you'd rather not go alone, I'm sure Carla could be recalled from her current case."

"No, Keith. I'll stay and take whatever comes. It doesn't matter so much anymore, as long as we keep our love intact. God knows Washington is accustomed to worse scandals than adultery."

His grave frown indicated another worry, however, which she sought to dispel. "Scotty is still too young to understand, Keith. When he's older, this will have passed. The estate is fairly secluded, and I'm sure we can trust Miss Vale to protect his innocence."

But still she paced the floor, wringing her hands, until he halted her as she passed his chair, and drew her down onto his lap. "You'll wear holes in the new carpet, darling."

"You can afford another, Mr. Curtis. Lord, the epithets Reed applies to you! Midas, Croesus, mogul, colossus, chief moneychanger of the Manhattan gold temples, Emperor of Wall Street. And those are some of the kinder ones."

"I don't know why he has singled me out this way." Keith pondered. "But if it's a personal feud, I'd rather settle it in the old tradition."

"By duel? Oh, no, Keith! Dueling is the most barbarous solution to any kind of quarrel."

"Not in the South or West, my dear. And definitely not in Texas, where heroes are made by the fast draw."

"Also killed by it," Devon said.

"Reed's bill will focus public attention on the large dramatic trusts, with me appearing as the villain." He paused, gazing at her seriously. "How will I look to you then? What will you think of me?"

"You know the answer to that, Keith."

Their mouths rushed together, driving all else from mind except physical union, and Keith rose with her in his arms and moved to the master bedroom. Nothing, they assured each other, could alter their love.

Chapter 28

Keith was in frequent conferences with his attorneys, Washington contacts, and advisers. Everyone knew that Keith Curtis, for some undisclosed reason, would be the principal of this unprecedented legislation. Financial and legal support, which he politely declined, was offered from capitalists in Boston, St. Louis, Baltimore, Chicago, and San Francisco.

"Why me?" Keith complained bitterly. "Why not Andrew Carnegie and his iron and steel monopoly? John Rockefeller, who is forcing many oil refiners to join his conglomeration or go bankrupt? The multimillionaire Morgans? Why not the lords of the shipyards, coal mines, textile mills, and factories, who work little children long hours in their sweatshops? When the Commodore died in January, he left an estimated two hundred million dollars, *very* little of which was accumulated honestly!

"Is it because I inherited much of my fortune, while most of the others began largely from scratch? That's one of our cherished national conceptions of a hero, isn't it? The fellow who pulls himself up by his own bootstraps! Never mind the methods he employs on his relentless climb up the ladder, the helpless people he steps on. Just so he boasts of making it alone."

"I know, darling," Devon pacified. "You represent old money, while most of your contemporaries portray the Horatio Alger ideal. It's human nature to envy people who inherit advantages."

"I'm also a Yankee, and Carter is still rebel enough to want my hide nailed to a Southern barn," Keith muttered. "The war impoverished his family, didn't it?"

"Along with hundreds of thousands of others," Devon said, "including mine."

"Well, I can't be held personally responsible for the way things developed, Devon. And because I don't publicize my philanthropies doesn't mean I'm Scrooge. If one of the other so-called moguls builds a library or endows a university, his family makes damned sure the public is aware of it. My benefactions are anonymous. So now I'm an enemy of the people! Promise me you won't attend the Senate hearings? I'd rather you didn't witness any of the action, and now you have the perfect escape in the Grants' announcement of their world tour. I'm sure the *Record* has already offered you that assignment?"

Devon nodded, admitting that it had its attractions, but she preferred to remain in Washington.

"Even as Mrs. Senator Carter?" he asked grimly.

"You know our marital status, Keith. We are no longer husband and wife, not really."

The subject came up again a few weeks later, when Reed insisted his wife accept the *Record*'s offer of a temporary foreign correspondency.

"Why?" she demanded.

"Because it's a great opportunity for you to travel at the paper's expense while doing something you enjoy."

"Oh, come now, Senator! You can speak plainer than that."

He scowled over the documents he was studying. "You're not obtuse, Devon. You understand my reasons well enough."

"Perhaps." She shrugged. "Perhaps not. Are the Hamptons coming on another of their frequent visits?"

Reed replied nonchalantly, "I'm going to Texas to help mend some fences."

"Cut by cattlemen in the nestors' wars?"

Her wit amused him, and he smiled slightly. "Political fences cut by sharp tongues in Austin. I should have attended the celebration in Fort Worth last year, when the railhead reached the town. Some folks, including my father, hinted that I'd contracted Potomac Fever and lost some of my fervor for my birthplace. False assumption, but it's time I returned for a visit."

"And of course there'll be some welcoming ceremonies for Senator Carter," Devon mocked, "sponsored by the influential Judge Hampton and his charming daughter?"

"Along with the governor and other distinguished Texans," he added, rebuking her.

"Texans, prominent or otherwise, don't include your Virginian wife, apparently."

"Goddammit, Devon! I know life in Texas was difficult for you, especially on the prairie, and you can't have much desire to go back. Now you have this marvelous chance for a grand tour, and I don't want to be responsible for depriving you of it. Wire the *Record* and pack your steamer trunks. According to the latest news, the Grants will depart—"

Devon interrupted, "May 17, on the *Indiana.* I'm aware of the Associated Press releases, Senator. Journalism is my profession, after all."

"And in your blood, you used to say," he reflected. "So how could you refuse now, unless the printer's ink has been drained from your system . . . or adulterated?"

"What is the subtlety of *that* remark?"

"None," he denied, "and I'm sorry. But you surprise me, Devon. I recall your eagerness to cover Nellie Grant's wedding and the Beecher-Tilton trial. Naturally, your reluctance now is somewhat puzzling."

She became defensive. "Those assignments were in this country!"

"And dull compared to those you could experience abroad."

She gazed at him, trying to pierce his armor. "I suppose you realize that the Grants' travels are expected to last about two years?"

"You can resign and sail home anytime you wish."

"Thank you," she snapped. "I would do so without your permission, if I pleased. But strangely enough, I thought you might want me by your side on your trip to Texas. You once told me that a wife was a valuable asset to a politician."

"Along with a family, which we never had."

"And is that my fault?"

"I didn't say that, Devon."

"But you implied it! I couldn't help the miscarriage, Reed, nor the fact that I never conceived again."

"You might have prevented the miscarriage by informing me of your pregnancy," he reasoned. "I wouldn't have left you alone on election day, nor allowed you to jounce in that damned old buggy over the prairie to the fire. Maybe you didn't consider the consequences, Devon, or think it important to tell me. Maybe you just didn't love me enough to want to bear my child?"

"Oh!" she cried. "What a cruel thing to say!"

"My apologies. And there's no point in probing old wounds, is there?"

"No doubt Nurse Hampton will be happy to apply her special brand of soothing balm to yours, Senator! However, I once entertained notions about reporting your journey."

"Pa is quite capable of that," he replied brusquely. "Besides, the *Prairie Post* is hardly worthy of your by-line, Miss Marshall."

Had he loved her as much as she once believed? Or was it merely infatuation that had flowered briefly? Without nurturing, the infatuation had simply deteriorated. Attempts at resurrection would be futile—a realization that had apparently come to Reed long before it had to her.

"What of your bill?" she inquired, for he had not mentioned it lately.

"Efforts are under way by powerful Republicans to block its introduction. Rumors are flying thick and fast. I've lost some Democratic support, but gained some, too—especially since Richard Coke resigned as governor of Texas to take a seat in the Senate. I anticipate much conspiracy, conniving, and God knows what else. I may even be assassinated by some maniac or some hireling. Nobody is taking this bill lightly, I can tell you that!"

"And you'd rather I were out of target range?"

He nodded. "I'd appreciate your best wishes, however, before you leave, Mrs. Carter."

"What happened to Miss Marshall?" she quipped.

He shrugged, shaking his head. "I wonder that myself, and I don't know the answer. I'm not even sure what happened to Reed Carter."

Starting upstairs to the room she now occupied alone, Devon pretended not to hear him. Nor did he try to delay her. Surely he was aware that a long separation abroad or elsewhere could constitute abandonment of his domicile, desertion, and grounds for divorce? There would be no need for messy mutual accusations, in that case. Was he concerned about her reputation now, or Melissa Hampton's?

PART IV

Chapter 29

Devon allowed herself some time in New York before the sailing date of the *Indiana,* and Keith put everything aside to be with her and their son at the estate. They named it in a charming ceremony while Scott, Miss Vale, and the domestic staff observed and applauded.

Holding bottles of vintage champagne and river water, they repeated in unison, "We christen this house Halcyon-on-Hudson. Bless it, O Lord, and all who live here. May they always enjoy health, happiness, peace, and harmony. Through your divine grace, may they share love and bliss, faith and unity, fidelity and devotion. Amen."

Then they embraced and broke the twin bottles on the tallest chimney, bearing a cruciform weathervane and towering like a spired steeple in the golden sunrise.

Congress had adjourned *sine die* in March, unusually early, and Reed had left promptly for Texas, where he would remain most of the summer.

Certainly Devon did not miss Washington now. Halcyon in spring with Keith and Scotty banished all else from her mind. She enjoyed the golden sprays of the forsythias, the delicate pink and white blossoms of the fruit orchards, and cut gorgeous bouquets of Persian lilacs and calla lilies for the house. English ivy made the lichened stone walls appear greener. Lars and Karl Hummel tilled the fields, which now produced feed for the animals. Wildflowers, like paints randomly splashed on a broad verdant canvas, brightened the meadows where Keith and Devon rode, their son astride his own mount between them. When once Scott trotted ahead, Devon admired his skill.

"How well he sits saddle, Keith! An exceptional rider for his age. Has he had many lessons?"

"A few from a horse master, but mostly from his father. He's learning to jump hedgerows and fences and will be ready to ride to hounds in a few years."

"In England?"

"Perhaps. But fox hunting is also popular in New England, you know."

That evening, in the midst of their lovemaking, a sudden violent spring thunderstorm struck, intensifying their physical pleasures, reminiscent of the occasion in the Catskill Mountain House when she had probably conceived their child. Devon heard the foghorn on the Hudson as if in a dream, and when finally they separated slightly, she wept quietly on his shoulder, dreading the imminent parting. Profoundly affected, Keith sought to reassure her.

"It may not be long, Devon. Once Carter makes his move in the Senate, we'll begin quiet divorce proceedings for you. He won't contest it. You know he'll be with Miss Hampton as much as possible in Texas, and is probably as anxious to settle this as we are. He might have proposed it himself, except for his public image."

"No matter how short, it will seem forever." She sighed, and Keith silently agreed.

The Childs mansion in Philadelphia was festively decorated for the bon-voyage party. The Grants' intimate and official friends had been invited. Some ladies of the press, who had spent eight years in Mrs. Grant's retinue, were certain it would be a more interesting affair than any which the First Lady would sponsor in the White House. Mrs. Rutherford B. Hayes—or "Lemonade Lucy" as she was called by the press—served no alcoholic beverages and seldom entertained.

Happily for Devon, Kate Field was also scheduled to report the tour and promised to persuade the steward to assign them adjacent or mutual quarters. Devon suspected that the astute journalist had long ago deduced her interest in Mr. Curtis. Miss Field was above petty gossip, however. Her columns dealt with fashion, travel, feminism, significant current events, social commentary, and the supernatural. It was due to her broad range of knowledge and cosmopolitan experience that the *Tribune* had commissioned her to accompany Ulysses and his "Penelope" on their odyssey.

The *Indiana*'s departure from New Castle, accompanied by an armada of naval escorts, commercial vessels, private yachts, and sailboats, was spectacular. There were steam whistles, fluttering flags, volleys of cannon and guns over the harbor. The well-wishers on the pier threw flowers, confetti, colorful streamers, and kisses to the Grants, who stood on deck with their nineteen-year-old son, Jesse.

The years in the presidency had taken their physical toll of the general, deepening the furrows of his face and grizzling his hair and beard. Julia's stoutness had increased considerably; her bosom appeared more buoyant than ever, and her ample hips had no need of the bustle on her dark blue faille travel costume. Silver threads glistened in her glossy black hair.

Although she seemed in exceptionally fine spirits, Devon sensed that it was an occasion of mingled joy and sadness for her, the scandals, blunders, and heartbreak of the Grant administration still poignantly fresh in her mind. Perhaps more than any other first lady, Julia Grant had loved the White House, enjoyed her duties as its mistress, and made more important changes than any of her predecessors. The transformation of the Red Room, scene of their final formal reception, had been entirely Julia's.

The *Sprite* sailed out of New Castle, heading back to New York, and despite all the activity around the *Indiana*, Devon recognized the *Sprite*'s distinctive whistle, blown in the Morse-code signal of "good-bye." She imagined Keith himself pulling the cord, and Scotty standing beside his father.

Chapter 30

The *Indiana* arrived in Liverpool to jubilant cheers on the docks and quays, bands playing the British and American anthems, and banners flying in the brisk breeze off the bay and the Irish Sea. A public holiday had been declared, and a triumphal arch and parade marked the entry into the city. There were an official welcoming speech and a grand banquet—a pattern that was to be repeated through Great Britain during the Grants' visit. Julia had left her native land with mixed emotions, but she beamed at the honors, satisfied that the general was being accorded the esteem he deserved.

"The English people appear to have longer memories than some Americans," she commented to the ladies of the press. "They realize that the Treaty of Washington, settling the grievous differences with the United Kingdom during the War Between the States, was ratified through my husband's efforts. And didn't he also veto the Inflation Bill, promote civil-service reform, work indefatigably for more and better educational facilities for the general population, and for the welfare of the Negro?" She deplored the inclination of people to forget a man's good deeds while dwelling long on his mistakes. "To those who might wonder how a brilliant militarist could have been so misled, I can only reply that Ulysses was loath to suspect evil of a friend, too honest in his own character to consider treachery in an associate."

The Union Jack, signifying that the sovereign was in residence, waved above the Round Tower of Windsor Castle, where the Grants were to be received. But Her Majesty was out riding when they arrived, and the master of the Queen's household escorted them to a large, magnificent apartment overlooking the Great Park. From its windows they could view the hummocky land and stretches of the royal forest. The horse-enthusiast general and his son were anxious to see the Royal Mews, and King Charles II's famous hunting lodge, Cumberland. Julia anticipated strolling in the enchanting royal gardens, along the Long Walk of splendid elms, and the beautiful avenue known as Queen Anne's Ride. Compared to this vast royal residence —one of many—the White House seemed small and humble, even insignificant.

Informed that the court was in mourning for the Queen of the Netherlands, Mrs. Grant was appropriately costumed in black satin with black lace ruching, and her cherished diamonds, many of which were gifts from her adoring husband. Physically she resembled her short, obese hostess, Queen Victoria.

Pretty in youth and during most of her marriage to her beloved consort, the dowager Queen at fifty-eight was fat and frumpish, her puffy cheeks nearly concealing her small eyes, and her triple chins draped in crepy folds over her regally high-collared black velvet robe. An exquisite jeweled diadem crowned her dark, graying head. She chatted pleasantly with Julia about Nellie Grant Sartoris, who had been presented to her at Buckingham Palace in 1872. But Victoria never patronized people whom she considered beneath her station, and she was invariably reserved with "foreign inferiors."

Hung with elaborately framed portraits of royal ancestors, the state gallery chosen for the presentation was no less overpowering than the great Oak Room into which Lord Derby escorted Julia for the banquet. Outside, in the quadrangle, the Grenadier Band played. After the Queen's early retirement, the evening took on more life. There was music and dancing in one of the drawing rooms. General Grant was bested at whist by the duchesses of Wellington and Roxbury. Lord Derby, the Iron Duke, and other nobles entertained Julia. Later, Prince Leopold challenged Jesse at Billiards and lost twenty royal shillings to him. This was the only place in the castle where smoking was allowed, and Grant enjoyed several cigars.

Briefing the American press the next day, Mr. Badeau, the Grants' official secretary and aide who issued all press releases, had to embarrassingly explain backstairs gossip about an unpleasant commotion created by the President's son over the dinner-seating arrangements. Expecting to dine with his parents at the Queen's table, Jesse had refused to sit with the royal household, and threatened to pack his bags and return to London. Julia had remained neutral, but Ulysses had supported the boy. Finally, Victoria conceded, or condescended, and invited Jesse to her table. But afterward she referred to him as "a very ill-mannered young Yankee, spoilt by his parents, who spoke of him as their pet."

On the way to their inn, Kate predicted that the incident would eventually be expanded out of all proportion and significance on both sides of the Atlantic, and Devon remarked that lese majesty seemed to have been invented for Queen Victoria.

"Prince Arthur was accorded every state courtesy and honor on his visit to America," she recalled, "and Jesse is no less a prince in his father's eyes. I admire Grant for defending him. Belligerent and arrogant youth or not, he's the son of a former President of the United States, not a servant to take his meals with the Queen's domestics!"

As soon as possible, the Grants went to Southampton to visit their daughter and son-in-law. And despite persistent rumors that all was not bliss between the couple, they appeared happy and content. Algy and Jesse drove over the pleasant countryside in one of Grant's many gifts, a smart trap and fine trotting horse, and Julia played with her grandchildren.

Admiring the lovely Sartoris home and gardens, Devon asked if Nellie had been to Sussex, the adjacent county.

"Oh, yes, Miss Marshall! Many times. It's some of the most beautiful country in England, pastoral and peaceful, rich in lore. I was telling Mother that they must see the magnificent cathedral at Chichester, and try to take a holiday at Brighton or Eastbourne, on the Channel. Some of Britain's most famous castles and baronial estates are in Sussex, none finer than Heathstone Manor. There are many historic ruins, too. I know Father will want to visit the site of the Battle of Hastings, where William the Conqueror defeated the Saxons. All great warriors do."

"Of course." Devon smiled. Was Nellie aware that some British scholars and historians considered Lee a greater military genius than Grant, and classed Lee as the Wellington of American generals, outranking even George Washington and Andrew Jackson?

* * *

In London again, the Grants were entertained by the Prince of Wales at Marlborough House. The breach between the Queen and her eldest son was common knowledge, and the two avoided each other as much as possible. One of Victoria's greatest disappointments was Edward's failure to achieve the high scholastic and moral standards set by his father, Prince Albert, after whose death the heir to the crown had become a rake and a royal scandal. He had numerous liaisons with theatrical and society coquettes before his marriage to Danish Princess Alexandra, and some were presumed to have continued even afterward. His appetite for food and drink was as prodigious as Henry VIII's, and he enjoyed smoking even more than Grant, averaging twelve cigars daily and at least twenty cigarettes.

Unlike his mother, Prince Edward did not shun publicity, nor become enraged over criticism and satires. The lovely lady journalists were welcomed at Marlborough House like invited guests. The prince's keen eye for feminine beauty more than once admired Miss Marshall's fairness and figure, enhanced by her ivory silk messaline gown and the Tiffany pearls from Keith, which she never dared don in Reed's presence. Devon met the brilliant and fascinating Disraeli, many dukes and earls, the famous English actress Lillie Langtry, and the ardent feminist Julia Ward Howe. Mrs. Grant, in iridescent moiré, renewed her acquaintance with the brocaded and jeweled Empress of Brazil, whom she had feted at the White House, and later remarked that the dinner was as delicious as any of Chef Melah's twenty-nine-course meals. The general was more interested in the painted battle scenes of Blenheim, Ramillies, and Malplaquet, by Laguerre, and discussing the long-past Crimean War, Indian Mutiny, Bismarck, and the Belgian atrocities currently shocking the civilized world. But he shied away from references to the War Between the States, insisting that the country was now thoroughly united.

Mistaken for a wealthy American heiress, Devon was pursued by several gentlemen and might have made some conquests, had she wished to. Instead, she signaled Kate to rescue her from a determined, slightly intoxicated lord, who seemed to think her career was a lark, declaring that "such a charming little creature couldn't possibly be engaged in a serious profession."

But Devon was busier than ever she had been in New York or Washington. Writing and dispatching her reports occupied her late into the night, allowing little time for leisure. She knew only that Reed was somewhere in Texas, and she addressed his mail in care of his father. To Keith she sent cablegrams signed with initials.

Miss Field did not restrict herself nearly so severely. "It's simply not possible to cover every single event for the Grants," she said, "so I've decided to select the most important for the *Tribune* and skip the rest. No wonder clever Olivia preferred to remain on the Washington scene. It's a lullaby, with Lemonade Lucy, and this is a cacophony."

"You're so right, Kate. I seldom get more than five hours of sleep, sometimes less. I must slow down."

"*After* the Pierreponts' reception, darling. We dare not miss that."

"No, indeed."

The notables at the American embassy that evening were too numerous to mention, and Devon had to be selective. The hostess was resplendent in silver lamé and emeralds. The lofty aigrette caught with diamonds in Mrs. Gladstone's hair matched her long-trained cerulean silk gown festooned with Honiton lace. The Duchess of Roxbury wore white brocade embroidered with brilliants and a regal coronet. Mrs. Grant had chosen a spectacular burgundy velvet with an intricately draped overskirt of bright yellow satin, described in the British journals as "gaudy."

"It was a bit much," Kate agreed. "Julia has a tendency to flaunt style rather than develop a flair. Even when she was young and attending my father's theater in St. Louis, she often dressed as if she belonged on the stage. Julia has always loved attention. She's the exact opposite of her shy spouse in that respect."

Nor did Grant share his wife's intense interest in the arts. He had to be coaxed to the opera. They heard Madame Albani sing *Martha* at Covent Garden, and the gracious diva surprised them by concluding her performance with "The Star-Spangled Banner." Tears of pride and joy shone in Julia's eyes as the house gaslights were flared, and the audience stood and applauded the uniformed general. It was an experience she would always cherish.

Many prominent Americans crossed the Atlantic that year, and most landed first in England. Senator Roscoe

Conkling, already thinking of the 1880 presidential elections, participated in some of the public ceremonies for the popular Grants. By more than coincidence, Kate Chase Sprague arrived on the same ship. Madame Demorest and Jenny June, associate editor of her fashion magazine and now a partner in her emporium, stopped in London on their way to France to plan the Demorest pavilion at the next World Exposition, to be held in Paris. Devon's hopes that the *Sprite* might sail up the Thames to the Pool faded when Keith's cablegram arrived at her hotel.

"WILL BE IN SARATOGA SPRINGS FOR SEASON AND RACING MEET. UNITED STATES HOTEL. BEST WISHES. KHC." This was where they had stayed on their memorable trip there, and Devon relived it vividly while lying in her lonely bed that night.

Insomnia made her lethargic the day the Grants went to Epsom Downs with the Prince of Wales. Edward was a great fancier of "the turf," as Englishmen termed all forms of this ancient sport.

"Why not wager a few bets?" Kate suggested, as Devon apologized for yawning. "Rooting for your horse might wake you up."

Devon smiled, thinking of Keith at Saratoga. Were Scotty and Miss Vale with him?

"Are you going on the tour of the manufacturing districts, Kate?"

"Lord, no! And I doubt that even faithful 'Penelope' will follow her Ulysses to every sooty factory and mill in Birmingham, and the grimy Newcastle coal mines. My fans want to read about castles and palaces, royalty, gorgeous clothes and jewels and glamorous galas. I'll gladly defer to the males of the profession on this expedition."

There was no evidence of the depressed international economy at Epsom Downs. One had to go to the city slums to realize it, see the poor and unemployed begging on the streets.

American papers brought distressing news of the bloody railroad strikes in Baltimore, Pittsburgh, St. Louis, Chicago, and other cities, killing and wounding many and forcing President Hayes to muster federal troops. In San Francisco, angry workers attacked the Chinese coolies, whom they considered responsible for the meager wages and abominable construction conditions on the Western rail systems. And there were Indian troubles, too. Reading of the Perce war against the United States in Idaho, Devon wondered if Reed might put aside his antimonopoly legislation and revive his bill calling for more forts in the West and better treaties with all the red tribes.

"I don't know about your editor," Kate mused, "but I'm sure mine expects some reports on a certain highly interesting couple visiting London now."

Kate Chase Sprague had been the darling of the English and European coteries for many years. People adored her charm, wit, style, and penchant for publicity. She was now appearing frequently on the arm of America's best-known senator. Moreover, Mrs. Sprague seemed not only willing but also anxious to have her presence broadcast, and many invitations were delivered to her Claridge's suite.

"My dear, how nice of you to call!" she greeted Devon, and immediately ordered tea. "With so many illustrious visitors in town, it's flattering to be noticed. I saw scores of them while driving in Hyde Park with Mrs. Pierrepont this morning. The Grants are certainly getting their share of attention from the British lions, aren't they? Perhaps short, dumpy Julia reminds them of their Queen."

Kate cared no more for Mrs. Grant than she had for Mrs. Lincoln. She had tolerated President Lincoln's eccentric, vindictive wife only because her father was Secretary of the Treasury in Lincoln's Cabinet. And she bore the Grants, whom she considered ostentatious and even vulgar, because of their position and Conkling's close friendship with them. "All America has read about Jesse's boorish conduct at Windsor Castle."

"He's just a high-spirited youth"—Devon smiled tactfully—"and there was too much fuss over the incident, anyway."

"I was presented to Her Majesty at fifteen, when my father was an Ohio senator, as well as to many crowned heads of Europe," Kate reflected, "and I certainly knew how to act in the presence of royalty. I was received at Buckingham Palace on several occasions during Father's tenure as Chief Justice, and entertained at Continental castles and palaces. Napoleon and Empress Eugenie invited me to a grand ball at the Tuileries. Oh, what glorious experiences I've had!"

And are still having, Devon thought, despite general press knowledge of the Spragues' financial failures. Part of the couple's marital discord centered on Kate's extravagance and obstinate refusal to lower her standard of living. She was now cutting deeply into her own inheritance. She had already disposed at auction of many of her father's valuable possessions from Edgewood, and sold some of her fabulous jewels. She no longer ordered Worth gowns or bonnets and shoes by the score. She had a clever modiste redesigning much of her wardrobe to comply with present fashion edicts, but no one could have guessed this from the clothes she was sporting in London.

Devon smiled and relaxed in the luxurious suite, savoring the delicious tea. Were the English privy to a secret of preparation unknown to others?

"Are you enjoying your visit here, Mrs. Sprague?"

"I always enjoy my trips abroad, Miss Marshall, and this is one of my favorite cities. I'd like to purchase a home in Mayfair, on Grosvenor or Berkeley Square. But that's not feasible at present, so Claridge's is the next best thing. As you know, Senator Conkling is also here—but he's not such a seasoned traveler, and I'm a sort of quasi-guide for him. We were at Westminster Abbey yesterday. The politician is roaming about the Houses of Parliament today. We'll take in some museums and galleries tomorrow. Isn't Prince Albert's new monument magnificent? Roscoe calls it Victoria's Taj Mahal to her beloved consort. Of course, he's most interested in the famous sights, but I plan to show him some of the lesser and humble ones, too, often missed by tourists." She rambled on, talking about many things, gazing at the reporter's idle hands. "You're not taking notes?"

"Mentally," Devon replied. "It's an art Miss Field taught me, and a great memory exercise." Also convenient, as her clever colleague advised, for ignoring trivia.

"I admire Kate Field tremendously. Such an intellectual, the Elizabeth Montagu and Mary Wollstonecraft of America."

"They are among her feminine idols. She wrote their biographies."

"Yes, I've read them. However, I think the Paris salons of the eighteenth century produced the most remarkable feminists, with political and social interests years ahead of their time. Mesdames Récamier and de Staël, for instance. I've been compared to those ladies myself, you know."

Devon nodded, spreading a biscuit with *paté de foie gras*. "How long will you be in England, Mrs. Sprague?"

"About six or seven more weeks, and then off to France." Her expressive gray-blue eyes spoke as eloquently as the gestures of her graceful hands. "Senator Conkling will be there, too. Print that, if you wish."

Her previous discretion was flung to the winds, and her contemporaries could think what they pleased. The Continent had always been broad-minded about *affaires d'amour*.

"I've often wondered why you are not more active in the women's movement, Mrs. Sprague," Devon ventured. "You've always been so closely connected with politics, and if you'd devote your wisdom and energies to promoting the cause, lecturing on suffrage . . ."

"Well, I'm certainly in favor of it, Miss Marshall. But it seems I always have too many other chestnuts in the fire, and I'm afraid some are hot enough to explode on my personal hearth." Pouring more tea, she inquired casually, "Where is Senator Carter?"

"In Texas."

"He doesn't mind your career?"

"Not really."

"It must be edifying, my dear. Doing something useful." She sighed ruefully. "Sometimes I feel rather useless, especially of late."

"Numerous publishers would leap at the opportunity to obtain your services," Devon told her. "You could eclipse every social correspondent in the country, and certainly on the Potomac."

Mrs. Sprague was well aware of her potential in journalism. Earning her own living might eventually become a necessity, but that did not appeal to her. "Senator Conkling and I are attending the Drury Lane Theater this evening," she said. "Will you be our guest?"

"Thank you kindly, but Miss Field and I have other commitments." Devon rose. "I'll be happy to include news of you in my reports to the *Record*, however."

"Please do, and I hope you'll come again, Miss Marshall. But do notify me in advance, if possible, so I'll be available. Roscoe and I have so many plans, and I promised him my undivided attention."

"Of course. Good afternoon, Mrs. Sprague. Give my regards to the senator."

Chapter 31

Gore Hampton was no novice in either political or romantic intrigue. His judgeships had been obtained through some highly irregular methods. In one instance he had eliminated his potential opponent in a deliberately provoked challenge to duel. In another, he had sentenced the man to prison on a false charge of harboring a runaway slave. He had never been faithful to one woman, and had cheated on his bride during their honeymoon in New Orleans, sneaking out several times to the brothels about which men in the gambling houses had boasted. Like the feudal lords of the Middle Ages, he had exercised the first-night privilege to deflower his comely virgin slaves on Hampton Plantation, ordering the husband out of the cabin and having him beaten if he dared defy the master. He had spawned numerous mulattoes who now wandered about the country, neither black nor white, scorned by the black race and exploited by lecherous whites. Hampton had experienced at one time or another most of the deviations listed in the accounts of Sodom and Gomorrah.

He had coveted and intimately fondled his daughter from puberty, but if his wife had realized this, she had been too timid to speak up. Often his hands had slipped into the girl's bodice to caress her lovely budding breasts, or beneath her petticoat, always warning her that she must never let Mother know about the little games they played. Melissa, whose father had always been her favorite parent, vowed silence and kept it. In her adolescence, his lust for her became almost unbearable, and he had to find other distractions. The war was over, his slaves had been freed, and he was also forced to consider his family's future.

Through collusion with a Union colonel during the military occupation of Texas, and later with the carpetbag regime, Gore Hampton had managed to retain his property —hundreds of acres of cultivated cotton fields and hundreds more of timberland—which he leased to friendly Yankees. He moved to Austin to ingratiate himself with the current government. There he built an imposing mansion on the Colorado River, conspired with the prevailing politicians, profited handsomely on his investments, and became one of the wealthiest and most influential citizens in Texas.

When his wife died, Melissa, then his only surviving child, was a beautiful young lady. His obsessive temptations to seduce her drove him to the brink of insanity and suicide. Marriage for Melissa was the proper solution, but he did not regard any of the prospects worthy of her.

Melissa was eighteen when Jason Carter's son arrived on the Austin scene. He was a suitable marital prospect in the judge's mind, but he was already married. Hampton knew his daughter better than anyone else, however. Melissa liked the new speaker of the Texas House, and she knew how to get what she wanted. The fact that she had fallen in love with Reed Carter was a nice bonus. Hampton knew full well what has going on between them. He was aware of their pony-cart ride to the hills above town while Devon Carter was in Washington, and their meeting on the riverboat during Mrs. Carter's recuperation at Hampton House. He was also aware that Carter had bedded Melissa on their visits to Washington. Gore hoped Reed was a potent stud, because Melissa was of his flesh and blood, and had inherited his nature.

Ordinarily, Hampton would have been murderously jealous of any other man getting to his little girl. But he was in his mid-fifties now, mellowing, and a "good piece of tail," as he phrased it, about twice a week, kept him satisfied. Thus, he gave Melissa every opportunity with young Carter. The senator's arrival alone in Austin indicated a shaky marriage. His announcement to the Texas press that Mrs. Carter was one of the few chosen chroniclers of the Grants' world tour was simply chivalry, and probably a cover-up for trouble between himself and Devon.

The official welcoming ceremonies, sponsored by the judge, included an invitation to be his guest at Hampton House. Not surprisingly, Senator Carter accepted. Also not surprisingly, Melissa was in his bed the first night. Hampton chuckled to himself. Daddy's little girl had had hot pantalets since twelve, and possibly earlier. She needed diddling regularly and could get it, with Carter planning to spend the entire summer in Texas. They would travel with Reed to visit his father. No matter that Jason lacked accommodations for all of them; they could stay in Fort Worth without creating any nasty suspicions. Wasn't a motherless girl's father her best chaperon?

"You're so good to me, Daddy," Melissa said one afternoon while Reed was elsewhere on the estate, "and so understanding. I was afraid you'd be angry if you ever found out about us."

"No, sugar, perish the thought. But you should worry about other folks finding out. You realize that, don't you?"

"Yes, Daddy. And we'll be ever so careful, although I'd love to make you a grandpa with him."

"Not yet, Melissa. Not till you're married. You make him take precautions, hear now?"

"Uh-huh."

They did not always take precautions, however. Sometimes Reed forgot, or it was just too good to interrupt, and Melissa would hold her breath for weeks. But nothing happened, which she considered a blessing from heaven. God was on their side. From childhood Melissa had been convinced that nobody, especially not God, would ever really harm her. The guardian angel her mother had believed protected a girl's virtue had been lax in that duty, but the thing that happened with that toad of a boy in her attic, resulting in abortion, had not actually hurt her. The kind old Mexican midwife had given her an opiate, alleviating the pain of the operation performed with a crochet needle. The aftereffects were no worse than menses. But she longed to give Reed children, and looked forward to presenting him with a bouncing boy for their firstborn.

"Do you like kids?" she asked him.

"Sure, and we'll have them, someday."

"I can't wait to marry you, Reed."

"Is that what you really want, Melissa?"

"More than anything else on earth!"

"Well, I don't think it'll be too much longer."

"How much?"

"A year or so, maybe."

"That seems an eternity."

He smiled, kissing her gently. "At your age, I imagine it does. But you're young and strong, Melissa, and will bear fine healthy babies." A twinge of pain crossed his face at the memory of Devon's miscarriage.

"Oh, yes!" she assured him. "And we'll have a baker's dozen. I'm not a weakling, Reed, like *her*. Good thing she didn't come back with you. Thin as she was the last time I saw her, the prairie wind would blow her away like a tumbleweed, or a hawk could scoop her up like a chicken." She always referred to his slender wife as skinny or puny.

The criticism caused a slight tension in his body and coldness in his attitude. "Melissa, you must understand something. I don't like to discuss Devon, especially not under these circumstances."

"But you don't love her anymore!" She waited, hanging on his silence. "Do you?"

"I don't know." He shrugged. "I honestly don't know."

"Oh, Reed, you can't! Not if you love me."

A puzzled frown. "That's what I tell myself, Melissa. But the truth is, I'm not positive. I'm thinking of her now, in fact, wondering how she is."

"If she loved you as a wife should, you wouldn't have to wonder, Reed. She'd be with you."

"That's true," he reluctantly acknowledged. "But she never lied to me about it, or pretended. I think she thought —we both did—that things would be different after marriage. But it takes more than living and sleeping together to have a good marriage. It takes something extra, and we didn't have it, Melissa. We just didn't have it."

"Then you're well rid of her!" Her fingers toyed on his chest, tapping light drumbeats, twirling the bronze hair into ringlets like an infant's, but it was too coarse to hold. "I wish I'd get pregnant, then you'd have to marry me."

His muscles flexed involuntarily. "Don't startle me, Melissa, even jokingly." He eyed her nude body. "Any symptoms?"

"No."

"You'd tell me, wouldn't you?"

"Immediately, darling." Her hands were on him again, more intimately. "Daddy knows about us."

Reed nodded, having suspected as much for some time. "But he doesn't seem to mind."

"Have you ever discussed it with him?"

"Euphemistically, in Washington. I wanted his reaction."

"And?"

"He counseled patience and discretion. When my Senate term expires, the state legislature will have to reelect me, you know." He paused. "But I'm not sure I want to remain in office that long, Lissy. I have a piece of legislation I'd like to get passed. And then I may resign. It's too damned much of a hassle in the Capital arena. I don't see how in hell my father stood it as long as he did. Of course, it was a different atmosphere then, and a good time for the Democrats. And Pa had no extracurricular affairs to distract him or make him feel unworthy of his position."

"Oh, Reed, you're not the only politician with a mistress!"

He laughed shortly. "How well I know that, honey!"

"What do you want?" Melissa asked softly.

"Peace of mind," he answered longingly, "and there's none on that part of the Potomac. Perhaps on the Colorado or the Red River—somewhere in Texas. I'll have to find it."

"I'll help you, Reed."

"I believe you will, Melissa. Eventually."

Accompanied by her father, they enjoyed a delightful holiday in Galveston. The obliging judge spent most of his leisure at the Tremont, the finest of the island resort's hotels, and gambling at a casino on the sophisticated Strand, while the young couple romped happily in the surf and on the long sparkling white-sand beach. Many tourists rented portable bathhouses, and the Hamptons' was a large, expensive model of Romany-striped canvas with a peaked top and bright yellow fringe that fluttered in the breeze from the Gulf of Mexico. Melissa hung up a tinkling glass wind chime and scattered several thick, comfortable cushions on the blanket-floor, as she imagined desert shieks decorated their tents while on a caravan journey.

The port was always busy. Ships flying the flags of many nations called for cotton, hides, tallow, wool, salt, sugar, rice, and sorghum from the numerous warehouses and storage sheds along the piers. Cattle on the hoof went to Cuba. The stevedores loading and unloading the various cargoes were mostly black. Many of the vessels that had formerly delivered slaves to the Texas markets now brought white peasant immigrants of many nationalities. River steamers went to Houston via the Buffalo Bayou, and up the navigable streams to other settlements. Shipowners and merchants had built enormous mansions, some of bizarre architecture, and gardens flourished in the semitropical climate—gorgeous oleanders, magnolias, jasmine, and roses, all the year round. Melissa spoke wistfully of a future summer home there. As she dreamed aloud, Reed gazed at the sails and smokestacks on the horizon and thought of his wandering wife.

The lovers discreetly awaited the evening exodus before strolling on the beach. Seagulls salvaged the edible jetsam and flotsam of the boaters and picnickers, and sandpipers stalked the insects. The perpetual breeze discouraged mosquitoes and gnats. An interlude of violet twilight followed the brilliant scarlet-and-saffron sunset, and then the moon appeared like a luminous silver balloon floating over the Gulf. Fireflies flashed, and the lighthouse keeper hoisted the lantern beacons. Waves broke, edging the shore with lacy white froth. They had built an elaborate sand structure, and Melissa sighed as it crumbled and dissolved.

"Oh, Reed, our castle! The surf destroyed it."

"We'll build another one. There's no limit on them, you know, and they always collapse with the tide. In hurricanes that happens to the real houses here, too—all except those stone fortresses belonging to the wealthy."

"Then we'll make ours a citadel, won't we?"

They frolicked like sprites, splashing each other gleefully, holding their breaths and floating on the huge buoyant swells, never venturing beyond shoulder-depth. There was no one to recognize them. Reed relaxed, forgetting his dignified office, his ambitious legislation, his faraway mate, and surrendered himself to pleasure. Melissa was vivacious and enchanting in the moonlight, the spume glistening on her firm pink body, her dark hair wet and tangled. Once she struck a graceful pose, crying, "Look at me! Venus rising from the sea . . . *with* arms!"

Then she ran out on the beach, giggling, challenging him to pursue her, and he gave immediate chase. She was a swift and agile runner, and Reed was panting by the time he caught her. Her pretended resistance and calculated wriggling against him further stimulated his now ravenous desire. They thrashed together on their discarded clothing, tasting the salt on each other's lips and tongues and flesh, Melissa crying and moaning and biting his shoulder in her ecstasy. Reed lost control in his own thunderous climax.

"Goddammit," he swore afterward, disgusted with himself. "I did it again, Lissy. I forgot again!"

"It's all right, darling. You couldn't help it. I held you."

"I could have broken away, I just didn't want to."

He lay on his back now, one arm under her shoulders, staring at the night sky. "I'm going to get a divorce, Melissa. I want to marry you."

"Oh, my love, that's my greatest wish! But you know what Daddy thinks?"

"Yes, that a divorce would threaten my career. But I've already told you how I feel about that, darling. It's not what I want for the rest of my life—our lives. If a divorce finishes me that way, so be it."

She hugged him. "Remember our first experience together?"

"Vividly. I couldn't resist the temptation then, any more than I could a while ago. In some respects, you were raped both times."

"No, dearest. *You* were seduced on both occasions, and did only what I longed for. I trust you enjoyed it as much as I?"

"You're a wonderful, fascinating girl," he said, "and have given me tremendous pleasure. I know you love me. And I feel the same way, Lissy. If I lost you now, my life wouldn't be worth living. It's as simple as that."

"Simple?"

"Yes. Legally, my wife has deserted me. I don't even know where she is now, except that she's abroad. I'm going to write her, in care of the *Record*, and ask for my freedom."

"You can't, Reed! Not yet. Daddy would blame me. Oh, please, don't do anything rash until after Congress convenes. You've worked so long and hard on your bill. You can't throw it all aside now. Your own father would tell you that, and would hate me for hurting you."

"Not if he knew the truth, Melissa. To my knowledge, he never touched another woman while my mother was alive, nor for a long period after her death. He did have affairs after that, though."

"Including Mrs. Winston?"

"I assume so. But Pa is a bachelor, and Carla a widow. Ours is a different situation. He's also in his sixties, and I'm in my thirties. We could have a long, happy life together."

"We will, darling. I promise you, we will."

Chapter 32

Fort Worth was hardly recognizable. The streets and square, almost idle when Reed had left, now swarmed with traffic and pedestrians. Homes were rising as rapidly as the carpenters could build them. There were new settlers, merchants, tradesmen, lumber mills, packing houses, a large new bank, and several more hotels. Main Street boasted gaslamps, sidewalks, and horsecars.

After the Hamptons were settled in the Mansion Hotel, the finest of the new hostelries, Reed rented a horse and rode out to the Carter homestead, passing hundreds of campers' tents along the way. What he found at the cabin made him regret his long delay in coming home. His father was obviously gravely ill, although reluctant to admit it.

"What's wrong, Pa, and why didn't you let me know?"

"Nothing's wrong, and how in hell could I let you know anything when you roam all over Texas!"

"I was only in Austin and Galveston, Pa. The Hamptons invited me to be their guest in both places."

"And I reckon I know why!"

"Don't presume, sir."

"Presume? I think your interest in the judge's daughter is an established fact, son!"

Reed glanced away at the prairie beyond the now glassed windows, from which Carla Winston had shot a pack of coyotes four years before. Remnants of the fire were still visible in the distance, resembling shadows. Mirages shimmered in the intense heat, dancing like St. Elmo's fire. "I love her," he said quietly.

"Love her? What're you saying? You're married!"

"Not lately, Pa." His features were suddenly grim. "Anyway, that's my business."

"Bullshit! It's your wife's business, and your constituents', and should be Gore Hampton's. Does he know about you and his little girl?"

242

He nodded slowly. "But she's not a child, Pa. And before you start condemning us, you should know the truth. Devon is not my wife anymore."

"She's still Mrs. Carter, isn't she?"

"In name only," Reed muttered. "We've been physically separated a long time, even before she was assigned to cover the Grants' world tour."

"Because you played her false? Began servicing that juicy little heifer?"

"I won't countenance your slurring Melissa Hampton, Pa. She loves me, which is more than Devon ever did."

"Then why did you marry her?"

"Oh, I don't know. Why did Sam Houston marry *his* first wife?"

"I never asked him, and he never talked much about it," Jason replied. "But one thing I do know: when she told him on their wedding night that she didn't love him but would try to be a good wife, he said proudly, 'No, thank you, ma'am. I won't have a white slave.' And he picked up his hat, left, and went to live with the Cherokees in Arkansas."

"Well, I'm not Sam Houston."

"That's a fact."

"I'm not Jason Carter, either."

"That's another fact." The old Senator indicated a packet of letters on the bureau. "Those are from your spouse, who didn't know where to write you. Aren't you interested enough to read them?"

"Not now. Let's close this debate for a while and deal with something else—something more important. You look like a ghost, Pa. You're ailing something fierce. Have you seen a doctor?"

Jason spat, missing the crockery jar he used for a spittoon. "What do doctors know about the human interior? All they know is what they can see and feel externally. Broken bones, boils, swollen prostate—things any veterinarian can treat. Tell an M.D. you've got a burning ache in your belly, and they don't know shit from chocolate."

"Is that your trouble? Dyspepsia?"

"If so, it's the worst and longest goddamn case in medical history! I must've boiled my innards out with bicarbonate and peppermint drops, and swallowed enough bitters and patent panaceas to cure a bloated buffalo."

A rosary, string of medals, and scapula hung on the

bedposts. A picture of Jesus Christ with an exposed and bleeding heart gazed benevolently from the wall. There was also a painted plaster statue of the Madonna on a crude pedestal, a votive candle and shaving mug of wildflowers at her feet.

"Have you converted to Catholicism, Pa?"

"Those are my handyman Miguel's religious symbols, his *encantos.* I didn't see what harm they could do, although they haven't worked any miracles yet." Jason eased himself to the edge of the bed, holding his stomach. "My guts started griping about six months ago and haven't stopped since. The pain is there day and night, relieved slightly when I drink pure cream or eat some lard or petroleum jelly. I suspect it's how a half-dead jackrabbit feels with a coyote gnawing his entrails. Occasionally I have nausea and bloody flux, too. In the beginning, whiskey would slack the pain some. Now it only aggravates it hellishly, as if the devil were twisting a red-hot poker in my vitals. I'm not printing the *Prairie Post* anymore, can't concentrate well enough. Anyway, Fort Worth has a fine newspaper and brilliant editor. It looks like my working days on anything are ending now. I can hardly climb in the saddle, much less ride any distance. As for roping, branding, herding . . ." He lamented these activities with a grave shake of his white head. "Ranching is over for me, son. Actually, I think life is just about over for me, too. I suspect I've got Old Nap—Napoleon's disease."

Reed stared at his father in disbelief. Jason was striving to suppress his pain. Reed knew a weaker-willed man would have been writhing in agony. Old Nap was cancer. Cancer had killed Napoleon Bonaparte. Maybe Jason still had some time, though. Perhaps there was hope . . . or at least some relief for him.

"Don't give up, Pa. You've never surrendered easily, and you'll whip this thing."

"Napoleon didn't beat it. Old Nap was his real Waterloo, chewing his guts out."

"But that doesn't happen to all its victims, Pa. Some survive. There are spas that can help. There's a sulfur spring not far from here."

"Mineral waters are mostly for rheumatism, son. Besides, I've already told you, I've been drinking concoctions of herbs, roots, leaves, swamp slime, pregnant-mare and cow urine, and God knows what else. Might as well have been red-eye for all the good they did. Been to two doctors, even took the train to consult a so-called stomach specialist in Dallas. He diagnosed an intestinal block and prescribed catharsis and emetics. Well, I was desperate enough to take the charlatan's advice, to my regret."

"No improvement?"

Jason snorted, spat again. "His dynamite laxative blew my bowels out, all right, almost literally, and one dose of his empirical compound was nearly fatal. I vomited bile and mucus and blood and got so weak I couldn't drag myself to the privy and had to use the chamberpot. I sent Miguel with an urgent message, and back came bismuth and paregoric . . . and constipation. Then more action from both ends—dysentery and vomiting. For a few days I was shitting and spewing up like those Yellowstone geysers in the Wyoming Territory. Ask Miguel what happened next. I fainted! For the first time in my life! He put me to bed and nursed me. Cooked gruel and soup and fed me with a spoon like a baby. That's one helluva fine hombre out there, and I'd already be six feet under without him."

"Lie down, Pa. Try to rest."

"Reckon I will," Jason agreed, but refused help, insisting he could manage alone. "Not quite that helpless yet. Still not wetting and messing my breeches, like some sick old folks. But I guess that's next."

Reed's boots paced the puncheons, his hands balled in his pockets, brow furrowed. The old rock, which he had once thought indestructible, was eroding—and rapidly. He was mortal, after all. Jason watched him through half-closed eyes, mouth clenched tightly in pain. Jamming on his Stetson, Reed went out to speak with Miguel Navidad, who was now sharecropping the land.

"How bad is he, Miguel?"

"Bad, Senor Reed. *Muy malo!* My *padre* go that way, and I know. El Patrón, he is dying. But he say he want to go with his *zapatos* on."

"And so he won't take off his boots, even to sleep," Reed surmised. "Tell me about your *padre*, Miguel. How long was he sick?

The Mexican leaned on the hoe, calculating on his fingers. Reed counted with him in Spanish to twelve months.

"One year, Miguel?"

"*Sí, señor*. But he no suffer much. Not like El Patrón. We give *remedio*."

"*Medicina?* What kind?"

Miguel shrugged, explaining that his *madre* had obtained the *remedios* from the Mexican equivalent of the Indian medicine man. The ingredients were always kept secret. "No cure Papa, but he go to heaven in peace, like the dove." He pondered a flock of wild pigeons winging overhead; then his black eyes saddened under his *sombrero*. "El Patrón, he no want *curandero*, so I bring him *espíritu* help and pray for the *milagro*. You see?"

Reed nodded. The symbols were visible everywhere in the cabin—talismans, amulets, charms. Jason didn't seem to mind. "*Gracias, amigo*. It'll take a miracle to cure him."

Miguel had a sudden inspiration. "There is a place of miracles in Guadalajara, Señor Reed. People crawl there on hands and knees, and rise and walk again."

Reed had heard of this sacred shrine and the pilgrimages there for over two hundred years. Our Lady of San Juan de Los Lagos was the Lourdes of Mexico. "Guadalajara is hundreds of miles away, Miguel. Pa couldn't travel that far, even if he believed . . . even if he would consent to go. But there is a sulfur spring about thirty miles east of here, where some folks claim to have been healed of various ailments. Of course, the water is not holy or blessed. It stinks, in fact. But if we could get Pa there and set up a temporary camp . . ."

The sharecropper hesitated. "Who will watch this place and work the land, Señor Senator?"

A series of miniature whirlwinds, called Texas *diablos*, were skipping across the prairie, swirling the red dust and loose dry tumbleweeds. Reed watched a few moments, then swore. "To hell with it! Turn the livestock loose, they'll feed themselves. The land will be here forever, Miguel, but Pa won't." He frowned, shaking his head dubiously. "It's worth a try, isn't it?"

"*Sí*," Miguel agreed, crossing himself for luck.

Before sundown that evening, Reed rode into town and found the Hamptons in the hotel dining room. The judge greeted him with a hearty handshake. "Why didn't you bring Jason? We could have had supper together. The food here doesn't compare to the Tremont's in Galveston, but it's edible. Sit down, Reed."

"Thank you, sir, but I'm not hungry." He signaled away

the approaching waiter. "The reason I didn't bring Pa is that he's ill."

Melissa touched his hand comfortingly. "Nothing serious, I hope?"

"It's chronic," Reed said. "Critical, and probably terminal."

"Good Lord!" Hampton exclaimed. "You mean he's been that sick for a while, and nobody knew?"

"Well, that's Pa's nature, sir. His troubles are his own, and he never inflicts them on others."

Hampton laid down his knife and fork on a half-eaten steak. His daughter abandoned her plate.

"Why don't you go upstairs, honey?" her father suggested. "Reed and I want to talk in the saloon."

"Yes, Daddy." Obedient for once in her life, Melissa promptly excused herself. Strangers' eyes, some leering, followed her up the stairway. Miss Hampton was the prettiest young woman in the Mansion Hotel.

Melissa was in bed when the judge knocked on her door later and requested her presence in the adjoining parlor. His recent propriety was puzzling. In the past he had simply entered her room and sat on the bed to converse with her, often holding her hand intimately and kissing her good night on the mouth before leaving. Was Daddy ailing too, or just aging? Her yellow muslin wrapper matched the satin ribbon holding back her dark, tousled hair. She refused to sleep in curlers or a snood. She had a sudden premonition.

"Jason Carter is dying, isn't he?"

"I'm afraid so, baby. Reed and that peon working the homestead want to take him to some mineral springs around here. I suggested the mud baths at Sour Lake, which helped Houston for a while before his death, or that fine spa with twenty-seven different efficacious waters near San Antonio, which General Lee frequented while stationed there. But neither Sam nor Robert had a malignancy. In any case, if I know the old Senator, he won't budge from his home. He'll die right there and would prefer to do it alone."

"That's for savages," Melissa protested. "We can't let him die alone, Daddy. We'll go there and do what we can."

"There's no place to stay, Lissy. I asked Reed. You

wouldn't believe the way Jason's been living on that prairie. 'Primitive' is the only word to describe it."

"Oh, it can't be that awful," Melissa insisted. "After all, Mrs. Carter stood it for a few months, didn't she, before they moved to Austin and Washington? And God knows, she's hardly the sturdy pioneer type!"

"Well, we'll soon know. I've told the desk clerk to order us a buggy from a livery stable for tomorrow morning."

They went, they saw, and Hampton was incredulous. But Melissa felt a grudging respect for Devon Carter, for enduring it as long as she had. She rolled up her sleeves and tried to clean and cook, hampered by inexperience. Household chores were alien to her, and she was grateful for Miguel's assistance. She acquitted herself favorably, however, determined to convince Reed of her domesticity.

Remembering the Carters' old Circle C Ranch and how it compared to this, the judge was elated that he had sided with the carpetbagger regime and retained his wealth. He'd have patronized the devil himself to avoid Carter's present straits! What had loyalty to the Confederacy gotten him? This sorry log pile and a few acres of desolation! The Hampton slaves had lived better and worked no harder. He hoped Reed would use his brains more advantageously. Melissa was accustomed to ease and luxury and would inherit a great fortune. Her dowry would be substantial enough to provide a fine home and every civilized comfort, and Hampton would brook no quibbling on Reed's part that might jeopardize her happiness.

The sooner Jason kicked the bucket, the better for all concerned, Hampton thought. Unappreciative old bastard, scowling at them, when they were only trying to help him.

"When're you planning to take him to those springs?" he asked Reed in the kitchen.

"Never!" Jason muttered from the bedroom. "And you can quit whispering. This isn't a wake."

"That's the spirit, Pa," Reed complimented. "You must be feeling stronger."

"Much," the old fellow lied. "Our guests can return to town now, if they wish. Why don't you escort them, son? Miguel and I can manage quite well. He sleeps with me, right here in this bed. And I don't want to hear any more about hauling me anywhere! I refuse to jounce over that rutted cow trail to that brimstone creek, bathe in that foul water that even cattle dying of thirst shun, or wallow like a pig in some mudhole. I don't care what Houston or Lee or anyone else did. I aim to stay here until I drop down dead. And then I don't want any fancy funeral or long-winded eulogies, and I don't care where I'm buried. Earth is earth, and the prairie would suit me fine."

It would not, however, suit his son, who planned to purchase a plot in Pioneers' Rest, the town cemetery on Cold Springs Road, and erect an appropriate monument. Reed had seen too many forgotten wilderness graves marked only with stone cairns and rotting stick crosses.

As Melissa approached with a bowl of hot chicken soup, Jason said, "Take it to the kitchen table, girl. I'm not an invalid. And set places for everybody, if you can find enough dishes. Miguel wrang an old hen's neck this morning, and you're going to taste some delicious cooking. He makes great rabbit-and-squirrel mulligan, too. Also good bread and tortillas. And his chili con carne is *excelente! Muy caliente,* eh, Miguel?"

"*Sí,* Señor Jason." The Mexican grinned at the others. "El Patrón, he like it hot."

Reed had eaten Miguel's chili and thought it would melt a cast-iron stomach. If his father could digest it . . . But, of course, he couldn't. Not anymore. The compliments were for Miguel's benefit, as Jason's show of strength was for his company's. Pure bravado. His legs wobbled unsteadily, his gaunt features wincing with every step, and the erectness of his once-tall ramrod-straight frame was clearly forced. But the compassionate Mexican refused to embarrass him by offering assistance. He understood the importance of dignity in dying. And he knew, better than anyone else present, how near the end really was for the old Senator. Two weeks, perhaps three. No more.

It was the strangest sensation Jason Carter had ever had. He was floating in space, gazing down upon the scene in the cabin. He recognized himself in the clumsy homemade bed, and his son and Miguel beside him. Reed's head was bowed, hands clasped over his spread knees. Miguel was on his knees, reciting his prayer beads. A blessed medallion was pinned to Jason's old gray nightshirt. Candles flickered on the mantelpiece and at the feet of the plaster Madonna. Jason could see the clock on the wall, its brass pendulum swinging rhythmically, distinctly hear the monotonous ticking. At intervals there was the sound of music—a thunderous pipe organ and a choir singing hymns.

His son spoke. "He doesn't appear to be suffering."

"*No, señor*. The peace of the angels is upon him. I give him *remedio*, like my *madre* give Papa."

"Morphine? The laudanum from the doctor?"

"No, something better. Something the Mexicans and the Indians know about for centuries."

"Peyote?"

Miguel nodded.

From his vantage point, Jason saw the nod. Earlier he had watched Miguel crush the bud from the mescaline cactus in a cup, and then spoon the juice down his throat while Reed was out of the cabin. Peyote, known to the Aztec and Toltec gods. Peyote, reserved for the Indian chiefs and medicine men to use only in ritual ceremonies to communicate with the Great Spirit—and to aid the tribal elders in the final crossing to the happy hunting ground.

After what seemed an interminable suspension, Jason beheld first a glorious light in the midnight darkness, and then a familiar and beloved lady in a white dress. She was smiling luminously and holding out her arms to him. It was his wife, as she had looked on their wedding day. Margaret, bless her dear sweet heart, had come to meet him.

Miguel was sobbing. "He is gone, Señor Reed."

"I know, my friend, I know. But I don't think he minded much, nor did he seem to pass alone. I think God—or someone—was there."

"Someone," Miguel agreed, making the Sign of the Cross and kissing the crucifix of his rosary. "*Sí, señor*. Someone."

Chapter 33

Devon was on the move too much for direct mail from the States to reach her. Even cablegrams were sometimes missed, or long delayed. She was in Scotland when finally she learned of Jason Carter's death through Carrie Hempstead's message from Reed. Devon immediately cabled her condolences, which were then telegraphed to Fort Worth. Devon had been genuinely fond of the old Senator and was pleased by the nice obituary printed in the *Record*. She regretted not being at the funeral. And she grieved, understanding that she would never see Jason again.

Scotland had special significance for General Grant, who was of Scottish ancestry. Bagpipes welcomed them to Granton, home of the clan. But her husband and son shied away from the kilts and tartan that Julia suggested they wear for the Speyside and Craigellache tour, where the family motto, "Stand Fast!" was much in evidence and had often inspired Grant during the American Civil War. After the Provost's greeting at Inverness, they proceeded to the Highlands. To enjoy this ruggedly beautiful region, Mrs. Grant donned sturdy brogans and skirts clearing her ankles. A storm was about to break as they reached Pentland Firth, in northern Scotland, and the misty autumn moors appeared dark and desolate, without the heather and ferns that brightened them in spring.

Partial to the romantic works of Sir Walter Scott, Devon was thrilled by the visit to his home, Abbotsford, in Edinburgh. And the entire party sang "Comin' Thro' the Rye" and "Auld Lang Syne" at the birthplace of Robert Burns, a humble farm cottage near Ayr.

The Duke of Argyle hosted the Grants at his estate in Inverary. The Duke and Duchess of Sutherland entertained them at Dunrobin Castle, where the baronial halls were decorated with hunting trophies of famous sportsmen. But the general, who disliked killing wild animals, declined the Duke's invitation to add his own name to the collection.

When Congress convened in mid-October, Devon was in Paris, where a long letter arrived from Keith. He was back in New York, after a festive season at Saratoga, and Miss Vale and Scotty were in the country.

Keith wrote eloquently of the celebrations of the hundredth anniversary of the Battle of Bemis Heights, and the Burgoyne Centennial: the long parades, some by torchlight, which the boy had especially enjoyed, the patriotic pageants and tableaus, picnics, orations, and entertainments. He had both won and lost money at the races and casinos. He missed her dreadfully, and had read of her father-in-law's passing. His Potomac contacts had informed him of the return of a certain senator from Texas, in the company of a certain judge and his daughter. The trio was ensconced in the Georgetown residence, presumably happy and still blissfully ignorant of its actual owner. He anticipated some Senate fireworks before the first of the year.

Like the Grants, Devon and Kate Field were staying at the elegant Hotel Bristol, on the Rue du Faubourg St. Honoré. Louis XV decor, absolute luxury, impeccable service, and the *Record* was picking up the tab. The city was as gay, exciting, and flamboyant as Janette Joie had described it while Devon was in her employ at the Boutique Chic in New York, except that it was no longer the capital of a monarchy. The Tuileries, where Napoleon III had held court, was in ruins now, burned by the Commune in 1871. The knowledge of this most recent French revolution, in which some twenty thousand Parisians were killed, undoubtedly influenced Grant's refusal to be honored with a military review by the marshal of France. It would be incongruous with his "mission of peace," as he called his visit.

Of the many soirees for the American celebrities in Paris, including the Marquis de Talleyrand's dinner, none surpassed Mrs. John Mackay's elaborate ball. On her vast and seemingly inexhaustible fortune from the great Comstock silver lode of Nevada, she lived in the fashion of continental aristocracy, in a magnificent residence on the Place d'Etoile. Colored lights and flambeaux illuminated the palatial gardens, which rivaled some of the châteaux of the Loire Valley. The servants wore crimson-and-gold livery.

European royalty and nobility were well represented, all in regal raiment: silver and gold brocades hand-loomed in Damascus, Genoese velvets, glistening French satins, radiant Lyons silks, exquisite laces, all *en train*, and dynasty jewels.

Astonished by the hostess's red-white-and-blue creation, said to be striped with genuine rubies and sapphires, Devon whispered to Kate, "Do you believe the gems are real?"

"Definitely. Mrs. Mackay told me she had the costume designed for this occasion, to represent our flag. Personally, I think it's rather vulgar. Why are Americans so ostentatious about their wealth?" Kate paused, as the majordomo announced the Marquis de Lafayette, the Baron de Rothschild, and Monsieur de Rochambeau. "Everybody who is anybody in France will be here this evening."

"Undoubtedly," Devon murmured, feeling like a peasant, as a *comtesse* swept in glittering from her diamond tiara to her diamond-encrusted slippers. "Suddenly I feel deprived, Kate."

"Nonsense, my dear. They're like circus horses sporting their show trappings. You are elegantly groomed. Ellen Demorest and Jenny June agree, and even Monsieur Worth is obviously admiring your gown and coiffure. Haven't you noticed the masculine attention? Some of the noblemen are actually leering. If you wished to make an alliance . . ."

"But I don't, Kate. I have the only attachment I want for the rest of my life."

Kate's delicate gesture encompassed their surroundings. "You're not impressed by all this? The tour is beginning to pall?"

"Oh, no! It's very educational."

"Still, your mind is often elsewhere, Devon. Once you thought my travels as a foreign correspondent were the epitome of excitement—a summit to which you aspired. Well, you're at the apex of your career now, Devon. But unless you relish it to the fullest, all your efforts will have been to no avail."

Julia's disappointment in the United States pavilion rising on the Trocadero grounds was echoed in the hired hack following her luxurious carriage. Although still unfinished, it showed little promise of competing with those of other countries. Great Britain was building a massive structure of many halls. Spain had simulated the Alhambra, and Switzerland built a gracefully spired and belfried chalet.

The Chinese and Japanese had chosen traditional designs. Tunisia would exhibit in a classic mosque, Algeria in a richly ornamented palace.

Was *this* how America would demonstrate her great progress? Devon wondered. After the Philadelphia Centennial, it was a mockery.

She cabled her dismay to Keith, suggesting he use his influence with the commission responsible. He responded: "The outer aspects are negligible. The interior exhibits will never be forgotten."

Her communications with Reed were unsatisfactory, affording little knowledge of his personal activities. His name appeared occasionally in the political columns of the Washington papers, where she read that both houses had observed periods of silence in his father's memory and there had been tributes to him on the floor. Social reporters noted the frequent presence in the Senate gallery of Senator Reed Carter's Texas houseguests, portly Judge Gore Hampton and his highly attractive young daughter, Melissa. The constant chaperonage of Miss Hampton's father averted even shrewd Olivia's suspicions.

Devon, like Jesse Grant, was growing homesick. As the Yule season approached and she saw children gazing at the toys in the decorated shop windows, she longed to return to New York. Instead, with the rest of the Grant entourage she boarded the American cruiser *Vandalia*, bound for Naples.

They arrived on a gloomy day, the splendid bay obscured by hovering gray mists, rare in sunny Italy. Vesuvius was sullenly silent, while a loaf of bread was retrieved from the laval ashes of a Pompeii bakery in the Grants' honor. Archaeologists, at work on the ruins since 1748, had recovered temples, homes, shops, baths, the forum, and an amphitheater. The art treasures fascinated Devon, particularly the gorgeous frescoes in brilliant blues and Pompeian reds. But she found the petrified bodies of people and their pets repulsive. She hoped the sun would shine before they left Naples.

Living out of trunks and hatboxes, her leisure was utilized in caring for her person and wardrobe, preparing articles, and gathering new material. She was currently reading a history of Egypt, where the Grants planned to spend the winter before returning again to Europe. She was also rereading Mark Twain's *Innocents Abroad*, which she felt aptly described her own situation. Her journals were becoming voluminous enough for a future book, which she hoped that Keith would encourage. It would provide a worthwhile project if she retired from journalism, and serene Halcyon-on-Hudson was the ideal place to pursue it. Had it been less than six months since she had been there with the two persons she loved most in the world?

Now the *Vandalia* sailed south, and they celebrated Christmas passing Palermo. Officers and crew had decorated the mast and hatchway with festive greenery and placed flowers and plants in Julia's cabin. The chaplain blessed the dinner of stuffed turkey and plum pudding, and the captain liberated the brig prisoners in the spirit of peace and goodwill. Grant proposed toasts to the loved ones at home, and invited everyone to join in the caroling. Devon's voice faltered on several hymns, and failed completely on "Silent Night."

She glimpsed Stromboli in the rain and listened later to the sailors' superstitions about the dangerous currents and whirlpools surrounding Scylla and Charybdis.

The Mediterranean was so rough on the approach to Alexandria that even the heavy warship rolled in the stormy troughs. The ladies were seasick. Mrs. Grant had to miss the official reception. But Grant, a hardy sailor, attended, and enjoyed a long conversation with one of the guests, Sir Henry Stanley, about his African explorations and heroic search for Dr. Livingstone.

A flotilla of small vessels followed the large, decorated flat-bottomed boat provided by the khedive for the journey up the Nile. Devon, in veiled pith helmet and tinted glasses, thought of Cleopatra and her handmaidens gliding on the great green river in her gilded barge.

She saw the temples and columns of Luxor, Karnak, Thebes, and the pyramids across the Nile from Memphis. She learned to haggle with crafty vendors in the marketplaces and eat strange and exotic foods. She saw tremendous wealth and dire poverty. The abuse of wives and daughters aroused her compassion and anger, as they toted heavy burdens in the streets, beat their laundry clean in the streams, and labored in the fields under the whip of their idle menfolk. "Women's plight," she said unhappily to Kate. "It's the same everywhere, isn't it?"

"For certain classes," Kate said. "Of course, if a sheikh

fancies a young beauty and whisks her off to his harem, her lot is much improved. That is probably every poor girl's dream. But she is still his servant, beholden to his commands, as enslaved as the eunuchs guarding the seraglio. If she displeases her master, she can be banished or killed. Worse, perhaps, her beauty may be cruelly marred, so that she is shunned by other men and forced to live by begging alms in the streets."

In Khartoum, where the governor general was their host, Grant was presented a magnificent Arabian steed on which to exhibit his horsemanship. Julia was fastened to a donkey, with attendants leading and flanking the animal—a comical sight, for she outweighed her mount by fifty pounds and could barely balance herself, even with help. The spectacle amused the men and infuriated the press ladies, to whom it appeared a deliberate indignity. If Julia had misgivings, they vanished in the splendid palace in Cairo, where she lounged on great velvet cushions, waited upon by giant Nubians. Slavery was an accepted way of life to the khedive.

Mrs. Grant shopped in the Cairo bazaars, where she purchased some fine cloth and ostrich plumes, an ivory-spoked fan, tortoiseshell combs, embroidered silk purses, leather gloves. Unaccompanied by an interpreter and unfamiliar with the monetary system, Julia was cheated by the sly merchants, overpaying for everything she bought. And in private, she admitted what Devon and Kate had suspected: she felt disdained and humiliated. "I do not believe our sex is of much importance here," she mused. "Tomorrow we leave for the Holy Land, and I wonder if it will be different there. I am reading the Bible again in preparation, and trust you ladies are, too."

"Oh, yes," Devon assured her.

Kate nodded, although her occult convictions were often in serious conflict with the Bible.

"Ulysses and I hope to arrive there merely as humble pilgrims. But as you know, crowds gather everywhere along our route, and I fear we shall be paraded into the Holy City like a conquering army."

Her fears materialized. The Turkish governor sent a contingent of mounted and armed men in colorful regalia, with banners and bands, and a multitude of cheering citizens to welcome them. Desert chiefs, always interested in great conquerors, had ridden long distances to hail Grant of Vicksburg. Snow had fallen in Jerusalem, and the ladies were bundled in cloaks, muffs, gloves, galoshes. It was a marked contrast to the warm, sunny plains of Sharon through which the caravan had recently passed.

In the Garden of Gethsemane, the ladies clutched blossoms from the Tree of Agony, after which they ascended Mount Olive to view the land of Moab, the Jordan Valley, and the Dead Sea.

As the men rode horses to Bethlehem, the women were again relegated to donkeys, and Kate murmured that perhaps it was fitting, since this was how the Virgin Mary had arrived there two thousand years ago.

"Except," noted Devon, "that Joseph was leading the ass, not mounted on a noble white steed!" Her own jack was balking, braying at Kate's jenny, and the attendants were beating both animals with olive branches.

Hushed reverence prevailed at the site of the Nativity. Greek monks guided them through the Church of the Holy Sepulcher, explaining that the manger in which the Christ Child was born was believed to be in a grotto under the basilica. Had Mary suffered great pain, labored in sorrow? Recalling her own travail, Devon wept despite her attempts at serenity.

Upon landing at Constantinople, international correspondents briefed Grant on the Russo-Turkish War and recent signing of the Treaty of San Stefano, which gave the Russian empire tremendous power in the Balkans. If this concerned the general in the city of the sultans, strategically located on the seven hills of the Bosporus, it did not dampen Julia's enthusiastic enjoyment of the ornate palaces, gilded domes and towers of the mosques, and the incomparable Byzantine Hagia Sophia with its luminous corona of forty windows and splendid interior of marble and gold mosaic. And Devon felt as if she were on a magic Turkish carpet! Here again, Mrs. Grant was spending freely in the markets at exorbitant prices, and her maid was desperately trying to alter her garments to accommodate her ever-expanding girth.

Devon could hardly wait to cable Keith from Greece. Let the King and Queen receive the dignitaries and light the Parthenon in their honor, *she* wanted to know what was happening in New York and Washington. Aware that a *Herald* correspondent was stationed in every major capital of the world, Devon sought the Athens source, introduced herself with her press credentials, and inquired about the States.

"Still there, far as I know," he drawled, resenting her status in the profession, but relenting slightly because of her genial personality. "Major yellow-fever epidemics struck some Mississippi River towns in January and February. Five thousand victims in Memphis and four thousand in New Orleans at the last count. Currency deflation reached its lowest point in history, and the dollar is worth only half of what it was ten years ago."

Sitting down at his desk again, he nonchalantly invited her to be seated on a hard chair, reminding Devon of her first job interview in New York. "Thank you," she said. "Anything new in Washington?"

He shrugged, pushing his hat farther back on his balding head. "That's not my beat. But according to the communiqués, it's the usual haranguing in Congress. A Texas senator introduced a bill against monopolies and is trying to drum up support to abolish them by law, which will happen when hell freezes over, of course. I don't know whether to admire his guts or pity his naiveté."

Devon only smiled at his comments. "Where is the nearest stationer, Mr. Morris?"

"Just around the corner, and all over the place. The Greeks are great ones for writing, you know." As Devon rose, he added snidely, "Give my regards to their majesties."

"I haven't met them."

His tongue clucked mockingly. "You mean you and Miss Field haven't been presented at court?"

"Why should we be? We're journalists, not courtiers."

"Or courtesans," he muttered.

"Beg pardon?"

"Nothing. Just clearing my throat."

"Well, thank you for the information."

"Yeah, sure. And here's a feminist tidbit I forgot. Senator A. A. Sargent introduced the Woman Suffrage Amendment early this year. It got nowhere, despite the ladies' march on the Capitol and the White House."

"Naturally not."

"Mrs. Hayes stayed inside with her knitting. Didn't even acknowledge their demonstration, much less greet them."

He grinned, chewing a Turkish cigar. "That's what I call class, Miss Marshall. A real lady."

Devon ignored the nettling. "Do you like your post here, Mr. Morris?"

"Not much," he replied. "It's nothing but ruins."

"Oh, I know! We encounter ruins everywhere we go, in this . . . and other lands," Devon said blandly, her expression calm. "Could *that* be what attracts so many tourists? Good day, sir, and good health!"

Chapter 34

Although the Senate could expedite legislation more rapidly than the House when so inclined, it could also delay it indefinitely. "You'd think some of our senators had been educated in the Roman Forum," Reed's father had once told him. "And devious and cunning—that's where you'll learn the true definitions of those words, son. Oh, you can introduce and get a bill passed, pronto, if it doesn't step on *any* influential toes, or threaten any important pocketbooks, and provided your party has the majority. You'll find out."

And he did. Although the Republicans dominated the Senate by only three members, they chaired the important committees, caucused in the cloakrooms and the marble halls, and watched out for one another in the chamber. Moreover, most of the Southern Democrats had been sent there while carpetbaggers were still in control of their respective states.

The Carter Antitrust Bill, years ahead of the times in legislative concept, lay on the Senate desk for weeks after its introduction the previous November, awaiting some powerful co-sponsors. It was clear to Senator Carter that he could never steer it through the various obstacles solo. His associate from Texas added his signature, as did a newly elected Louisiana Democrat. But there was much deliberation over which of the seventy cumbersome committees to refer it to, although even the pageboys knew it rightfully belonged in Interstate Commerce. The procrastination served its purpose, enabling the opposition to muster allies and devise counteraction. Reed decided to take the bull by the horns and apprise the press of the devious games of the Senate.

At one point, he told his aide, "Sometimes I think the Fathers of the country erred in the constitutional design of Congress, and did not actually intend it to function in the fashion it often does. There are too many impediments and loopholes in it, especially in the structure of the Senate."

Mason Forbes listened attentively to the proposed strategy.

"Spread the gospel and begin with the liberal journals of New York, where most of the leviathans of wealth and monopoly reside. Circulate pamphets and petitions. Find a paper, no matter how small and seemingly insignificant, that will print a list of the ten richest men in America, headed by the colossus whose worth the *Wall Street Journal* estimates at close to half a billion. The telephone is just a novelty now, but soon it will be a necessity in business and homes. And when Thomas Edison perfects that incandescent bulb he's working on, imagine what electricity will do for the nation—and for those able to finance and control its production."

Forbes nodded sagely. "There'll be a whole new gang of robber barons."

Reed grimaced. "The *same* ones, Mason. Doesn't the cream always rise to the top and become butter for the privileged ten percent, leaving skimmed milk for the rest?"

The course was charted. Forbes set himself up as a freelance reporter interested only in the welfare of the oppressed masses, a sort of press *amicus curiae*, who wished to defend their constitutional rights and prevent their continued exploitation. He hung around the factories, mills, mines, railyards, docks. No wary worker would acknowledge his presence while on duty. But afterward, in saloons, tongues primed with a few beers or shots of whiskey, they poured out their grievances. On invitation Forbes visited a few of their homes and witnessed large families living in incredible squalor—rented shacks of one or two rooms, vermin-infested slum tenements, or pitiful company housing—eternally indebted to their landlords' commissaries for the food and clothing they were forced to purchase on credit.

Forbes provided petitions for the eligible voters to circulate and send in frank-marked envelopes to their senators and congressmen. In the fervor of martyrs and crusaders, some declared themselves ready and willing to make any sacrifices, endure anything to improve their lot. Others urged violence, in anger and frustration. But the majority, remembering the futility and despair of the terrible railroad strikes of the previous summer, trudged wearily home, fell into exhausted sleep, and either forgot the petitions or destroyed them in fear of reprisals. With hungry mouths to feed, they could not risk losing their jobs or being blackballed at a time when work was still difficult to find. Furthermore, the defeated labor organizations had sharply declined in the last decade, from thirty national unions with a fairly active membership of over three hundred thousand, to nine largely sedentary brotherhoods of less than fifty thousand intimidated and cowed members.

"Their voices seem to have been effectively silenced," Forbes reported to Senator Carter. "Moreover, they realize that for every man who would lose his livelihood in active protest, there are twenty or thirty starving immigrants to replace him at less pay and even worse conditions. As for the fairly comfortable and secure portion of the populace, they are content with the status quo. What now, sir?"

"Hit the snakes on the head," Reed replied fiercely. "Buy advertising in the major cities. I'll get a loan from Gore Hampton to finance it, and maybe the agitation will result in enough contributions to reimburse him."

"Yes, sir," Mason said, dubious of the latter, since the people most concerned in the matter needed their money for vital necessities.

Keith was livid when the first advertisement appeared in the New York *Graphic*. Like a roster of wanted criminals, it had his name at the top, and contained information about the Curtis Enterprises which he had thought confidential. But most infuriating was the blatant, unsubstantiated charge that "the millionaires all have high-and-mighty politicians in their gold-lined hip pockets and armies of lobbyists to severely cripple legislation not to their advantage." The languishing Carter antitrust bill, bound in a maze of senatorial red tape and apparently doomed to oblivion, was cited as a prime victim of their sinister power.

Alert correspondents in and out of the Senate press gallery began to take notice. The bold young Texan was often declared "out of order" on the floor and sent to his seat, and there were no fervent patrons or champions to take up the torch. But Senator Carter's determination aroused interest, and garnered publicity. Perhaps the apathetic citizenry would eventually get the message.

His principal adversary, on the other hand, had valid reasons to avoid a public confrontation. Keith Curtis declined to meet with reporters during banking or Stock Exchange hours, although he encountered them on the granite steps of the Curtis Bank. Always, Keith's responses were courteous. "If the senator from Texas will waive his congressional immunity, he will find himself involved in the greatest libel suit ever instituted in the legal annals of this country. Good afternoon, gentlemen. I'm late for an urgent appointment."

His carriage stood at the curb, the footman holding the door open. Several reporters ran alongside the vehicle as it left Wall Street, shouting out questions that were politely ignored, while the occupant appeared to study some papers from his gold-monogrammed morocco portfolio.

Scott was playing in Gramercy Park with several other youngsters, while Miss Vale sat on a convenient bench reading a biography of Mary, Queen of Scots. Keith used his golden key to admit himself to the exclusive enclave available only to the residents of the area, who paid for the privilege.

It was Friday afternoon, the March weather was mild, and Scott was eager to go to the country for the weekend. This was the pattern they had been following since Devon's departure. The household staff of the town mansion, including the stately English butler, were all exceedingly fond of the young master, sometimes increasing the less indulgent governess's tasks. Cook, for instance, was inclined to give him sweets between meals, while the maids allowed him to slide down the banisters or rummage in the attic and basement. They picked up his toys and clothes when he forgot them.

The child ran to his father now, waiting to be picked up, and Keith pretended to puff and stagger as he swung him up to his shoulder. "You're getting too big for this, Scotty. Daddy can hardly lift you."

"Oh, Daddy, you're teasing! Mother is lots bigger, and I've seen you carry her around, climbing the stairs, sometimes even running."

"You have, have you? And what did you think of that?"

"That you like to play with Mommy as much as with me."

Keith smiled. "Well, you're right, Scotty—though Mother and I play in different ways. Adults have different games, which you will eventually discover for yourself."

"Do grown-ups have as much fun as kids, Daddy?"

"I think so, yes. But they also have more problems, son. So don't wish to be out of childhood." Keith set him on his feet and signaled Miss Vale. "Captain Bowers has the *Sprite* ready to sail, Scott. Shall we go to the country?"

"Oh, yes, sir! Right away." Scott paused, gazing up at the tall figure beside him. "I wish Mother could be with us. *When* is she coming back?"

"Soon, I hope," Keith told him.

"I miss her, Daddy. All the time."

"So do I, Scott. But we must make the best of it."

"Because we're men?"

Keith laughed, tousling his curly head. "That's as good a reason as any, son."

Chapter 35

By early spring the *Vandalia* was plying toward Italy again, and the travelers were still going strong. Except for an occasional *mal de mer* on rough seas, Julia had not suffered so much as a cold. And Ulysses, now forty pounds heavier than when he left the White House, appeared ruddy and in excellent health.

Curious about this much-heralded American general compared to Garibaldi by Italian officers of the Risorgimento, King Victor Emmanuel invited them to his palace. And during the long audience with Pope Pius IX, son Jesse idled on St. Peter's piazza pondering the statues of the Bernini colonnade. But the basilica, Sistine Chapel, grotto, and vast museums of the Vatican could only be cursorily glimpsed in the allotted time.

It would require months, even years, to explore the whole city, Devon thought, as day after day the reporters followed their subjects through the Rome of the Caesars: the Colosseum, Forum, arches, columns, theaters, and temples.

For Devon, Rome was the ultimate experience, and she made random jaunts alone during the afternoon siestas, while the shops were closed and the others rested in their hotels. Everywhere were monuments, statuary, galleries, piazzas, gorgeous gardens, fantastic fountains splashing and tinkling. Tossing the traditional coin into Trevi, she wished fervently to return to Rome on a honeymoon with Keith. As in Paris, artists sketched in the streets and exhibited on the sidewalks. She encountered the dark flashing eyes and flirtatious Casonavian smiles of many romantic Latin Rogues. The natives loved music and singing, and not every fine voice belonged to a trained professional. Devon had heard sweet serenades on the Venetian canals during the Grants' tour there and from the boatsmen on the River Arno in Florence. In Milan, aspiring troubadours and divas congregated around La Scala, dreaming of discovery.

After witnessing the opening of the World's Fair in Paris, the odyssey proceeded to Germany. Prince Otto von Bismarck replaced Kaiser Wilhelm, who was recuperating from a recent assassination attempt, as their official host. General Grant was especially eager to meet this renowned warrior, who called at their Berlin hotel in full military uniform and gilded helmet, at sixty-three still the impressive image of the Iron Chancellor. Bismarck arranged a review of the Prussian Guard and a mock battle on the Tempelhof grounds, which was rendered more realistic by a sudden violent thunderstorm. Watching from the canvas shelter, Devon wondered if Grant remembered the rainy, muddy campaign of Virginia in his march on Richmond.

Later that evening, at a brilliant reception at Bismarck's palace, Mrs. Grant met and chatted amicably with his charming wife, Princess Johanna.

Government officials escorted the celebrated visitors throughout their considerable sojourn in Germany: to the famous Baden-Baden spa, the fabled Black Forest, and the grandest of the grand castles at Heidelberg.

In their shared quarters on the cruiser en route to Denmark, Devon and Kate studied their guidebooks on the Scandinavian countries and discussed the schedule. In Copenhagen, the King and Queen were to receive the Grants at Bernstoff Castle. But royal presentations were no longer a novelty, and superstitious Kate was more excited over the prospective visit to Elsinore, scene of *Hamlet*. "You must carry a copy there, to feel the true mood," she told Devon, "and Julia has already announced her intention to do so. Of course, you've seen the play?"

"Oh, yes. Many times. Edwin Booth's Hamlet was the best."

"Well, he's certainly the prince of American Shakespearean actors," Kate acknowledged. "But I think his abilities have been somewhat impaired by his brother's horrible disgrace of the family. John Wilkes Booth's crime is a terrible shadow to live under." She broke off, sighing. "I had thought the Grants would at least have called on Mrs. Lincoln in France. It's tragic the way she's living there now, a pitiful exile, forgotten."

Devon nodded, writing in her notebook. "Mrs. Grant claims she was not aware she was there."

"Perhaps not. But most American tourists know she's in Pau. It seems rather odd that the Grants didn't."

From Denmark they sailed to Sweden, then across the Baltic Sea to Russia. Imperial St. Petersburg was at the zenith of its splendor, splendor reflected in the reception at the Czar's palace. The Grand Duke Alexis, more handsome even than Devon remembered from his visit to the White House, was again bedecked in elegant uniform, ribbons, and gold lace. She wrote a great deal about this phase of the journey. Nowhere on the Continent was there greater pomp. The former first citizens of the United States were treated like royalty, offered the use of the imperial yacht, and Julia accepted everything as their due, rueful that their critical countrymen could not witness the esteem accorded them by powerful foreign rulers.

It was now July, and in Washington Congress was preparing to adjourn *sine die*.

Devon had been abroad one year and had received fewer than a dozen letters from her husband, forwarded through the *Record*, all so impersonal they could have been printed in any conservative journal. It was in Washington newspapers that Devon learned he was on a speaking junket in New England. Later, she would discover that the people and press were listening to Reed Carter.

In Philadelphia, Reed spoke in Independence Square. In Boston, he chose Bunker Hill and the Common. The courthouse grounds of Baltimore; Bowling Green, where George Washington had delivered revolutionary orations to the colonists, was the logical site in New York. He condemned "those monstrous monopolists who control the country, and all its assets and resources. Make no mistake, my friends, these men affect your future, and probably the rest of your days!"

Alert reporters quickly recognized the feud between Senator Carter and Manhattan capitalist Keith Curtis, and pounced on it, exaggerating it. Cartoonists had great fun depicting the Texan in exaggerated Western duds, with tengallon hat, spurred boots, and double-holstered gun belt, shooting from the hip. Thomas Nast drew him more imaginatively, with a protruding tongue in the shape of a pistol rapidly firing bullet-shaped words at the caricatured faces of his targets.

Elder politicians compared his soapbox stumping and

rhetorical technique to his late father's and Sam Houston's, and thought he sounded like a man with presidential aspirations. His opponents planted hecklers in the audience, called him an upstart, and challenged him to debates. Conservative editors asked if Senator Carter was against all monopolies everywhere, or only those in the industrial North. Was he also proposing a limit to the bales of cotton and hay, tons of wheat and corn, acres of tobacco and rice and sugarcane the agricultural South could produce? How many horses, cows, sheep should Texas ranchers be allowed to own? And how had the Confederate veteran felt when he was fighting to protect the Southern planters' monopolization of human beings in slavery?

But liberals and visionaries conceded that Senator Reed Carter had a valid argument: conglomerations, combines, and cartels under various disguises were indeed rapidly expanding and were usurping capital and industry, diminishing initiative to private enterprise.

Devon was in glorious Vienna, writing about Emperor Franz Josef's lavish reception at Schönbrunn Palace, the tour on the Danube in the royal yacht, the special performance of the famous white Lippizaner horses in the Grants' honor, when the *Record*'s ominous cablegram was delivered to her hotel room: REGRET TO INFORM YOU SENATOR CARTER INJURED. EXTENT AND CIRCUMSTANCES UNCERTAIN AS YET. HOPEFULLY NO CAUSE FOR ALARM BUT PLEASE ADVISE OF YOUR IMMEDIATE INTENTIONS. BEST REGARDS. CARRIE AND STAFF.

Devon prepared to leave Europe as fast as arrangements could be made.

She agonized all during the long Atlantic crossing, and tried to divert herself by polishing her article on Austria. But once again, only the highlights of this superb country, unsurpassed for scenery and history, architecture and art, could be touched in an article.

And terrible realizations kept intruding. *Reed may already be dead and buried. Or permanently afflicted.* Was she a poor widow? A wife with a handicapped husband? She paced the cabin floor or stood at the porthole, longing to see the familiar shores.

Exhausted, ravaged by worry, she remained in New York long enough only to clear customs before going on to

Washington. Grabbing several newspapers, she was both horrified and relieved to read that Senator Reed Carter was reported to be recovering satisfactorily from the recent attempt on his life. *Accident?* My God, it had been an assassination attempt! Had Carrie been unaware of the facts when she sent the message, or had she thought to spare Devon?

She found Reed with his left arm in a sling, caucusing in the library with Gore Hampton and Mason Forbes. He seemed more surprised to see her than either of the others.

"Come in, Mrs. Carter! What brings you here?"

After the anxiety Devon had suffered, his affected nonchalance was infuriating. "I heard you were hurt."

He joked briefly about the exaggeration tendencies of the press. "No cause for obituaries yet, my dear."

The judge and Forbes paid their respects, then excused themselves to leave the Carters alone. But soon Miss Hampton appeared, carrying a small tray with a glass of water and vial of pills.

"Time for your medicine," she blithely announced. "Oh, hello there! I thought I recognized your voice."

Reed obediently swallowed the pills, and Devon waited for Melissa to depart. Instead, Melissa parked near her patient, a vigilant nurse and immovable object. Devon tried to ignore her presence.

"Perhaps you'll be kind enough to enlighten me in detail, Reed."

Reed shrugged, smiling grimly. "It's stale news now, happened three weeks ago. As you know, there's nothing deader than yesterday's paper."

Melissa indicated a stack of clippings in a wire basket on the study table. "It made headlines."

"The fact remains that someone tried to kill you, Reed! Who, when, where, how, why?"

"My, my! You *are* a reporter," observed Melissa.

Reluctance to discuss it was apparent from Reed's abruptness. "A lunatic. August 15. In Pittsburgh. With a derringer. And who knows why? Maybe he didn't like my speech, voice, looks. He was a poor shot, fortunately. Just winged me, didn't even graze the bone. Infection set in. I ran some fever for a week or so, but I'm healing now." He glanced gratefully at Melissa. "I had good care."

"Thank you, Nurse Hampton, for ministering to my husband," Devon said cryptically. "Were you there when it happened?"

"Not on the scene, but Daddy was. Reed speaks in some rough sections of industrial towns, where ladies don't belong."

"Did they catch the man?"

"Yes, he's in police custody now," Reed replied.

"Do you think he was hired?"

"No. If that were the case, he'd be dead. Hired assassins who bungle the job can give evidence. In my opinion, he's simply a maniac and belongs in an asylum. You needn't have left your assignment, Devon. The doctor assures me that I'll recuperate without permanent damage."

"We've been reading your articles," Melissa interjected. "It must be real exciting, all that hobnobbing with the high and mighty."

"Yes," Devon agreed. "But I was an interested observer, primarily, not a participant."

"A shame this little incident interrupted your chronicles," Reed drawled. "But you can resume the odyssey, can't you?"

"When and if I wish. The *Record* is currently using an international news service, and Tish Lambeth could substitute for me. The Grants plan to stay in Europe through the winter, visiting Spain and Portugal before sailing for the Orient."

"Oh, well," Melissa said brightly, "then you'll have plenty of time to catch up with them, won't you?"

It was a blunt nudge, and Devon resented it. Why did this tactless wench always make her feel like an intruder in her own home? There was one effective *coup de grâce* at her disposal, but neither she nor Keith could employ it. Still, she longed now to inform Reed that the principal object of his vitriolic statements was also the provider of this charming rendezvous for him and his lady friend.

"Are the Hamptons your permanent guests?"

Her tone created an indignant rise in Melissa's bosom, so enticingly displayed above her deep décolletage. "I reckon you don't know what's going on around here, ma'am."

"I reckon I have a fair idea, miss."

"How could you, when you've been traipsing over the

world for more than a year? Reed's a national hero now! Ballads and poems and stories are being written about him. Folks are saying he should run for president. If he does, Daddy'll manage his campaign, along with Mr. Forbes."

"Now, Melissa," Reed temporized, "you know I have no such intentions. The hysteria of songs and plays does not particularly impress me. Nor can I possibly accept all the invitations to speak at county fairs, labor picnics, turkey shoots, logrolling and hog-calling contests."

"You may change your mind, Senator."

"No," he said emphatically, adamantly. "I think the stumping accomplished my purpose, sparking enough public interest to force some concrete action on my bill." He changed the subject. "Why don't you see about tea? Devon's had a long trip."

"Yes, and she does look all tuckered out, doesn't she?"

Melissa stood, smoothing her sheer chartreuse gown, appearing fresh and youthful despite the late-summer heat. "I'll give Cook orders concerning dinner, too, since we have an extra guest."

She left the door open, but Devon promptly closed it. "So *I'm* an extra guest? There's also a new domestic staff, none of whom recognize me. Miss Hampton is in full control here now, isn't she?"

"A house like this needs a woman's management," he said, "and Melissa's very competent. She ran a much larger one, Hampton House, from the age of fifteen. Furthermore, a senator requires an official hostess on occasion. She's quite accomplished in that respect, too."

"Oh, she's obviously experienced in many things," Devon quipped, "the most important of which you neglected to mention, Senator Carter! She's also your personal mistress."

Reed reached for the liquor decanter on his desk, declining her proffered assistance. Holding the container between his knees, he removed the crystal stopper and poured a neat drink. To her astonishment, he nodded without shame. "We both knew the state of our marriage before you went abroad, Devon. Several times I wanted to request a divorce, but was dissuaded."

"By your judicious mentor?"

"The judge has greater political ambitions for me than I have for myself," he answered seriously. "His daughter, however, wants only our future happiness, in whatever life we choose, separately or together. Naturally, we prefer the latter, which is legally impossible at present."

"You mean politically inexpedient?" She paused, flipping through some of the news clippings, letters, telegrams, and invitations in the basket. "What happened to all your honor, Reed? You've fallen prey to the same moral lapses you used to deplore in other mortals."

He sipped his bourbon pensively. "I've fallen in love, Devon. If that's a crime, I'm guilty. But I haven't succumbed to the vices I've always condemned in public officials. And part of my personal human failure is your responsibility, my dear. Had you loved me, as I did you, another woman could never have breached our marriage. I worshiped you, Devon. You were my ideal of womanhood. I desired a perfect union for us. I campaigned for the Texas House to please you and Pa. I accepted the speakership because I wanted your pride in me even more than my father's. And what happened? Within two months you were on your way to cover the wedding of the daughter of a president we both despised when he was fighting General Lee!"

"As you know, there's no place for prejudice in journalism, Reed."

"No," he agreed with a ponderous sigh. "But there's a definite place for a wife, Devon, at her husband's side. That's what the marital vows are all about, Mrs. Carter. But my mate wasn't always where she belonged. God, how I needed you in Austin! But you were on the Potomac, while I was on the Colorado. In New York and Philadelphia, when I needed you in Washington. And then abroad. . . ."

"The last was at your request," she reminded. And someone else's, she thought wistfully.

Oh, Lord, the irony of it! To think that she had become the legal obstruction that Keith's wife had once been in their relationship. But it was not really she, but the ambitious judge, who was against a divorce. After a long pause she said quietly, "In any event, rest assured that I will not stand in your way. I shall leave this house promptly, thus substantiating legitimate grounds of desertion for your divorce petition. And the sooner, the better."

She was hastily gathering up her belongings as Melissa

reappeared with a laden tea cart wheeled by a uniformed maid.

"You're not staying for refreshment?" Melissa inquired hospitably, as she might of a casual caller who seemed suddenly anxious to depart.

"I'm sorry, no," Devon replied, furious at the quaver in her voice. "I had forgotten another appointment."

"In Washington?"

"New York."

"But that's three hundred miles away!"

Devon glared at her. "I know the distance."

Reed drawled, "You've traveled it often enough, haven't you, madam? And if there's no available seat on the train, no doubt you'll find comfortable accommodations locally?"

Devon did not dare pursue that, suspecting that he was aware of the Clairmont and her acquaintance with the owner. "I've slept on trains before. Best wishes for your continued recuperation, Senator. Good-bye, Miss Hampton. Please give your father and Mr. Forbes my regrets."

Melissa glanced curiously at Reed, who was pouring another drink. "I don't understand."

"Really?" Devon mocked, determined to avoid a scene before the servant. "Well, then, let Senator Carter explain it to you. Just leave my luggage in the foyer, out of your way. I'll send a porter for it." As Reed rose, she said firmly, "Pray don't bother, sir. I'll show myself out. Good afternoon!"

PART V

Chapter 36

Only twice had Devon been inside the Curtis residence on Gramercy Park South, and both occasions were seared into her memory. The first was a presentation of imported Paris lingerie, which she had modeled for the mistress of the brownstone mansion.

Never would she forget her first sight of Esther Curtis in a canopied bed on a queenly dais, with a customized wheelchair nearby. Her garments, the linens, the puffed-and-shirred lining of the tester were coordinated shades of blue satin gleaming against her carefully coiffed raven hair, intense purple eyes, and flawless white skin. She was languid, pale, pampered, exotically beautiful . . . and apparently paralyzed. She impatiently awaited the demonstration and purchased almost every offering. That experience had been a nightmare. The master of the house returned early enough to witness part of the display of intimate boudoir apparel.

Devon's other visit to Gramercy Park had been even more unpleasant. That time she had been unwittingly lured there on the deceptive promise of an exclusive interview with the First Lady while the Grants were guests of the Curtises in New York. Esther had shrewdly deduced the identity of her husband's lovely young mistress. Learning of the fallacious invitation, Keith had been furious and attempted to warn Devon to ignore it, but his message had not reached her in time, and she had walked naively into the trap. President and Mrs. Grant had departed that morning for another destination, and the hideous confrontation with Esther had so mortified Devon as to affect her health for months afterward.

Now, as a cab delivered her to the address after midnight, the gruesome drama recurred lucidly, and her hand hesitated on the bronze knocker. She had spent the evening on the train, dozing intermittently in her seat, reaching the

New Jersey station at eleven o'clock. The Manhattan-bound passengers were ferried across the Hudson River in the light of a full moon.

Unless away on business, Keith should be here now. The elderly butler answered the door in robe and slippers. Now completely gray and slightly stooped, with failing vision, he did not immediately recognize her.

"Is Mr. Curtis in?" she asked.

"Mr. Curtis has retired, miss. Are you aware of the time?"

"Yes, but I think he'll see me, if you'll be kind enough to give him my name: Devon Marshall."

Recognition dawned, and Hadley apologized for forgetting his spectacles. "Come in, please, Miss Marshall. I'll tell Mr. Curtis you're here."

"Thank you, Hadley."

Devon waited in the gaslighted foyer, and within minutes Keith was embracing her. "When did you land, darling?"

She tried to speak and lost her voice. She shook her head mutely, burst into tears, and collapsed against him. Keith carried her to his rooms, sorry he had dismissed Hadley so perfunctorily. Placing Devon on his bed, he chafed her wrists, tapped her cheeks gently, repeated her name softly. As she revived, opening her eyes and smiling at him, he braced her shoulders with one arm and coaxed some cognac down her throat. Satisfied that she was conscious, he propped her against the pillows and blotted her tearstained face with a towel.

"I received your cablegram, Devon, but you didn't state the ship or arrival date. I'd have met you, of course."

"I didn't know the details at the time," she explained. "We docked before dawn yesterday, and I went immediately to Washington."

He stroked her hand. "The wound wasn't serious. Has there been a change?"

"No, except for the better."

"Then why did you go there first?"

"I . . . I thought it was my duty."

Her poignant expression enlightened him more than her voice, and he urged her to sip more brandy. "You're exhausted, Devon. How long since you've slept and eaten?"

"I napped an hour or so on the train, but haven't had a full meal since Carrie's cable. I was in Vienna then. I ate lightly on the voyage, afraid my nervousness would make me queasy."

"I'll wake a maid and order something for you."

Her hand stayed his on the bell cord. "Not yet, Keith. My stomach is still in knots. Don't wake anyone. Is Scotty here?"

"No. I've been leaving him at Halcyon since . . . well, for the past few months. How do you feel now?"

"Better, just being with you again."

"Do you want to tell me what happened in Washington?"

Devon nodded, chewing her lower lip. "They're living in the house together. Her father is with them, of course, so it appears quite proper. But there's an entirely new domestic staff. Miss Hampton is running the place as if she were its mistress. Reed was surprised to see me, and a bit sheepish. But not too embarrassed to discuss the matter frankly and broach divorce. But I'm sure you realize the effect of the assassination attempt on his political career?"

"Oh, yes," he said gravely. "The press has had a jolly good time with both of us for months now. Congress will have to reckon with his bill now. But the legislative process can be slow and tedious. It may take years, even decades."

Devon sighed. "I'm inclined to believe that's Gore Hampton's plan, Keith—to keep the issue alive until the next Democratic convention. By then, Reed's name will be a household word. He could be a strong candidate for the presidency."

"Oh, yes," Keith conceded. "Champion of the poor and oppressed, defender of the rights of the common man. That lunatic made a hero of him!" He frowned, pacing now, hands balled into fists in his dressing-gown pockets. "But maybe the assassin wasn't so crazy after all, when he took that shot. Maybe he had no intention of killing him."

Devon stared at him, nonplussed. Was she hearing him correctly? "What are you saying, Keith?"

He paused, profiled in the bureau mirror. "There may be a reason for what happened, Devon. A method to the so-called madness."

She shook her head vehemently. "Oh, no, Keith! Reed would never be involved in a conspiracy like that!"

"I don't think so, either, Devon. But it might have been instigated without his consent. Because a man is basically honest doesn't say the same about all his associates. President Grant was surrounded by thieves and scoundrels who betrayed him. Politicians often shift loyalty, using one another to their own advantage."

He took a deep breath and continued, "I've had Gore Hampton investigated, and he's hardly a sterling character. Scruples have never hampered his personal ambitions. He has ruined many people, friends and foes alike, when they dared to oppose him. He's a born political boss. And what better way to prove his power than to rocket a fairly unknown Texas senator into the White House?"

"What better way?" Devon agreed. "But if he hired someone to risk Reed's life just for publicity, the hireling could implicate the judge. He'll be brought to trial, won't he?"

Her sophistication and naiveté were often paradoxical. "My adorable innocent! You don't imagine that Hampton would be foolish enough to arrange it *personally*, do you? A few thousand dollars could buy dozens of intermediaries. And if that's the case, the trigger man will never go to court. He will be expediently eliminated, through an accident or 'suicide.' Mark my words, Devon. The poor devil in that Pittsburgh dungeon is doomed to death, one way or another."

Devon would not put it past Gore Hampton. He was capable of any treachery. In a monarchy, he would either be the primary power behind the throne or the principal conspirator intriguing to overthrow it. In a democracy, he could manipulate the presidency. Thank God Reed had no aspirations in that direction—or did he?

Keith was remorseful. "I've upset you, and you were disturbed enough. I'm sorry, Devon. This is just a theory and I have no proof. I could be wrong. I hope I am. I regret the shooting and am glad it wasn't fatal, but it hasn't changed my personal feelings toward Carter."

"Interesting," Devon concurred, confident that Reed would ultimately succeed. Whatever his faults and weaknesses, he was not stupid, greedy, or ruthlessly ambitious. And whatever odious game the judge was playing, his daughter was the stake, and Daddy surely would not compromise or destroy the man his little girl loved and longed to marry.

The hall clock chimed three, its musical tones echoing through the silent house. "It's almost dawn," Keith said, pacing again. "I'll dress and go downstairs."

"Is that what you want to do?"

"Devon, you're tired and need some rest. I should have put you in a guest room."

A slight smile. "Why didn't you?"

"Good question. I acted impulsively, the way you did."

"I was confused, Keith. I had my key to the Clairmont and could have spent the night there. But I just had to get out of Washington. Did I do wrong?"

"Of course not, darling. I'm happy you came directly to me."

"Love brought me," she murmured.

He approached her, smiling tentatively. "Are these accommodations to your liking, ma'am? And shall I go or stay?"

She smiled and patted the mattress, then extended her arms.

Chapter 37

When she awoke, the sun was up. Keith was gone, but a perfect red rosebud, its long stem carefully dethorned, lay on the pillow beside her. A note, written on his monogrammed stationery, rested beneath it: "Dearest Love: For all the reasons you know so well, my humble thanks. You were sleeping so peacefully, I couldn't bear to disturb you. Make yourself at home. I'll return as early as possible. Forever yours, K."

Devon smiled, inhaling the exquisite fragrance of the Persian rose, which, she knew, made the finest attar and most lasting sachets. She brushed the velvety petals across her cheeks and lips and breasts, remembering his kisses and caresses. How like him to leave only a single token, personally selected and pared!

Later, she would dress and have a light breakfast, such as she had become accustomed to in Europe. But now she just wanted to stay in Keith's rooms, savoring their reunion. She bathed in his marble tub, coiffed her hair with his military brushes, and slipped on his gray silk robe, laughing at her reflection in the mirror.

Below the windows, across the street, gardeners were working in the park, mowing and rolling the emerald lawn, pruning shrubs, watering flowers. Children, tended by vigilant nurses and governesses, played behind the securely locked gates of the iron pickets, and Devon visualized Scotty and Miss Vale among them. The gold-plated key necessary for admittance lay on Keith's bureau, near a framed photograph of father and son taken by Mathew Brady. Devon hugged it to her breast, thinking wistfully of the weekend trip to Halcyon.

Moving into the study, she touched the quill on the desk which had penned the sweet note, the jade-handled letter opener, and shook the glass-ball paperweight Keith had bought at the Philadelphia Centennial. The encapsulated crystal chips created a blizzard over the white coral mountain, down which a tiny boyish image coasted on a bright sled, all in minute, realistic detail. It was a symbol of their relationship, the solid rock of their love, the storms periodically enveloping it, the unaware child at the center.

Over tea and croissants in the solarium, Devon read the papers. The Grants were still in Austria. Roscoe Conkling, recently returned from the Paris Exposition to a hero's welcome in his native state, condemned President Hayes' statement that civil-service appointments should be made on merit, not on patronage. Kate Chase Sprague, arriving on the same ship, had gone to Castle Canonchet, the Spragues' summer home on Narragansett Bay, and met with physical violence from her drunkenly enraged husband, who had attempted to throw her out of the second-floor bedroom window and threatened to kill her lover. St. Patrick's Cathedral, years in the building, was finally ready for dedication, its twin Gothic spires now a Fifth Avenue landmark. But the Brooklyn Bridge was still far from completion, delayed by constructional and financial problems, and costing many workers' lives.

Impatient for Keith's return, Devon explored the house of which she would eventually be mistress. A delightful surprise awaited her in the drawing room, where a life-size portrait of their son had recently been hung, and she stood a long while admiring it. The artist had managed to capture his spectacular good looks, without nullifying his aristocratic features. One hand was casually tucked in the pocket of his blue twill blazer with brass buttons and embroidered marine insignia; the other held a yacht cap against his long-trousered legs. There was a glint of mischief in his gray-green eyes. Her baby was growing up, and suddenly she longed passionately for another child.

Esther's large, elegant white-and-gold suite was unoccupied. Sealing it after her death, as Keith had once considered, would have been ineffectual. Bitter memories could not be obliterated by bolted doors. He simply tried to ignore that section of the third floor, glancing away when he passed the hall entrance.

To Devon, however, the suite must be dealt with. The ghosts must be exorcised, the past relegated to its proper place. She turned the Dresden doorknob decisively and walked in. The bed was neatly made with its elaborate counterpane and tasseled bolster, the blind slats angled to admit some light. The wheelchair and other personal articles had been removed, along with the contents of the closets, wardrobes, and drawers. But Devon thought the entire apartment should be redecorated, from ceiling to floor.

She raised several windows to welcome sunshine and fresh air into the gloom and to dispel the musty atmosphere. She heard birds twittering in the park, and the exuberant voices of youngsters. There were no strange sounds in here, and no specters. Wherever Esther was now, she was not in this room.

And yet, at that very moment, their lives were being affected by the dead woman, as if from the grave. A sudden chill enveloped Devon, prickling her spine, and she recalled the mad laughter and shrieking of that terrible confrontation in the parlor. She closed the windows promptly and left the suite.

Keith was in his office, conferring with his lawyers, when his secretary knocked and handed him the message that had just come over his private telegraph line: PLEASE COME IMMEDIATELY. HEATHER VALE.

No explanation. But Keith knew the governess, her unshakable composure and ability to cope with anything. Evidently this demanded his presence.

"Excuse me, gentlemen," he said, rising. "This meeting will have to be continued at another time. Please proceed as far as possible on the information I have provided."

Notifying Captain Bowers to prepare to sail within the hour, he rushed to Gramercy Park. "Something has happened at Halcyon," he told Devon as she met him in the foyer. "We're leaving immediately."

His face was blanched under his tan, and she thought he was withholding the truth from her. "Is it Scotty?"

"I don't know, Devon. Miss Vale just wired me to come at once. The carriage is waiting to take us to the *Sprite*."

Devon dashed upstairs for her portmanteau, praying that Scotty was all right.

The coachman drove rapidly through the congested streets, the footman yelling at the drivers of other vehicles to make way. The yacht's boilers were steaming, the gangplank laid for boarding.

"Full speed," Keith ordered as Bowers saluted him.

"Aye, sir!"

Rufus was in the main salon with some hastily prepared

food and a carafe of hot coffee. Neither could eat, but Keith laced his coffee with brandy, and urged Devon to take some in hers. They could not sit still long enough to drink it, however, and walked together, apart, in circles, pausing occasionally to gaze through the portside glass expanse at the Jersey palisades. Manhattan Island was on the starboard side.

"Miss Vale should have been specific," Devon fretted.

"I'm sure she had her reasons, Devon. There are six people at Halcyon. Any of them could have had an accident. Or maybe the place caught fire."

Devon had a horrifying vision of the house in flames, Scotty trapped inside. Then she mulled other dreadful possibilities. Perhaps Scott had been thrown from his horse, or had fallen out of a tree. A spinal or brain injury could cripple his body, affect his mind. He might never walk again! She flogged herself with hysterical religious convictions that God had chosen to punish their adultery through their child. The sins of the parents . . .

"Darling, stop wringing your hands. You'll twist your fingers off. Don't jump to tragic conclusions."

"Well, what do *you* think happened?"

He shrugged. "Guessing is useless. Anyway, we'll know soon. Bowers is throttling the engines for landing."

The house was visible above the escarpment and hanging alpine gardens of ferns and vines. There was no evidence of fire, but panic reigned. Mrs. Sommes was running about distractedly, her daughter, Enid, stammering and blubbering. And for once, Miss Vale's equanimity had deserted her entirely.

"Oh, Mr. Curtis, I hope the telegram didn't disturb you too much. But I had to send it. Master Scott is missing!"

Devon gasped. Keith demanded, "Missing since when?"

"Recess this morning. You know, I always allow him a recreation period after early lessons and before luncheon. Well, he went out to play and hasn't returned."

"Was he riding?"

"Afoot, sir, and the collie was with him. But the dog came home alone, limping with a thorn in his paw."

"Where are Karl and Lars?"

"Searching for Scott. He must have ventured off the property and lost his way."

"Was he punished for any reason, Miss Vale?"

"No, sir. He was an exceptionally fine student today,

earning high marks on all his tests. I rewarded him with a longer recess. He was not trying to escape discipline, sir."

Devon cried anxiously, "Saddle some horses, Keith."

"We'll ask Captain Bowers and the crew to join the search. What direction did Scott go in, Miss Vale?"

"That's the trouble, sir. No one is certain. The Hummels were busy in the barn and stables, and Mrs. Sommes, Enid, and I were in the house. Master Scott and Bumper were romping in the meadow when last seen. Perhaps he went to the woods, to that brook where he caught his first fish."

"I gave strict orders to everyone on this place!" Keith raged. "The child was never to go near the water alone!"

"Yes, sir. But you also said we were not to hover over him constantly. And he has never done anything like this before."

"Children are unpredictable, Miss Vale."

"Indeed, sir." She looked at Devon, her eyes pleading for understanding. "I'm so sorry, madam. But I'm confident he'll be found safe."

Keith grabbed a hunter's horn off the wall. "Come along, Devon, if you want to ride with me. Miss Vale, deliver my request to Captain Bowers, please."

"Right away, sir"

Bumper, named for his clumsy habit of knocking into things, whimpered when they passed, as if realizing that he had failed in his duty to guard his young master.

Scott was familiar with the sound of the horn, which carried for miles, and Keith blew it intermittently as they rode. "If he's in hearing range, he should respond."

As often happens in crises, some inner strength enabled Devon to stabilize her emotions sufficiently to function as more of a help than hindrance. Keith had enough problems without adding her anxieties.

After an hour of fruitless effort, the horn sounded eerie to Devon. "He's not in the vicinity, Keith."

"I'm afraid not, Devon."

"What if we don't find him before dark? Bumper should be beaten for leaving him!"

"What good would that do?"

"But he should have held on to him, somehow."

"I think I'd better alert the community, Devon. Organize a search party. Call in professional help, too—trackers and bloodhounds. You go to the house and wait. I'll ride to the village. Maybe someone has seen him."

"Would they know him, if they had?"

The question gave him pause. That was one of the drawbacks of seclusion. Protecting his privacy, he had not encouraged visits from neighbors, and Scott did not attend the local school. The isolation of Halcyon might prove to be more of a hazard than a precaution to his son's safety.

A terrible idea, which he dared not reveal to the distraught mother, had already entered his mind: that the publicity about his great wealth may have inspired someone to abduct his heir for ransom.

"We'll see," he muttered, spurring his mount and heading for the public road. Galloping toward the village, Keith hailed a farmer hauling supplies from the market. The man stared at him blankly, until he introduced himself and mentioned his estate. "Oh, yeah. You're that Curtis fella, with the yacht and private landing, ain't you? All that money! We heard of you. I'm Zebulon Benson, Zeb for short."

"Nice to know you, Mr. Benson."

"What can I do for you, sir?"

"My young son is missing. Apparently he strayed from my place about ten o'clock this morning and hasn't been found yet. He's eight years old, has dark curly hair and hazel eyes, and was wearing a brown linen suit, white shirt, and brown tie."

"Naw, I ain't seen no kid fits that description," Benson said. "But I got four of my own—two boys and two girls—and they're always running off somewhere, or hiding in the hayloft. They get home before supper, though. Come feeding time, hungry youngsters and animals alike know where the feed trough is."

"Thank you, sir. And if you should see Scott, please send word to Halcyon."

"Is that how you pronounce it? Me and the missus call it Haly Con. Where do you city folks get fancy names like that, anyway?"

Keith quickly explained. "A halcyon is a bird of the kingfisher species, Mr. Benson. It nests in high places, usually near water, and is supposed to symbolize serenity. It calms storms during the incubation of its young."

The farmer clucked his tongue. "Imagine that! You learn something new every day. I'll keep a sharp eye out for Scott. Sure hope you find him soon."

"Thank you, sir. I'd be most appreciative. Good day."

"Good luck," Benson replied, moving on.

Farther along, Keith saw a woman working in her vegetable garden, and made inquiry. But the only boy of that age she had noticed that day was barefoot, in overalls and faded gingham shirt, carrying a cane fishing pole and can of worms. She did, however, offer an encouraging suggestion. "Peddlers come around now and then, in vans painted like circus and minstrel wagons, and children follow them like the Pied Piper. Maybe that's what your kid done?"

"Did a vendor pass here this morning?"

"Might have, while I was visiting my neighbor, Hallie Burns. They usually ring a bell to attract attention, but we could have been too busy talking to hear. Then, there's another fella been sort of camping hereabouts the last month or so, first one spot and then another, painting pictures. Queer sort, keeps to himself mostly, don't speak much to nobody."

"Can you describe him, ma'am?"

"Never been close to him. Kind of tall and slim, with a full reddish beard. Wears shabby clothes, a slouchy hat splattered with colors, and coughs frequently. I guess he sells the pictures, and moves on when he gets enough painted. Some folks will do anything rather than work for a living."

"Do you think he may have been using my place?"

"Would seem likely, the woods and brook and stone bridges and all. I hear your house is a fine old Dutch mansion, and you got some beautiful gardens, even hanging off the river cliff."

"It's also posted property," Keith said.

"No-trespassing signs don't mean nothing, mister, if a body wants to ignore 'em. You can crawl over and under fences, you know, and climb stiles. But I don't see no harm in just painting the scenery, do you? God made nature for everybody to enjoy."

"True," Keith agreed. He thanked her hurriedly and proceeded to the village.

The land above Washington Heights and around Inwood was some of the wildest of Manhattan Island. The views from its western heights were spectacular, sweeping miles of the blue Hudson and striking terra-cotta palisades. Its rugged inaccessibility had aided General Washington in the defense of the region. If Scott had wandered or been taken into this remote wilderness, he might never be found. The woods were dense enough to conceal an army. There were marshy lowlands, and steep bluffs over which an unsuspecting pedestrian could tumble into the river, and be carried by the strong currents to the harbor and out to sea.

As bells were the best alarm to alert the villagers, Keith sought the pastor of the nearest church and related his plight. "Lord have mercy," the minister prayed, rushing toward the belfry. "We'll do what we can, Mr. Curtis. I was about to ring vespers, anyway. It's getting on toward evening."

"I know, Reverend. That's what worries me most."

Chapter 38

Riding in the yellow-and-blue van pulled by a sorrel horse was an adventure for the little boy. He was not allowed to sit on the seat with the driver. Instead, for some reason beyond his comprehension, he had been placed in the covered section shielded by a frayed canvas curtain, with the art paraphernalia—canvases, easels, palettes, brushes, boxes containing tubes of bright-colored oils and tiny pots of watercolors, and bottles and jars of odorous turpentine.

"Could I please sit with you, sir?" he asked plaintively. "I want to see where we're going."

"That's not necessary, kid. Just be quiet and try not to bother me. I've got other things on my mind."

"But you promised to show me something wonderful."

"Never mind that now."

"May I play with some of this stuff?"

"No, don't touch anything. My equipment costs money, and I don't have much to spare. I'm not rich, like your daddy."

"You know my daddy?"

"Yeah, I know him." His voice sounded ominous. "I met him once, a long time ago." He paused thoughtfully, frowning as if in pain. "A damn long time ago, but I'll never forget him."

"You mustn't curse."

"Shit," he muttered.

"That's ugly, too."

"Hold the language lesson, boy, and tell me your mama's name."

"Daddy calls her Devon."

"You mean 'darling'?"

"That, too. But I think her first name is Devon, and she writes stories for a newspaper. But she's far away now, in Europe. That's across the Atlantic Ocean."

290

"I know where Europe is, kid."

And indeed he did. He had wandered the Continent for years, like a gypsy, traveling mostly alone. But there were thousands of artists there, with far greater talent than his, and their works sold on the streets and in the markets for pennies, often traded for bread, cheese, sausage, or wine. Many either starved to death in the slums or sought other means of livelihood. Handsome young males often became gigolos, kept by patrons of both sexes for social and sexual amusements. But anyone like himself who could not function adequately under such circumstances had a difficult time of it.

After several years of roaming, he had returned to America in steerage, broke, disillusioned, ill with a hacking cough and intermittent chills and fever. He landed in Boston and tried to paint in New England again. But how many Maine seascapes and lighthouses, Cape Code piers and dunes, Connecticut barns and saltbox houses, covered bridges, Congregational churches, and town-square bandstands could the market absorb? His best work, his only commendable accomplishment, had been produced in Boston, when he had a lovely raven-haired inspiration who lived in a Bulfinch mansion with violet-tinted windowpanes on Louisburg Square. She was the only woman he had ever loved. When he lost her, he had lost himself, his art, his interest in life. He could hardly paint at all anymore. He had become what Curtis had classed him on that cataclysmic occasion when he had burst into his attic studio on Tompkins Square: a paint dauber! Even so, painting was the only thing he knew how to do, the only thing he cared about . . . until now.

"My mother is traveling in Europe with President and Mrs. Grant," Scott said, repeating what his father had told him.

"The ex-President, boy. Rutherford B. Hayes is in the White House now. Didn't your nanny tell you that?"

"A nanny is a nurse for babies," Scott objected indignantly. "Miss Vale is my *governess*."

"Your old man thinks you're too good for public schools, or even private ones, eh? The millionaire doesn't want his spawn associating with riffraff."

"Why are you so angry, mister? I haven't done anything to you. I thought we were friends, and it was your idea to take me for a ride in your wagon."

The man laughed raucously. " 'Ride' is right, kid! You don't know the half of it."

"My name is Scott."

"I know that. Master Scott Heathstone Curtis, and you're the son of that wealthy Wall Street tycoon whose name has been in the newspapers so much lately. You should be worth quite a tidy fortune to me."

"If you need money, sir, borrow some from my daddy. He'll lend it to you, at interest. He owns a big bank and lots of gold and silver and jewels."

"Isn't that just dandy?"

It seemed to the child that they had been traveling for hours. "When will we reach that wonderful place?"

"Before dark. Hush, now, and take a nap. There's a blanket, and a little food and water. Eat if you're hungry, then go to sleep."

"I've outgrown naps, sir."

"And obedience? Do as you're told!"

"Yes, sir."

Scott didn't understand any of this. The man had seemed nice and kind when working near Halcyon, making friends with Scotty and Bumper, petting the dog and tossing sticks for him to fetch. During recent weeks he had been sketching the arched stone bridge across the brook, climbing the fence stile to enter the property. His paint-spattered smock, faded breeches tucked into scuffed calf-high boots fascinated the curious boy, but more so his peculiar, nearly orange whiskers, which contrasted startlingly with his pale hair.

"Why do you wear that funny beard?" Scott had asked.

"You think it's funny?"

"Well, it's not the color of your hair."

The painter had grinned and laughed. "Maybe it's false, sonny. Pull on it and see."

Scott curiously obliged. "No, it's real."

More laughter. "You like me, kid?"

"I like to watch you paint. May I see the pictures in your wagon?"

"If you want. But be careful, don't rip any. I sell them."

"Oh, I shan't harm them, sir, just look at them."

"I had an exhibit once, in a fine Manhattan studio. Your daddy wanted to buy one of my pictures, but I wouldn't sell it."

"Why not?"

"It's a long story, which you're too young to appreciate. I'm busy now, and you'd best run along."

"I suppose so, before Miss Vale or one of the Hummels come hunting me."

"The Hummels?"

"Our handymen."

"Handy at what?"

"Working on the place."

"I see. Well, then, don't tarry."

"May I come again tomorrow?"

He shrugged. "It's your property."

The next day, after his lessons, Scott and Bumper were back. The collie lay in the shade of an oak, while his little master skipped rocks on the brook, intrepidly walked the railing, picked wild berries from a bush, and talked with his new friend. But when he asked his name, the reply was brusque. "None."

"Everybody has a name, mister."

"And so did I, once, but no longer. An artist's name has no meaning unless he's famous. Then his signature on a painting can command big money. My pictures are not valuable, so I rarely sign them anymore. And even if I did, it could be my name or that of a duck."

"A duck?" Several tame ones glided on the clear stream, quacking and searching for bugs. "I don't understand, sir."

"You wouldn't," he muttered, splashing some crimson oil on the canvas. "Only two people would really understand, and one is dead." His hands trembled as he removed the ruined canvas, folded the easel, and left.

Day after day, Scott was drawn to the scene. Once he told his governess about the stranger he had met in the woods, amusing her with his improbable description, which she regarded as childish fantasy. Her charge possessed a vivid imagination and was always inventing imaginary characters, including elves and leprechauns. Miss Vale did not question him about these fantasies, which all youngsters had.

Now the gaudy wagon rumbled along the backwoods lanes paralleling the main road. After nibbling an apple, some cheese, and bread, its small captive occupant fell asleep. He awoke in a wretched little house in the Bronx. He had no idea where he was, nor when he had arrived. Apparently he had been carried into the shack by the stranger. The tattered shades had been drawn, and he was lighting some candles, which sputtered in the necks of empty wine bottles.

Never had Scott been in such filth. Dust and trash covered the meager furnishings. The floor was littered, the brass bed unmade, dirty garments draped helter-skelter on pegs and rickety chairs. Everywhere were pictures in various stages of completion, standing or lying in corners, some damaged beyond repair, others slashed and hacked to pieces in frustration. Some finished ones hung on the rough, unpainted board walls, and a few were even covered for protection. A washstand held a scum-ringed bowl and cracked water pitcher, and when Scott mentioned that he had to use the bathroom, he was gruffly told, "Go outside, nobody will see you."

"It's getting late, mister. You better take me home now."

"Shut up and go! Or do it in your pants, I don't care. But remember, you have no other clothes, and you may be here for a while."

"Why?"

An odd grin. "Because you're going to be my guest, laddie. That's why."

"For how long?"

"I'll decide that."

"I . . . I'd rather be at Halcyon, sir."

"Naturally. It's a fine estate, with every convenience, no doubt. But you'll not be leaving here soon, so forget it and behave yourself. That way, you won't get hurt."

"I thought you liked me and we were friends?"

"I'm nobody's friend, boy. Understand?"

Scott nodded, walked outside, and stayed near the rotting stoop. Trees, bushes, weeds, and vines obscured him from human sight, for no neighbors were visible. Debris was scattered about the fenceless, unkempt yard, and the stench of garbage and raw sewage was sickening. The house looked as if it had been put together from shipping crates and tar paper. The last rays of the sun struck the sycamore trunk behind which he modestly relieved his bladder. Flies, gnats, and mosquitoes buzzed and droned annoyingly about him. Hurriedly fastening his trousers, he went back inside. His host was drinking red wine from a squat wicker-encased bottle.

"Don't you use a glass, sir?"

He scoffed, gesturing toward a bin of dirty dishes and cutlery. Pots and skillets of spoiled food stood on the rusting stove. "You see any crystal goblets? Fine furniture? I'm a poor man, not like that wealthy son of a . . . not like your father."

"Does my daddy know where you live?"

Wine trickled down his chin into his ugly facial brush. It would be a relief to scrape the damn itchy thing off: it had served its purpose as a disguise, and no one could guess it had been dyed. He had shunned familiar places while growing the beard, trading with different merchants.

"You think your daddy would visit a place like this?"

"If he knew I was here."

"Ah, but he won't know that, my lad. Not until I want him to, anyway. You've been snatched. Know what that means?"

Scott shook his head.

"Good, because I haven't devised any plan yet. This ingenious idea just occurred to me recently. What a great way to punish that bastard. Make him suffer . . . and pay!"

"You used another bad word."

"Bastard? That's not such a bad word, Scott. It simply means a fatherless child, denied by his papa. The world is full of them. But there are other kinds of bastards, too, and I'm acquainted with many. Also a few bitches, which are female dogs, although some women belong in the same category." He gulped more wine, swishing it in his mouth and throat like a gargle. "You don't know what I'm babbling about, do you? Well, I can't explain the facts of life to you now. But I am interested in your birth. I know you can't remember the event, or when your father married your mother."

Mallard thought of Esther's obituaries in the New York and Boston papers. Keith Curtis had been listed as her surviving husband. This child was too young to be the one she was undoubtedly carrying the day that suspicious, snooping son of a bitch had surprised them at the St. Marks Place studio, violently attacking his wife's lover and causing the fall down the steep attic stairway which had injured Esther so terribly. Had she recovered sufficiently to bear Curtis an heir later on? Then perhaps he had married again after her death, to give his son a stepmother. . . .

In a sudden temperamental rage, Mallard yanked the dusty sheet from a large framed portrait of an extraordinarily beautiful black-haired woman who was largely

naked except for some artistically arranged gauze draperies.

"You ever see this lady before?"

Scott cocked his head to study the exotic oval face, with
its vague, enigmatic smile, long dark tresses cascading over
bare milky shoulders. "I don't think so, sir. She's quite
pretty, though. But why isn't she wearing a dress, instead
of those veils?"

"Salome." He grinned ruefully. "She should be carrying
the head of John the Baptist on a platter."

"What?"

"Nothing. She's not your mother, then?"

"Oh, no, sir! My mother has blond hair. Her eyes are
not purple, either, they're green. And she would never be
painted without any clothes on! She's very beautiful."

"I see." Curtis' mistress, no doubt, and this was their
natural son, their love child, born long before Esther's
merciful departure from this earth. Should be worth a million to Curtis, at least. Maybe two or three . . . or more!

Mallard didn't eat much that evening, although he fed
the child as best he could before ordering him to bed. Scott
went obediently, wincing at the soiled mattress and feather-
filled sacks rank with sweat.

"Should I say my prayers, Mr. Artist?"

"Stop calling me that! Go ahead and pray, if you want.
Just don't ask me to listen. I don't care what rich brats ask
God for, and I know well enough what the poor ones want.
Close your eyes and go to dreamland now, or I'll paddle
your ass."

Like a caged animal, Mallard paced the creaky floor of
the shack until after midnight, calmed little by the wine.
Most of what he earned was spent for cheap burgundy,
very little for food. He had no appetite.

Now that he had struck a fabulous gold lode, what was
the safest mining procedure? It was much too early and
risky to mail a ransom note. Besides, he wanted the old
boy to worry, to despair of ever seeing his son again. Why
not? Hadn't Curtis put him through hell, an agony of uncertainty, not knowing what had happened to Esther, how
badly she had been hurt, unable to find out? Mallard owed
him. Oh, yes.

Strange how Curtis could understand his own love, but
not Esther's for someone else! And so the fruit of his
mistress's womb had fallen into the hands of his bitterest

foe. The irony evoked a riotous, humorless laughter that rumbled through the silent shanty and the deep, dark woods. The child moved uneasily, his eyelids fluttering. Good! Let the boy suffer, too. Let them all suffer a little of what he and Esther had been tortured by—separation and despair!

Mallard coughed and spat up a clot of bloody phlegm. Could a million dollars cure him, even if he went West? He knew his disease. It was the same ailment that had killed Edgar Allan Poe's young wife, whom the desperate poet had brought to the supposedly salubrious climate of the Bronx in 1848. But her consumption had progressed rapidly, as was his.

"Well, Mr. Millionaire, I hope your physical and mental torture equal what I went through when you separated Esther and me! That was my baby she miscarried, not yours. It was my seed, and we both knew it. But your enormous ego couldn't bear that, could it? An aristocrat could never be a peasant's cuckold or accept a penniless paint dauber's spawn as his own! Nevertheless, she loved me, and neither you nor her family could change that. Esther Diane Stanfield loved Giles Mallard!" he shouted at the ceiling. "You hear that, you rich son of a bitch! Your wife loved *me*! Hear that, mighty King of Wall Street!"

Much later, he flopped on the bed beside the sleeping child and passed out.

Chapter 39

The volunteers were organized into units, each led by natives familiar with the region. Each was promised compensation for his time and effort, plus an incentive bonus if the child were found. Equipped with lanterns and torches, they moved slowly into the twilit woods, shouting the boy's name through the groves, across the ravines and meadows, along the lanes and orchards and fields. Roused from supper tables and later from sleep, residents emerged, some in night attire, to offer assistance.

But the obstacles were enormous, and Keith began to despair. They might be hunting in the wrong areas. If abducted, Scott might already have been transported by water to some other location, across the Hudson to New Jersey, the East River to Long Island, the Sound to Connecticut. And he dared not contemplate the other potentialities. Toward midnight, fog began to drift over the vicinity, encompassing the trees like damp gray cocoons, impenetrable to even the brightest lights, forcing a halt to the search.

"No point going on now, Mr. Curtis," one guide told Keith. "Better wait till the fog lifts, if it does. I've seen these heavy ones linger for days. I reckon you have too, if you're familiar with this island."

"You're right, Mr. Wooten. We may as well camp here until morning. Build a bonfire in a clearing. The others will follow suit. I understand you've conducted many searches, sir?"

"A fair number. Mostly for kids, but several for women who had lost their bearings."

"All successful rescues?"

"Afraid not, Mr. Curtis. The ladies were found, because they had the sense to stay put. But youngsters get scared and desperate and keep wandering until . . . Well, only three were discovered alive. Seven were never located at all. I'm sorry, but those are the facts. The odds are against you. And I'm sure you realize that your son may not be lost . . . exactly?"

Keith nodded. "As soon as it's light enough, I'll go home. There may have been some developments there by now."

"We'll continue searching until you learn something definite."

"I'd appreciate that, Mr. Wooten. Please make sure that I get the name of every participant."

"Yes, sir. Most have already signed the roster at the church, but others have joined along the way. It's wonderful how folks respond in these crises. Well, I see the fellows have a nice fire started. Some have supplies. Frankly, I could use a slug of rum. How about you?"

"Might as well."

But Keith merely smoked, gazing into the flames, as if his own person were being consumed.

Hearing hoofbeats at dawn, Devon rushed outside and peered through the ghostly mists, praying that Keith would emerge with Scotty in the saddle. But he was alone, and reluctant to meet her anxious eyes.

"No luck yet, Devon. But the search will continue. Anything here?"

"No," she quavered. "Captain Bowers and the crew, the Hummels, and some neighbors are south and east of the property." She had watched the glowing lights far into the night, until they became vague, indistinct, flickering like fireflies, finally disappearing in the fog. "Come inside. You must be exhausted."

Mrs. Sommes prepared breakfast for everyone, insisting that they take some nourishment, if only buttered toast. Devon choked down a slice with milk, while Keith drank several cups of strong black coffee.

"I've telegraphed the Pinkerton agency," he said. "They should be here soon. I've also ordered bloodhounds and professional trackers." He pondered the effect of his next words before uttering them. "There are other possibilities that we must consider."

Devon shook her head vehemently, clamping her hands over her ears. "I don't want to hear them!"

"Devon! Listen to me!"

"I refuse to believe he's dead, Keith! I'd know it, I'd feel it."

"We must—"

"Scotty's alive," she insisted.

"This is an island, Devon, surrounded by deep water."

"He can swim."

"Oh, darling, for God's sake! A child in the Hudson? He may have found an abandoned dinghy or scull and tried to reach one of the islands."

"Why would he do such a thing?"

"Adventure, of course. Boys thrive on it. I used to roam, when I could escape adults long enough."

"But surely not at Scotty's age?"

"Oh, yes. Even younger. I was about six the first time I ventured off. I got as far as the Battery before I was caught. My governess was discharged, and I had a male tutor. But that didn't keep me from trying it again. I was wild about ships and the harbor. I longed to ride the ferries. Scott can handle a rowboat fairly well, but not a leaky one."

He glanced away to avoid the tears brimming in her eyes. Then he went on. "On my way to the village yesterday, I met a local lady who offered a plausible suggestion. She said that peddlers come through here frequently, and children tend to follow them."

"I suppose *you* did that, too?" she sniffed.

"Every chance I got. Medicine and minstrel vans were my favorites, because they usually had entertainment between spiels for the products. Kids are attracted to danger and excitement. They'll chase off to fires, play with snakes, take up with strangers, sneak under circus tents. I used to envy the boys hanging on milk and ice wagons, and even the ragpicker's son ringing his father's bell and chanting his beggar's song in the streets. I wanted to go to sea on a raft, walk the ledge around Croton Reservoir, camp in Central Park, and God knows what else."

Devon realized his intentions, and loved him for it. She smiled poignantly, touching his hand. "You must have given your mother some gray hair! But you don't believe any of those things happened to Scotty, do you?"

The time had come, he decided, to broach the horrible prospect that had plagued him from the beginning. "We can't rule out abduction, Devon. And if that's the case, we know why, don't we? And who is largely responsible. My wealth has been exaggerated, publicized over the entire country. When a man's fortune is estimated at half a billion and more, how much is his only child worth to him— and to an abductor?"

"Dear Lord," Devon murmured tremulously. "If Reed has caused this, I'll kill him, Keith! I swear I will."

"No," he said grimly, "I will, Devon. And I suspected it yesterday—that's why I've called detectives. If Scott is being held for ransom, we have no choice now except to wait for contact. Oh, God, if only they don't harm him! I'll pay any amount of money, do anything to get him back alive and unhurt."

At nine o'clock two Pinkerton operatives arrived and went into conference with Keith. They were young men, in their thirties, and well-trained. Their experience with abduction cases, however, was limited to cadavers. Under Robert Pinkerton's supervision, they had aided in the recovery of the corpse of the millionaire merchant A. T. Stewart, stolen from its crypt by graverobbers and held for payment. They had also assisted the United States Secret Service in tracing the ghouls who had attempted to steal Abraham Lincoln's remains from the marble sarcophagus in the Springfield Memorial.

The Halcyon and *Sprite* employees were questioned in private and cleared of suspicion.

Preferring subtle and secretive methods of operation, the Pinkerton men did not recommend the use of bloodhounds. But Keith had already gotten some dogs, and their shrill baying nearly drove Devon to distraction. How must fugitive slaves have felt, tracked this way through fields and swamps! Some distance from the fence boundary, the hounds frantically circled a spot where a four-wheeled vehicle and horse or mule had recently stood. The dogs yelped and strained at their leashes. Here they lost the scent and could not be coaxed to leave.

Keith was summoned to the scene. "This is undoubtedly where your son was last on the ground, sir. Apparently he was taken aboard the contraption. And probably not by a peddler."

"Is that an assumption?"

"Deduction," one of the operatives replied, explaining, "Precautions were obviously taken to obscure the wheel and hoof marks. It's a common trick, attaching branches and other brush to the rear to obliterate traces, especially in dry weather. More difficult, naturally, in damp earth, which would leave substantial indentations. But this evidence is sufficient, Mr. Curtis. I believe the boy was taken."

His partner concurred, and they went in different directions, seeking clues. Keith returned to the house.

Keith's close friend Dr. Ramsey Blake heard the news upon arriving for the weekend at his country estate in Washington Heights. He rushed immediately to Halcyon. "I'm so sorry about this," he said, extending his hand. "Can I help in any way?"

"You can sedate his mother," Keith replied.

"She's here?"

"Yes, and verging on collapse."

"No wonder. I'll remain as long as I'm needed. Another physician is caring for my patients."

"Thank you, Ramsey. I've got my hands full."

"Would you like something for your own nerves?"

"No, I need a clear head."

The case was now creating headlines in New York.

MILLIONAIRE'S SON MISSING!

INTENSIVE SEARCH FOR CURTIS HEIR!

REWARD FOR INFORMATION CONCERNING YOUNG SCION!

BANKER'S BOY STILL LOST!

Reporters arrived by train and steamboat, in buggies and on horseback. This was precisely the kind of publicity Keith had hoped to avoid, but with so many people involved, secrecy was impossible. He pleaded with the journalists to leave, lest their presence jeopardize the child's safety. He said he did not believe his son had been kidnapped, but had merely wandered away.

"But it's been three days now, sir."

"Not quite, and children have been missing longer," Keith replied. "They stray from home and lose their sense of direction. He may be staying with strangers who are unaware of the situation."

Most understood his unspoken fears and tried to cooperate. "Then it's advisable to print his description, sir, and mention the reward. Money is magic."

"It can also be a curse," Keith said.

The newsman grinned. "That's what my editor says every time I ask for a salary hike. But cash can flush out information, Mr. Curtis."

"And suppress it, Mr. Hines."

"Is the law helping any?"

"The local constable has a posse in the search."

"What about professional detectives?"

"We're considering that as a last resort." The truth might frighten off the abductors. "That's all, gentlemen. Please be good enough to retire to the village, or elsewhere, and await further news. You'll be promptly notified when anything happens."

"Does the reward apply to the press, sir?"

"To anyone furnishing useful information," Keith called over his shoulder before entering the house. The doctor met him at the base of the stairs.

"Are they still here?"

Keith sighed heavily. "It's their job. How is she, Ramsey?"

"Resting now. I gave her a stronger sedative. Miss Vale, too. Neither had slept much in the last thirty-six hours." He added with professional scrutiny, "How long since you've been to bed, my friend?"

"No matter." Keith shrugged indifferently. "I couldn't sleep under these circumstances."

"Nevertheless, you must get *some* rest, Keith. A few hours, at least. I'd also like to examine your heart. You're risking apoplexy. And right now, you look fifty years old!"

"Is that all? I feel a hundred."

"I'm serious, man."

"You think I'm joking? If I lose that boy . . ."

Ramsey nodded sympathetically. "It'll probably kill you, *and* his mother. But we can't let that happen, Keith. Regardless of the outcome, neither of you can simply lie down and die. Or fall dead from worry. You need each other more now than ever before. Here's some medical advice. It may seem callous, but listen anyway. Start another pregnancy as quickly as possible."

Keith scowled. "Hell, Ramsey! I can't even think of sex now, and I doubt that she could, either."

"Why not? Isn't that how you became parents?"

"You don't understand."

"Oh, yes, I do. Think of love, not lust. Get some rest, go through the proper preliminaries, and nature will assist you. Devon will sleep six or eight hours. Be beside her when she wakes, Keith."

Keith smiled. "I understand Ramsey. And thanks."

Chapter 40

Mallard felt a timid tugging at his clothes. He opened swollen eyes and almost immediately began to cough severely, nearly strangling. It alarmed the child, who imagined it was vomit from an upset stomach. Mallard spat into the slopjar beside the bed, and when his throat had cleared somewhat, asked hoarsely, "What're you wanting so goddamn early?"

"It's morning, I'm hungry."

"There's some bread in the box in the kitchen."

"No, sir. There isn't any more bread. Can you bake some more?"

"If there's any flour and lard. But I have no sugar or yeast. How about pancakes? I think there's a can of molasses in the cupboard."

"That would be fine, sir. I like pancakes, with lots of butter and maple syrup."

"Well, I don't have lots of anything, boy, and I can't cook worth a hoot. I make hoecakes and douse 'em in blackstrap."

"What's blackstrap?"

"Not maple syrup! It's cheap molasses, the dregs of sorghum vats. But edible."

"That's all right, Mr. Artist. I'll help you cook"

"I told you not to call me that!"

"But I don't know your name, sir. You never told me."

"Your highfalutin' father once called me a paint dauber, so how about Mr. Dauber? Or Mr. Duck?" Wrenching himself painfully off the bed, he worked his hands and mouth together and waddled comically across the room. "Quack, quack, quack!"

Scott was tickled. "You're funny."

"I'm glad you think so, kid. And I'll tell you something else. You're not a bad egg, considering you must be spoiled rotten."

"Miss Vale punishes me when I'm not what she calls 'a perfect little gentleman.' "

"As compared to a crown prince, no doubt."

"Well, I can't get into too much mischief when she's in charge. Daddy is not quite so strict, and Mother lets me do what I like, mostly. But she's not around so much."

"Get a pail, Scott. We have to dip some water from the rain barrels outside."

"Why do you keep those rusty old screens and canvas covers over them?"

"Filters for leaves and other debris. Birds roost and mess on the roof." He scanned the sky through the dense woodlands. The trees sighed, moaned in the slightest wind, and branches scraped the shanty. "The supply is running low, but a good shower would replenish it. There's a spring-fed brook nearby for emergencies. Come back inside and give me a hand."

After placing the battered buckets on the floor, Mallard checked the fire chamber of the ancient iron range. Scooping a hollow in the dead coals and ashes, he inserted some kindling twigs and sprinkled on a few drops of turpentine before striking a match. Flames flared, and he adjusted the damper on the crooked stovepipe poking through the ceiling. Daylight was visible through the holes in the roof. A stevedore had given him a keg of pitch one day while he was sketching on the docks, but Mallard lacked the energy to climb up and patch the cracks.

"Can you wash dishes, Scott?"

"Oh, sure. I watched Mrs. Sommes and Enid do it many times."

"Who are they?"

"The housekeeper and maid at Halcyon. We have other servants in town."

"Born with the proverbial spoon in your mouth, eh? I'll heat some water. Go easy on the soap, I'm down to my last two bars."

Just then Mallard was seized by another attack, so violent that he staggered outside and clutched a tree for support, heaving and gasping for breath. Blood spewed from his mouth onto the bark. Scott brought him a cup of wine, which seemed to alleviate these horrifying attacks.

"Thanks, sport. Like I said, you're a good egg. Reckon you could finish those buckwheats I started? They're ready to cook. Just put some grease on the griddle and fry 'em golden brown on both sides. Later, I'll shave and go to the village. Some storekeepers let me trade my goods for theirs."

Back in the kitchen, the boy wrestled with breakfast, apologizing for burning the first batch. "You can draw with charcoal, Scott, but you can't eat it. Turn the next ones sooner."

"How many would you like, sir?"

"None." Mallard was scrounging for a hidden bottle of wine, relieved when he found it. He kept several demijohns buried in a chest under the house, like treasure. He never touched them, anticipating the final emergency. "I'll just have some more medicine."

"May I go to town with you, sir?" Scott inquired, his face puckering at the refusal.

"You have to watch the place, laddie. And don't cry! You're too big for that. Crying is for babies. Hey, look at those fine flapjacks! You've got the knack now. No cowboy could make better ones. I doubt even the chuck-wagon cook could."

Those were familiar words to Scott, used by his mother in stories she had told him while he had the measles in Washington. Cowboys, he imagined, were as strong and tough as the wild mustangs they caught. "I'm not a sissy," he declared, firming his little jaw.

"I knew that the first time I saw you," Mallard said solemnly. "And you must promise not to leave the house while I'm away. You might get lost, you see, and the wolves would eat you alive. The woods are full of them."

"Really? My father never told me that."

"He forgot, or didn't know. There are also snakes, so poisonous their bites kill in minutes." He snapped his fingers impressively. "Just like that! And I wouldn't want anything bad to happen to you, Scott. I like you too much, I really do." This, at least, was true.

"I'll stay inside, sir, and lock the doors."

"Shall we shake hands on it? That's a solemn vow, you know, like swearing on the Bible."

Mallard sorted through his stock of unframed canvases tacked on cheap balsam stretchers, rolled up in brown-paper tubes, or merely tied with string. Some appeared to have been conceived and executed by a madman in a nightmare: demons overpowering angels; satyrs and nymphs in orgies; fanged and snarling jungle beasts locked in fierce combat; the elements rampaging in dark skies; gnarled trees; nocturnal scenes with ominous, lurking shadows.

"No use trying to barter any of these," he decided ruefully. "They'd scare folks around here."

The still-life watercolors or seascapes would bring food today.

"Tell me, Scott, of all the pictures you've seen, which do you like best?"

Without hesitation he indicated the skaters on Jamaica Pond, and the feverish red splotches on the artist's otherwise pallid face flamed. It was the same one Curtis had wanted to buy!

Mallard could not part with it, even after he had read of Esther's death. It would be like selling a part of himself and, worse, a part of her.

"Congratulations, Master Curtis. You have good taste in art."

His intense brooding puzzled the child, who found himself gazing at the portrait on the wall. The elongated violet eyes seemed to meet his. "That lady up there is on the pond, isn't she?"

"Add uncanny perception to your other attributes," Mallard muttered. "Yes, she inspired it, and I couldn't sell either of those pictures, even if I were starving in a gutter. Besides, they're damned good and remind me that I wasn't always second-rate." He sighed. "I wonder what'll become of them when I'm gone?" After a long silence, Mallard said quietly, "We're all animals in the Creator's zoo, Scott, even though you can't always see our bars."

"Is that why you painted that big golden bird in the cage with a person's face and body?"

"You've seen pretty birds in cages?"

"Yes, sir."

"Well, there's a place in New York City where beautiful girls earn their living by sitting in fancy cages. They wear feathered costumes and masks if they don't want to be recognized. Some don't mind, others do. That particular one obviously hated it, which is why I decided to paint her. She didn't belong in a cage, stared at by men."

"Then why did she do it?"

"I suppose she was broke and desperate. I don't know how she escaped that cage, but I went there two evenings to sketch her, then missed a few, and when I went back again, she was gone. Someone had freed her, I guess."

Sometime later, Scott helped him carry the paintings to the van, and Mallard left him.

At the Crossroads Store, where he occasionally bartered his work, Mallard affected ignorance when the proprietor indicated the New York *Herald* spread on the counter, and the reward posters in his windows. "You ain't heard about that missing boy?"

"I've been sick again," he explained. "What's all the fuss about? Kids run away every day."

"Not millionaire's sons. You can have the paper, if you like. I've already read it."

"Thanks." Mallard coughed. "Can you use any of these, Mr. Lumis? I have to eat."

"And drink, eh?"

"I'm not a teetotaler."

"Me, either. Yeah, I believe I can sell some of this batch. What do you need?"

"Some staples: flour, sugar, lard, so forth. I could use some bacon, stew meat, and a soup bone, too, and fresh produce, if you have any. Also some potatoes, lentils, dried fruit, and canned goods."

"Figuring on going into hibernation?"

"My sickness weakens me for long periods of time, and I must be prepared."

"Too bad you can't find that Curtis boy, collect that big reward. Then your money troubles would be over, at least. They're hunting him at Marble Hill now, in the caves and quarries. Waste of time, if you ask me. Most likely he drowned. Happens to plenty of folks every year, and no trace of 'em is ever discovered. Their bodies get chopped up in the paddlewheels and screw propellers of the steamers. Fishermen sometimes recover pieces of them."

The gregarious merchant prattled on as he gathered items together. "How long you been laid up this time?"

"Several months."

"Too sick to shave, eh? Grew a beard?"

Mallard rubbed his raw, nicked chin. "Un-huh. Couldn't stand it any longer, though, and my razor was dull. But I was tired of looking like Robinson Crusoe."

"Wasn't he a pirate?"

"Not exactly."

"You better get to another climate before winter," Lumis advised, as Mallard suppressed his coughing. "Ever hear about that nature fella, Edward Muir? How he was dying of lung fever when he went West, and he improved so much he began exploring the Territories. He's cured now! Mountain and desert climate done it."

"Sunshine and fresh air didn't cure Chopin."

"Who?"

"Oh, just a Polish musician, sir. Consumption seems to be an occupational hazard of poor artists. Physicians have been recommending a change of climate for better health since Hippocrates."

"I didn't think they was letting in unhealthy immigrants no more," Lumis said.

Mallard was pondering the glass jars of peppermint sticks, licorice whips, gumdrops, and jawbreakers. The Curtis kid was probably accustomed to imported bonbons. Would it arouse suspicion to ask for some sweets? Since his teeth were decaying, and sweets produced toothaches, he no longer ate them himself. But he had promised Scott a treat. "You got any cookies or pastries, Mr. Lumis? I've suddenly developed a craving."

"Maybe you're pregnant?" Lumis laughed, enjoying his own humor. Mallard grinned slightly. "No bakery goods, except on Saturday, when the Widow Eisler brings in her cakes and pies. Take some candy?"

"All right. Mix up a dime's worth. And if you have a bar of chocolate . . . ?"

"Sure," the old man said, pitying him. "What you doing for that cough?"

"Brewing mullein and sassafras leaves with cherry bark."

"Put a couple of drops of creosote in it and rub your chest with camphor oil. I'll give you a little of each. Some folks swear by them remedies."

"That's kind of you, sir, and I'm grateful."

"Ah, well, if it helps . . ."

Mallard rolled up the newspaper, tucking it under his arm. "I think I'll take your advice about leaving this island, too. Work my way west, doing odd jobs." He affected a confident smile. "I can always paint, if only houses and barns."

"And storefronts? Mine'll be needing a new coat before long. We can discuss price next time you're in. . . ."

True to his word, Scott had not left the premises. Indeed, he had passed the time cleaning up as best he could.

"Good boy," Mallard complimented, presenting him the

small bag of candy. "Anybody come around while I was away?"

"No, sir. Maybe nobody knows this place is here."

"That's the whole idea, laddie. Privacy is essential to my work. Eat some candy now, while I read this newspaper. Be careful of the hard pieces. Don't hurt your nice teeth."

Christ, he sounded like a parent! He was getting too fond of the kid, and he'd better make a decision soon.

Chapter 41

Devon was managing to function, but hideous nightmares disturbed her sedated sleep. Exhaustion forced Keith to bed a few hours each night, where he thrashed and muttered and moaned in his dreams. Numerous letters containing false information were delivered to newspapers and the Curtis Bank, in the hope of collecting the reward, now increased to a million dollars. The Manhattan police precincts received similar messages, along with crank confessions.

The estate already seemed to be in mourning. The servants moved quietly in the house. The handymen performed their chores largely in silence. The governess went into partial seclusion in her room, praying and castigating herself. All felt a sense of deep failure. Most difficult to bear, however, was the uncertainty.

Over a week had passed when Carla Winston arrived, and she and Devon wept in each other's arms.

"Oh, Carla, I'm so glad you've come!" Devon cried. "Maybe you can help."

"That's my intention, dear. I was on a case in Illinois when I heard the news, and begged to resign."

Carla did not mention that Mr. Curtis had requested her services, for she would have come anyway.

"I keep thinking of Scotty dead," Devon sobbed, as Carla tried to soothe her.

"You mustn't do that, Devon. A positive attitude is essential. We'll find Scotty."

"But there's been no word yet!"

"It takes time to formulate schemes," Carla explained. "If the perpetrators applied half the energy and ingenuity to legitimate work, they could be highly successful businessmen. The news angle must be considered, too. Publicity imposes caution."

Devon sighed. "Then this crime was committed in vain, and suspicion may be averted by—"

"On the contrary," Carla interrupted. "The culprits may simply reverse the procedure: try to collect the substantial reward, rather than a ransom, and become wealthy heroes instead of hunted outlaws."

She glanced at Keith, who was listening thoughtfully, and he nodded. "That's a plausible theory, Carla."

"And since the money is doubled if the boy is delivered unharmed, it's to their benefit to keep him healthy."

Carla's presence comforted them both. Dr. Blake was greatly relieved. Devon had been perilously close to real illness. He assured Keith that it was now a matter of physical endurance.

"I'll continue mild sedation and gradually reduce the dosage," he said. "Keep up her strength with nourishing food and rest. And your own, too. You've lost at least twenty pounds."

"Then I needn't worry about a middle-age paunch."

"Middle age? Nonsense! You're in your prime, man, and Devon hasn't even reached hers. Bear that in mind when you retire tonight. . . ."

Carla repeated her colleagues' routine questioning of the household staff, concentrating primarily on the governess. "Think hard now, Miss Vale. The fact that Scott apparently went willingly with his abductor indicates that he knew him at least slightly. I speak of one, because, while others may be involved, it's unlikely they would have exposed themselves at first. Most likely, someone gained his confidence weeks or even months in advance."

"But he had been cautioned repeatedly against strangers, Mrs. Winston."

"Indicating that the person approached him first as a friend, and worked at establishing friendly relations."

"Well, he was allowed the freedom of the estate, as long as he did not go near deep water or beyond the designated boundaries. He often rode alone, or roamed with his collie, but the Hummel brothers were supposed to be aware of his position at those times. I don't ride, you see, and they do. I'm not excusing my laxity, however. I should have made certain that Karl or Lars was checking on him more closely that day."

"Hindsight won't aid us much now," Carla reasoned

gently. "But since your charge was closer to you than anyone except his parents, he may have confided something to shed light on this mystery. You might have disregarded it as childish babbling, yet it could be important. Did he mention meeting anyone on the premises, Miss Vale? A wanderer? A stranger, either man or woman?"

"That's difficult to evaluate."

"Why?"

"Because he had the normal fantasies of children," Miss Vale replied. "The imaginary adventures and companions. Fictional and legendary characters sometimes became quite real to him, and myth difficult to distinguish from fact. For instance, while Mr. Curtis was teaching him archery, he fancied himself riding and hunting with Robin Hood, and testing his bow-and-arrow skills with William Tell. On his father's yacht, he pretended to be the captain, studying the instruments under guidance and taking the helm. When he heard a train whistle, he was the engineer. In England last year, he was a knight of the realm and had all sorts of adventures, especially at Heathstone Manor. Several weeks ago he spoke of an acquaintance with a painter. But his description was so absurd, I paid no serious attention."

Keith bounded out of his chair. "Why haven't you mentioned this before, Miss Vale?"

"As I said, sir, it seemed too ridiculous to be true. Scott claimed the man had long whitish hair hanging from beneath a slouchy hat, rusty-red whiskers, and wore breeches and boots like a cavalier. Naturally, he made it all up."

"No!" Keith declared. "I was told that an itinerant painter fitting *that* description was seen around here recently!"

Heather's hand flew to her throat. "Who could he have been?"

"The kidnapper in disguise, using painting as a ploy to trespass on this property. And you didn't consider it important enough to tell me or the other agents? Good Lord, woman!"

"Forgive me, Mr. Curtis, but I simply did not suppose such a curious creature existed. I was humoring Master Scott in pretending I did. Besides, he only referred to the man once, and then appeared to forget it. And so did I."

"We're trying to discover clues, Miss Vale! Leads! Anything, no matter how seemingly silly! The neighbor who described the man to me said he traveled in a van, and the bloodhounds tracked Scotty's scent to where he was apparently taken aboard."

The governess began to weep. "I shall never forgive myself. And I deserve immediate discharge."

"What would that accomplish now?" Keith relented, retrieving his composure. "We may have a suspect, at least."

Carla agreed, and asked to borrow a horse.

"Of course," he told her. "Whatever you need."

"I want to examine the place you mentioned. Then I shall ride every day over the area. The vehicle should be sighted eventually, unless it rolled over a cliff. I'm aware of the numerous reports of a man and small boy seen crossing every local body of water in every conceivable craft, at every hour of the day and night. I'm inclined to ignore them, although investigations are routinely conducted."

She paused, then said, "Notoriety is the most likely cause for the delay of a ransom demand. The culprit might be skeptical about succeeding at his game, and undecided about his next move. He might also be a fundamentally decent human being who acted on a desperate impulse, and has had a change of heart. If so, the child might just be left somewhere, near a village."

Pacing, she continued. "That is why all lines of communication must be kept open . . . and a discreet reporter could be of great assistance."

"Unfortunately," Keith lamented, "not many members of the fourth estate are discreet."

Carla addressed Devon. "Is the *Record* aware of your presence here?"

"No, I don't think so. My editor thinks I'm in Washington with my wounded husband."

"I wonder who's investigating the shooting?"

"No one is now," Keith answered. "The suspect is dead. I didn't think he'd ever go to trial."

"I didn't either," Carla said flatly.

Devon's jaw dropped, and before she could speak, Keith handed her the Washington *Star*, folded to the correct page. She quickly scanned the dateline and long column.

PITTSBURGH (AP)—Harvey Hawks, attempted assassin of Sen. Reed Carter, Dem. of Texas, was discovered hanging in his prison cell at dawn yesterday. His own suspenders, attached to a ceiling beam reached by standing on his cot, formed the noose.

Hawks was scheduled to face a grand jury next week for possible indictment.

The suspect, alias Neal Harmon, alias Henry Shaw, had served several prison terms for various felonies, including arson, forgery, and grand theft. But he contended that he never intended to kill Senator Carter, merely to scare him. Hawks had denied that he was a member of, or party to, any conspiracy against the senator and had acted entirely on his own initiative.

The prison physician, Dr. Francis Denton, who pronounced Hawks dead of a broken neck at 5 A.M. yesterday, suggested that an earlier medical examination indicated some severe mental derangement.

Warden Karnes stated that Hawks was a strange and lonely fellow. He had no known family or any visitors during his incarceration, part of which was spent incommunicado and in solitary confinement.

When reached at his Georgetown residence in Washington, the recuperating Senator Carter had no comment on Hawks's action. His friend and political adviser, Judge Gore Hampton of Austin, Texas, remarked only that "The poor soul [Hawks] was evidently insane."

The body of Harvey Hawks will be interred without ceremony in an unidentified potter's field. His death closes the police files on the Carter case.

Olivia's article in the same edition stated:

One way or another, Senator Reed Carter continues to make news.

This reporter, present on the recent headline-catapulting occasion concerning the Harvey Hawks suicide, preferred to discuss other matters, some of which obviously discomfited Carter. Upon questioning, Carter expressed sincere sorrow and regret over the disappearance of the young son of Keith H. Curtis, the New York financier with whom he has been in public contest. He deplored the tragedy, but doubted that the Carter-Curtis feud and publicity over it had precipitated the child's disappearance.

Concerning rumors now rife in the Capital of a romance with Judge Hampton's attractive young daughter, Melissa, both of whom are his current houseguests, and a possible divorce from his largely absentee journalist wife, Carter replied noncommittally: "I'm sure the press will have the details of any such action long before I have."

Mrs. Carter, who writes under her maiden name for another journal, had been abroad over a year with the Grant tour, when she was informed of the attempted assassination of her famous husband. She returned promptly to America. But if in Washington at this time, she was unavailable for comment.

Miss Hampton suggested that Mrs. Carter, née Devon Marshall, might be in New York covering the mysterious disappearance of the young heir to the vast Curtis fortune, although she has not been glimpsed among the vigilant correspondents keeping a news watch in the village near the palatial estate, Halcyon-on-Hudson. Reliable and informed sources believe, however, that the lady is the privileged guest of Mr. Curtis and has been promised an exclusive story when the case finally breaks.

"I'm sorry," Keith apologized, as Devon sighed and tossed the paper aside.

"About Olivia's prattle? I've told you before, that part of my life is over and doesn't matter anymore. It's almost like reading about strangers, people I scarcely know. Only Scotty matters to me now. And you."

Keith embraced and kissed her. "Love will carry us through this ordeal, Devon. And if there's a merciful God in heaven, we'll get our child back!"

"Yes," she murmured. "And perhaps another one, too. And then we'll go away, Keith. Far away, where no one can ever hurt us again."

They had forgotten their compassionate audience, both of whom left the room quietly, in tears.

Several more days passed, and Devon's faith did not waver. She functioned adequately. She was neither a recluse nor a raving maniac. She took charge of the household and encouraged the distraught governess, once a rampart of poise and efficiency, to forsake her self-imposed exile. Devon believed, as did everyone observing her, that she was under some special divine guidance. Perhaps God did bestow a special grace upon mothers.

Newspapers were no longer kept from her. In the *Record*, she read Tish Lambeth's reports on the Grants. They were currently traveling in the Iberian Peninsula, being royally entertained by the rulers of Spain and Portugal. Tish was much impressed by Julia's meeting with James Russell Lowell, the American minister in Madrid. She admired Mrs. Grant's adaptability, her discussions with noble ladies and warriors alike, her graciousness to all. General Grant, who usually avoided subjects on which he was not well-versed, was grateful for his wife's versatility. And Miss Lambeth, once a plodding reporter, was developing flair.

The women's movement increased and diversified its activities, the goal now encompassing more than suffrage. Miss Anthony and Mrs. Stanton continued to lecture and write, and to petition Congress.

Two of the most fervent workers were missing, however. The Claflin sisters had sailed for England in August. Vanderbilt had bequeathed "certain unspecified large sums of money" to Victoria to further her research in spiritualism and psychic phenomena.

The entire family and staff of servants arrived in Liverpool in six first-class staterooms, and leased an elaborate mansion in a fashionable suburb of London. And it seemed likely that they would remain abroad for a while, since a wealthy suitor had become enamored of the beautiful Vicky, and a nobleman of the delightful Tennie. The Claflin sisters once again, had landed on their feet.

Chapter 42

"Eat hearty," Mallard encouraged, placing a bowl of steaming vegetable soup before his captive guest. "The perishable food won't keep long without ice, so we must eat it quickly. You can have mine. I have no appetite today."

"You had none yesterday, either," Scott reminded, "and the beef stew was pretty good."

"I'm glad you enjoyed it. But I'm feeling bad again. I must lie down."

"That's all right, sir. I'll clean up the dishes."

Mallard patted his head fondly before leaving the table. "How proud your father must be of you, Little Prince, and with every reason!"

His temperature had soared, as it invariably did in the afternoon. The chills came oftener now, and the coughing was more violent, as if his lungs were about to be expelled. He suspected the end was near and wondered why he was not more fearful. He began to feel a curious relief and a resignation tantamount to peace. Whether or not he soon faced spiritual judgment did not especially concern him. Hell, or whatever awaited sinners, could be no worse than the agonies he had suffered on the earth. He had already done considerable expiation.

"Can I do anything for you, sir?" Scott asked later, terribly concerned.

"If you would be so kind, pour some cool water into the basin and wet some rags for my face."

Scott obliged. "You're hot with fever, sir. I think you need a doctor."

"It's too late for that, sonny, even if one were handy. My goose is cooked. I mean, the sitting duck is now a dying duck."

Human death had little reality for Scott, who had never witnessed it. He had never seen a corpse in a casket or attended a funeral. He did not understand what was happening to his peculiar friend.

"Would you like some wine, Mr. Duck?"

Weak laughter sputtered from the swollen lips. "Very much. I finished the last in the cupboard, and it's time to rob my emergency cache." He tried to rise, fell back on the bed, heaving. "Jesus, I'm burning up! Wring out another cool cloth, please, if you can find one. There should be a couple of old huck towels in that pile of dirty clothes."

"We really should wash those things in the brook, sir, when you're able."

"We will, then. Ah, that feels better." Mallard relaxed slightly, closing his eyes. But his breath was shallow and raspy, and he intermittently clutched at his chest and grimaced. "Tell me, Scotty. Do you think you could find your way out of this place alone?"

"To where, sir?"

"The nearest farm or village, *any*where where there are people?"

"If there's a road, and it's not too far, I think I could."

That was the trouble. There was no clearly defined lane, only tracks strewn with brush. And the nearest farm was over two miles away.

"Forget it," Mallard told him. "You're safer here, I guess."

"How long have I been here, sir?"

"Not as long as it probably seems to you, Scotty. Only two weeks. And I wish I could get you home now, somehow. Maybe tomorrow I'll have the strength. If so, I'll write a note for you, and take you within sight of someone's home. They'll notify your daddy, and he'll come for you."

"What will you do then?"

The bony shoulders twitched. "Fall on my own sword."

"You have a sword?"

"No. It's just an expression, lad. Don't bother about me. I'm a skewered duck, awaiting the final roasting in Hades. I did something terribly wrong in taking you away, and your dad could punish me. But I won't last long enough for that. Do you understand what I'm saying?"

Scott nodded vaguely. "Sort of."

"What I did, boy, was steal you. Your father's very rich and would pay a fortune for your return. That's called ransom."

"Like a king's ransom?"

"Close enough. I needed money desperately. You see that. But I won't have much use for it now, and I don't want anything bad to happen to you. Will you tell your daddy that I was good to you? That I didn't beat you, or blindfold you, or tie you up? I fed and cared for you as best I could, and tried to keep you clean, even though I had to bathe you in a barrel."

"Yes, sir. That was fun, being scrubbed in a barrel. And just wearing my birthday suit, while my clothes dried."

Mallard forced a smile. "You're something, Scott. Really something. If I'd had a son like you . . . But I didn't, and never will. I never had anything I ever wanted. Never."

"I'll ask my daddy to help you get it."

"Oh, Scotty." Mallard averted his face, unable to meet his eyes.

Toward evening Mallard rallied slightly, part of the puzzling syndrome of this disease that had baffled medicine for centuries. Death always appeared most imminent in the afternoon: the fever raged at its highest point and the coughing was most severe. Mallard's had shaken the bed alarmingly, rattled the dishes, threatened to collapse the thin walls. He expected each seizure to be his last. But he lived.

Shifting its orbit, the late-September sun struck the earth at a different angle and began to alter the landscape. The artist's trained eye could detect the subtle alterations from the windows. Tiny golden veins etched the elm foliage in an exquisite tracery, as if wrought by a gilt-dipped feather, and the scarlet maples wore a subdued blush. The pigments on his palette were dry and crusty, but he knew which shades would blend to make the burnished copper of autumn oaks, and the rusty crimsons of sycamores and hickories. The holly and hawthorn berries, pale yellow now, would turn turkey red in November. The hemlocks remained eternally green, and Mallard thought longingly of Socrates' poison cup. How had he prepared it strong enough for instant death?

Suddenly he remembered his liquor cellar. "Will you help me do some treasure hunting, Scotty, under the house?"

"Like pirates? Captain Kidd and his crew used to plunder in this region."

"I think the first pirates were the explorers who swindled

the Indians out of this country for a few dollars and worthless baubles," Mallard declared. "But we won't be committing piracy, just retrieving a box I buried myself. I'll show you where to dig. Just watch out for snakes and spiders."

With painful effort and desperate determination, Mallard moved outside, clasping the small hand that offered its strength. He picked up a long, thin branch and swept it languidly under the floor, brushing away stringy webs and flushing out a pair of raccoons.

"Where's the shovel, sir?"

"Don't have any. Just use a sturdy stick and your hands. There's only a few inches of dirt covering the hoard."

"From buccaneers?" This had become an adventure.

"Right." Mallard tried to dig, but had to stop after a few seconds. "It's right here under this corner, mate. I'll be the captain and supervise."

"Aye, aye, sir!"

Scott saluted and continued alone, unearthing the old wood coffer and squeaking open the lid. The dusty bottles were pleasantly cool, and Mallard placed one to his febrile cheek with the tender touch of a lover. Vintage stock, this had been pilfered from a French cargo left unattended on an East River dock.

"Eureka!" Scott cried elatedly. "That's what you say when you find gold, sir."

"I know, partner, and this fine sherry is liquid gold to me!" He coughed, leaning against the worm-tunneled walls. "Will you salvage the treasure for me? Carry the prizes in, one at a time, and be very careful, please. Don't break any. Line them up beside the bed, where I can reach them. I hope you haven't misplaced the corkscrew."

"No, sir. It's on the table, where you left it."

"Hurry, now," Mallard urged, "and empty the cache before dark!"

"All of it? There are seven bottles, sir."

"Every single one is precious, my friend. We've reached El Dorado, where I shall die happy."

That evening Mallard consumed two demijohns of wine, and Scott had his first experience with delirium tremens, more horrifying than anything he had encountered in his strange captivity.

"Close up the house, boy!"

"It is closed, sir."

"Not that broken window. Bats are flying in!"

"I don't see any, sir."

"You must be blind, then! They're coming from a nearby cave. Cover that hole, quick!"

Scott blocked the open space with a stretched canvas. "Are they gone now?"

"Not all of them! A couple are hanging on the ceiling, staring at me, just waiting to swoop. If they get tangled in our hair, we'll have to cut 'em out with a knife. Think you can do that?"

"I don't know, sir. I don't see any bats."

"Better hope they're not vampires! They'll suck your blood, and you'll die. Jesus, there's a whole flock in here now! Get the broom and drive 'em outside."

The astonished boy ran to fetch the broom, swiping furiously at the invisible invaders. "I think I got them, sir."

"You sure? Well, shut the door and stuff some rags under it. Snakes and bugs are crawling in now!"

"Where?"

"Coming across the floor . . . green and black and slimy! They're starting to clumb the walls . . ."

"The snakes?"

"And beetles and locusts. Listen to their noise!"

"Those are crickets, sir, and they're outside in the woods. Birds are singing, too."

"Light more candles. Insects fear fire."

"Not moths."

"Do as I say!"

"Right away, sir." Scott scurried for the matches, flaring the wicks of several wax stubs. "Is this better?"

Mallard gulped more wine. "How'd that goddamn squirrel get inside?"

"There's no squirrel, Mr. Duck."

"Don't tell me that! The son of a bitch is sitting on the bedstead, chewing an acorn, his cheeks puffed out like a chipmunk's. Maybe it is a chipmunk. No, it's a squirrel, and he's chattering at me, getting ready to leap! Drive him away!"

"How?"

"With a stick, of course."

Scott swung an imaginary club. "Shoo! Go away, get out, we don't want you here!" He opened the door and then banged it shut. "There, now, sir. They're all gone. The bats, snakes, bugs, squirrel, chipmunk, and there's no way for them to enter again, I promise you."

"Good boy." Mallard was huddling in the bed, peering from under a pillow. "Thank you for protecting me."

"Would you like to eat something now, sir? You might like the dried apricots. I prefer the apples and peaches."

"Take whatever you want, Scotty. It's all yours, everything of mine belongs to you now. I'm willing it to you, my little friend. Get me a pencil and paper, so I can write my last will and testament."

"You don't have to do that, Mr. Duck."

"I want to, kid. My pictures, the best of the lot and any others you like—all yours. The van and horse, too, if old Maudie hasn't run away. I don't own this place. Just squatting, like they do out West. But all my other worldly possessions are yours. For taking such fine care of me. Help me open another bottle of wine."

The child hesitated. "Maybe you've had enough for today, sir. Tomorrow—"

"Tomorrow I won't have any need of this medicine." Mallard winced. "Tomorrow I'll be a dead duck, laddie. The grim reaper's coming for me tonight." He began to retch again, spitting up bright red blood, and Scott tried to direct his head over the chamberpot.

Although frightened as never before in his life, he managed well enough. Having no experience to equal this horror, he could scarcely believe it was all really happening. It was for that reason that Scott didn't mind too much. Mostly, he was worried about his unhappy friend.

Mallard was shivering, groaning, twisting convulsively. Now the hallucinatory tormentors were pestering him physically, and he begged the boy to beat them off.

"For Chrissake, do something!"

Scott obeyed, wielding a pillow and stamping his feet loudly around the room. "I'm killing them all, sir. Every last one."

"They're clever. They'll hide under the bed and come out later, when they think we're asleep. Sweep 'em out from under there, you hear? Squash 'em."

"Yes, sir! I've gotten most of them already, but if you notice any stray ones . . ."

"Oh, Jesus! The bats are back, they're back!"

"Just one. Don't worry." Scott smashed the broom hard

against the wall, splattering frayed straw. "There! I fixed him."

Suddenly the delirious patient was reciting remembered bits of Scripture, drama, poetry, philosophy. He was walking through a valley, and lying down in green pastures. He was inquiring curiously about the sting of death. An invisible raven was perched above his chamber door. He saw the fluttering candle shadows as hunchbacks ringing bells in Notre-Dame Cathedral, as old men with scythes, as dancing skeletons. He was debating with Plato, then whispering to the dark-haired lady in the portrait.

Although the evening was cooler than the afternoon, it was still unbearably warm in the closed shack, and the odors were nauseating. Even Scott's strong stomach rebelled, and he feared he might throw up. Mallard was fouling his bed, as a lame bird does its nest. Finishing the burgundy, he dropped the bottle on the floor. His thrashing ceased. Soon he was snoring.

Scott scrounged through the soiled articles for a possible pallet. He discovered an old blanket with "U.S. Army" stamped in black letters on the faded, moth-riddled wool. He slept on it, pretending he was a soldier lost in the field. Confident his troops would find him soon.

Chapter 43

Carla Winston had been searching for several days, riding from dawn to sunset, and checking regional maps at night. There were reasonably comfortable lodgings along the routes, but she had learned to carry emergency supplies in her saddlebags, where she also toted an extra weapon and ammunition. Following the tracks that began where the bloodhounds had lost the scent had proved futile.

Sections of the Bronx seemed as primitive as territory Carla had traveled beyond the Mississippi, and the wooded terrain as difficult to explore as mountains. She recalled the terrible night with Devon in the Carters' Texas prairie cabin, fighting the hungry coyotes. And how Carla had worried during the boating accident in Austin.

In the line of duty, Carla had fawned upon Judge Hampton, whom she distrusted, and had even endured his lecherous advances, eluding him by artful pretense.

But Carla had never been as deeply involved in a case as she was in this one. Poor little boy! Would she find him? Not the least of her agony was the memory of her beloved Jason Carter, and the realization of his connection with the boy. To be sure, Jason had not known of the child's existence. But Devon connected Jason to Scott, somehow, and Carla had never loved anyone as fiercely as she had loved the old Senator. She could not fail to find Devon's son!

Dear God, she prayed, cantering along a Bronx lane, let me find Scott Curtis. Send me a hint, a clue, and I'll be eternally grateful. I ask these favors in your holy name.

Some fifty yards ahead, where the trace forked, she glimpsed a faded sign and directional arrow: CROSSROADS STORE. ONE MILE ON RIGHT. It was not listed on the map and might easily have been missed, except for the advertisement partially concealed by a low-hanging branch of the tree to which it was attached. Intuitively, Carla spurred her mount.

Like most rural merchants, the proprietor handled a wide range of products. Among other items, the windows displayed an anatomical truss on a dusty dummy, a plaster-of-paris foot patched with bunion and corn aids, a pickle-kraut crock, an iron Dutch oven. And several paintings. Not good, the art, but not actually bad, either. Mediocre. Some pictures appeared to have been painted over others, either for lack of new canvas or more bizarre reasons. One concealed a possible self-portrait in a cluster of Berkshire birches, the gaunt, cynical, sardonic features barely visible. Another had the same tormented face, virtually a hollow-eyed skull, disguised in a Vermont landscape. How unusual!

Carla had to check it out. It could be a lead; indeed, it could be *the* lead!

A bell announced her, and the owner, wearing a garter-sleeved shirt and canvas apron over trousers, emerged from the stockroom.

"May I help you, ma'am?"

"Are the pictures on display for sale?"

"Everything in this place is for sale," Lumis answered. "Price subject to negotiation. You like any of 'em?"

"Some show promise. Past promise, though, I think. Not future."

"That describes the painter pretty well," he remarked, shaking his head sadly. "He traded 'em to me for food and medicine."

"Medicine?"

"He's sick, poor devil. Lung fever in the worst way. Can't last much longer."

"You accepted the paintings on commission, then?"

"No, like I said, for necessities. The fella's kicking the bucket. I advised him to go West, to a healthier climate. And he might try, painting his way. But I don't think he'll make it."

"Too bad," Carla murmured.

"He's got no use for pictures no more, just for money. You want to make an offer?"

Carla examined the merchandise, pretending indecision. "Do you have his address, by the way?"

"Naw, he's a rover. Paints here and there, and moves on again. I only seen him twice."

"When was the last time?"

"About two weeks ago. I gave him more supplies than

his stuff is worth. Felt sorry for him. I'll be lucky to fetch a buck apiece for 'em." He frowned, embarrassed by his confession.

"What's his name?"

Lumis scratched his head. "I ain't sure. Don't believe he ever told me, actually. If so, I can't remember."

"Thank you kindly, Mr. Lumis."

"How'd you know my name?"

"It's on the building. 'Oscar Lumis, Proprietor.' "

He grinned sheepishly. "Reckon I forgot that. Wouldn't take no sleuth to discover my handle, would it?"

Carla smiled slightly, looking closely at another of the paintings, recognizing the arched stone bridge over the meandering Halcyon brook. The artist had been to Halcyon. He was either the abductor or a cohort. "How does he travel?"

"In a sorry old van pulled by a swaybacked nag," Lumis said, straightening canned goods. "Ain't the friendliest person in the world, neither. You got to buy words from him, almost. I think he lives on them wheels, and expects 'em to haul him westward." He peered at Carla, attracted to her pretty face. "You like that picture, ma'am? Take it, as a gift."

"That's extremely kind of you, sir. But I'll have to return for it. I'm just out riding today, you see, and couldn't carry it easily on horseback."

"I'll keep it for you, then. Come back soon, now?"

"Soon." Carla smiled.

Her befuddled admirer simpered. "Where you from?"

"Norfolk, Virginia. Presently the guest of friends in Washington Heights. They have a fine stable, and I enjoy riding in the country."

"Well, you're a long way from there now, ma'am. Better head back, if you expect to make it before dark."

"You're right."

"Don't forget to return for the picture," Lumis reminded as Carla opened the door. "I gave him two pounds of sugar, a sack of flour, and other staples. Even some candy for his sweet tooth."

"How generous! Good day, Mr, Lumis."

He bowed from the waist, clumsily gallant. To his chagrin, another customer arrived, preventing his following her outside.

The pieces of the puzzle were falling into place, the

mystery solving itself, including the pacification sweets. The suspect had lived in the vicinity recently, and probably still did, not well enough yet to travel long distances. He was broke, and what better way to get hold of some money than through ransom? But evidently severe illness had put kinks in his plans. This renewed Carla's hope that Scott was also still alive.

As she rode along, she noticed some staked and piled brush. An abandoned lane? If private, who would bar the entrance? A week ago, the greenery would have appeared to be growing there, and easily ignored. Now it was withered, shedding, a cause for curiosity.

Carla dismounted, cleared a path for Galahad, then remounted. Here and there other hacked-off bushes and branches formed senseless barriers in the weeded ruts, which surely did not lead to a cultivated farm or occupied homestead. Who would live in this wilderness? Drawing rein and lifting her binoculars, she spied a dilapidated shack nestled in a thick grove, unpainted, blending into the trees. A rusty, crooked stovepipe thrust through the variegated leaves at a crazy angle, a fire hazard. No smoke was visible, nor any other signs of habitation.

Should she go in alone, or get help? Contact with the other detectives was impossible, since they were working in different localities. She must notify Mr. Curtis from the nearest telegraph station. Not knowing what they might find in the house, she did not want Devon present. She trusted that he alone would receive the telegram. She would simply wait for him in the village.

Chapter 44

Carla secured the frothing Galahad to a hitching post on the village square, near a water trough, and dispatched a coded message to the Curtis estate, a message which meant nothing to the telegrapher. Then she sat on an ancient wood bench carved with names, gazing at a Minuteman statue befouled by a century of unpatriotic pigeons. She was thinking nostalgically of its Southern counterpart—a bronze, marble, or granite image of a great Confederate hero, erected by the local citizens and meticulously maintained. It was frequently revered with ceremonies and wreaths and speeches, while a band played "Dixie." Rosters of the community's Civil War dead were read, along with the battles in which they had fallen. The large cities of the North, where she had traveled, were proudest of their connections with colonial independence.

Keith galloped up bareheaded, in fawn-colored breeches and open-throated white linen shirt, the dark glossy coat of his champion bay speckled with salt crystals. Instantly he was out of the saddle and striding rapidly toward Carla.

"Tell me, without any pretty words," he began, mopping his perspiring brow. "Is he alive?"

"I don't know," she answered. "I don't even know if this *is* the hideout, but there are indications . . ." She paused, apprising him once again of Pinkerton rules, such as communication with the Manhattan office, and *modus operandi* in the field, to be dispensed with only when human safety was involved. "Professional ethics, you understand?"

As Keith nodded, she continued: "The local peace officer is unavailable, however, and a poorly organized citizens' group anxious to collect the reward could be highly detrimental."

"Absolutely. We dare not risk it."

"Then it's just us, you and me, for the present. I'm glad you came prepared," she added, observing the pistol stuck in his belt and the hunting rifle in the saddle scabbard. "With a tall Stetson and high-heeled boots, you'd resemble a Texan . . . I mean, Westerner."

Keith scowled slightly at the banter, although appreciating its intent. Carla thought to allay his anxiety, lest rashness lead to a calamity. "You're the expert, Carla. What strategy do you recommend?"

"Extreme caution. I must warn you, there's an uncanny silence about the place. I detected only one whinny, which may have come from a stray horse. I observed no plausible vehicle. What aroused my suspicion was the apparently deliberate attempt to conceal the lane entrance. Since it does not lead to a resident farm or private estate, why bother to camouflage its existence?" Another pause for emphasis. "It could indicate that the suspect has already left, leaving the victim behind, bound, without food or water, making survival impossible. Or."

"—dead and buried," Keith interrupted. "I realize that, Carla, and have been preparing myself to accept the worst."

"And Devon?"

"She places tremendous faith in God and in maternal instinct."

Carla feigned a smile. "It's a gift most women have, mothers or not." She gave him a piercing look, then said simply, "Shall we start now?"

"I see no logic in further delay."

"Nor I. Mount up."

They arrived at the location within an hour, maneuvered around the obstacles, and halted midway along the rutted path. Except for the twittering of birds and the scurrying of small creatures, the awesome silence still prevailed. No familiar domestic animal or human sound.

"What do you think?" Carla asked warily.

Keith hesitated, much of his optimism vanishing. "Abandoned. How could anyone live long under these circumstances?"

Carla chose not to enlighten him about the primitive conditions under which the Carters had existed before moving from their desolate prairie cabin to the state capital. "Nevertheless, I believe we should proceed, sir."

"Of course. Miracles do happen."

The stench of rotting garbage and the privy assaulted them. Vultures were already wheeling expectantly overhead, roosting confidently in the trees and on the roof—an ominous sign. Able to scent death for miles, the scavengers flocked to the scene.

The horses' hooves rustled the fallen leaves. And even as they approached within fifty feet of the ramshackle shelter, there was no noise or movement inside.

Signaling to Keith, Carla whispered, "Let's dismount and stalk. You take the right side, I'll take the left. Have your gun ready."

They proceeded quietly on foot, concealed by the dense growth, circling the house and nodding to each other at sight of the van, partially obscured by brush. This was the identical van described to Keith by the neighbor working in her garden. Carla executed more silent signals and instructions: she would try the front door while he guarded the back.

Neither entry was bolted. Carla turned the main knob cautiously, cocked derringer in hand. Mice darted across the kitchen floor into their holes. Roaches and ants swarmed over the table and cold range, feeding on the spoiled food. Maggots squirmed in the kettles of stew. Ignoring the filth, Carla stepped over the narrow threshold into the bedroom and stifled a horrified gasp. Of the many terrible things she had witnessed in her profession, few equaled this.

The emaciated man on the bed was too ill to stir, possibly in a coma. Blood covered the mattress and pillows, drooled from his nose and mouth, caked his unshaven face, and matted his long yellow-white hair. His breath was laborious, shallow, rattling.

The child was sprawled facedown on a dirty blanket in the corner. Carla bent to touch him; he was quite warm, perspiration curling the dark hair in ringlets on his neck and forehead. He was thin, feverish—but alive! Thank God! Alive!

Opening the rear door, she beckoned to Keith, who leaped over the tumbling steps, as incredulous at the scene as she had been. He recognized the piteous figure on the gory bed, but did not notice the pallet until his vision had adjusted to the dim room. All but one candle had consumed itself, leaving a smoky haze.

Carla retreated quickly outdoors as Keith fell to his knees, and clasping his sleeping son in his arms, wept loudly. Fear, grief, loss, dissolved into joy. He held the boy tighter, unable to contain himself. Soon Scott woke, rubbing drowsy eyes, afraid it was only a dream. He began haltingly, "Daddy? Is it you, Daddy?"

"Yes, Scott, yes! It's me, Daddy. You're safe now." He was kissing and hugging him again, "Are you all right, son?"

"Pretty much. But poor Mr. Duck is terribly sick, Daddy, and needs help badly. I tried to care for him for several days. But he just lies there spitting up blood, and he won't eat. He won't even drink the wine anymore."

"Mr. Duck?"

"I think that's his name. But he has others, too. Mr. Drake and Mr. Paint Dauber. He's an artist, Daddy, and said he knew you."

"He did, once. Long ago."

Keith gazed at the near-nude of his late wife, remembering the Tompkins Square studio, the bitter fight, Esther's fall down the steep stairway trying to protect her lover, who had refused to defend himself lest he endanger his artistic hands. He recalled, rapidly, all the horrors that followed. In this portrait, she was almost as naked as she had been on the rainy afternoon he discovered them together in the wretched attic. Long blue-black hair cascading on her bare white shoulders, cherry-tipped nipples, purple eyes, and that enigmatic smile. Cunning had been her strongest characteristic, and the bitch had succeeded in torturing him even from the grave. Certainly she had destroyed that poor bastard, now on his deathbed.

"I told Mr. Duck you'd help him, Daddy."

"I'll send a doctor," Keith promised, certain that Mallard would expire shortly. "And the law. They'll know what to do."

"He willed me everything, Daddy. He wrote it on a sheet of paper. You want to see?"

"Later, Scott. Guess who's with me?"

"Mother?" he asked, hardly daring to voice the hope.

"No, she wasn't feeling well. But she's at Halcyon now, waiting for us."

Scott's eyes brightened. "She's back from Europe?"

"Yes, she's back. Scott, do you remember meeting Mrs. Winston in Washington, when you had the measles?"

"Yes, sir."

"Well, she rode out with me and will go back to Halcyon with us," Keith said. "Everyone will be so glad to see you again. Mommy, Miss Vale, Mrs. Sommes and Enid, Lars and Karl, and all your pets."

Carla had remained outside, to regain her composure and give her client time to do the same.

"I can hardly wait to see them!" Scott cried. "Do you want any of this stuff, Daddy? It's all mine now. Some of the pictures are nice. Mr. Duck said you wanted to buy the skating picture, once. You might look at it."

"All right, son."

Keith removed the ragged, dingy sheet and looked at the best of Mallard's work, *Jamaica Pond*. And there was a masked girl in a tawny bird-of-paradise costume, perched on a velvet swing in a gilded cage. The mouth, the sweet unforgettable mouth, was Devon's. But neither of them needed these painful reminders.

Mallard twitched, struggling to rise. His hooded eyes blinked in surprise that he was still alive, however tenuously.

Keith threw open the doors and windows and stood pondering the virtual corpse of the rival he had once envied and despised. But he sent Scott outside to Carla before asking, "Giles Mallard?"

"Keith Curtis?"

"Yes. Can you speak?"

A nod. "And so we meet again? That's a wonderful boy you have, Curtis."

"I know that, Mallard. And the reason for your unspeakable action is obvious. But I do want to thank you for not harming him."

The debilitated man tried to raise to his elbows, failed, and lay down again. "I . . . I never intended to hurt him. I . . . I just needed some money. Then this devilish disease took fiendish, octopus hold of me . . . and I knew I was dying. But I couldn't send him home alone. I was afraid he'd get lost. I had grown quite fond of him. He did his best to nurse me . . ."

"I'll get medical help for you," Keith promised grimly.

"Don't bother. This attack is fatal. I'm practically dead now."

"Better conserve your strength, man."

"For what? More pain and punishment? You should have killed me that day in Manhattan. You'd have done a great favor. I . . . I think I actually died then, anyway. I loved her, you know, above all else on this foul earth. . . ."

"I believe you." Keith nodded stoically.

"When I . . . I read of her death . . . Well . . . that finished me." He hemorrhaged blood over the bed and himself, spattering Keith's clothes and boots. "Where's the boy?"

"Outside, with a friend."

"Good." More convulsions. "I wrote out a will to him. As you can see, there's little of value to anyone in your position. But there are several worthy paintings. Take them, please. That's all I own. I . . . I've been bartering and even prostituting my talent to live . . ."

"Perhaps we could devise a stretcher and get you out of here," Keith began.

"No, no! Take the child and go. I only hope I haven't contaminated him. I ordered him away when I was coughing. He is healthy and well-nourished, and this is largely a curse of poverty and neglect." A film was glazing his blue eyes. "Don't pity me, Curtis, or speak of forgiveness. I still hate your guts, too much even for a handshake. Just get the hell out of here, will you?"

"Sure."

Removing Esther's portrait, Keith stacked it with that of the ice skaters and the masked and caged golden girl. Then he went outside and scattered the buzzards. Carla and Scott were watching a squirrel hoarding acorns.

"Is Mr. Duck better, Daddy?"

"Some," Keith fibbed, motioning to Carla, while the boy's attention was turned to their horses. "There are three paintings I want you to destroy. I've put them together in the kitchen. Rip the canvases from the frames, douse them with kerosene or turpentine, and set them on fire. We'll wait for you down the lane."

Keith lifted his son into the saddle, then swung himself astride. "Mrs. Winston will catch up with us shortly. She has something to do here first," he explained, starting off in a slow trot.

"Oh, Daddy, I'm so glad we're going home. And Mother's there! Will she be with us long this time?"

"I think so, Scott. She has no reason to leave us at all anymore."

"She won't be working?"

"Well, not for a while, anyway. Maybe never. At least, not the way she did before."

"Then we'll be together *always*! Won't we, Daddy? Forever and ever!"

"I hope so, son," Keith answered, pressing the small back to his broad chest. The tears came again.

The child smiled, glancing up at the sky with gratitude. "I guess God heard my prayers, after all."

EPILOGUE
Spring, 1879

Devon felt she had been born again. She and Keith shared love, peace, and gratitude. Thanksgiving and Christmas were celebrated as they had never been celebrated. They were *together*, at long last, a happy family anticipating another member. But this birth would occur legitimately, to Mrs. Keith Heathstone Curtis, who wore her new wedding ring with pride.

Now Devon sat on the rear terrace, Miss Vale nearby, smiling as Keith and Scott rode across the green meadows sprinkled with brilliant wildflowers and across the recently planted fields. The collie ran alongside the horses. Two new calves, several lambs, and a pair of frisky colts romped in the grass under the watchful eyes of their proud mothers. Kittens meowed and puppies yapped on the lawn, playing together, too young to realize that they were supposed to be enemies. What a fertile place this is! Devon mused, conscious of the strong movements in her womb.

"You look happy," Miss Vale commented.

"Oh, I am! Never more so. Isn't this a lovely day?" She took no notice of the guards and fierce watchdogs constantly patrolling the property, or of the extra-high fences and locked gates erected since the tragedy, nor of the fact that Keith himself was always armed, though never conspicuously.

"We've all been blessed, Mrs. Curtis."

Mrs. Curtis. Having despaired of ever hearing herself addressed that way, Devon rejoiced in the sound of it.

"Would you like some refreshment, Heather? Mrs. Sommes just brought a fresh pot of tea and some cakes."

"Thank you. Allow me to pour, please?"

In her seventh month of pregnancy, Devon was somewhat awkward, and delighted to delegate the privilege.

The wicker table and rack were heaped with recent newspapers, journals, and magazines to keep her abreast of events in America and abroad. Wall Street, of course, was pleased that the government had resumed specie payments, suspended in 1861, restoring confidence in the federal fiscal policies and the national economy. Senator Reed Carter's antitrust bill had been defeated, even though the Democrats controlled both houses of Congress for the first time since 1858. True to his word, Reed had resigned his Senate seat and departed for Texas with the Hamptons, still ignorant of the actual owner of the Georgetown residence, which was now for sale at a handsome profit. On their trips to Washington, the Curtises could always stay at the Clairmont, in the elaborate twelve-room penthouse suite, with its lovely terraces and roof garden and panoramic view. The Curtis attorneys were currently managing Curtis business affairs on the Potomac, however, for Keith refused to leave Devon's side until the baby was born.

Heather Vale was elated that female lawyers had won the right to argue cases before the Supreme Court and were now also being admitted to some excellent medical schools, thanks to the determination of Dr. Elizabeth Blackwell. "We'll win the franchise someday, too," she predicted. "Women have already gained a few freedoms. At least we needn't abide by the harsh Napoleonic Code governing wives in France."

Just recently Devon had gotten news of a different kind: Dr. Blake's stethoscope had detected two distinct heartbeats in her uterus. Twins! "Ramsey better be present for this delivery!" she joked to Keith.

"Don't worry, darling. He'll be in residence for two weeks before the expected date, and at least one week afterward."

Already they were examining references and interviewing prospective nannies. Once the big event occurred and Devon was able to travel long distances, they planned a holiday in England, at Heathstone Manor. Scott was eager to return to the vast baronial estate, and they would be carrying an entourage along on the *Sprite*, which had been equipped for additional accommodations. It was virtually a passenger ship now, nearly as large and well-fortified as the military cruisers on which the Grants were still sailing around the world.

Besieged by sudden urges, Keith resorted instead to mundane matters, the industrial and scientific achievements of which Devon was already aware. The regular telephone exchange established in New Haven, Connecticut, and the Edison Electric Light Company now under construction in New York City were concerns in which the Curtis Enterprises were heavily involved. Public-street lighting had been installed in Cleveland, Ohio. Wabash, Indiana boasted of being completely illuminated by the marvelous incandescent bulb.

"Telephone communications between large cities will eventually be commonplace. The spectacular novelties previewed at the Centennial have become realities, Devon. The Age of Wonders has dawned, and we're living in it!" Pausing, he kissed the sacred ring on her left hand. "But the greatest wonder in my life is finally having you, Mrs. Curtis."

"You've expressed my sentiments perfectly, Mr. Curtis. How can I possibly follow that tribute?"

"With love," he murmured.

"You know what the doctor said," she cautioned, although she was as eager for lovemaking as he was.

"I wouldn't risk hurting you or the babes. But did you ever think how wonderful it is just to hold someone you love, to touch them and speak to them?"

"Many times," Devon confessed, "especially when it was impossible, because miles separated us. But that's not the case anymore."

"It never will be again, if I can help it."

"Whither thou goest?"

He nodded, embracing her tenderly. "That's one of my favorite biblical passages."

"Mine also," she agreed, clinging to him. "Must we really obey doctor's orders? He did suggest alternatives, you know. Certain positions and procedures."

"Stop seducing me! You always were the most provocative temptress I've ever known, even when you pretended not to care."

"I always cared, Keith, always. . . ."

For several months now Scotty had been observing Devon's increasing bulk, centered primarily in her abdominal region. "You'll be too big to fit in the saddle, Mother."

"I already am, darling. I fear the poor animal would become swaybacked and splayfooted under my present load. Try these delicious cream puffs!"

"My taste runs to different sweets," Keith remarked, winking intimately. "But Scott may have one, if it won't interfere with his appetite for dinner. I'll just have a cup of tea."

"Did you enjoy your ride?" Devon asked as Miss Vale served them.

"Oh, yes, ma'am! We always do. Too bad you couldn't join us. We missed you."

"Well, it'll be a while yet, dear."

"You have to lose some weight first?"

"In a manner of speaking."

"What does that mean?"

Keith glanced at the governess. "Your pupil needs some instruction, Miss Vale."

She blushed. "Oh, sir! Not the birds and the bees! I've always considered that a parental duty. Particularly the father's, where a boy is concerned."

He laughed, relieving her embarrassment. "Don't trouble yourself on that account, Miss Vale. I was referring to the three R's. I'll handle the other department in due course."

But Scott had already learned a few facts of nature on his own: female animals swelled before the birth of their young. He assumed the same was true of human beings. "Mother's going to have a baby, isn't she?" he inquired nonchalantly.

"That's right," Keith answered in the same tone. "In about two months."

"I hope it's a brother!"

"Brother or sister, we'll love the baby in either case."

"Of course, sir. And it's about time, don't you think? I've been an only child for *years* now. It's a wonder I'm not spoiled rotten."

His parents laughed, and Keith tousled his dark curls. "A wonder, indeed! And I heartily agree—an addition to the family is long overdue. But I'm confident we'll make up for lost time," he said, offering Devon another pastry. "Go ahead, my love. You're eating for three, remember."

"Two," the governess corrected.

"You have your arithmetic, Miss Vale, and I have mine —and Dr. Blake's."

"Oh? *Oh!* Yes, indeed, sir!" And beckoning to Scott, who grabbed a chocolate eclair, she called, "Come along, Master Scott. You've had your afternoon recess, and it's time now for more lessons."

Miss Vale swept her charge along the terrace to the door, while Devon and Keith sat watching, smiling, their hands slowly reaching for each other.